Praise for *Taste Me*

"Filled with steamy and erotic sex scenes, fantastic world-building, and sexy and compelling characters."

—*Minding Spot*

"The chemistry between the leading characters makes it a worthy read… and the female protagonist brings girl power to the genre."

—*RT Book Reviews*

"This is what a powerful and very sensual paranormal novel is all about! Mixing up futuristic, paranormal, intrigue, and all-consuming sex, Ms. Hogan fashioned characters that rival some of the most prominent paranormal authors today."

—*Night Owl Reviews* Reviewer Top Pick

"Utterly stimulating… sex, drugs, and rock 'n' roll the paranormal way… *Taste Me* is a thrilling introduction to both a fascinating new series and a brilliant new author in Tamara Hogan."

—*Dark Divas Reviews*

"In this sexy romp of a story, incubi, sirens, Valkyries, vampires, werewolves, and faeries live undetected alongside humankind… Hogan has brought the supernatural to life in a very unique way."

—*Romance Fiction on Suite101*

"Edgy with a fresh feel."

—*Anna's Book Blog*

CHASE ME

TAMARA HOGAN

sourcebooks
casablanca

Published by Sourcebooks Casablanca, an imprint of Sourcebooks, Inc.
P.O. Box 4410, Naperville, Illinois 60567-4410
(630) 961-3900
FAX: (630) 961-2168
www.sourcebooks.com

Printed and bound in the United States of America
VP 10 9 8 7 6 5 4 3 2 1

The role that coffee shops play in many authors' writing routines cannot be overstated, and this morning when I approached my regular haunt, I received a nasty punch to the gut: a sign on the door saying that they'd soon be closing their doors for good. So this book is dedicated to Bev, Karen, and the crew at The Coffee Corner, who've kept me caffeinated and encouraged since the day I first wandered in with an idea, a spiral notebook, and a dream that had been sitting on the back burner for far too long.

Support your mom-and-pop coffee shops, y'all.

THE UNDERWORLD COUNCIL

INCUBUS—Elliott Sebastiani*	Second: Antonia Sebastiani
SIREN—Claudette Fontaine	Second: Scarlett Fontaine
WERE—Krispin Woolf	Second: Jacoby Woolf
VAMPIRE—Valerian	Second: Wyland
VALKYRIE—Alka Schlessinger	Second: Lorin Schlessinger
HUMANITY—(Vacant)	Emeritus: Carl Sagan (1934-1996)
SEC/TECH—Lukas Sebastiani	Second: Jack Kirkland
*President	

Chapter 1

GABE LUPINSKY WHISTLED AS HE KICKED OFF HIS snow-covered dress shoes and hung his coat and suit jacket on empty hooks in his parents' mudroom.

He'd done it. He'd actually done it. Maybe things were finally looking up.

"Gabe, is that you?" Glynna called.

"Yeah." He entered the big country kitchen to find his younger sister hopping barefoot across the cold tile floor.

She wasn't wearing her prosthetic. Again.

"I know, I know. Don't say it." She hugged him, probably as much to stave off his nagging as to say hello. "So? The announcement was today, right? Did you hear?" Eyeing him, she bounced up and down in his arms. "You know. Hurry up and tell me. Cruelty to handicapped people. My foot is freezing."

"Handicapped, my ass," he muttered. "Why don't you wear some damn slippers? And some clothes, while you're at it?" Releasing her, he followed her into the carpeted living room. It was snowing outside, a classic March squall, yet Glynna wore shorts that barely peeked out from under the hem of her oversized Minnesota Vikings T-shirt. The void where her lower left leg should be—had never been—was evident.

"Problems with the new prosthetic?" he asked. "You know there's a break-in period. If you don't wear it, it just extends the process."

She shot him a look. "I think I know that."

Gabe let the snippy response slide. He'd lost count of how many prosthetics Glynna had broken in and outgrown over her lifetime. Though his sister was an adult—barely—watching her deal with the inevitable bruises and pressure sores still made his heart ache as much now as it had when she was a little girl.

"I'll put it back on after we talk with Mom and Dad." Glynna sat down and pulled a fuzzy purple slipper on her foot, leaving the sweatpants lying over the arm of the big L-shaped leather couch.

Sisters were a mystery he knew he'd never solve. "Have you heard from Gideon and Gwen?" He and his siblings all got together once a week to talk to their parents, who were one month into a half-year trip of the Asian subcontinent, gathering material for their next travel book.

"Gideon caught a case and won't be here. Gwen's on her way. You are *not* going to make me wait until she gets here."

He couldn't hide the grin for long. "Yeah, I got it."

"Ha, I knew it! I knew it! Congratulations!" She launched herself off the couch and hugged him again, pogoing up and down with excitement. "Director of Physical Sciences at Sebastiani Labs. Do you get a bigger office? Underground parking? A big-ass raise?"

He smiled, shaking his head. "Remember that the position's temporary, just while Alka's on sabbatical." Yeah, the position *was* temporary, but he'd beaten out Alka's own daughter for the job. Satisfaction warmed him like a crackling fire.

"Well, gawd knows you're bossy enough to actually

be the boss." She hopped back to the kitchen they'd just left. "Let's break out the bubbly!"

As he followed, Gabe reached under his glasses to rub his tired eyes. He'd racked up too many late nights and too much screen time preparing for the grueling series of interviews, and it wasn't like he'd get a break from the pace. That was the gig, and he wanted it more than he'd wanted anything in a long, long time.

He'd wanted it, he'd worked for it, and he'd gotten it. Yes, things were finally looking up.

Glynna pulled a bottle from the fridge, hopped to the sink, and popped a cork. When the sparkling wine frothed up over the bottle's lip, she quickly slurped. "No use wasting good Prosecco."

As she poured two flutes, he covertly glanced around the room. His parents had been comfortable leaving Glynna, who still lived at home, holding down the fort while they were gone, but he and Gideon had privately decided to… keep an eye on things, just in case. So far, neither he nor Gideon had heard about loud parties or rowdy gatherings—none loud enough to cause the neighbors to complain, at any rate. The kitchen was spotlessly clean, probably because the pile of empty pizza boxes he'd seen stacked in the mudroom rivaled the Leaning Tower of Pisa for height.

He walked over to the refrigerator and opened it, raising a brow but not commenting on the magnet near the handle that read, "Why buy the pig if you just want some sausage?" A pint of half-and-half, lots of condiments, some Leann Chin takeout, cold pizza… and not much else. There wasn't a piece of fruit or a vegetable in sight. "When did you last grocery shop?"

"Quit snooping."

The letters on the half-and-half carton blurred, and he rubbed his eyes again, squinting into the dimness. "This lightbulb's burning out. I'll bring a new one next time I come over."

"Whatever. It looks fine to me."

The back door opened and closed. Gwen poked her head in from the mudroom, shrugging out of her long down coat. "Am I late?"

Glynna glanced at the clock. "Nope, but hurry up."

There was a muffled double-thump as Gwen's heavy winter boots hit the floor. A couple of seconds later, she entered the kitchen, dropping her bulging briefcase on the kitchen table. She eyed the open bottle and champagne flutes. "I hope we're celebrating?"

"Yes!" Glynna burst out before he could answer. "He got the job!"

"I knew it. Congratulations, Gabe." Her hug was more subdued than Glynna's was but no less heartfelt.

"Thanks, but remember, it's temporary. Alka will be back later in the fall."

"Say again?"

He pulled his head back so she could read his lips. "Remember that it's temporary."

"Well, Elliott Sebastiani hasn't accomplished what he has by not recognizing and nurturing talent. You're on your way."

Gabe shrugged. No doubt Sebastiani Labs' CEO had signed off on Alka's decision since Gabe would report to him while she was gone. It was a fabulous opportunity, true, but now it was up to him to execute, to prove, day in and day out, that they'd made the right decision.

His first opportunity to make a good impression would be tomorrow when he, Alka, and Mr. Sebastiani discussed how to restructure his current workload. Earlier today, when Alka had told him the job was his, she'd unknowingly eased his mind about his biggest concern: her daughter, Lorin. Thankfully, Lorin planned on spending the summer in northern Minnesota, working the archaeological site where, it was theorized, their ancestors had settled after being marooned on the planet eons ago. Yeah, he and Lorin would have to touch base occasionally, but she'd be out of sight, out of mind for most of her mother's absence.

Thankfully.

"Here." Glynna handed them both a delicate flute. "It's time to call the 'rents."

They went to their parents' study, a comfortable room cluttered with papers, books, and souvenirs from their travels. Wolves dominated the decor—matted prints of wolves in the wild, figurines carved of wood, jade, and ivory, and candid family snapshots. Glynna sat at the computer and, with a few clicks and keystrokes, placed the call to their parents, who'd somehow managed to find reliable electricity and broadband in Nepal.

"Been burning the midnight oil already?" Gwen asked.

"Huh?"

"You've been rubbing your eyes since I got here."

He jerked his hand out from under the thick lenses of his glasses. He blinked hard, but the damn shadows wouldn't clear. "Can we get some more light in here?"

Gwen looked at him strangely.

"There they are!" Glynna cried. "Hi, Mom and Dad!"

"Hello, my darlings!" His mother's voice sounded a

little choppy, but being they were calling from the freaking Himalayas, who could complain?

"Gabe got the promotion!"

So much for *his* news. As Glynna chattered away, he winced, raising a hand to his stinging left eye. Was there any aspirin in the house? Because he could really—*Ouch.* He caught his breath as the sting became a stab. Something… snapped. "Shit." Doubling over, he slapped his hand over the hot, lancing pain.

"Gabe?" He heard his mother's worried voice.

He collapsed onto a nearby chair. *Jesus.* Someone was skewering his eye with a rusty blade.

"Gabe?" Gwen touched his wrist. "What is it?"

"Pain," he gritted out. "In my eye."

"Glynna, call the ambulance—"

"No ambulance."

"Gabe—"

"Call Dr. Mueller." Gabe rattled off his ophthalmologist's phone number.

"What's going on?" his mother demanded from half a world away.

Gingerly opening his eyes, Gabe peered at the screen and tried to shove down the panic. He could hear the worry in her voice, but he couldn't see her mouth.

The black sinkhole in his field of vision swallowed her lower face whole.

———※———

Lorin Schlessinger stumbled into her chilly cabin, tracking clods of mud across the rough plank floor, entirely focused on the precious cargo she carried, swaddled in a large piece of treated chamois.

Shouldering the heavy door closed, she nudged the fabric aside to make sure she wasn't hallucinating. *Nope. Still there.* She carefully set the luminescent silver metal box, about the size of a fisherman's tackle box, on the wooden table next to her laptop. The box was unexpectedly light for its size, and accidentally hitting it with the stake she'd tried to hammer into the ground hadn't scratched its surface.

She was late for her meeting, but… damn, what a reason for tardiness. After years of backbreaking work—hell, *generations* of backbreaking work—had the unforgiving ground finally surrendered not just concrete evidence of their ancestors, but the Holy Grail of concrete evidence?

Noah Pritchard's command box. Knees suddenly wobbly, she lowered herself onto one of the table's straight-backed chairs and scrubbed her fists against her numb cheekbones. *Breathe. In and out.*

She gazed at the box, marveling at the serene, almost phosphorescent, glow. She wasn't aware of any local metal possessing such properties, but she was no metallurgist. Someone back at Sebastiani Labs would have to help identify the composition—once she let the thing out of her sight.

It was sheer dumb luck she'd found the box at all. She'd driven up to the Isabella dig ahead of the rest of the crew to wake the northern Minnesota archaeological site up from its long winter nap, hauling canned goods to the cookhouse, turning on the electricity and such. After evicting some squirrels from the outhouse, she'd gotten that indescribable itch between her shoulder blades—*get up to the dig site*—and hiked the third of a mile from base camp up to the swatch of unforgiving, iron-laced land where her parents had discovered the petroglyphs depicting their ancestors' violent arrival on the planet, confirming their oral histories.

Remnants of last night's late May snow still nestled in the shadowy northern lee of a few rocks and trees, but her experienced eye—and the mud on her boots—told her that the ground had thawed enough to start repairing the pit.

Her first sight of the protective tarp last year's dig crew had laid over the hole made her adrenaline jump. As she expected, the soil underneath the tarp was a muddy, rocky mess. Frost heaves had shoved most of their carefully placed stakes right out of the ground, but other than that, it looked like the site had wintered well. Once school was out and this year's crew arrived, the real work could begin, and the half-exposed hearth they'd uncovered in the southeast corner of the grid late last fall would once again get her personal attention. With a wistful look at the shallow hole, Lorin turned her back and made herself pick up her hammer. Repair first, explore later.

She had no idea how long she'd been pounding stakes when one of them simply shattered instead of slicing neatly into the ground. She picked up her trowel to dislodge what she was sure was a pesky piece of iron ore, but when the corner of the box emerged, glinting in the struggling sun, it was all she could do to remember her training, to not just claw the thing out of the muddy ground with her bare hands. Instead, she'd taken a deep, shaky breath, mentally and physically stepped back, and forced herself to place the measuring devices she carried in her backpack. She took pictures of the box *in situ* as she excavated, finally lifting it from its sleeping place and stumbling back to the cabin.

Lorin shivered, rubbing her dirty hands together for warmth. The sun had set, taking the temperature down with it. She switched on several lanterns, throwing light into every corner of the rustic cabin, and then set a match to the kindling and newspapers she'd laid in the cabin's potbellied stove earlier in the day. Before long, the kindling was crackling merrily, and she poured water into the battered blue iron basin to wash her hands and forearms.

She gazed at the box glowing on the table in its soft chamois nest, her eyes narrowing. She hadn't wiped it down yet. Where was the dirt, the mud?

How odd.

She didn't have time to analyze that now, or to sweep up the mess she'd made on the floor. She was late. Moving quickly to the small table serving as the cabin's desk-cum-kitchen table, Lorin punched the power button on her laptop and swiped her now-clean fingertip across its biometric fingerprint pad. Sitting down, she looked to the ceiling, issued a quick but heartfelt plea to the tech gods, and engaged the Council's proprietary conferencing software. Here in the Minnesota north woods, comm links and cell coverage were spotty at best. Lorin glanced at her battered watch. *Damn it.* She should have tested the sat link before going up to the dig to repair stakes.

But if she'd done that, she wouldn't have found the box.

Apparently the gods were in a benevolent mood. Her screen snapped to life, multiple windows popping open, reflecting the Council meeting agenda, a chat room, and video feeds providing views of the speaker and the entire boardroom table. On-screen, she watched her holographic body shimmer into her assigned seat next to her mother.

Ugh, she had mud all over her face. She might as well step away to wipe it off, because Krispin Woolf had the floor, and he was pontificating about—ah, who the hell cared? The WerePack Alpha's opinions and perspectives, rarely reasonable to begin with, had veered more wildly out of synch with his fellow Council members ever since his daughter Andi had been assaulted the previous year.

It didn't help that the perpetrator, a deeply disturbed off-planet incubus named Stephen, had escaped and hadn't been recaptured yet.

"I'm sure that Dr. Tyson's qualifications are stellar, but he's… human."

Even three hundred miles north of the Sebastiani Labs Chanhassen boardroom, Lorin heard the slur in Krispin Woolf's voice. "No offense," Woolf added with a glance at the Council's sole human representative, Security and Technology Second Jack Kirkland.

"None taken," Jack responded.

Lukas Sebastiani, the Security and Technology First, leaned into the table, his powerful incubus body coiled with tension.

Crap, what have I missed? The meeting had barely started, and Lukas already looked ready to blow.

"Krispin, we're evaluating candidates for the Humanity Chair. Hu-man-i-ty," he emphasized between gritted teeth. "Every single one of the candidates will be human. That's the point."

As Krispin once again repeated his objection to filling the Humanity seat, which had been empty since Carl Sagan's death, Lorin noticed Jack tap something on his mini. Probably urging Lukas to throttle back. The WerePack Alpha specialized in being a pain in everyone's ass—especially Lukas's. The tension between Lukas and Krispin had been escalating ever since Stephen had somehow escaped from their most secure holding cell.

It wasn't as if Lukas had personally allowed Stephen to escape. Lorin looked at Claudette and Scarlett Fontaine sitting side by side on the other side of the table. The sirens had been impacted by Stephen's crimes even more than the Woolfs had been. Stephen had killed Claudette's daughter and Scarlett's sister Annika on his rampage, but not only did the Fontaines not blame Lukas, Scarlett had become his bondmate.

On-screen, Lukas's nostrils flared at a particularly bigoted comment. Jack's face was rigid with distaste. Today, the two men seemed to share nothing in common except their oversized bodies. Lukas usually exuded a casual, rugged presence, but today his aura seemed dark and barely leashed. Jack, sitting next to him, was blond Armani elegance.

Beef and Cake. Lorin knew that despite their nicknames, first impressions could be deceptive. She and Jack were occasional sparring partners, and any human who could hold his own against a Valkyrie was no pushover. Lukas, despite his size, was an absolute marshmallow with those he loved, and if anything, his recent bonding had simply softened his center even more.

Elliott Sebastiani finally tapped on the boardroom

table with the unusual palm-sized rock that had served
as the Council president's gavel for as long as anyone
could remember. "Order, please," he said impatiently.
The tension between Lukas and Krispin was long running, ongoing, and never ending, but even if he privately
agreed with his son, Elliott was a stickler for procedure.
"Ten minutes for the WerePack Alpha."

If sticking to procedure put a time limit on Krispin
Woolf's remarks, all the better.

As Krispin expounded upon the apparent gaps in
Dr. Tyson's resume, Lorin watched the other Council
members mentally push back from the boardroom
table. Most of the Firsts had schooled their faces into
expressions of polite neutrality, but the Seconds, several of them new to their positions, either weren't as
successful at it or simply didn't care who saw their
reaction. Sitting next to his father, WerePack Second
Jacoby Woolf seemed frozen in place as he listened to
his father's frighteningly rational-sounding, yet bigoted, assessment. Scarlett Fontaine focused on Lukas,
worry chasing over her pale redhead features. Teenaged
Incubus Second Antonia Sebastiani's expression simply said, "WTF, dude."

Lorin opened a private message box.

[LSchlessinger]: Hi, Mom.

In the room view camera, Lorin saw her mother reach
for her laptop. Her huge jade and bone bracelet clattered.

"Alka, do you mind?" Krispin Woolf shot her a
dirty look.

Her mother removed the priceless bracelet and set
it on the boardroom table with a polite smile. She then
typed as noisily as she could.

[ASchlessinger]: Hello, dear. How was the drive up?

Lorin sighed. She was twenty-seven years old, and her mother still worried when she traveled by herself.

[LSchlessinger]: No ice on the roads, no freezing rain, no snow. No flat tires or blown radiator hoses. No marauding bears. No serial killers hiding in the bathroom at the rest stop.

[ASchlessinger]: No need to be nasty. How is the site?

[LSchlessinger]: Mud Bowl City. I... found something.

[ASchlessinger]: You started digging? Lorin. You know better.

[LSchlessinger]: Mom—

[ASchlessinger]: You know how important preparation is...

[LSchlessinger]: Mom—

[ASchlessinger]: You have to follow procedure, Lorin—

[LSchlessinger]: MOM. I found it WHILE I was repairing the grid.

Lorin watched her mother pause and purse her lips. She cursed under her breath and finally responded.

[ASchlessinger]: What's "it"?

Lorin glanced at the box gleaming on the table.

[LSchlessinger]: Let me open a private cam session...

Lorin activated the supplemental webcam, opened a stream to her mother, and tried not to squirm in her chair as she waited.

"Despite what the younger Mr. Sebastiani says, filling the Humanity seat places us at more risk, not less."

Lukas sat up. "Krispin, with today's technology and social media saturation, it's becoming more and more of a challenge to stay under humanity's radar. It's just a

matter of time before our true origins are revealed," he
said. "We need to start preparing the way for—"

"We all know your assessment of risk isn't exactly
foolproof these days."

Hoo boy. Did Krispin Woolf have a death wish?

Her mother abruptly straightened in her seat. Leaning
in closer to her laptop screen, she raised her hand and
tried to touch. "Oh, my. Oh, my stars."

Krispin Woolf cut off his harangue. "Alka, perhaps
you'd like to share whatever it is that you find so fascinating with the rest of us?"

"Certainly," her mother responded, her face full of
pride. "Lorin?"

"One moment, please," she responded evenly, fingers shaking as she took control of the meeting's conferencing software, initiating the sequence that would
change the webcam stream she'd been sharing with
her mother from private to public so everyone at the
meeting could see the box. A small smile crept up the
corners of her mouth.

Suck it, Krispin.

As she waited for the software to engage, she fidgeted
in the hard-backed kitchen chair. The greenish-silvery
box glowed on the table like an otherworldly thing, and
it was all she could do not to stroke it with her fingers.
"Damn it, hurry up," she muttered. She was an arm's
length away from announcing the find of the freaking
millennia, and the damn technology was moving at a
glacial pace.

After years of digging, after decades of begging for
tidbits of a budget, the Schlessingers finally had something to show for it.

A chilly breeze whistled through a gap in the cabin's old pine logs. Lorin shivered again and pulled her head more deeply into the neckline of her flannel shirt. "One more moment," she repeated. "Software is coming up now." Lorin smoothed the folds of the chamois. Unable to resist, she ran her finger very lightly along the edge of the button positioned at the center of the box's latch. Smooth to the touch, slippery, like warm ice, looking as if it would open at a—

"Whoa." The webcam engaged, giving everyone a close-up view as the lid of the box rose as if lifted by an invisible hand.

"Lorin! No!" Her mother's horror was evident, even through the tinny laptop speakers.

Biohazard protocol. Lorin shoved back from the table, tipping the chair over with a clatter, and dove to the corner of the cabin farthest from the table.

Not that a dozen feet meant anything at all if opening the box had released some alien toxin into the air.

Chapter 2

"SO YOU'RE THE SACRIFICIAL LAMB?" LORIN STALKED over to Lukas Sebastiani, who stood on the other side of the simple flat deck that broadened the entry to the cabin she'd been forced to stay in since yesterday. The afternoon sun was doing its best, but she buttoned her light insulated jacket before looking up to his face. "Any last words you want me to pass on to Scarlett before I throttle you?"

Lukas held up a grease-stained takeout bag and shook it. "Bacon cheeseburgers and onion rings."

"From Gordy's Hi-Hat?" As peace offerings went, it was a good one. "Damn you. Gimme."

Lukas extended the bag. She snatched it, quickly sat down at the wood picnic table, and dove in. She stuffed an onion ring into her mouth, nearly moaning with pleasure. Miracle of miracles, they were piping hot.

She winced. The crooks of her elbows stung.

"What?"

Lorin flexed the arm that wasn't delivering the precious grease to her mouth. "I swear, Wyland used the largest gauge needles he could find to take my blood."

"You're lucky he used needles and not fangs. Suck it up and deal."

"Hmmph," she grumbled around a convenient mouthful of food.

The quarantine team hadn't found anything toxic in

the cabin, or in the dirt up at the site, and there wasn't an area of her body that hadn't been examined, probed, and Roto-Rootered from here to kingdom come. After countless claustrophobic hours stuck in either the cabin or the mobile med trailer, she finally had a clean bill of health—a provisional clean bill of health, at any rate. Some of the lab tests Wyland insisted upon performing were so esoteric the results wouldn't be back for weeks.

Her old friend certainly knew her weaknesses— hence the food—but she also knew his. The pleasant expression on Lukas's face wasn't quite natural.

Something was up.

She reached into the bag for the first foil-wrapped burger. "Just so you know, I'm onto you. But I'm going to eat these burgers while they're hot."

"Lorin—"

"Is it safe to come over yet?" another voice called. Rafe Sebastiani rounded the corner of the cabin with his languid, lanky saunter, hands in his pockets. Before she could swallow and return his greeting, Chico Perez also appeared.

"Well played," she murmured to Lukas around the first delicious bite. With his choice of peace offering and traveling companions, it was clear that Lukas had taken her species' hyperactive adrenal system into account. After being confined to the cabin for nearly two days, she had to burn off some of the energy that had built up in her system, or else she'd jitter away.

Food, fight, and fuck—the Valkyrie trifecta. Lukas had covered all the bases—or so he thought. Apparently Rafe hadn't told his brother that they'd discontinued their arrangement.

Interesting.

She stopped eating long enough to stand and hug the two men, and then—what the hell—hugged that traitor Lukas as well. "I'm not sharing," she informed them all. "If you're hungry, there's food in the cabin."

"Excellent." Chico quickly ducked inside.

Rafe touched her shoulder to get her attention. "How are you?" His concern was evident on his face.

Rafe looked… tired. What was going on with him? When he'd told her that the "benefits" part of their "friends with benefits" relationship wasn't working for him anymore, she hadn't pressed, hadn't asked him why—even though his decision had left her seriously in the lurch. Maybe she should have. "I'm fine now that I can get outside and move," she said aloud. "Embarrassed as hell, though. I'm just sorry that an accident turned into such a big honkin' production." She glanced at Lukas. "Did the media pick anything up?"

"Nothing so far," he responded. "The quarantine and med units were pretty well-camouflaged."

Lorin nodded. The mobile labs looked like any other recreational vehicle driving up north for the weekend, right down to the children's bicycles bungee-corded to the back. Dipping her hand back into the paper bag, she came back with nothing but paper napkins. Ugh. She'd eaten three burgers and two orders of onion rings all by herself. She'd pay for it later with heartburn.

One more thing to blame on Lukas.

Snatching one of the napkins, she wiped the grease off her mouth and hid a smile. Time to yank her old friend's chain, just a little bit.

Lorin patted her full belly. "So, that took care of food.

What's next?" Her gaze dropped to Lukas's lips as she moved her own hand slightly south. "Fight or… fuck?"

Lukas shifted uncomfortably, glancing at his brother, flaring his nostrils to get a bead on her emotional energy.

"You know what will happen if I don't burn off some of this energy," she said silkily. "Do you want me to stroke out here and now?"

Finally he held out his hands. "I'll fight you, sure, but—"

Lorin burst into merry peals of laughter. Rafe joined in. "You are such a bitch," Lukas muttered.

"You deserved it. Stop pimping out your brother."

Lukas looked at Rafe. "Why aren't you dragging her into the cabin already?"

Rafe opened his mouth to answer, then closed it again.

What the hell was going on with Rafe? Damn it, she should have insisted on an explanation. And now Lukas had a puzzled expression on his face. He'd picked it up too.

"Hey." Chico emerged from the cabin licking Cheetos dust from his fingers. "What's it gonna be?"

Lorin sighed. She had to bleed off some of the excess energy her confinement had created, and they all knew it. Sex with Rafe—sex with any of them—wasn't an option.

"I'll fight you," Lukas repeated.

Lorin seriously considered his offer. She'd get in a few good licks before he defeated her, and whapping Lukas upside the head even once had definite appeal. *Nah.* When she sparred with Lukas, she had to fight defensively; he was just too physically dominant. Today, she didn't want to think that much. She just wanted to beat on something.

Lorin extended her clenched fist to Chico. The were-wolf grinned and bopped it with his own. "Bring it on."

———

Gabe bumped along the rutted dirt path someone had mistakenly informed him was a road, wincing when something scraped the undercarriage of his Beemer. He hadn't seen a sign of civilization since taking a left at the ramshackle watering hole squatting by the intersection where the asphalt ended and the gravel began.

He should have stopped at Tubby's Municipal Liquor Store when he'd had the chance, because this road was going to drive him to drink. He'd canceled a date for this—a setup by his brother, sure, but it was an authentic date, his first since his diagnosis—hell, the first since he and Kayla had broken up half a year ago. He'd scored reservations at a great downtown restaurant, and had orchestra seats for the latest Broadway touring show. He was under no illusion that Elyssa had bondmate potential; she was gorgeous, fun, and wasn't looking for anything serious. As Gideon had said, Gabe had to get back in the saddle somehow. But when Elliott Sebastiani had asked him to handle this epic shit-storm personally, in that oh-so-charismatic tone that made him feel like the most capable person in the world? Yeah, he'd caved. Even with possible sex on the agenda, he'd caved.

One more thing to blame Lorin Schlessinger for.

Bright sunlight dimmed to shadow as he drove into a tunnel created by pine trees taller than telephone poles. As he removed his clip-on sunglasses, a rogue branch swished along his passenger side, undoubtedly drooling sap on his new car's paint job.

"Shit." He hadn't even reached his destination yet, and this was already the assignment from hell. Dead bugs spattered his windshield, nearly obscuring his vision after an ill-advised attempt to swipe them away with the windshield wipers. And this was just the beginning. Once he got to his destination, he'd experience all the joys of camping. Mosquitoes. Ticks. Frost warnings and wilting heat.

Lorin Schlessinger.

Gabe sighed heavily. Elliott Sebastiani owed him—big-time.

Mood now mine-shaft dark, Gabe thought about acceptable ways to make Elliott pay. A budget increase? An equipment upgrade for the Metallurgy lab? Hazard pay? A sabbatical, as soon as Alka returned from hers? The upcoming months were going to be absolute bloody hell. He knew this as well as he knew his parents' itinerary, or the melting point of gold.

Regardless of Elliott's vote of confidence, he really wasn't comfortable being away from Sebastiani Labs for the entire summer, even with technology keeping him in regular touch with his team. He was still getting up the learning curve on his new responsibilities. Lorin, previously his peer on the org chart, was now reporting to him. He didn't know if there was any truth to the rumor that Lorin had been offered the position first. If she had, she'd declined it—and it was just as well. Her administrative skills were atrocious.

But this? Gabe whistled under his breath. The Valkyrie Princess had gotten herself into some deep shit this time. Elliott was completely right to insist on more direct supervision, but given that Alka hadn't left yet, he hadn't anticipated supplying the supervision himself.

Damn it, Alka.

Gabe didn't quite know what he was damning Alka for—honing her daughter's prodigious talents with such focus and precision? Letting Lorin get away with her perception that status reports, schedules, job queues, or priorities didn't apply to her? Leaving her post without giving him insight into how he, a werewolf mutt with dodgy lineage, was supposed to manage a reporting relationship with the Valkyrie Second? Giving birth to such an annoying creature in the first place?

He was clearheaded and rational. Lorin was headstrong and impetuous. She argued with him for sport. And… she was so damn talented. *Imagine, Noah Pritchard's command box.* Despite her protocol screwup, the Valkyrie Princess just might have made the archaeological find of the ages. Though he hadn't seen the box for himself yet, Elliott had told him that the metal had some highly unusual properties. Gabe couldn't wait to get his hands on it.

But the timing was horrible.

Now, almost five muscle-cramping hours later, he finally saw the landmark—a weathered wooden sign reading "Noah's Ark Wilderness Camp"—and turned onto the private road. Before long, he reached the "church camp," a scatter of buildings in a space cleared of pine trees. Gravel crunched under his tires as he parked between Lorin's rattletrap truck and the black Impala he knew belonged to Lukas Sebastiani.

Had Lukas given Lorin the happy news yet? As a Valkyrie, the urge to argue and fight was bred into her very bones, and her first instinct would be to kill the messenger. Gabe didn't envy the man. He clipped his sunglasses back onto his thick-lensed rimless glasses, knocked back the last cold mouthful of gas station cappuccino, and slowly got out of the car. As he stretched his arms to the sky, a howl split the air.

A wolf.

"Is that all you got? You fight like a girl," Gabe heard a male voice taunt. "C'mon, baby, show me some sweetness."

After a second of silence, he heard a higher berserker's yell—female—followed by the sound of flesh hitting flesh.

Gabe's skin crawled. His brain skittered to scenes from every horror flick he'd ever seen. Reaching into the backseat of his car, he grabbed the first likely looking weapon—weenie-roasting sticks—and broke into a run.

Where the hell was Sebastiani? Gabe pounded his way through the pine trees in his driving loafers, shoving at the branches slapping his face and torso, coming to an abrupt halt when he reached a grassy clearing about the size of a basketball court.

Lorin was under attack, all right—but if the unholy grin on her face was anything to go by, she was enjoying herself immensely.

He loosened his grip on the weenie-roasting sticks. Gabe didn't recognize the man Lorin was sparring with, but he'd found Lukas Sebastiani. The big man stood at the edge of the clearing, watching the fight with an amused—and relieved?—look on his face. His brother Rafe stood at his side, cheering Lorin on with clear partisanship.

His temper spiked. Gabe wasn't as jacked in to the Underworld Council grapevine as his sisters were, but even he knew that Lorin Schlessinger and Rafe Sebastiani were lovers. If he had to deal with incubi pheromones stinking the place up all summer long, he was definitely going to demand hazard pay.

Looking at Rafe's long, blond hair, his aristocratic features, the wicked grin, and the old-school aviator sunglasses that Gabe longed to be able to wear… of course Lorin was sleeping with him. The incubus was a physical ideal, and if his outrageous reputation was anything to go by, he pretty much slept with whomever he wanted.

So why sleep with Lorin Schlessinger?

Okay, that wasn't quite fair. Despite her ferocious expression—teeth bared, a fresh scrape on her chin— Lorin was far from ugly. If pressed, Gabe would have to admit that, yeah, Lorin's body was pretty much a physical ideal—if one's physical ideal ran along the lines of Amazonian beach volleyball players, and his usually did not. He preferred the women he dated to be smaller, more feminine, and definitely better groomed. When Lorin deigned to attend department meetings, arriving late more often than not, her streaky blond hair usually looked like she'd just stalked out of the ocean with a surfboard tucked under her arm. Never mind that they were landlocked.

The man's bare heel connected with Lorin's right cheekbone. Gabe winced as her head snapped back at the impact. How could Rafe stand to watch this?

On the other hand, how could he resist? Lorin was stripped down to clingy black leggings, a sports bra that should have been ugly but wasn't, and nothing else. Her taut, bare stomach was coated with mud, and he sucked in his own in response. She had better defined abs than he did. Time to get back to the gym.

Except there was no gym here, at the ass end of nowhere.

His breath caught as she tripped on a rock jutting out of the ground. The man capitalized, diving on top of her as she fell.

"Damn you, Chico," Lorin growled, twisting her face out of the mud.

Rafe tipped his head back and hooted. "He's got you now, babe."

"As if." Teeth gritted, Lorin scrabbled onto her elbows and threw the man off her body with a bump and grind of her tightly muscled butt.

Gabe swallowed and pushed his glasses further up his nose. Chico. Must be Chico Perez. Perez, a werewolf, was a Sebastiani Security operative. His brother Gideon had mentioned working with him to apprehend Annika Fontaine's killer last year.

Lorin crowed as she maneuvered Chico onto his back, pinning him to the ground with her body weight. Though he was as scraped and muddy as Lorin, Perez looked like he was having the time of his life. He squirmed a little for form's sake, but it was clear the fight was over.

"Draw?" Chico wheezed.

"As if," Lorin replied without heat, flopping off of him. Lying side by side on their backs in the muddy grass, they sucked in air.

Was that what she looked like after—*No*. He was in tough shape if he was thinking about Lorin Schlessinger and sex at the same time. And even if he, in some alternate universe, considered the option? Lorin worked for him now, and she was so far out of his league that it wasn't even funny.

"Hey, Gabe." Lukas came over, extending his hand.

"Lukas."

Lorin sat up. "Lupinsky." She spat his name like dirt was in her mouth. "What the hell are you doing here?"

Gabe glanced at Lukas, who shook his head no with an apologetic expression on his face.

Damn it. He looked at Lorin. "I'm your new site manager."

Chapter 3

THE PHONE RANG. LORIN SET THE CHEF'S KNIFE DOWN next to a growing mound of peppers and onions that would adorn her breakfast pizza and peeked at Caller ID.

Elliott.

With a heavy sigh and a sinking stomach, she put the phone on speaker. She might as well pace while her ass was being chewed. "Hi, Elliott. You're up early on a Sunday morning."

While they exchanged pleasantries, her gaze shifted out the window to Gabe's tent, glowing a cheerful bright blue in the tepid morning sun. At least it wasn't falling down around his ears. Last night, after they'd all returned from having pizza at Tubby's, Gabe had refused the other men's offer to help set up the two-room monstrosity. She knew he'd survived the night because he'd knocked on her door ten minutes ago, all rumpled and grumpy, asking where he could wash up.

Yeah, given the frost on the ground, pointing toward the lake without saying a word had been a little bitchy—but his expression had been absolutely priceless.

And if he stayed on the walking path, he'd bump right into the hot sauna. If he veered off the path or took another route? Lorin shrugged. He'd learn to follow directions, or deal with the consequences. Guilt nudged her with a fingertip. With his BMW and his driving loafers and cappuccino habit, Gabriel Lupinsky had "city boy" written all over him. She could have given him a space heater last night. She could have asked if his sleeping bag was rated for the weather.

She hadn't.

Whether he'd selected his campsite by knowledge or by accident, Gabe had chosen an ideal location to set up his home away from home. With the tent tucked under the overhanging branches of a big pine tree, he'd have some shelter from the wind and rain, and the branches would supply essential shade once the hot, humid days of summer arrived. He was a hundred-foot extension cord's distance away from the building housing their communal dining hall and workroom. The outhouse was a fair distance away, and the bunkhouse where the student crewmembers stayed was on the other side of the clearing altogether—which was a good thing, because their raucous video game battles sometimes raged long into the night.

"Lorin? Did you drop?"

Crap. Lorin turned away from the window. Elliott Sebastiani might be the closest thing to a father figure she had, but he was also her boss, and her president. "I'm here, Elliott." She sighed. "Let me have it."

She held her tongue as he coached her in the most diplomatic language imaginable, killing her with kindness. Why couldn't he just holler and yell, get it over with? But that wasn't his way. Hollering and yelling was *her* way. Anger was hot and cleansing, a cauterization that healed cleanly.

And it expended the pent-up energy that plagued her kind. She'd already been for one jog this morning, and thanks to Gabe Lupinsky, she felt another one coming on strong. By the end of the summer, she was going to be in the best shape of her life.

Men. Within the past twenty-four hours, every man she'd come into contact with had pissed her off. Lukas, despite his peace offering, had driven up to the site primarily to handle her. Chico had given her the workout she needed but had stolen her last bag of Cheetos as payment. And what the hell had Rafe been up to, giving her that soft kiss that everyone—except her—certainly misinterpreted? If Gabe's long-suffering expression was any clue, he sure had.

This morning, she wanted to give every person with a penis a FastPass to hell. She might make an exception for Elliott. Maybe.

"Elliott, have you watched the playback?" She certainly had, analyzing the video where she'd accidentally opened the command box as carefully as an FBI agent did the Zapruder film. "There's no way such a light touch should've opened the box."

"Accident or not, watching you dive into that corner gave us all some bad moments." Elliott's sigh was audible. "You were all alone up there, Lorin. Five hours away by car, two by chopper, which we couldn't have used anyway because it would have drawn all kinds of the wrong attention. What if you'd been injured? Killed? What if this accident had happened when your student crew was there? What could the body count have been?" He paused, giving the vivid visual time to seep into her consciousness like toxic waste. "Imagine the headlines: 'Suicide Pact At Northern Minnesota Church Camp.' The media would have been the least of our worries."

Over the crappy landline, silence hummed. Lorin heard Elliott take another deep breath, then slowly exhale. "It's been a really… bad year, Lorin. We can't lose you too."

Lorin swallowed hard. Even now, thinking about Annika Fontaine's death sliced.

"Finding the box is a game-changer, Lorin, especially if what we suspect of its origins is accurate."

"Okay, I get that. But why the watchdog?" Why *this* watchdog? "He's a program manager, a paper pusher, for Freyja's sake."

"I see you're conveniently forgetting that you report to him now." Elliott's voice was drier than the Mojave Desert.

"You know what I mean, Elliott," she muttered, looking at the beamed ceiling. "He hasn't worked in the field for ages. He's deadweight."

"Not to me," Elliott responded. "I need day-to-day—strike that—hour-to-hour visibility into this project. Gabe gives me that visibility, without impacting your progress." He paused. "Lorin, you're a stellar archaeologist. You have a preternatural talent for unearthing things, but we all know that administration isn't exactly your forte. Gabe, on the other hand, excels at administration. I need him there, if only for my own peace of mind."

"What about my peace of mind?" she snapped. "We drive each other nuts, Elliott." How could he sound so logical, so reasonable, when her thoughts were anything but?

"Will you submit daily status reports for the archive? Will you carry a sat phone 24/7, and actually answer it when it rings? No," he said, answering his own question, "not if your past performance is any indication." After another pause, he asked, "Don't you think it might be beneficial to have a geologist and metallurgist of Gabe's caliber available on-site?"

"Paige Scott is coming back this year."

"Ms. Scott is a talented young woman with a lot of potential, but she's still a grad student. Do you begrudge her the opportunity to work with Gabe?"

Lorin squeezed her eyes closed. Answering yes would make her look like a selfish pig. Damn it, damn it, damn it. She was well and truly stuck.

There was a knock on the door—two perfunctory taps, a courtesy, no more. "Speak of the devil. Gabe is here." Taking the phone off speaker, she opened the door.

Gabe's body temporarily blocked out the sun. "Very funny." Barely waiting for her to wave him inside, he stalked toward her coffeepot.

His teeth weren't chattering and his lips weren't blue, so he must have found the sauna. Wearing jeans, a black fleece pullover, and leather work boots, with a day's beard and his black hair slicked back from his forehead, he looked nothing like the urbane man she was used to seeing in Sebastiani Labs' hallways and conference rooms. Though the boots looked like they were fresh from the box, his jeans were clearly old friends, molding his long legs and admittedly excellent ass. She'd almost bought the jacket he wore for herself because its pile was so thick and luxurious. She'd virtuously passed.

Lorin pursed her lips, reconsidering. If he'd shopped for most of his supplies at the same place he bought his jacket, he just might be okay. Ah hell, what was she thinking? No doubt he'd researched his gear thoroughly. He probably had a cost/benefit analysis stored somewhere on the laptop she'd seen him unload from his car.

"I'll be done here in a moment." Lorin arched a brow at the coffee he'd already poured for himself into a mug that said *Bitch Is the New Black*. "Make yourself at home."

As she wound down her conversation with Elliott, she watched Gabe do just that, poking around the cabin, examining her woodstove, her coffee cup collection, taking in the unmade bed with a quick glance. Making his way over to the small bookshelf, he unerringly picked up the single most heinous picture of her in existence, the one her mother refused to put away despite years of pitiful begging. That summer, puberty had struck with a vengeance, and the picture had captured her with gangly limbs, huge feet, glasses, braces, and an unfortunate afro perm.

Gabe was grinning like a fool.

She snatched the picture from his hands and slapped it facedown on the shelf.

"Um… wow." Gabe sat down at the table, smiling around the lip of his coffee mug.

On the phone, Elliott said, "I expect you and Gabe to play nice, Lorin."

Her stomach jumped. "Yes, Elliott."

"I mean it. Don't torture the man. No fighting."

She eyed Gabe. "What if he throws the first punch?"

Elliott's sigh was less patient this time. "Lorin, his job is going to be tough enough without you provoking him. Just stay out of his way. Do what you do best, and let Gabe do the same."

Stay out of his way? How was she supposed to do that when he sat sprawled at her table like he owned it? As she watched, Gabe removed his glasses and cleaned the lenses with a small cloth he pulled from his pocket. It was like he'd removed body armor. As he stared myopically at nothing, she could see the flecks of silver in his icy blue eyes.

Sleet falling on Lake Superior.

She turned her back on him. "Okay, Elliott, I get it. Take care, and enjoy your Sunday. Okay. Kisses to Claudette. Bye." The clatter of the handset sounded unnaturally loud in the small cabin.

"Tattling to the boss already?"

She stalked away from the phone, picked up the chef's knife, and chose her next victim, a plump Vidalia onion. The first chop sounded like a falling guillotine. When she looked at Gabe again, his glasses were back where they belonged. "For your information, Elliott called me."

"Okay." His stomach growled audibly.

Guilt poked her again. No doubt her mother would be horrified at the hospitality she'd shown Gabe thus far. "Would you like to have some breakfast?"

"Thank you—as long as you're eating too. Less chance of being poisoned that way."

She rolled her eyes at him.

"What's on the menu?"

"Breakfast pizza—a flatbread Mom and I learned to make when we spent some time at a dig in Ethiopia when I was young," she answered. "It's one of my favorite comfort foods—" *Lorin, you're babbling. Just shut up.*

But of course he'd picked up on the edge in her voice, and now he was watching her much too closely. "You've had a stressful few days, that's for sure. Being quarantined isn't an experience you forget."

She flicked a glance his way before turning her attention back to her onion. Sounded like there was a bigger story there.

"Well, now that Wyland's cleared you, you can dig and run and… fight to your heart's content." When he cleared his throat and started asking detailed technical questions about the sauna he'd just used, she knew she'd imagined the huskiness in his voice.

"It's a wood/solar hybrid," she told him. "We converted part of our grid to solar a couple of years ago." When she walked past him to rinse her hands at the washbowl, she smelled her own shampoo. Somehow, on him, its crisp rosemary-mint scent seemed darker, less civilized.

He stretched a yard of leg under the table, crossing his booted feet at the ankles. "I was never so glad to see a building in my life." He shot her a wry look over the rim of the steaming mug. "I was certain you were trying to kill me off with hypothermia."

"Don't think it didn't cross my mind." She wiped her dripping hands. "But don't worry. If I wanted you dead, you'd see me coming."

Gabe's hand jerked, sloshing a tiny bit of coffee. "Sorry," he muttered, catching the spilled liquid with a quick lap of his tongue before it dripped on to the table.

Lorin's gaze locked on his mouth, and her sex gave a voracious clench. *Oh, hell no.* She knew she was hard up, but Gabe Lupinsky? Slick, ambitious, *annoying* Gabe Lupinsky? No.

But her traitorous body wasn't listening to common sense, because rough and ready looked damn good on him. Unlike the corporate Gabe Lupinsky she had no problem ignoring when they were both at work, this Gabe hadn't shaved, had towel-damp hair, and wore faded jeans that cupped him as faithfully as a lover's hand. For a desk jockey, he had a pretty great body.

She assessed the subtle flexing of his forearm muscles as he drank the coffee. He had a pretty great body, period. He must work out, somehow. What did Gabe Lupinsky do when he wasn't crunching numbers, squinting at a laptop screen, herding cats, and generally making her life miserable?

Gabe nudged an adjacent chair away from the table with the toe of his boot, indicating that she should sit down. "We need to talk."

"Yes, we do." Lorin sat but chose the chair across the table, trying to ignore the heat blooming between her thighs. Great body or not, they had to get a few things straight. Her mother wasn't here to protect their find, so it was up to her to do it. "Reporting relationship be damned, you're not in charge here."

His face clouded with the first hint of temper. She hadn't known he had one.

"Lorin, do you really think I want to be here, spending the summer living in a tent, with no decent coffee in a fifty-mile radius except here in your cabin?" Gabe rubbed his neck with his hand, looked at the beamed ceiling, then back at her. "You're the one who screwed up. Don't blame me for how Elliott chose to respond."

Okay, that smarted. "Have you seen the playback?"

"Not yet. I'm still waiting on clearance."

She hoped Gabe thoroughly enjoyed the microscopic background check Lukas would perform before giving him access to the Underworld Council network. "Well, there's no way that the box should have opened. I barely touched it. The metal is… unusual."

"That much I've been told. I can't wait to examine it." At her narrowed eyes, he added, "Lorin, who did you think would analyze your find?"

Him. No matter how much he annoyed her, Gabe was the most skilled metallurgist and all-around geologist at Sebastiani Labs. Of course he'd be working with her on this project. She sighed and fidgeted in the chair. "Okay, cards on the table. You annoy me. A lot."

"Same goes," he immediately responded.

"Someone mark it on the calendar—we finally agree on something."

Gabe took another sip of coffee, clearly considering his words before he spoke. "Listen. You don't want me here, and I don't want to be here. I'll stay out of your way as much as I can. But we *will* present a united front to Elliott. I don't care what kind of nepotistic connections you have to Elliott Sebastiani. I don't care that you're the Valkyrie Second. You report to me, and unfortunately, shit flows up the food chain as well as down. Your screwup is my screwup." His gaze speared into her. "We won't make another one of such magnitude."

Her breath caught, but not with anger or fear. No, fear would be preferable. This was lust—sheet-rolling, wall-banging, bone-incinerating lust. Who knew that Gabe could be so… alpha?

He sighed. "Lorin, I have no intention of getting in

your way on day-to-day operations—I'm buried up to my ass in my own work. But you can use me here."

Lorin pictured his long, rangy body stretched out on her bed, those oddly sexy glasses dropped carelessly to the floor. She could think of a lot of ways she could use him—

He cleared his throat and stood, his neck flushed with ruddy color. "Maybe now would be a good time for you to give me a tour, fill me in on how things work here."

"Good idea." Breakfast be damned, she needed to get out of this cabin before she did something monumentally stupid. She stood too, crossing her arms over her pebbled nipples. "I can show you where we keep the space heaters."

"Space heaters." After a fleeting dirty look, he quickly schooled his expression. She had to give him points for control.

A phone blipped at Gabe's waist. "Excuse me, I have to take this."

Lorin's eyes widened as he removed a Bat Phone from the leather carrier. "How the hell did you get one of those?" Lorin didn't want one of the coveted Sebastiani Labs prototypes for herself, but the fact that Gabe had snagged one before she had a chance to turn one down smarted.

He grinned like the Cheshire Cat.

Game on.

—∿∿—

Several hours later, Gabe sat in the outer room of his two-room tent, taking a breather before he started working again. Lorin had given him a quick tour of the site, pointing out the bunkhouse, the outhouse—Jesus, he was going to be using an outhouse all summer—but they'd spent most of the time in the site's largest building, which housed a good-sized workroom on one side and eating facilities on the other. He'd immediately commandeered the one dusty desk in the workroom as his primary workspace.

They'd spent too much time in a tiny space Lorin called the Control Room, about the size of the stingiest networking closet at Sebastiani Labs. The room housed not only the backbone of the site's computer network, but the brains of the idiosyncratic electrical grid. Earlier in his career, Gabe had happily rappelled into sphincter-tight crevasses and caves. Why had a six-by-six room felt so claustrophobic?

Lorin had been as ready to leave as he'd been, and he was finally, thankfully, alone in his tent, his home away from home for the summer. He was the proud borrower of not one but two space heaters, and a thick extension cord now snaked along the perimeter of the tent, providing him with electricity that he promised himself he'd use as sparingly as possible.

Now that he had firsthand experience with the conditions Lorin was dealing with, he'd cut her a little more slack the next time she called in late for a meeting. Network connectivity was dodgy, and the electricity, Lorin had told him, could be hit or miss. He'd been glad to see that the backup generator was gassed up and ready for action. Most of the devices he considered essential for daily life would be useless without electricity.

His phone blipped, and he snatched it off his waist. Tilting his head slightly to the left, circumventing the void in his field of vision, he opened the video his parents sent to him and his siblings. Gabe grinned as he watched his mother, in wolf form, pose in front of the shatter-topped mountains that time had shoved to the sky. It had taken every bit of his negotiating skill to stop his mother from coming home while his retina problems were being diagnosed.

"I'm coming, I'm coming," he heard his father mutter. The picture jittered as he set the camera down on a rock. After a pause, his father trotted over to join her on four legs.

His parents looked healthy. Their fur was shiny, and they were moving well. The terrain they were covering was some of the most rugged and desolate on the planet, and the fact that his mother was navigating on three legs chilled his blood. But she and Glynna had never known anything else.

At least he had all his limbs.

Gabe stood abruptly. He had a steep learning curve on how the dig operated, and the filing cabinets he'd seen in the workshop office seemed as likely a place to start as any. Delving into files would also help him stay away from Lorin long enough to get his thoughts and unruly body under control. Exiting the tent and zipping it closed behind him, he walked to the workroom. Where *was* Lorin, anyway? She'd disappeared after helping him lay the extension cord in his tent. What was she doing?

It was… too quiet. He was used to the hustle and bustle of the city. What the hell did people do up here if they weren't working? On the quick tour Lorin had given him earlier, she'd pointed out her running trails and the dock that the crew would help put in at the lake after they arrived. The local watering hole they'd eaten at last night, Tubby's, was the closest thing to a social opportunity he'd seen. It was too depressing for words.

Well, he had his computer and a pile of technical journals. He could always catch up on his reading.

He could also remind himself of all of the reasons why sleeping with Lorin Schlessinger would be monumentally stupid—the first point being he was her boss. She reported to him, at least on paper. He'd never dated a co-worker, and he wasn't about to break his rule with the Valkyrie Princess.

As he opened the workroom door, the phone gave a single blip, quickly followed by a second. High priority emails. Plucking the phone from its holder, he squinted and skimmed, a smile growing as he read. Lukas had finally authorized his access to the Underworld Council's confidential workspace, and Elliott's email approved Gabe's request to retrofit Sebastiani Labs' most secure facilities, a lab located in SL's sub-basement, for this project. He tapped back a quick response to Elliott, confirming the timeline and thanking him for the speed of his response. Another blip; another message from Lukas: Lorin will help you config your Council_Net access.

Yeah, right. He'd have to find her first. No, first things first. With a wince, Gabe opened the workroom's sole file cabinet very slowly. "Hmm." Instead of the unorganized mess he'd expected, crisp manila file folders lined up like soldiers on parade. He flipped through the files. Status reports. Geological assays. Budget. He pulled the file labeled "Training Records" and quickly flipped through its pages. Processes, procedures, confidentiality agreements, advanced first aid training… the records were current, complete, and clearly Alka's work, thank god. Gabe was particularly glad to see the exhaustive inventory list of first aid materials, because Underworld Memorial was a good three hundred miles to the south, and they couldn't exactly call a local doctor if someone got hurt. The injury log cited minor cuts and scrapes, a sprain here and there, a broken finger last season. Most of the entries were made in Lorin's crabbed handwriting, and most of the injuries she logged were her own. He imagined her swearing up a storm as she did so.

He touched a bloody smudge at the top of a page. He leaned down to sniff it, and jerked his head back when he realized what he was doing. Shoving the file back in the cabinet, he bypassed the Budget file and pulled Assays. He paged through the records slowly. Previous years' crews had performed all the right geological tests, utilizing radar, sonar, and various metal detection techniques. His own department had assisted, and—yes— there was his own signature at the bottom of the most recent report.

The command box Lorin found hadn't pinged anywhere, and it should have. What properties did the metal have that it had evaded detection despite the technology they'd thrown at it?

The metallurgist in him was definitely intrigued. And damn it, so was the man.

Chapter 4

"NO RUNNING WATER, WOOD HEAT, AND COLD AS THE moons of Gennadia Prime," Beddoe muttered, shivering in his inadequate skinsuit. The gleaming panels resting atop the buildings indicated that they'd started to learn how to harness the power of their nearest star, but *Dia*, Minchin hadn't mentioned how primitive the conditions were. He blew on his chilled fingers as he assessed the domicile's stubborn closure. The entrance hadn't opened at his voice command or touch, and the near-translucent wash of data scrolling along his peripheral vision wasn't helping. *Door. Tree. Roof. Dirt. Rocks. Lock.*

"I know it's a lock. Directions to open."

Door. Lock.

The door stayed stubbornly closed. "Dia."

His uplink to the Core provided him with little more information than he could discern perfectly well for himself: his vitals, the molecular composition of the strange items he encountered in this even stranger place, and the simple names these simple people had given to their simple things. In one of the countless small economies he'd instituted on board the *TonTon*, he'd budgeted and expensed for unlimited access to the Core, but instead of connecting, he'd shuttled the funds to his personal account. If there were massive holes in his knowledge base, he had only himself to blame.

Why in the name of the multiverse would the *Arkapaedis*'s homing beacon have blipped *here*?

He could really use Minchin's help, but he could hardly trust his first officer with this delicate task. Minchin had his uses, but the man was certainly his uncle Lorcan's spy, and the last thing Beddoe wanted his boss to know was that the homing beacon for the legendary lost *Arkapaedis* had popped on an inconsequential mudball in a territory so remote that the very assignment was considered a punishment route. But he'd get the last laugh. Yes, he would. Once he found the *Ark* and claimed the astronomical finder's fee, he'd be able to buy this unknown jewel of a territory outright. Its treasure trove of water and resources would be his to use. His to sell.

If he could find and disable the beacon, he could buy himself some time. If he couldn't, it wouldn't be long before the quadrant would be crawling with pirates and salvagers who wouldn't care what damage they left behind.

Voices approaching. A woman and a man. He chanced taking one last look through the domicile's small window, seeing a raised sleeping pallet—*bed*—what he thought was a heating device, open shelves laden with supplies. The small fortune in clean water, sitting in clear view of whomever passed by, made his fingers itch.

Beddoe exhaled, surprised he couldn't see his breath. They relieved their bodily wastes into a hole in the ground but bathed with clean water. To use such a precious resource for mere body hygiene was an act punishable by death on his homeworld.

Luckily for them, he wasn't a particularly law-abiding man.

He scrambled around the corner of the domicile and out of sight just as the man and woman emerged from the tall stalks of vegetation. As he watched, the woman said something he couldn't hear. The man didn't respond, which seemed to annoy the woman even further.

"Damn it, I can't believe this!" she yelled. "So much for not interfering with day-to-day operations."

The man looked baffled. "Lorin, I just want to take some soil samples. You can work around me, can't you?"

Beddoe raised a brow. The Core's language translation module was doing a better job than he expected it would—and though it was missing a word here and there, the woman's tone was universally recognizable.

Just as he thought she might actually strike the man, she growled in frustration, about-faced, and strode away. The man stared after her, shook his head, then ducked into the flimsy shelter he'd searched earlier, zipping it closed behind him.

Beddoe felt an odd communion with the man wearing the vision correction appliance. He'd have a hard time looking away from those buttocks too.

Peering from around a tall stalk, he watched her approach the door in her heavy boots, her footfalls loud against the platform. Shooting one final glance back to the man's shelter, she extracted a ring of jingling metal pieces from her jacket pocket. Selecting one, she inserted it into the tiny jagged slot.

Mechanical lock—a truly ancient technology. It figured.

The man and the woman were both very pleasant to look at. Despite his obvious vision defects, there were always customers for the man's type of tall, dark, and handsome—but it was the woman who drew his own connoisseur's eye. Her long hair was not blond or brown, but a streaky combination of both. She had a classic figure, with breasts and hips that would more than fill a man's hands. Stunning facial structure, with a particularly stubborn jawline. Beautiful, really. She was almost as tall as the man and looked like she could take a lot of physical damage. He could think of several *TonTon* clients with rather… exotic tastes who would empty their personal accounts to spend some time with this one.

He wouldn't mind breaking her in himself.

A vibration pulsed against his wrist as she slammed the door closed behind her. He sighed. Just as well. He pushed the button acknowledging his readiness to return to the ship. Darkness was falling, and the temperature with it—

Something bumped his foot.

His T-Mach was in his hand before he was aware of having grabbed it. He aimed, hesitated, but slowly lowered his weapon. The animal—small, deep-space dark, with a distinctive white stripe—wasn't attacking, and firing his weapon so close to the woman's shelter would draw attention he didn't want. "Identify."

After a short pause, the creature's molecular composition scrolled across his field of vision—and that was all. As he cursed his limited data, a familiar stinging chill washed over his body. Timeless beats later, he shimmered onto the bridge of the pleasure cruiser *TonTon*, locked in orbit a planet and a dimension away.

"Welcome back, Sirrah." Xantha Ta'al, his second

officer, rose from the command chair and stood at attention, acknowledging his return—and his still-drawn weapon—with a careful nod of her head.

He nodded back just as neutrally, hiding the fangs that had just descended into his mouth with a brutal shove. Minchin should be sitting in the command chair, not Ta'al. Minchin was cutting too many corners, powerful uncle be damned. "Where's Minchin?"

Ta'al pushed keys on the console, her fingers moving with lightning speed. "Entertainer's residence, Captain."

Beddoe cursed under his breath. Minchin spent far too much time with the incubus Stephen, who'd recently been reacquired after a lengthy escape to the planet's surface.

"We appear to have a stowaway, Captain." Ta'al indicated the black-and-white creature sniffing at his feet.

Was that amusement in Ta'al's voice? No, it couldn't possibly be. The woman, a stoic Valkyr, was as emotionless and as reliable as an automaton. "It had contact with me when I transported. Send it back down."

"Aye, Sirrah." As she flicked the controls, the animal lifted its tail, spraying something from its back end an instant before it disappeared.

A thousand dying suns, what was... The noxious odor came straight from the bowels of hell. "Toxin?" he gasped.

He already knew the answer. They were going to die.

The unflappable Ta'al coughed, and though her eyes had to be as blurry as his were, her fingers flew at the con. "Bridge contained," she choked out. More keystrokes. "Assessing composition." Time dragged as Ta'al studied the console and finally spoke. "Negative."

"What?"

"Negative for toxicity," she repeated, coughing again. "Noxious, certainly. Most disagreeable. A very effective defense mechanism."

Choking, Beddoe strode blindly to the elevator. "I'll leave cleanup in your capable hands. Please keep the scent out of the customer areas. I'll be with Minchin in Stephen's quarters."

"Yes, Captain."

Immediate response, respectful tone, implacable facial expression. How had such an excellent officer fallen into his hands? "Ta'al." Despite her streaming eyes, she met his gaze squarely. "I am pleased with your performance. Consider your probationary period complete."

Ah, there it was—a flicker of expression, the slightest lift of an eyebrow. "Thank you, Captain."

"Carry on."

With a few flicks of her fingers, Ta'al reversed containment, reactivating the elevator. Stepping inside, Beddoe took deep, grateful breaths of clean air. The doors closed and the elevator descended, each ticking number carrying him further away from that bedeviled scent, and closer to Minchin—and whatever damage he'd already done to Stephen.

His first officer was absolute hell on his profit margin, and that he could not abide.

~~~

Gabe stood in front of the bank of old TV sets lined up on hand-me-down coffee tables in the living room area of the bunkhouse, a snarl of black wires in his hands. "No wonder your budget is so outrageous," he called to Lorin, who was in the other room snapping sheets onto beds. Three different video game systems? Things sure had changed since he was a grad student working in the field.

Although it was evening, Lorin emerged from the other room wiping sweat from her hairline, dressed in a pair of those saggy-waisted cargo shorts she seemed to live in, and a tank top that bared her muscular shoulders and arms. Gabe had shed his light coat when they'd entered the bunkhouse, but he was still glad for his long-sleeved sweatshirt. The woman must have a blast furnace for a metabolism.

Walking to the battered refrigerator, she grabbed one of the Diet Cokes they'd loaded earlier, opened it, and drank thirstily. Swiping a wrist over her mouth, she said, "Most of the gaming gear is donated. Some of the students leave supplies here for future groups to use after their own field season is over." She nudged the refrigerator with her boot. "Donated. The TVs are donated. Almost everything in here except the mattresses has either been donated or left behind by work crews over the years. You might have noticed there's not a lot of nightlife in the area." She looked around and shrugged. "It might not have all the comforts of home, but—"

"Pretty damn close." Gabe appraised the bunkhouse, which over the years had taken on more of the patina of a frat house than an up-north hunting shack. In the living area, a trio of sagging, mismatched couches faced the bank of televisions, surrounding a big wood table scabbed with dings and water rings, perfectly positioned for feet or the next beer. A beautiful shallow pottery bowl—Rafe Sebastiani's work?—sat on the center of the table, filled with remote controls, pinecones, condom packets, and spare change.

The readers in the group would probably prefer one of the two overstuffed chairs cozied up next to the table and lamp near the window. Bookshelves covered one full wall, loaded with board games, comic books and graphic novels, DVDs, random rocks, video games, photographs, and yes, even some books. The bare-bones kitchen to his left featured a battered sink with cold running water, a microwave, a toaster, a toaster oven, some mismatched dishes, and two full-sized refrigerators.

There was no hot running water and no indoor toilet, but with unlimited free Internet, video games, beer, pizza, and condoms, Gabe could see why the Schlessingers had hundreds of students applying for summer field positions.

Gabe peered into the other room, briefly considered claiming one of the bunks for himself, but just as quickly discarded the idea. He valued silence, and none would be had here.

"Want to take a run before hanging it up for the day?"

Gabe couldn't help the snap of his head. They'd been working like dogs all damn day, getting the site ready for the crewmembers who'd start straggling in tomorrow, and she still had enough leftover energy to run? All he wanted to do was flop onto one of these hideous couches and not get up for hours. "Sure," he said instead. If she had the energy to run, so did he, damn it. "Let me change and meet you at your cabin in five."

She slammed the rest of the can of pop. "On our way back, we can swing by the sauna." Dropping the empty can in the recycling bin, she sauntered out the door while he stood locked in place.

Sauna? Did she mean… bathe? Together? His face heated, and blood pooled in his groin. He knew that saunas were a historically communal bathing ritual, brought here by the Iron Range's Scandinavian immigrants, but… just how authentic did she mean this sauna to be?

Authenticity be damned. He was going to wear his swimming trunks, which, thankfully, were very, very baggy. If she sauntered into the hot, cedar-scented enclosure wearing nothing but her birthday suit, he'd find a way to deal. Somehow.

Back at the tent, he changed quickly into his running gear and joined Lorin on the cabin's deck. She had changed and was already stretching, wearing viciously expensive running shoes and clingy black leggings with a snag running from the left knee to ankle. On her next bend from the waist, she stayed down, a disgusted look on her face as she glanced at his feet.

Gabe fought his eyes away from the taut globes of her ass. "What?"

"You have really big feet."

"So do you. What's your point?"

"Just figures," she said moodily, shifting over to give him some room to stretch.

Out of the corner of his eye, he watched Lorin brace her hands against the picnic table and lean into a quadriceps lunge. Her muscles flexed and rippled as she deepened the stretch, deeper, deeper, until her crotch nearly rested on the heel of her running shoe.

She didn't so much move as… flow from one movement to the other. What would she look like writhing underneath him, lost in the throes of passion? What would it feel like to have those legs twined around him as she shook apart in his arms? *Absolutely spectacular.*

Gabe cursed as his body responded. The sweatpants wouldn't camouflage his condition very long. For a split second, he felt like a pimple-faced pup again, but he shoved the guilt away. An erection was an autonomic physiological response, nothing he could control. They were both adults here. A woman as beautiful as Lorin Schlessinger had certainly seen more than her share of inconvenient erections.

She pointed to the deck. "Footprints."

She hadn't noticed his condition; she hadn't even been looking at him. Gabe didn't know whether to be relieved or insulted. He crouched down beside her. Sure enough, there were muddy footprints on the deck in front of the window.

"Looky-loos." At his raised eyebrow, Lorin flapped her hand toward the nearby town. "Trespassers. We get a couple every year, usually kids on a dare, or someone who's drunk, on foot, stumbling home from Tubby's." She narrowed her eyes. "Though usually not this early in the season."

Gabe examined the muddy footprints. The trespasser had a slightly smaller foot than he or Lorin did, and wore shoes with virtually no tread. The prints tracked from the cabin door to the window, and then trailed off the deck into the birch and pine trees. "There's no mud today. Whoever it was must have been here yesterday. Anything missing from the cabin?"

"Not that I've noticed, but I wasn't looking, either. I lock the door when I leave camp."

As she went into the cabin to check her possessions, Gabe examined the cabin's lock and doorknob. No pry-marks. The metal was smooth and unscratched.

Lorin came to the doorway, standing so close that even through the top notes of sunscreen and bug dope, he could smell her warm skin. "Doesn't look jimmied," he said, stepping back.

"How about you? Missing anything?"

"Shit," Gabe muttered. Trotting back to the flimsy tent, he mentally ticked off his valuables. The prototype Bat Phone never left his body, even when he jogged. His laptop was stored in a locked file cabinet in the workshop, and he'd used it not two hours ago. Sweeping the zippered door open, he quickly scanned the few possessions he'd brought. Over in the corner, his duffel bag slouched, agape. He jammed his hand into it and fished around, past his own sunscreen, bug dope, and a small first aid kit, until he felt the hard clamshell case of his backup glasses, and the magnifying glass he sometimes needed for reading. His prescription eyedrops were still there. A sigh of relief escaped.

"Wow," Lorin said from behind him. "What a mess."

She was right. Like a teenager dithering about his first date, he hadn't been able to figure out what to wear to go running—and bathing—with Lorin, and his clothing was strewn all over his bedroll and the floor. "It doesn't look like anything's missing," he said after a cursory search of the rest of his tent. "Most of the scientific equipment I brought is still locked in the trunk of my car."

Lorin sighed. "We haven't had to be too concerned about physical security around here before."

"We are now," he stated. "The data on our laptops alone is worth a bloody fortune to anyone who wants inside information about Sebastiani Labs. Imagine what could happen if someone hacked yours, with Council communications on it. The locks I've seen up here so far are pretty damn flimsy."

"I'll call Lukas, see what he recommends," she finally responded. "There *is* such a thing as safety in numbers. The grad students will be arriving tomorrow, and after they do, you'll have a hard time finding anyplace to go without tripping over someone else. This quiet, this… privacy will soon be a thing of the past."

Thank gawd. Right about now, Gabe would appreciate having more people around. Anything to cut through this… tension that now wafted between them, as stubborn as wood smoke.

"Let's check out the dig site."

Gabe followed Lorin out of the tent. She locked her cabin, the workroom, and the bunkhouse before zipping the key ring in her jacket pocket, and then led them on a steady, single-file jog down a trail winding through the tall tamaracks and jack pines. Years of fallen needles carpeted the trail. Birds chirped, and something rustled in the underbrush. He focused on his footing, avoiding the strewn pinecones. Anything to keep his eyes off her ass.

Lorin slowed as the trail dumped out to a clearing, to the excavation site that looked nothing like it had in Alka's season-ending status report last fall. That site had been neat and orderly, with the active area's grids laid out with military precision, and shaded by protective overhead tarps. Now it was a muddy mess, and the shallow pit's north wall was partially caved in. Off to the west, the treasure that the site had spit up years ago—the residence, dug into the side of a hill, with its priceless wall of glyphs—was protected by the pole barn that Alka had erected around its entrance.

Lorin worked her way over to the corner of the pit where he knew she'd found the command box, put her hands on her hips, and sighed. "I can't tell whether anyone else has been up here or not. When I found the command box, I was on my feet, my knees, my stomach."

Gabe's thoughts skittered to Lorin sparring with Chico Perez, her toned stomach streaked with mud.

"We should be just about done with overnight frost," she continued. "Once we know the dirt won't liquefy under our feet, we'll be able to grid this area off again."

He pointed to a corner of the knee-deep hole, approximately twenty feet square, where a large ring of boulders was surrounded by rotted wood logs, too precisely placed to be random. "That's the cooking ring?"

Lorin nodded. "Excavated last year. The charred wood dates back about a thousand years. I found the command box over there," she said, indicating the other side of the pit. She fell silent as she stared.

He shivered, and not with the evening chill. If her theory was right, their ancestors' ship had crashed nearby. People had lived here, died here. They were standing on hallowed ground. "Any indication of burial mounds?" he asked, loath to speak into the hushed silence.

"Not that we've found," she responded softly, "but there's a lot of the property that we haven't yet explored. The radiocarbon dating aligns with our oral histories. Written records pick up in the early twelfth century, and most of those come from Europe. Wyland and Bailey are doing what they can to digitize and store what we have, but some of the documents are crumbling to dust right in front of us."

Gabe listened carefully, all senses on alert. It wasn't often that anyone not on the Council received any visibility into its inner workings. He'd been so busy dealing with Lorin as an epic pain in his ass, and more sensitive body parts, that he'd forgotten that she represented her species—hell, she represented *all* of them—as a Council member. It had to be a crushing responsibility.

He had to ask. "Why is a human working on our archives?" Prior to Bailey Brown's arrival on the scene, Lukas's business partner Jack Kirkland was the only human alive with confirmed knowledge of their existence. Dr. Brown's very presence at Sebastiani Labs had lit up the office grapevine for weeks. One day he'd helped the little human shove a cart groaning with computer equipment over the lip of the elevator that led to Sebastiani Labs' sub-basement, where the backbone of its network resided.

"Because she's the best," Lorin said simply. "She actually works for Lukas, and he's billing Elliott through the nose for her time."

"Quite a gig," Gabe said. "Knowing Jack Kirkland certainly can't hurt." He couldn't keep the cynicism out of his voice.

"Bailey would die before disappointing him. He's her family."

After an uncomfortable silence, Lorin gestured to the fire pit. "Mike and Paige will continue this work when they arrive."

"They were here last year?"

Lorin nodded. "Most of the crew is returning this year."

"No humans on the crew, right?"

"Nope."

He nodded with approval. "Nice to have some experienced hands." Yesterday Gabe had pulled and reviewed their applications himself. Mike Gill's scholastic interest was forensic anthropology, and by all indications he was an impressive student, but Gabe's long-dormant teaching instincts were piqued by Paige Scott, a faerie geologist who didn't yet realize she'd be working on the discovery of the ages. Ms. Scott had done some very solid work last summer—potentially leadership-caliber work. Her signature had appeared on the most recent sonar, radar, and magnetic and metal detection assays, and her field reports were meticulously written. If he could trust Paige's work, the box Lorin had found a couple of days ago hadn't caused even the slightest ping during last year's ground-penetrating radar sweep.

What kind of properties did such a metal have that it evaded all their tests? Gabe couldn't wait to get back to SL and get his hands on the thing. If the schedule he and Julianna had worked out held, he'd have to wait a couple of weeks, but the thrill of the academic hunt already coursed through him, made him shift on his feet.

The discovery of the ages. The Lupinsky family, those damaged mutts, would have their place in the history book. A mere footnote, to be sure, but his name would be linked with Lorin's for all posterity. The idea both satisfied and disturbed him.

"You're shivering," Lorin said. "Let's head for the sauna."

Gabe swallowed to lubricate his suddenly dry throat. "Okay."

Lorin led the way, backtracking on the trail they'd taken to get here, and veering off on a side trail that led to the sauna sitting at the edge of the site's small lake. "We'll put the dock in and the raft out once it gets a little bit warmer," Lorin said, indicating several large tarp-covered mounds near the shore.

He followed her into the sauna, a weathered wooden building that definitely looked like it had been there awhile, shivering in pleasure as cedar-scented heat bled into him. The sauna had the traditional two-room configuration, a changing area and steaming area, with a door in between. The changing area had a curtain that could be drawn to provide privacy, but it was frayed and dusty with disuse. Storage cubbies tic-tac-toed up one wall, and three were currently in use. He'd brought his swimsuit and his toiletries up earlier, and Lorin's things already filled two squares. Amongst the shampoo, conditioner, lotion, and other detritus of femininity was a tiny mound of *Baywatch*-red fabric that hadn't been there yesterday.

Swimsuits, then.

His eyes widened as Lorin reached for the zipper of her fleece jacket. Did she mean to strip down right here in front of him? Nudity wasn't necessarily sexual in their society, but… sometimes it damn well was. He glanced at the curtain in quiet panic. How would he ever be able to face her across a conference room table if he saw her naked? If she saw him naked?

He swallowed with a quiet click. If she could do this, so could he.

Gabe toed off his running shoes, placing them neatly next to hers. Socks next. Taking a deep breath, he reached for the zipper of his jacket—just as Lorin shrugged hers off with a lithe movement that would be engraved on his retinas for a long time to come.

She closed her eyes momentarily, shivering with obvious pleasure. "Doesn't that heat feel fabulous already?" She folded the jacket and reached past him to place it in a cubby.

When their bodies touched, she jerked back like she'd touched a live wire. With her jacket off, clad only in a duo of tank tops, her nipples pebbled under his gaze. Snatching her swimsuit from the cubby, she released the curtain from its ancient moorings, drawing it across the changing area with a puff of dust and a screech of rusty metal hoops. "Hurry up, I'm freezing."

Gabe hurriedly undressed. Hearing her do the same without being able to see her was almost worse, because his imagination was aflame. While Lorin chattered about the summer crew's qualifications, he stared at the long, narrow bones of her feet, the high arches, the toes tipped with pansy-purple polish.

Not at all what he expected from Lorin Schlessinger. "Do you need some help over there? Hurry up."

He glared at his unruly cock, currently standing at attention. Damn her for lobbing such an incendiary comment over this flimsy, ineffectual wall. She had to know where his testosterone-poisoned brain would go. Did she think him so neutered that he wouldn't take her up on it? His cheekbones throbbed as he let the silence lengthen.

You can't take her up on it, asshole. She reports to you—and she's the Valkyrie Second. He might temporarily outrank her at work, but in every other way that counted, she was fathoms out of his league.

"Coming," he said through the gravel in his throat. Let her make of his comment what she would. He quickly stripped off his clothes, folded them, and stepped into his swim trunks. He took a deep, cleansing breath and looked down at his groin. At least the baggy surf shorts provided some coverage.

He swished back the curtain and choked back a groan. Lorin was bent over in the bathing area, pouring warm water over her hair, her sighs of pleasure audible over the splat of falling water hitting the concrete floor. His eyes zoomed in, fetish-close, on her ass, on the skimpy red bikini bottom that revealed as much as they concealed.

Gabe closed his eyes. He was a dead man.

Chapter 5

"LORIN, WE CAN'T SEE YOU. COULD YOU MOVE CLOSER to Gabe?"

I'm practically in his lap already. "Sure," she replied to Willem Lund, who was helming the hastily called meeting from the Sebastiani Labs boardroom. When she'd suggested to Gabe that they dial in to the meeting from the workroom, her only thought had been keeping Gabe out of her cabin, its floor space dominated by the sturdy double bed. Gabe's laptop had an integrated camera—ideal for the conferencing needs of the person at the keys—but for two people? Completely inadequate. "Should have brought my own," she muttered, shifting the chair closer to Gabe.

"Why didn't you?" Gabe took a big slug off his— *her*—thermal coffee mug.

He'd missed a patch when he shaved that morning. Five black bristly hairs stood at the side of his Adam's apple.

"Lorin, we still can't see you," Elliott called.

She tore her gaze from Gabe's moving throat.

Shit. Someone needed to commit her to the nearest psychiatric facility. Her idea to take a nice, friendly sauna with Gabe last night had been utter freaking lunacy. Who could have predicted that Gabe Lupinsky would look so great nearly naked? For all the excess yardage in those unexpectedly exuberant surf shorts he'd worn, the thin fabric clung quite faithfully to his dimensions. She'd wanted to take him in her hands. She wanted to see him, taste him.

Take him.

"Sitting side by side won't work," Gabe said. "Your shoulders are almost as wide as mine are." He pushed her chair, with her in it, forward a few inches. "There. Now lean in."

His damp, warm breath drifted across her neck. The position put Gabe not two inches behind her. The heat of his body bled into hers.

"That's better," Willem said.

Better for whom? Lorin disguised her reflexive shiver by tipping her head and scratching under her ear.

"Fighting already, I see." Elliott's amused voice made Lorin suspect that he knew the true source of their tension.

Gabe shifted his weight in the squeaky-wheeled office chair, clearly uncomfortable.

It was all her fault.

Last night during their sauna, Gabe had prattled on about their breakdown of responsibilities, their processes and procedures, with an erection tenting his shorts, asking cogent, focused questions, mentioning their reporting relationship a lot more often than necessary.

How convenient for Gabe that he could ignore basic biological functions, could ignore... her not-very-subtle pass.

She closed her eyes in mortification.

"Could you stop squirming?" Gabe grumbled from behind her.

Lukas looked up from his mini, nostrils twitching.

Damn it.

"I know some of us have other meetings in a half hour, so let's get started," Willem said. "Recording started. Let's take roll, please. Elliot Sebastiani."

"Here."

"Lukas Sebastiani, Jack Kirkland, and Bailey Brown, representing Sebastiani Security."

There was a trio of responses from the side of the table closest to the window where the Sebastiani Security contingent sat together. The slight blurring in the windows at their backs indicated the security shades were fully engaged. "Good to see you when you're not diving for the corner, Lorin," Jack added with a smile.

She smiled back. "Hi, Jack."

Beside her, Gabe cleared his throat.

"Wyland."

"Present."

From across the table, Bailey mouthed something that looked a lot like "unfortunately."

"And Julianna Benton from Physical Sciences Ops. Welcome."

"I'm glad to be here," Julianna said. The gorgeous redhead was Alka's—now Gabe's—operations manager.

Gabe leaned forward, placing his hand on Lorin's shoulder for balance. "Apologies for the short notice, Jules." To the room at large, he said, "Julianna will be coordinating some of our work while I'm on-site here with Lorin."

Lorin's head whipped to Lukas. "Security clearance?"

"Completed and upgraded late last night," he responded around a jaw-cracking yawn. "You should have a copy in your Council email."

Of course she did. And her question to Lukas simply exposed the fact she hadn't even cracked her laptop open that morning, much less read her email. Upon waking, she'd been in such a twitchy state that, after two self-administered orgasms, she'd gone for a punishing run, barely making it to the workroom in time for the meeting. And despite the light burning in Gabe's tent long into the night last night, this morning he looked disgustingly poised and alert. Somehow, he'd managed to get his Council work environment installed, configured, and functioning without her help.

Just how much work had he knocked off last night while she'd been taking care of… business? She was out of the loop, and it was her own damn fault.

Lorin shifted her weight to the side as Gabe leaned in to use the keyboard, opening a chat window with Julianna. On-screen, Lorin noticed Julianna's tiny smile as she read what Gabe quietly typed.

How… *cozy*. Was there more than business between them? The more she thought about it, the more it made sense. Last night in the sauna, after declining her clumsy pass, Gabe had kept a careful distance between them. Mr. Scruples wouldn't screw around on his girlfriend.

Her face flamed, but she kept her tone cool. "There's no reason for Gabe to be stuck here when the box—and the action—is down there," she said. She turned toward him, bumping into his chest with her shoulder. "Go home, Gabe. Where you belong."

Their gazes locked in a private battle. "For the time being, I belong right here."

"Yes," Elliott seconded. "Lukas and I feel better

knowing there are two of you there, especially with the visitor you recently had."

"Nothing on that footprint so far," Lukas added. "We'll keep on it."

Lorin blinked. When had Gabe sent Lukas—

"Shall we look at the agenda Gabe sent?" Willem said.

An agenda? Of course Gabe had sent an agenda—and the first thing on it was a quick review of her own quarantine results. All the tests had, so far, come back negative. Her clean bill of health was great news, but the fact it had been mentioned at all simply re-emphasized that she'd made a huge mistake in the first place. Julianna's sympathetic expression made her feel even more stupid. Wyland continued with an update on the box itself, which had been catalogued, carefully crated, and placed in the archives until they were ready to examine it.

Gabe was up next, and the rest of the meeting went very smoothly—too smoothly. The details Gabe walked them through were well thought-out, exhaustive, and smacked of fait accompli: while Gabe and Lorin worked the dig for two more weeks, Julianna would coordinate a retrofit of the secure lab located in Sebastiani Labs' sub-basement. Once the buildout was complete, they'd run the box through a battery of tests. After reviewing the results, the box would be carefully opened, and the items inside extracted, carefully catalogued, and then analyzed.

"Lorin will coordinate expansion of the grid in the area where the box was found," Gabe said, looking at his watch. "The summer crew starts arriving in a few hours."

"We're keeping the discovery of the box confidential for now, correct?" she verified.

At her side, she felt as much as saw Gabe nod.

Elliott concurred. "No need to tell the students anything specific until we know what we're dealing with."

She sighed. "I know it's the right decision, but these workers were selected for their brains. It's going to be a challenge." Shooting a glance at Gabe, she said, "Explaining Gabe's presence here will be challenging enough."

Elliott's hooded gaze encompassed them both. "I have every confidence that the two of you will come up with a convincing explanation."

At her side, Gabe sat up straighter. He'd felt it too. Elliott's patented "nested Russian doll" requests were powerful—an order at the core, couched as a request, wrapped in an expression of confidence that made his employees kill themselves to fulfill his expectations.

Gabe leaned forward, pressing his hard, muscular chest against her shoulder blade, quirking a smile and gesturing with his hand while he and Julianna discussed the specific chemicals, tools, and equipment Gabe required for his work. His voice vibrated through her torso, painfully acute, but she couldn't quite seem to find the muscular will to shift her body away, or to ask him to move. There was a smudged fingerprint at the rim of his glasses, and she could smell the coffee on his breath when he laughed.

As the meeting went on, there were no disagreements, because Gabe gave everyone an opportunity to build upon the plan. He asked for input. He accepted feedback gracefully. Though Lukas scowled, no doubt mentally beating the bushes for risks he hadn't yet seen or considered, Elliott, seated at the head of the boardroom table, smiled like a pasha.

Lorin sat silent and numb. He'd thought of everything. In a mere twenty minutes, she'd officially and totally lost control of her mother's project, her own contributions relegated to tasks and sub-tasks on a freaking project plan.

Finally, Julianna snapped her stylus into her e-tablet with a decisive click. "Gabe, I'll have an updated lab status to you by noon." She turned toward Elliott Sebastiani. "Thank you for the opportunity to work on this project, sir. And Lorin?" Julianna's gaze met hers from the open window on the desktop. "Congratulations on your find."

There was no wordless warning in Julianna's expression, no evidence that she knew Lorin was fighting not to jump her lover's bones. Gorgeous, smart, and… nice. She had no defense against nice.

Lorin thanked Julianna, choking out something she hoped was appropriate, and then shoved out of the chair, its legs screeching against the floor. "Excuse me," she said, walking quickly to the door.

"Lorin?"

She kept walking, ignoring the question in Gabe's voice. "I'll be up at the site."

Ducking out, she hurried down the stairs. With each step away from the workroom, she lengthened her stride. Before she was halfway across the compound, she was running full-out, running like the wind.

⁓

Gabe threw his pen down on the battered desk in disgust, his concentration shot. What was wrong with Lorin? He'd expected some fight from her at the meeting, some healthy give-and-take. He'd looked forward to it. But she'd been too quiet, and when she left, she'd looked positively... wounded.

Just when he thought he had a bead on the woman, she did a one-eighty on him.

His Bat Phone chirped. He plucked it off the desk, looked at the display window, and swore. Something must have gone to hell in a handbasket for Lukas to be calling him not a half hour after they'd all left the same meeting.

"Lukas. What's wrong?"

A pause on the other end. "Why does everyone always ask that?"

"Lukas, you manage risk for a living. Go figure. What's up?"

"Just wanted to let you know that the footprint run finished and came up empty."

Gabe heard Lukas's vocal shrug and sighed. Even if they managed to identify the make of the shoe, they would then have to match the shoe to its owner—and all this for a piddly trespassing charge that probably wouldn't stick.

"You said there was no indication that the person got into Lorin's cabin? Nothing missing?"

"No," Gabe replied. "The lock wasn't tampered with, as far as I could tell. Lorin mentioned that it's not unusual for them to get the occasional curious local wandering through. Whoever it was could have just smashed the window if he really wanted to steal something."

Lukas responded with a noncommittal "hmm."

"Well, keep your eyes peeled." He cleared his throat. "So, have you seen Lorin?"

The hair rose on Gabe's neck and forearms, a prickle of primal awareness. "Do you need to talk to her? Is she not picking up?"

"Like she's even carrying her phone."

"Do you need me to pass along a message? Is Alka okay?" Gabe's stomach churned like a washing machine. Alka was gearing up for her long-planned trip to Peru and Chile, but she wasn't scheduled to leave until next week sometime.

"Yes, yes, everyone's fine. I didn't mean to worry you." Lukas fell silent, worrying him even more. "Are you seeing anyone right now?"

"What?" Gabe's eyebrows flew into his hairline. "Lorin just made the find of the millennia, and you want to talk about my sex life?" *Or lack thereof?*

"Ah, shit," Lukas muttered over a thunk in the background. Gabe winced as he visualized the other man's heavy boots being propped onto something delicate—probably Elliott Sebastiani's prized Eames table.

"I told Scarlett she should call you instead."

"What?"

Lukas sighed audibly. "Did you notice how agitated Lorin was at the meeting?"

"She usually is. Agitated, I mean. By me."

"She was agitated—and aroused—by you."

"What?" Blood rushed to his face and parts farther south. "Lukas—"

"You two were spilling so much sexual energy during the meeting that I had trouble concentrating. Lorin really needs to get laid. So, if you're not seeing anyone…" Lukas's voice trailed off casually.

Gabe's eyes bulged. Was Lukas really suggesting—

"She's a Valkyrie, remember?" Lukas interrupted. "You have to do something, Gabe, because she's bouncing off the walls."

Do something? Like have sex with Lorin? "Are you serious? I think your brother might have a slight problem with what you're suggesting."

"Nah, Lorin and Rafe aren't sleeping together anymore," Lukas responded. "So, she isn't involved with anyone right now, and I know you and Kayla broke things off awhile ago. If you aren't seeing anyone, maybe the two of you can… scratch a mutual itch."

Lorin wasn't sleeping with Rafe Sebastiani. The information bounced in Gabe's brain like a pinball on a hot table.

No. Gabe yanked the mental reins. Who Lorin was or wasn't sleeping with didn't matter—despite the incendiary offer she'd made to him in the sauna last night.

Food, fight, fuck. How many times had he heard the Valkyrie adage? It had new significance to him now, because damn it, Lukas was right—Lorin had a problem. He mentally scrolled through the options. Lorin appeared to have the food part handled. Fight? He shook his head. Nope. He'd run with her, sure—but hit her? Fight with her? Nuh-uh, not gonna happen. But fuck? Oh yeah, he could imagine that. Had imagined it, over and over again, in dozens of variations.

"I know you want her, Gabe."

It would be useless to deny such a thing to an incubus of Lukas's skill. "Who wouldn't?"

"So, what's the problem?"

"Lukas, she reports to me."

"So?"

"I provide her with work direction. I sign off on her budget, her salary, her bonuses, until Alka gets back."

"And as a member of the Council, she makes decisions impacting all of our species on a regular basis. She could have you arrested with a single phone call." Amusement filled his voice. "Do you really think she's worried about bonus money?"

Probably not, and their relative financial standing was just one more roadblock standing between them. "How about the fact that she finds me as annoying as I find her?"

Lukas had the balls to laugh at him. "Sexual tension, man. Off-the-scale sexual tension."

He'd have to take Lukas's word for it. He hadn't had sex in so long that he'd almost forgotten what sexual tension felt like. "Don't you think Lorin can find her own partner?"

"Sure she could, but you're both there, both healthy, unattached adults who are attracted to each other. She has to leach off some energy somehow. I'd rather she does it with you than with some random guy she picks up at Tubby's."

Now he knew why she'd made a pass last night. Lorin didn't necessarily want to sleep with him; she just had to sleep with somebody. The very thought of Lorin picking up a stranger at a dive bar enraged him. "So this is… a risk management recommendation."

"If you like." Lukas's voice was dry as dirt. "She wants you. You want her. She needs to leach off some energy—soon—or she'll be worthless. Sounds like a win/win to me."

"I'll take your recommendation under advisement."

Now that Lukas had planted the idea of having sex with Lorin in Gabe's head, he wouldn't be able to think about anything else.

"One more thing." Gabe blinked at Lukas's suddenly serious tone. "You might want to reassure Lorin that she still has a leadership role on this project. She didn't say much of anything at the meeting."

"Yeah." Everyone had offered feedback on the plan except the one person whose feedback was most important.

He'd blown it.

He said as much to Lukas, who didn't disagree. "We're always doing something that women find highly annoying. A blanket apology goes a long, long way."

"A long way towards what?"

Lukas's knowing laughter rang in his ear. "Goodbye, Gabe."

Chapter 6

"PAIGE! GOOD TO SEE YOU!"

Crap. Lorin had returned, but his apology would have to wait. Gabe stopped in the doorway of the workroom and watched Lorin wrap her arms around the smallest woman he'd ever seen. Dressed in shades of pink from head to toe, the top of Paige Scott's head barely came up to Lorin's chest, and then only with an assist from the dandelion-fluff white-blond ponytail perched on top of her head.

"Ewww, you're all sweaty," Paige complained. "Have you been running?"

Gabe caught the annoyed look Lorin shot his way before she answered. "Chopping wood for the sauna."

Lorin had shed the soft fleece jacket she'd been wearing earlier and was stripped down to a duo of tank tops. Although it was barely sixty degrees outside, her skin glistened with perspiration.

When did sweaty women start turning him on?

"Gabe," Lorin called. "You might as well come over and meet Paige."

Gabe approached the two women. This was his ace geology and metallurgy grad? Her tiny hands didn't look capable of picking up a pickax, much less wielding one.

"Gabe, this is Paige Scott, here for her third season. Paige, this is Gabe Lupinsky, who'll be… working with us this summer."

"Hello," he said, extending his hand to the smaller woman. They hadn't talked about a cover story yet, but Lorin's vague introduction would probably work well enough for now. When Paige lifted her gaze to his, his smile froze, just for a second. Her irises, snapping with intelligence and bravado, were a distinct pinkish-red. "Ms. Scott, it's a pleasure to meet you."

"Please call me Paige," she said, squeezing the hell out of his hand. "It's an honor to meet you, Dr. Lupinsky. I'm familiar with your work."

"And I'm familiar with yours," he replied, retrieving his hand. The faerie's pink canvas high tops were adorned with tiny black skulls. Gabe was relieved to see some outward sign of edge, even if it was cosmetic. Standing next to Lorin, Paige Scott looked like she'd float away with a puff of the breeze. "Nice job on the assays and maps."

"Thank you. Topography's not my specialty, but I did what I could." Paige stepped back, encompassing Gabe and Lorin with a single look. "So."

"Hmm?"

Gabe sighed. The faux-innocent expression on Lorin's face wouldn't fool a toddler, much less a curve-breaker like Paige Scott.

Paige snagged a piece of her fluffy hair, twirling the lock around her forefinger as she considered them. "The assays are unremarkable. Our most significant find last season was a fire pit and some deer and rabbit bones. So, what's up? What is Dr. Gabriel Lupinsky from Sebastiani Labs doing here?"

A look of panic chased across Lorin's face. "Well, you know my mother is on sabbatical—"

"Lorin." Gabe rested his hand on her forearm. Lorin stiffened but didn't move away.

Paige's gaze ping-ponged between them. "Ah."

"What?" Lorin nearly squeaked, yanking her arm back.

"You're lovers," Paige said.

It could work, Gabe thought. It could work very well. A relationship between them was a perfectly logical conclusion for someone to draw. Why not use the obvious sexual tension between them for a useful purpose?

You want to touch her, his libido taunted.

What the hell are you doing? his common sense warned.

Gabe disregarded common sense and slid his arm around Lorin's waist, resting his hand familiarly on her hip. "Busted," he said with a smile, digging his fingers into her resilient flesh as she tried to tug away. "It's new yet," he explained to Paige as he wrapped his other arm around Lorin, dropping a kiss onto the tip of her nose for good measure. "I wanted to learn more about where Lorin worked. It's been ages since I worked a dig, so I volunteered."

Lorin's right thigh visibly twitched. Probably fighting the urge to knee him in the crotch. She yanked out of his arms with a growl.

Paige rolled her eyes at her reaction. "Lorin, chill. What's the biggie? It's not like you'll be the only people knocking boots here this summer."

The sound of tires against gravel got their attention, when a faded black Explorer emerged from the tunnel of trees.

"Crap," Paige muttered.

"He's seen you," Lorin said. "You'd better hurry."

"Yeah," Paige quickly agreed. "Catch you later. Nice to meet you, Dr. Lupinsky." Before Gabe could reply,

Paige picked up her bag and took off at a run, carrying the duffel containing a summer's worth of gear like it weighed nothing.

The linebacker-sized guy wedged behind the wheel of the truck didn't look happy. He skidded the truck to a stop with an impressive spray of rocks, opened the driver's door, snagged a pillow off the passenger seat, and hit the ground running, leaving the truck idling.

"Too much ground to make up, Mike," Lorin hooted. "She's got you."

Mike grunted a response as he blew past them, carrying the pillow like a football. They both watched as the big redhead bolted into the bunkhouse.

"Okay, I'll bite," Gabe said. "What's that about?"

"Remember that big bed in the bunkhouse?"

He nodded. Lorin had looked absolutely spectacular bent over it, snapping clean sheets onto the corners.

"The crewmember who puts a personal item on the bed first gets it for the season." When voices exploded from the bunkhouse's open door, Lorin smiled like the Cheshire Cat. "Sounds like she held him off."

Sure enough, Mike poked his head from the bunk-house door. "Lorin, c'mon, help me out here. I'm bigger than she is. I need the room."

Paige appeared beside him, grinning as she rubbed her shoulder.

Had the guy actually tackled her? He was well over double her body weight. Gabe shot a glance at Lorin, but she didn't look outraged on Paige's behalf, or even particularly concerned.

"Nothing I can do, Mike," Lorin called back. "You know the rules."

"You snooze, you lose," Paige crowed. "And I'm going to be snoozing in a double bed all summer long." As she turned on her heel, she murmured something to Mike, too soft for them to hear. Mike narrowed his eyes and slowly followed her into the bunkhouse.

Lorin watched them with a pensive expression on her face.

"What's wrong?"

"She's had a crush on him for ages, but he treats her like a little sister." Lorin sighed. "Well, they'll have to work it out. And speaking of which." Her voice took on a muscularity it hadn't had just a few seconds ago.

He was obviously tetched in the head, because suddenly he was really turned on.

He planted his feet and faced her. What was coming? A slap to the face? A fist to the gut? An epic cockpunch?

He probably owed her a free shot.

"What the hell were you thinking?" she hissed. Her hands didn't move, other than to clench into white-knuckled fists at her side. "We're lovers? Who's going to believe that?" Before he could defend the idea, she was off and running. "City boy, let's get something straight right now. I might temporarily report to you, but in all the ways that matter, I'm in charge." She shot him a look that sliced. "Yeah, I made a mistake opening the box, and your presence here is my metaphorical spanking. I get it. But this is my mother's dig. My dig. Not yours. Never yours."

His thoughts were snagged back on "spanking," but he yanked them to heel. He had to set a couple of things straight, right now. "You're right. I'm sorry. And I'm also sorry about the meeting earlier today. I know I should have—"

"—talked to me first?" she spat out. "Had the courtesy to discuss 'our plan' with me before presenting it to everyone else as a done deal?"

"Yes." His prompt agreement startled her into silence, so he took advantage of the lull. "Last night, after the sauna, I was… wired. I couldn't sleep. You were in your cabin for the night, the lights off. My brain wouldn't shut down, so I… worked, like I frequently do. You were gone when I woke up this morning, and you didn't return to the compound until just before the meeting started. I considered rescheduling the meeting, but you know as well as I do how tough it is to find an opening on Elliott's calendar." He shrugged. "I should have discussed it with you first, and I didn't. I'm sorry."

Lorin scowled at him, and then nodded. "Thank you. And for what it's worth, it's a decent plan." She paused, seeming to consider her words. "When you first got here, you said we needed to present a united front. You're right, but it goes both ways. Please remember that Schlessingers have run this dig—without you—for decades. We'll run it after you're gone."

It was his turn to nod and extend a conciliatory hand. "Okay. Truce?"

"Ooh, not yet, bucko," she snapped. "What the hell were you thinking, kissing me like that in front of Paige?"

A jolt raced down his spine as he parsed her words. Might she be open to him kissing her in private? "You left the meeting before we could talk about a cover story. When Paige jumped to the conclusion she did, I… went with it." He managed a shrug. "If she believed it, the others probably will."

Her incredulous expression made his stomach clench. Of course it wasn't believable. Lorin Schlessinger slept with the pick of the litter, not mutts who were legally blind without their glasses. "Let the crew think you're slumming for the summer," he said with a cheerfulness he didn't feel.

"Oh, please," she scoffed. "Last night I practically threw myself at you, and you let me know in no uncertain terms you just weren't interested."

His jaw dropped. "Not interested? Are you really that dense?"

"It's okay, really," she interrupted with a remote smile. "It really is. It's entirely your choice, and you said 'no' in every way that mattered. But given that you did, why is pretending to be my lover a solution you're comfortable with?"

Were all Valkyries so oblivious? Screw his scruples. Spearing one hand into her sweat-dampened hair and clamping the other on her ass, he yanked her body against his. Lorin's widened eyes made it clear that, if she missed it last night, she certainly noticed his erection now. "Make no mistake about it, Lorin," he nearly growled. "I want to eat you alive."

"Same goes." She eyed his mouth. "So what's the problem?"

When her hips snuggled against his, he choked back a groan. Their nearly equal heights aligned their bodies perfectly. "You report to me."

"A technicality. I turned the job down before it was offered to you."

Okay, rumor confirmed.

"Come on, Gabe. Your management style is so

hands-off it isn't even funny. Mom's been on sabbatical nearly a month already and I've barely heard from you."

He'd been too busy dealing with his eyes and climbing the steep learning curve on his new responsibilities, but he wasn't about to tell her that. "Hands off?" He flexed his fingers against her firm hips, so muscular, yet so quintessentially female. Now that his hands were on her—and her hands were on him—all the reasons he'd denied himself last night simply floated away. When her fingers twined in the belt loop at the back of his jeans, he felt the subtle, diabolical tug all the way down to his balls. *Concentrate.* "Your mother and I communicate rather frequently. We need to do the same."

"I'm not my mother," she said, trailing her finger over his ass.

"No shit." He'd never felt the need to strip Alka Schlessinger bare.

Lorin's snort of laughter made clear her thoughts had traveled down the same sick track.

He steeled himself against the shivers caused by her clever, clever finger. "We're in an odd situation here, Lorin. You and I haven't had a chance to hammer out our new working relationship yet, and here we are, practically living in each other's back pockets, working on what could be the biggest find in our people's history. This situation is complicated enough without us—"

"Sleeping together?" She shrugged. "What's so complicated about it? You want me, I want you."

She wanted him. She'd said it out loud. A sudden energy swirled through his system, tense and invigorating, like he was about to dive off a cliff without having checked the waters below. "We have students to supervise."

Her mossy green eyes lit with amusement. "You act like they're in kindergarten, Gabe. They're adults who work independently for long stretches of time, and who—believe it or not—have sex lives of their own." Stepping closer, Lorin pressed her lips to the corner of his mouth. Licked him. "We could disappear a half-dozen times a day and no one would even notice."

A half-dozen times a day? Gabe nearly groaned aloud, but his mouth was too busy chasing her agile tongue. He didn't know whether to be thrilled or intimidated by the prospect of satisfying this woman. Lukas had suggested that Lorin was in a sex drought of her own. How long had it been since she and Rafe had—

No. Thinking about the pleasures Lorin had experienced in the sex demon's bed was a one-way ticket to performance anxiety. He might not be as smooth as the other man, but he had some skills of his own.

Impatient with the chase, he slammed his mouth over hers and speared his tongue into the dark, damp cavern. Her strong fingers clenched his ass with bruising strength, pressing his erection more firmly into the humid notch between her legs. A growl rumbled out of his chest. He grabbed back with shaking hands.

He'd never wanted a woman so much in his life.

"Damn it," Lorin breathed against his lips as a caravan of vehicles crunched into the parking lot. "They might be adults, but they don't need to watch us go at it in the parking lot, either." She reluctantly drew away, raking his frame with an avaricious gaze that felt like the stroke of a hand. "Later?"

Ah, hell. He was going to do this. Was already doing this. "Yes."

"When?" she asked. "Where?"

A car backfired. "Where should I park, Lorin?" a dark-haired, sharp-featured guy called from the driver's window of an old Skylark. "I'm leaking oil."

"Damn," Lorin muttered. "Park over to the far side of the lot, Nathan." She pointed to where she wanted him to go. "Hi, Ellenore," she called to a gamine redhead with a centerfold body who'd just stepped from a red Miata.

Didn't Lorin hire any ugly people?

Over in the parking lot, crewmembers gathered around Nathan's now-smoking car. "Go take care of business," he said. "I'm going to—"

"Take care of business?" she said with a grin, staring at the front of his pants.

"You're evil."

"You can handle it," she said as she walked backwards toward the parking lot. "Later."

Were her words a threat, a promise, or both? Suddenly Gabe couldn't wait to find out.

———

"You're making a mess." Nathan held out his hand as yet another hamburger fell apart on the grill under Lorin's hand. "Let me."

Across the room, Gabe's laughter rang out again. "Fine." She slapped the spatula into his hand.

Gabe and Paige sat across from each other at the end of one of the picnic tables in the cookhouse dining room, and if the laughter they shared was any indication, they were hitting it off very well indeed. As Lorin watched, Paige licked at the ketchup dripping off a loaded hamburger while Gabe scrawled in the open notebook sitting next to his silverware.

Instead of crawling up the walls like she was, Gabe was working. And laughing. With someone other than her.

Another Tinker Bell giggle from Paige. There was a sparkle in her eyes, a confidence and flirtatiousness in her body language, that another woman could recognize a mile off.

Damn.

"What's left to cook, Lorin?" Nathan asked.

Lorin steeled herself and looked down at the list. Whether she was annoyed or not, people needed to eat. "One steak, medium, for Ellenore. Two steaks, extra rare, for Mike. And a veggie burger for Gretchen."

Nathan rolled his eyes. "Like those two are interested in eating."

"Hmm?"

Nathan gestured with his head. "Look."

Mike, her bone guy, and Gretchen, a first-year crew-member who'd be their primary artifact cataloguer, sat across from each other, their heads nearly touching as they talked. Their feet tangled together under the table.

"Okay, that didn't take long." She darted a look at Paige. The young faerie's excessive vivaciousness had a cause—and, thankfully, it wasn't Gabe.

Nathan shook his head as he slapped raw steaks onto the grill. "Vamp and siren. This ought to be interesting."

Lorin didn't respond. Hookups weren't unusual when healthy and hormonal young people lived together in such close proximity for months at a time. Factor in the idiosyncrasies of their species—shifting werewolves, vamps who could glamour others into compliance with a look, incubi and succubi who absorbed emotional energy for sustenance and emitted luscious pheromones in response, sirens who amplified emotional responses with their voices, and faeries with their off-the-charts empathic abilities? Hookup city.

She was the only Valkyrie on the crew this year, which left her no one to spar with. She and Mike had tried last summer, but the experiment had been an utter failure. Mike hadn't been able to tackle a woman—even one as strong as she was.

"Okay, here you go." Nathan transferred the steaks and the lonely veggie burger onto a platter and handed it to her. "I'm King of the Grill," he crowed, holding the spatula like a scepter. "I like this gig."

"I'll remember that." Lorin tried to assign crewmembers to work they liked to perform. If only the crew had a neat freak who loved washing dishes and cleaning outhouses. So far, no luck.

Tonight was Paige's night to do dishes.

Lorin delivered people's food, circulating around the dining room, making sure she talked to everyone, especially Gretchen. Lorin laughed at her good-natured grumbling about the outhouse and black hole–sized drop-offs in cell phone coverage.

Finally there was no one else to talk to. After reminding Gretchen about the safety and procedures session tomorrow morning, she walked over to Gabe and Paige. Van Halen's "Hot for Teacher" floated through her head as she approached their table. Gabe laughed indulgently as Paige told a joke that had been as old as the proverbial hills back when Valerian was in short pants.

"Oh, hi, Lorin," Paige said, looking up with a smile. She stood up, picking up her tray and indicating her now-open seat. "He's all yours. Alas, it's my night for dishes. I hate doing dishes."

"I do too," Lorin commiserated, taking Paige's seat. "You'll have them knocked off in no time."

"This year I came prepared." Paige jutted out a hip, displaying a pair of hot pink rubber gloves with frilly decorative cuffs hanging out of her back jeans pocket. "So, Dr. Lupinsky—"

"Paige, I told you to call me Gabe," Gabe interrupted. "We'll be working together all summer."

The younger woman flushed a delicate shade of shell pink. "Okay. Gabe. I'll pull that white paper you suggested and see what Miller has to say about the ductile properties of iron ore versus taconite." She looked back and forth between Gabe and Lorin. "Um, see you two tomorrow. Have fun."

Silence resumed after she left. Finally Gabe cleared his throat, indicating the Bat Phone resting on top of his notebook with a jerky hand. "Did you see the updated schedule Jules sent?"

Good. He was as tense as she was. "No, I was up at the site all afternoon." And if he said one word about her not being up-to-date on her email, she'd blow. The crew would have sun protection tomorrow because she and Nathan had put up the gazebos, and the tarps they'd erected over the pit would block both the sun and snoopy overhead satellites.

A huge crash came from the kitchen as something large and metal dropped to the floor. After a second, hoots and applause broke out.

"I pinged you this afternoon, and you didn't respond," Gabe said.

"I didn't have my phone with me—"

"That has to change, Lorin. What if the problem was more urgent than someone not knowing where to find biodegradable toilet paper? We found more, by the way."

"So sorry about your asses."

A ruddy flush climbed his neck. "The toilet paper isn't the issue," Gabe gritted. "You don't answer email, you don't pick up the phone, you don't return texts. In case you missed the memo, Lorin, this is the reason I'm here. Elliott needs a reliable line of communication. You don't even try to provide one."

She glared at him. "The real problem is your expectation that I return your emails and phone calls within minutes, even when the communication just isn't all that urgent. Toilet paper? Really? Would it have killed someone to walk up to the site?"

Gabe seemed to be choosing his words carefully. "It would be more convenient if—"

"—more convenient for you, maybe. I was busy erecting tarps so we can start working tomorrow. Boss."

Gabe leaned in. "Point taken, and quit the 'boss' crap. We both know that you could have me hauled off in chains with a click of a mouse. You outrank me in every way that matters."

In her mind's eye, she imagined him bound at the wrists and stripped to the waist, awaiting the Council's judgment. She crossed her arms over her suddenly stiff nipples. "I couldn't actually do that, you know. Have you hauled away, I mean. There are processes and procedures up the wazoo—"

"Funny how you value some processes and procedures more than others."

"Well, some processes make sense, and some are
stupid."

"The point I was trying to make," Gabe said, still
clenching his teeth, "is that we need to hammer out the
parameters of our working relationship. I need you to carry
a phone at all times." He leaned in close again, dropping
his voice to a barely audible rumble she felt clear to her
core. "Lorin, think. Your latest find changes the game
completely. We've already had a trespasser, and we can't
tell the crew what's going on. We're each other's only
backup. We—you and me—have to be in lockstep on this."

They stared at each other, and Lorin finally sighed her
acceptance. "You're so annoying when you're right."

He eyed her. "Then I'm going to annoy you a lot."

Before she could respond, Paige's high-pitched
screech sliced through the air as she scooted out of the
kitchen. "Nathan, don't you dare!" A shower of water
from the sink sprayer followed her, dousing the side of
her head and splashing all over the floor.

"Is it always like this?" Gabe asked with a sigh. "There
hasn't been a moment of silence since they arrived."

Lorin considered. "I run. A lot."

"Me too."

"Join me tomorrow morning?" she asked. "Getting
away from the site would give us a chance to talk without the crew overhearing us."

"Good idea. Sure."

A day's growth of beard once again darkened the
planes of his face. Despite his city boy mien, despite
those ridiculously sexy glasses, he looked rough and

ready, scruffy around the edges. Good enough to nibble on—or gobble down whole.

What did Gabe's wolf look like? After mere hours on site, Nathan had already shifted and taken off into the woods on four legs. Gabe had been here for days. If he'd shifted, she hadn't seen it.

"Nathan, stop it!"

Lorin cleared her throat. Paige's voice reminded her that she and Gabe still had some business to take care of. "We need to talk."

"You've changed your mind about sleeping together," he replied. "I completely under—"

"Are you crazy? No, this is about Paige." She took a deep breath. "Be careful with her, Gabe."

"What?"

"The laughing, the joking? Don't flirt with her, Gabe." The minute she said the words, she regretted them. She sounded like a jealous shrew.

Gabe's face darkened, like a thunderstorm gaining strength as it blew across the prairie. "What kind of degenerate do you think I am?"

Though Gabe hadn't raised his voice by much, heads turned at his tone. "Ooh, lover's quarrel," Mike called.

"Shut up," Lorin snapped at Mike without taking her eyes off Gabe. "I can't hear myself think in here. Let's take this outside."

"Oh, by all means. Let's." Gabe's subsonic growl vibrated through her rib cage. His ice floe eyes locked with hers, his pupils expanding, pushing the chilly blue away until all that remained were hot pools of black. Though the width of the table was still between them, she could feel the heat pumping off his body.

His nostrils twitched, just the slightest bit. Damn his werewolf hide, of course he could smell how much she wanted him.

Adrenaline mixed with annoyance as she waited for him to clear his dinner tray. He slowly and deliberately threw his paper napkin into the burn bin, put food scraps into the compost pile, and finally pushed the tray itself through to the dish alcove.

"Thanks, Gabe!" Paige called.

Her stomach jumped at the younger woman's cheerful voice. *Maybe you* are *a jealous shrew.*

Gabe stalked back to the picnic table, scooping up his belongings without looking at her. He shoved the Bat Phone into the deep front pocket of his cargo pants.

Her breath snagged in her throat. He was rampantly, outrageously erect.

They walked to the door. "After you," he said with a mocking sweep of his arm. His mild tone of voice was completely at odds with the turmoil roiling in his eyes. His face seemed sharper, more feral.

It was all she could do to choke back a moan.

As they walked out of the cookhouse together, Lorin heard someone—Mike?—say, "I'm taking bets. Fight or fuck?"

"Fuck, definitely."

"Fight, then fuck."

"They're totally going to do it."

The door slammed shut behind them. Leaving the heat of the cookhouse, the chill of the evening slapped her cheeks. She was primed, her fists and sex both clenched tight.

Gabe didn't take four strides before he whirled back towards her. "What the hell are you suggesting?"

Yes, Mr. Discipline had a temper after all. She… liked it. "Gabe, I didn't mean to… I'm not suggesting that—" She broke off, huffing a breath she could see in the night air, and rested a conciliatory hand on his forearm. "Gabe, I know you weren't flirting with her. I know that. But *she* was flirting with *you*, and Paige is… fragile right now."

"Cotton candy."

"What?"

"She reminds me of cotton candy."

Lorin nodded, acknowledging his description. "Physically, she's tougher than she looks, but emotionally?" She shrugged. "She's had a massive crush on Mike since last season, and now he's obviously interested in Gretchen." She paused. "You aren't—weren't—doing anything inappropriate. But please, be careful with her."

"Like every man here doesn't stare at your ass when you walk by," Gabe muttered. The air between them seemed to simmer. "And why would Paige flirt with me when she knows—thinks—we're lovers?"

"Think of it in terms of pack dynamics. You're clearly the alpha male in terms of age, experience, power, looks. Flirting with you, garnering your attention, is a public salve to her battered ego." The slightest grin curved her lips. "It's really nothing personal."

After a several-second silence, he said, "There might have been a compliment buried in that statement somewhere, but I'm not sure."

Her smile grew without her permission. "All I'm asking is that you step carefully as you work with her.

It would be… unfortunate if she misinterpreted your professional interest."

Suddenly he was standing right in front of her, stopping just before their bodies touched. "You can't honestly think I'm interested in Paige."

Her eyelids drifted closed. His pissed-off growl was just fucking lethal.

He gave her a mild shake, tilting his head slightly to the left as he looked at her. "Lorin, answer me." Behind the lenses of his glasses, his gaze drilled into hers.

There was nowhere for her to hide. "She's adorable, innocent as all get-out," she finally answered. "Small enough to tuck in your pocket. Men seem to find that attractive." She'd never felt so gigantic in her life.

"She looks like she'd break if you touched her," Gabe murmured against the whorl of her ear. "If things got a little rough."

He plastered his body to hers, walking her backwards until the knots of the cookhouse's wood logs dug into her back. Hot breath condensed on her neck as Gabe nibbled down to the sensitive intersection where neck met shoulder. She gasped as he settled in to suckle and nip.

Lorin locked her knees as they threatened to buckle under her. City boy had a… very talented mouth. She speared her fingers into his silky black hair, dragging his head toward hers, diving at his mouth to sample every bit of his dark flavor. When she clamped her hand on his ass, his low, rumbly growl became an audible groan.

Too many layers between them. She needed to touch him, wanted his hands on her—

"Hey, you two. Get a room."

They sprang apart as Mike strolled out of the cook-house, followed by Gretchen and the rest of the crew. Paige brought up the rear, locking the door behind her and offering them a subdued "good night" as she passed. The night filled with chatter as the crew walked en masse past the fire pit to the bunkhouse, finally leaving them alone again.

The air snapped and hummed like a live electrical line had dropped between them. "My cabin," she breathed. "Now."

His only response was a curt nod.

Not touching, they walked across the compound, picking up speed the closer they got to the cabin. As they jumped the single step up to the cabin's wooden platform, Gabe tensed and reached for his pants. Lorin's blood flashed to a boil. Was he unzipping his pants? Right here, where anyone could see him? She whipped her head back and forth to make sure they were alone. If he wanted to put on a show, she was more than willing to watch.

Nope, he reached for his pocket instead. Condoms? "I have condoms in the cabin," she said impatiently. "Plenty of them. Hurry."

Quickly opening her door, she turned back to find Gabe glaring at his Bat Phone. "You've got to be fucking kidding me," he muttered, reading the display window. When he looked at her, his expression bordered on physical pain. "It's Elliott. I have to take this."

Damn. Depending on the topic, Gabe could be on the phone for hours.

"Lorin…" Under the single bulb illuminating the entrance to the cabin, Gabe's face was tight with frustration.

"I'll leave the door open," she whispered. "Come back when you're done."

"You are *not* leaving this door unlocked."

"How has this alpha streak of yours escaped me for so long?" Reaching into her jacket pocket, she extracted her key ring, removed one, and slapped it into his hand.

He stared at it, then at her.

"Gabe."

He blinked. "What?"

"The phone?" she said, indicating it with a nod.

"Shit." He punched a button and rumbled a greeting to Elliott.

"Gabe, there are some definite benefits to going off the grid."

He heard her, but his only response was the dirty look he shot her as he stalked to his tent.

Chapter 7

"It's almost impossible for Lorcan to make an honest profit in the natural resources sector right now."

A merry laugh. "Since when does honesty have anything to do with it?"

Beddoe eavesdropped on the conversation behind him while he talked with a couple for whom he'd performed a bonding ceremony at the beginning of the voyage. The financial analysts chatting too loudly behind him worked for Lorcan too. The women were *TonTon* regulars, and the information they sometimes spilled about Lorcan's investments in the raucous natural resources sector had benefitted Beddoe's personal portfolio on many occasions.

The ladies' glasses were nearly empty. That wouldn't do. "Please enjoy yourselves," he said to the besotted couple, turning his attention to the women. Benna's garment, a curve-hugging column tiled with thousands of bronze mirrored squares, threw light in all directions. Ramping up his glamour, he greeted them with courtly kisses on both cheeks, and then gestured to their vessels. "Another libation, ladies?"

"Yes, thank you," the shorter woman said, raising her glass to her lips to empty it. A voluptuous beauty with platinum hair, Willa's pale blue dress nearly matched her skin tone, such a close match that at first glance she appeared unclothed—no doubt the effect she intended.

She cruised a talon-sharp fingernail down the chest of his dress uniform. "You take such good care of us, Beddoe," she crooned. "Who… takes care of you?"

He had very reliable information about her erotic preferences, and the prospect of that fingernail repeatedly scoring the tender skin of his privates curdled his stomach. Beddoe schooled his face into an expression of rueful, worldly disappointment. "Ah, Willa, I'm afraid the *TonTon* is a jealous and demanding mistress." Lifting her wandering hand off his uniform, he kissed her blue-skinned knuckles. His fangs tingled at the proximity of her iron-laden blood, but he'd sooner drink from a garbage scow than this one. "Allow me to convey your request to the server." With a quick, courtly bow, he backed out of the range of that lethal fingernail.

The soft pluck of twelve strings drifted through the delicately scented air, unobtrusively accompanying conversations held in a babel of dialects. The extravagantly garbed guests availed themselves of the *TonTon's* extensive collection of intoxicants, and delicacies from dozens of worlds glistened on serving platters. While the server prepared fresh drinks, Beddoe assessed the room with a critical eye. When your livelihood depended on people willingly parting with their coin, coin had to be invested first. Every detail was refined to perfection; no aspect of presentation could be neglected.

Welcome aboard. Take your ease. What do you desire? It's yours—for a price.

Luckily for Beddoe, there was an endless stream of gamblers and sexual adventurers willing to pay a very high price for their pleasure.

Most of the guests paid absolutely no attention to the

stunning panorama on the other side of the huge hull window. Ta'al was piloting the cloaked ship in a slow, circuitous route for the sightseers tonight, far enough away from the system so that features of individual planets blurred. But down on the Third, darkness sliced across the large northern land mass. In his mind, this wild territory and its precious, clean water was already his. He almost had enough coin to pay the exorbitant claim stake that would finally free him from Lorcan's yoke.

Almost.

The beacon had blipped once, very strongly, then had inexplicably disappeared. Had anyone else picked up the signal? It was just a matter of time before the quadrant swarmed with scientists, profiteers, and all manner of fortune hunters, including Lorcan himself.

He had to get down to the surface again—but first, business. Beddoe gestured his newest employee toward him. As impeccably attired as the guests he mingled with, the wildly attractive young man wore a discreet pin on his lapel indicating that he was available for the guests' entertainment. The spoiled youngest son of a scion of industry, he still saw paying off his debt through sexual servitude as an exciting lark. Beddoe glanced at the large screen flickering on the wall opposite the hull window. Stephen, four floors below, listlessly serviced a giant of a woman with his tongue, his body half obscured by her huge, pillowy thighs.

Unfortunately, new employees' enthusiasm didn't last very long.

The young man approached. "Yes, Captain?" His flashing white teeth rivaled the investment banker's reflective dress for brightness.

"Could you bring these to the ladies?" Beddoe indicated the two women. "They might enjoy your company."

"Certainly, Captain."

The young man delivered the drinks and engaged the women in conversation. It didn't take long for Willa to pounce, stroking the lethal fingernail down his jacket front. The man shifted closer, murmuring to her, bending his head slightly so his hair flopped rakishly over one eye. *Yes, excellent.* Benna wandered away, leaving them alone.

More murmured conversation. Two nods. Negotiations complete.

As the young man leaned in for a kiss to seal the deal, Willa's fingernail sliced through his vest lacings, continuing mercilessly south. When the young man's eyes bulged, Beddoe's ballocks pulled up against his body in sympathy.

Hand still on his sac, Willa tugged him to a privacy pod, the door quickly snapping closed behind them.

Welcome to the TonTon, boy.

A throat clearing near the entrance captured his attention, and when Beddoe saw who it was, satisfaction overflowed like bubbly ambrosia. "Welcome, Sirrah," he said, greeting Ambassador Armand Tierney Ta'a'pet with a firm handshake, drawing him into the room. Yesterday the taciturn politician had lost enough coin at the Fein du Chin tables to fuel the *TonTon* for a week.

He couldn't cover his debt.

"Captain." Ta'a'pet acknowledged his greeting with a curt nod. "This is an… unusual place to discuss business."

"Let's leave business for another day, Ambassador. Tonight, let's simply enjoy." Beddoe escorted the ambassador to the selection of alcoholic beverages, powders, herbs, vials, and injectors attractively displayed on trays. "May I offer you a libation, Ambassador?"

Ta'a'pet chose a cigarillo. After lighting it himself, Beddoe drew the man into conversation. Though the ambassador relaxed only slightly—one didn't amass his fortune or wield his power without knowing how to quickly adapt to different surroundings—Beddoe noticed the Valkyr ambassador kept his back to the room, studiously avoiding Stephen's performance, and ignoring the dozen or so privacy pods that rimmed the perimeter of the room.

"Should you desire privacy, Ambassador, the unit at the end of the row has been reserved for your use," Beddoe informed him quietly. Each privacy pod was furnished with a soft lounger, a screen, and a variety of erotic accoutrements.

The ambassador's eyes fired with interest—quickly hidden, but not quickly enough.

Subtle, subtle. He was in the business of providing excellent personal service. And if, during the course of providing that service, he happened to record the ambassador enjoying some of the *TonTon's* more exotic pleasures? Even better business.

A sharp sound from the screen drew everyone's attention. "Faster," the woman ordered Stephen, whose right buttock now sported a raised, bloody stripe. She held a riding crop in her large hand.

"Yes, madame," Stephen said listlessly.

Beddoe couldn't tell if the flush on the woman's round, doughy face was from pleasure, rage, or a mixture of both. The woman was the bondmate of his

most reliable liquor vendor. The vendor had requested
a session with Stephen as payment for his most recent
delivery and was watching the performance from one of
the privacy pods.

He sighed as he watched Stephen lap between the
woman's legs with a distinct lack of enthusiasm. Beddoe
half expected the door to burst open, the vendor screaming for a refund. Damage control time. "Please enjoy
yourself, Ambassador," he murmured with a respectful
bow, moving in the direction of the vendor's pod.

Something had to be done about Stephen. Ever since
his recapture, the incubus had been a shadow of his former self. The wicked, naughty glint that clients used to
find so appealing was gone, as was his legendary stamina. He jerked at the slightest sound and rarely came
out of his quarters except for his regular health check.
Through some misadventure he wouldn't speak of, his
head bore permanent scars he refused to have removed.
He often rubbed at his chest, at some silent pain, though
repeated scans revealed no abnormalities.

Stephen had lost his puckish joy—always his most
marketable commodity.

CRACK.

Madame hit Stephen harder this time, but the expression on his face still didn't change.

"Again?" she threatened.

No reaction from Stephen.

CRACK. CRACK. CRACK. Soon Stephen's back
and buttocks were slick with blood. Beddoe considered
cutting the feed but decided against it. Most guests' eyes
were positively glued to the screen. The woman's mate
hadn't left his pod.

Dia. Any hope he had that Stephen might help him build his personal account more quickly flew out the hull window. The incubus would be out of service for days as he healed.

"Captain." Minchin's tone was barely respectful, and he didn't even try to disguise his interest in the scene playing out on the screen behind his captain.

Anger rose like a Coriolis storm. Lorcan's worthless nephew was the one who'd allowed Stephen to escape down to the surface of the Third in the first place. His price? A world-class tongue bath. Beddoe yearned to deposit the man on the coldest, most remote outpost he could possibly find, but he couldn't—and Minchin knew it—but earlier in the day, Beddoe had assigned his first officer an endless list of menial tasks and confined him to the ship.

The stakes were way too high to allow this stupid man to roam at will.

When Beddoe snapped his fingers, Minchin finally dragged his gaze away from Stephen—and if looks could kill, Beddoe would be a crumpled heap on the floor.

"My uncle would like to speak with you," the vampire said. "Now."

Beddoe swallowed back sour bile. His previous first officer, who'd also been his lover, had been reassigned to another ship in Lorcan's fleet because this entitled *japarr* needed toughening up. The very thought made his blood boil.

"Captain. He said now."

"Acknowledged."

Minchin's lip twitched, displaying the tip of a pointed incisor. Beddoe's own fangs shoved down at the flagrant insubordination. He took one step forward. Another. Then he crowded into the other vamp's space until their noses nearly touched. He smelled herb and fear on the other man's breath. "Are you issuing a challenge?"

After a slight hesitation, Minchin dropped his gaze, bent his head, and took one step back.

It wouldn't be long before Minchin challenged instead of retreated. But not here, and not now.

On screen, the vendor's bondmate spasmed and shrieked, her hand buried between her own thighs. Stephen, slumped on the floor at the foot of the bed, was bloody and unmoving. As the screen dimmed, the milling guests made their way to the privacy pods to watch the last act: the whispered-about *TonTon* alien abduction finale. Unfortunately, the man Minchin had acquired from the surface for tonight's performance was a popular television meteorologist whose absence had already been noted. Very sloppy work.

"See to our guests' comfort," he ordered the first officer. Though the assignment was more of a reward than a punishment, it couldn't be helped. He, unfortunately, had to contact Lorcan. "Minchin. After the guests depart, you will clean the privacy pods with your own hands."

The thought of the first officer scrubbing a galaxy of bodily fluids filled him with great satisfaction.

Minchin's lip twitched at the menial order. Beddoe stared at him until the first officer nodded, adding a hasty, "Yes, Sirrah."

After the guests disappeared into the privacy pods, he thanked the libation server for his usual impeccable service and walked to the door. When the first hoarse shouts and the sounds of physical struggle emanated from the still-dark screen, he turned around momentarily. The lights came up on a performance space stage-dressed in gleaming metal, bubbling test tubes, and large trays festooned with probes and medical tools. A monitor on a levered arm hovered over the brightly lit examining table.

The doors whisked open and four *TonTon* employees wearing bug-eyed Aanadari protection suits carried in a thrashing, kicking, naked man. It took the strength of all four employees to finally get the man lashed down. Bids from the guests in the privacy pods scrolled across the monitor suspended above the examining table. Several enthusiastic guests, including Ambassador Ta'a'pet, had already selected which implement they wanted to see used on the man first.

His preferences were duly recorded and stored along with everyone else's.

After a short wait, one of the employees theatrically picked up the largest probe on the tray. Scoffing at the ambassador's lack of imagination, Beddoe nonetheless made a note to send a gift assortment of similar devices to the man's personal quarters.

Beddoe hailed Lorcan as he left the room, the door swishing closed on the man's first shriek.

———※———

Paige boosted herself up onto the big workroom table, leaned over, and peered at the yellowing topological map. "Where did you find this? It's, like, ancient."

According to the date Alka had scribbled in the map's corner, she'd drawn it when Gabe was a teenager, which probably made him "like, ancient" too. After yet another night spent tossing and turning on a blow-up mattress in a chilly tent, this morning he felt every one of his years.

While Lorin and the crew worked at the primary site, he'd spent the morning digging through the treasure trove of old maps he'd found standing upright in a cardboard box. He'd hit the jackpot, finding a topological map of the entire property, not just the area the crew was actively working. The map was hand-drawn but very detailed and meticulously done. The fact that the maps weren't being preserved more carefully was an issue that had to be addressed, but right now he was too busy kicking his own ass for not bringing ground-penetrating radar equipment with him from Sebastiani Labs. "Are you aware of any survey work that's been done over here?"

"Way over there? No. Why do you ask?"

Good question. How could he explain why the northern portion of the property tugged his attention so much? He'd jogged past the area three times now, and every single time he felt a tingle at the base of his skull. Something about the area was just… off.

"About a mile away," Paige mused. "No road."

"Deer trails."

Paige glanced at him. "Not a problem for a wolf."

He made a noncommittal sound that neither confirmed nor denied her assumption that he'd explored the area on four legs. Because of his vision problems, Gabe hadn't shifted in so long he'd almost forgotten what his wolf looked like.

"Maybe Lorin knows," Paige said, twirling a piece of blond fluff around her forefinger. "I've never been that far away from the compound myself. And to run there?" She shuddered. "I'll never understand why you and Lorin spend so much time running when there are perfectly good couches to nap on."

Unrelieved horniness. "It's great cardio," he said aloud. "Someday, when you're 'ancient,' maintaining your body will become—"

"Gabe, there's exercise, and then there's just crazy," Paige mumbled around a wad of grape bubble gum. "Lorin's already been running twice today, and she was just out clearing brush with Mike and Nathan."

Burning off energy because he'd left her hanging last night. He leaned his hips against the table so Paige wouldn't see how vigorously his "ancient" body was reacting to the thought of Lorin wearing shorts, a T-shirt, steel-toed boots, and sweat.

Apparently he now found lumberjacks highly erotic.

Gabe carefully rolled up the fragile map, half kicking, half congratulating himself for not joining her last night. Thank the universe for ringing phones. If Elliott hadn't interrupted them, he would have done something mindless without thinking it through first, and then tortured himself with Monday-morning quarterbacking afterward. He couldn't be ruled by his dick on this one, even if it shouted, "Yeah, you can, you dumb shit" at the top of its hormone-addled lungs.

She maddened him. Mesmerized him. Challenged him. Made him hard as a diamond-tipped drill bit.

Gabe released a deep breath he wasn't aware he was holding. He'd thought it through, and… he was going to sleep with Lorin Schlessinger—if she was still talking to him.

Yeah, he was going to do this. Lorin was a jittery mess, the demands of her Valkyrie physiology slowly but surely making themselves known. For his part, Gabe hadn't had sex since he and Kayla had broken up.

Sleeping with Lorin was, as Elliott would say, a $1 + 1 = 3$ solution.

Damn Lukas for planting this fool idea in his head. Now that the seed had been planted, it wove insidious roots. But the alternative? Lorin getting her physical needs met with someone else? Gabe's fists clenched. *Unthinkable.*

The snap of Paige's gum jolted his brain back to practical matters. Before he and Lorin could sleep together, they had to talk, set some ground rules—if she was still interested. Leaving her hanging last night might well have nipped his foray into sexual harassment in the bud before it even started. Lorin might well have changed her mind—

Rosemary mint. Sea salt. Sun-baked sweat.

Lorin leaned against the frame of the open workroom door. She wore another of her endless supply of fleece zip-up jackets with the clingy black leggings she favored for running, and that definitely favored her back. Her quads subtly flexed as she shifted her weight. He nearly groaned as he imagined them vised around him while he bottomed out in her body.

Her green eyes burned with annoyance, and with a hunger she didn't bother to hide.

"Paige, let's call it a day," he said, not breaking his gaze from Lorin. He could smell her humid need from here. "Thanks for the information. We'll pick this up again tomorrow."

Paige scowled at the rolled-up map Gabe held. "I hate missing things."

"We don't know that anything's been missed."

"What's going on?" Lorin asked, levering her weight off the doorjamb and sauntering into the workroom.

Sex on the prowl. Gabe shifted his weight as the zipper of his jeans bit into some damn tender flesh. Was that why every man on the dig favored baggy cargo pants?

"Gabe had some questions about an area of the property that I'm not familiar with," Paige said as she dropped from the table to the floor. "Maybe you can help."

"They're about to start *Harold and Kumar Go To White Castle* in the bunkhouse," Lorin said.

"Nathan's turn to pick the movie?" At Lorin's nod, Paige rolled her eyes. "I think I'll pass. You two have plans?" She looked back and forth between them and smirked. "Of course you have plans. I'll just leave you… to it. See you tomorrow!" she called over her shoulder as she left.

Lorin approached the long wooden table that bisected the workroom and leaned against the other side. Gabe's nostrils quivered with scents: her after-dinner coffee, pinesap, and wild, wet arousal. Saliva pooled in his mouth.

"What did you and Paige find?" she asked.

Shove it down. Gabe cleared his throat and carefully unrolled the map again, pointing to the area he and Paige had been looking at. "I'm curious about this area to the north."

When Lorin carefully touched the brittle edge of the map, Gabe felt like she'd stroked his very body. The movement was completely unconscious, which made it all the more provocative.

"That's part of our property, but it hasn't been assessed in any detail. Our focus for the last decade or so has been the petroglyph cave, and the current site. And"—Lorin shot a quick glance over her shoulder, lowering her voice—"now that the box has been discovered there?" She shrugged. "I don't see our focus, or frankly our budget, stretching any further afield right now."

"If that box is what we think it is, you'll be in a strong position to lobby for more funds."

"We'd have to go to the Council, go head-to-head with Krispin Woolf." Lorin's eyes lit with challenge. "Is that something you'd be willing to do?"

It was an important consideration. Krispin Woolf wasn't known for temperate reactions, and disagreeing with the WerePack Alpha—*his* alpha—could have long-lasting implications. "I really hate politics," he muttered.

"But you're so good at it."

He wasn't sure whether her comment was a slur or a compliment. "You're dressed for running," he said, shifting away from the table. "Feel like running to the north? Maybe you'll notice something I haven't."

Lorin's gaze flicked down to his bulging groin, then back to his face. "I would think you might find running a challenge at the moment."

"I think I can manage." *She was staring at his lips. Jesus.* He cleared his throat again. "Let's get away from camp for a while. We need to talk."

"Okay. Need to change?"

His jeans had a stranglehold on his dick. "Yeah. It'll only take me a minute."

"Don't rush on my account."

The suggestive twist in her voice contradicted her words. There was every reason to rush. "Ladies first," he said, gesturing toward the door with his hand.

"I'm no lady." She sauntered out in front of him. "Don't forget the lights."

He about-faced and slapped at the switch. Damn it, she had him as addled as a juvenile getting his first sniff of tail. Time to get his brain back in the driver's seat, at least for a while. He'd change, get them away from camp, and they'd have the conversation they needed to have. Then he'd—

"Hi, guys." Mike and Gretchen stood in the building's entryway, hand in hand. "Ready to lock up for the night? We're done with cleanup."

Hell. He hadn't even thought about locking up, or that there might still be people in the dining area next door.

"Hi there," Lorin replied. "Are you going to the bunkhouse to watch the movie?"

"Nathan's choice, right?" Mike glanced at Gretchen. "*Harold and Kumar*. Want to go to Tubby's instead?"

"Sure." The young siren's single-word response was an erotic novel.

Gabe reached for the vulnerable slice of skin at the small of Lorin's back. She stilled at his touch. "Have fun," he said.

Mike eyed them both and grinned knowingly. "You too."

The younger couple walked away still holding hands, their shoulders brushing as they strolled down the tree-lined road leading away from the site. When Lorin cleared her throat and stepped away, Gabe was almost relieved. She was nervous too.

Crossing the compound, they finally reached Gabe's bright blue tent. "I'll just be a second," he said as he unzipped the door.

"Hurry." Lorin wasn't a siren, but the demand in her voice hit him like a roundhouse kick.

Gabe shouldered into the tent's back room and assessed his workout clothes. What could he wear that wouldn't get him laughed off the site before he and Lorin got to someplace more private? Something that could be stripped off quickly in the event that she was as hungry for him as he was for her?

It wasn't possible, but a man could dream.

He picked up a clean jock and just as quickly dropped it back onto the pile. He wasn't even going to try to wrestle his unruly anatomy into the blasted thing. Grabbing a pair of compression shorts instead, Gabe stripped out of his boots and jeans and worked the clingy fabric up over his legs and his raging erection, layering a pair of faded maroon sweatpants over them. The T-shirt and fleece jacket he was already wearing would work just fine.

His thoughts raced as he laced his running shoes. Should he bring a blanket? Give her something soft to lie on while he lost himself in her? Somehow, such premeditated thoughts seemed way too presumptuous— even though every cell in his body was certain they'd have sex before they returned to the compound.

The hair on his legs stood on end, scraping against the soft cotton. He was going to have sex. With Lorin Schlessinger. Out there in the woods. Probably not what Gideon had in mind when he'd urged Gabe to end his sex drought.

Reaching into the dark corner of his duffel bag, he snatched a condom out of the box he'd almost left at home, tucking the small packet into his jacket pocket. Then he cursed and grabbed three more.

"Hurry up. It's getting dark."

He exhaled into his hand to check his breath. Not minty fresh, but…

"Gabe. Are you knitting a new pair of socks in there?"

"I'm coming, I'm coming." Striding to the tent's flapping door, he almost tripped when he saw Lorin, legs straddled and bent over at the waist, touching her palms to the ground as she warmed up. Zipping the tent door closed, he turned away and did a few perfunctory stretches of his own. If he let himself stare at her flexing ass, he'd dive on her like a slavering beast—privacy be damned. "Come on, let's get going."

"Okay. Sure we need to talk first?" She jogged backwards, putting too much space between them. "I'll still respect you in the morning, you know."

He made himself match her tone. "That would imply that you respect me now, and we both know *that* isn't true."

A tiny smile tilted the corners of her mouth—not confirming or denying his words.

The woman drove him nuts.

What did she expect from this, from him? Just a quick, medicinal roll in the pine needles to bleed off some of her excess energy?

Did she really expect so little?

Probably. Her last lover, Rafe Sebastiani, had been a gorgeous, hedonistic sex demon, and he… wasn't. Never before had he been so conscious of the weight of the glasses resting on the bridge of his nose, or how long it had been since he'd been to the gym.

"It's just sex, Gabe." Her smoky alto voice sounded

slightly annoyed. "Do we need to negotiate a bloody contract first?"

His lizard brain slithered into fantasy mode, with Lorin wearing a tight pencil skirt and stilettos, nibbling on a pen, as she stated the number of orgasms she expected per sexual encounter, and the penalties that would accrue if she didn't receive them. "Details are important," he said.

Was that rough, growly voice his?

Her breath hitched; her pupils dilated. "You *are* very detail-oriented."

The heat in her voice was going to strip him bare.

"Can you talk and run at the same time? In the name of efficiency?" She shot him a final challenging glance, pivoted, and took off like a gazelle, disappearing into the tunnel of pines.

Testosterone and adrenaline raged like class-five rapids.

Chase. Taste. Take.

He sprinted after her, more alive than he'd felt in ages.

～⁓～

Lorin's feet pounded down the deer trail leading to the shattered rise that had caught Gabe's attention. Squirrels rustled in the underbrush, scurrying to safety as she approached. An owl hooted a complaint from a nearby pine. The sound of her own breath, whooshing in and out of her lungs, sounded unnaturally loud in dusk's dim hush.

Where was Gabe? Freyja help her, what would she do about this knee-knocking need if he changed his mind again?

Behind her, branches cracked. A muttered curse. *Ah, finally.* She lifted her forearm to protect her face from the slap of low-hanging branches as she picked up the pace, her muscles warming, flexing, flowing. The rise was just ahead. She was more than ready for—

A hand latched on to her upper arm, spinning her around and yanking her against a rock-hard body.

Gabe.

In the near-dark, their faces inches apart, she stared. There were pine needles in his hair, and a branch had whipped a red weal across his cheekbone. His breath came in puffs she could see and feel. "Caught me," she murmured.

His big, blunt-fingered hand clamped onto her ass in response.

Lorin flexed against it, testing him. Testing herself. His fingers clenched back immediately, pressing her more firmly against his groin, his erection pushing at her through the layers of constricting clothing. "Still want to talk first?" she gasped.

He opened his mouth. Cursed again—and crashed his lips to hers, devouring her with perfect succulent pressure.

Lorin clutched at his hair. Who would have guessed that Gabe Lupinsky had such a wicked, talented mouth? She could wallow in his decadent, primal taste for hours—some other time. Right now, she needed him inside her like she needed her next breath.

Lips still locked together, she tried to pull him down to the soft moss, but Gabe pinned her against a nearby birch clump with his body instead. Before she could figure out how he'd managed it, her feet were off the ground, her back scraping against bark, and her legs scrabbling for purchase around his waist.

As she crossed her ankles behind his back, Gabe

leaned into her spread legs with his full body weight, pressing her back into the cradle created by the trio of trees. Her moan of delight floated into the thick night air, and she rubbed greedily against the blunt ridge of flesh pushing under his soft cotton sweatpants.

She'd never spared a single, lascivious thought to the body Gabriel Lupinsky covered with his conservative clothes as he glared at her across conference room tables back at Sebastiani Labs. Now, as she writhed against his rock-hard flesh, she knew she'd never be able to scrub his dimensions from her mind.

Freyja help her. He was... spectacular.

Damn it.

"Gabe." She scraped her breasts against the layers of fleece and cotton separating their chests. Supporting her weight, he lowered his head and nuzzled against her aching nipple with his cheek. *Not enough.* She shoved her jacket and shirt up under her armpits, exposing her torso to the chilled night air. She needed to feel his skin against hers, feel the scratch of his beard—

Gabe unsnapped the front fastening of her bra with a dexterity that she filed away for later thought. Then, time sputtered and stalled as he explored her aching flesh with hands, lips, and teeth.

Lorin shuddered against his mouth, her bare back scraping against the papery birch bark. She was a hair-breadth from coming, and they both still had all of their clothes on. She wanted to feel him, hot and pulsing, in her hands. "Hurry," she demanded. Her hands tugged at the drawstring at his waist.

This first time, she wanted him inside her when she came.

Gabe lifted his head from her breast, his jawline lit by the sliver of moon peeking out from behind the night-time clouds. His eyes were glittering silver slits behind his glasses.

Her stomach jumped. She'd had a werewolf lover or two in her time, but something about the feral hunger on Gabe's face twisted her in a knot. If she didn't get him inside her soon, she'd combust.

Trusting him to support her weight, her hands burrowed under the waistband of the sweats and shoved the layers down, out of her way. His cock leapt into her hands, hot, hard, and heavy, throbbing with tensile strength. She needed him inside her, now. She needed to ride him like her life depended upon it.

She groaned aloud. Right now, she thought it just might.

He removed one arm from under her butt, supporting her with the other as he yanked at the waistband of her running tights. She clutched at tree branches. *Damn stirrup heels.* What had she been thinking? She'd have to take off her running shoes to get the blasted things off.

"Hang on," Gabe bit out, wrapping her legs tightly around his body. Reaching into his jacket pocket, he took out a Swiss Army knife and clicked it open. Spandex snapped, sagged, disappeared, and they were finally touching, skin to skin, his cock tucking between her legs like a custom fit.

"Shit." When he pulled back, chilly air kissed her damp crevices.

"What?" She dug into his ass with her heels. "Get back here."

"Condom. Condoms," he muttered. "In my pocket."

Good thing one of them had a brain. She knew she

was healthy and protected against pregnancy, but they hadn't exactly had a chance to exchange sexual histories. "Hurry."

He snatched a condom from his jacket pocket, ripped the package open with his teeth, and donned it one-handed.

She raised a mental brow. She'd never heard any gossip about Gabe's sexual prowess on the Sebastiani Labs grapevine, hadn't heard any morning-after whispers in the ladies room at Underbelly, but… damn, Lupinsky had some moves.

She moaned as his heavy shaft nudged her hungry entrance. "Put me down," she said. "I'm too heavy." He was strong, but there was no way he'd be able to support her weight long enough for the long, rough ride she craved.

He buried his head at the crook of her neck instead. His breathing was rough and uneven as his sharp teeth strummed up the sensitive cord of her neck.

"Gabe." Damn it, she'd give him maximum points for foreplay, but right now she wanted his big cock, filling her to the brim, nailing her against this tree. "Now."

He lifted his head and met her eyes. And did as she ordered.

Their groans twisted together as Gabe pressed in and stretched her wide. He stopped for a second, gritting his teeth, suspending her on a rack of pleasure. She writhed, trying to get more of him, but her precarious position didn't give her a lot of leverage. Sacrificing her handhold on his shoulders, she skated her hands down the muscles of his back, clutched his ass, and pulled.

Gabe groaned, his knees giving a single, precarious quake, but he steadied quickly. "Lorin." He kissed her, a gentle brush of the lips that inexplicably made her eyes sting. "You can stop this now, with a single word."

As if. Her skin was about to burst off her frame. She rolled her hips, gaining another precious inch of his cock. They both groaned. "Gabe," she gasped, waiting for the rest of its blunt glide.

It didn't happen.

Gabe dragged in a ragged breath. His face was all planes and shadows, his cheekbones as sharp as the knife he'd used to bare her body to his.

"Please."

He boosted her body a couple of key inches—almost withdrawing from her body in the process—but before she could react, he surged, deeply, driving into her body with long, desperate strokes she could do nothing but receive.

Lorin clutched a tree branch with one hand and Gabe's fleece-covered shoulder with another, scissoring her legs more tightly around his churning hips. She didn't know if it was the angle, the precarious position, his size, or some combination of the three—but damned if he wasn't hitting every skittering nerve ending she had, and a few she hadn't known about.

She grasped his shoulders—the only solid thing in the universe.

Their eyes met. Locked.

Faster, faster.

She tensed then caught her breath. "Gabe." As she shattered, the tension that had plagued her for days spiraled up, up, and away, an explosion of glittery butterflies taking flight between her thighs.

A growl. Two rough thrusts. One more, even deeper,

that pushed the breath from her body and rolled her eyes back in her head. Gabe's rangy body stuttered and stilled. His face tightened.

And he tossed his head to the sky and howled.

Chapter 8

BEDDOE DIDN'T NEED THE TINY RED LIGHT FLASHING IN his peripheral vision to know his blood pressure was dangerously high. Approaching his personal quarters at the end of the walkway, he faced the entrance for an identification scan. "Welcome, Beddoe," it acknowledged, opening the door with a click and a swoosh. Stepping inside, he waited for the door to close, for the lock to activate, for the soundproofing to engage.

Then he slammed his fist into the wall.

"Dia!" Withdrawing his hand from the hole he'd just created, he sucked his stinging knuckles. His internal organs sat up and took notice as the dark taste of blood swirled on his tongue.

He needed to feed.

Walking to the chiller, he loosened the stranglehold his uniform jacket had on his neck. Lorcan had wanted to talk to him, all right. The bastard had raised the *TonTon's* profit target. "A stretch goal," Lorcan had stated in his oozing, slimy voice. "Challenging but achievable, yes?"

"Yes," he'd automatically agreed, even as his ballocks tried to burrow into his body for protection. One did not refuse Lorcan and live to tell the tale.

Snatching a bag of blood from the chiller, Beddoe raised it to his mouth, his fangs puncturing the receptacle with a soft pop. As he suckled, the strain slowly leached from his body. Lorcan clearly suspected something was amiss, but he must not have proof. If Lorcan had evidence that Beddoe was skimming, he'd already be dead.

Lorcan hadn't mentioned the beacon. Could the *TonTon* actually have been the only ship close enough to have picked up the *Arkapaedis*'s short, weak blip? Could he be that lucky?

No. A smart man created his own luck. He needed to get back down to the surface, find that beacon, and shut it down—once and for all. Buy himself some time.

Still suckling at the bag, he opened his storage unit and assessed the small collection of Earth attire he'd cobbled together from several of the larger entertainers Minchin had recently acquired. He'd learned his lesson from his last trip to the surface. This time, he'd dress for warmth. He finally selected stiff, dark blue leg coverings very much like the vision-impaired man had been wearing, an oddly bubbled long-sleeved shirt that pulled over the head, and the dark jacket made of a synthetic substance so light, soft, and warm that he'd taken to wearing it in the privacy of his own quarters.

Placing the garments on his sleeping pallet, he drained the bag, stripped to the skin, and took a second bag of blood into the body care unit with him. Being it was full dark on the surface, he programmed only moderate UV protection. "Begin." As warm chemicals misted over his body, he made short work of the second bag. Rich, thick nourishment surged through his system, sharpening his thoughts, chasing away the nerves Lorcan's call had wrought. How could he deliver the financial performance Lorcan demanded without impacting his own portfolio? How could he cut expenditures without impacting the customer's experience? Environmental controls in the staff and crew quarters were at the extremes of tolerance as it was, and both the time- and d-drives were overdue for retrofit.

"Remove body hair?" the cleansing unit asked.

"Negative." The man he'd seen arguing with the strapping woman down on the surface had sported a shadow of facial growth. A slightly unkempt look might allow him to blend better once he reached the surface.

"Cleansing complete."

Exiting the body care unit, he dressed in the strange clothes, struggled with the closures of the stiff, ankle-height animal-hide footwear—*boots*—and placed his Mach on the table beside his sleeping mat. He couldn't risk taking technology to the surface without gathering more data on the culture's current capabilities. Almost unconsciously, his fingertips skimmed the outline of his useless complant, barely discernible under his skin. In retrospect, his decision to divert the astronomical Core access fee to his anonymous account had been criminally shortsighted.

He was data-blind. He couldn't remember the last time he'd had to rely strictly upon his own powers of observation to complete a mission.

Punching a button on the comm panel he'd barely missed hitting with his fist, he asked Ta'al to meet him in Transport.

He could no longer trust his physical safety to Minchin.

Leaving the blessed heat of his quarters, he strode to Transport, gave Ta'al the coordinates, and stepped onto the pad. "Retrieval in three local cycles, please. You have the con."

"Yes, Sirrah." If Ta'al had questions about why she was being placed in command during his absence instead of Minchin, she didn't ask them, and if she was at all nervous about scattering her captain's molecules across the Void and trusting they'd reassemble correctly at the desired destination, it didn't show. Her pilot's hands were steady at the controls.

"Engage," he ordered.

"Aye. Engaging."

Beddoe stiffened his knees and tightened his sphincter as the transporter's cool, stinging energy washed over him in an uncomfortable wave. Time and consciousness winked away, returning as he shimmered into place on the surface behind a building that blazed with light, pulsed with sound, and positively reeked. He rubbed his arms, waiting for full feeling to return to his limbs. The aftermath of transport felt like pinbugs on the march, each one taking a tiny bite of his—

A screech of metal against metal. Someone was coming.

Beddoe clumsily crouched behind the large blue garbage receptacle, barely avoiding the widening slice of light as the door opened. Rock crunched underfoot as someone approached and threw something. The receptacle vibrated against his shoulder as whatever had been thrown hit with a soft thud.

Beddoe breathed slowly and quietly, ignoring his muscles' burning protest as he held the brutal crouch. He heard a soft scrape, followed by a barely audible crackle. The unmistakable scent stung his nostrils. *Dia*, the person was smoking herb. His shaking legs would never hold him that long. He had to—

An eerie howl echoed from the foliage.

"Goddamn timber wolves," the man muttered. He threw his herb to the ground and quickly returned to the building. The moment the door slammed closed behind him, Beddoe let his legs collapse, the small, cold rocks biting into his buttocks through the stiff fabric.

Another howl. Beddoe scrambled to his feet, rubbing at his sore knees and thighs. Seeking shelter seemed more prudent than walking, alone, through the dark tunnel of trees leading to the location where the beacon had last blipped.

Once he was confident his legs would hold his weight, he strode to the front of the building. A roughly carved sign over the door read "Tubby's." The door didn't open when he approached. He extended his arm, clasped the handle, and pulled.

The building's warmth enveloped him the minute he entered, but the smells trapped in the room were almost enough to make him turn around and take his chances with the howling animal outside: malty yeast. Primitive liquor. Perfumes and unguents covering sweat and other body scents. The light source audibly buzzed and emitted a noxious chemical odor. He smelled herb, and—

"Excuse us," a young woman murmured politely as she and a big male brushed past, hand-in-hand, smelling of very recent sex.

Vampyr. The male was unmistakably Vampyr; the tingling in his fangs confirmed it. Like recognized like. It had always been so.

Near-translucent data scrolled across the bottom of his field of vision. *Humanoid male. Humanoid female.*

Wrong. His data had some very dangerous gaps.

The couple approached the long, narrow table

bisecting the room and spoke to the wildly bearded man standing on the other side. Turning, the man tugged on a lever, dispensing straw-colored liquid—*beer*—into a drink vessel. While they waited, the couple spoke to a very small woman sitting at the long table.

The little one didn't look particularly happy to see them. "Go, sit," she said. Picking up her own drink vessel, she waved a hand at the large screen mounted over the long counter, where stick-wielding men glided over a hard, white surface on bladed boots. "I'm watching the game."

The Vampyr frowned, but once the bearded man placed the brown, malty beverages on the table, he and the larger female departed, sitting at a table for two in the darkened corner.

Leaving the tiny female all alone.

His interest was piqued. Despite her stature, she was a woman, not a girl. Her breasts were small but well-formed, her hips slight but rounded in sexual maturity. Her near-white hair was… quite extraordinary, and to a man in his line of business that was saying something. A certain segment of his client base would absolutely love her.

He could calculate the profit already.

Clearing his throat, he approached, levering himself onto one of the row of odd backless seats. He left one empty seat between him and the woman, who busily sucked on a small red fruit impaled on a tiny spear.

"What can I getcha?" the giant of a man said from behind the oblong table. His grizzly gray facial hair cascaded to a barrel chest covered by a vividly colored red-and-black checked shirt.

Beddoe looked at the row of colorful bottles, at the mechanical levers. The yeasty smell of the beer was making his stomach roll in a most unpleasant manner. What could he drink that wouldn't make him ill? Gesturing to the small woman, he said, "I'll have what she's having."

The big man smirked. "One raspberry cosmo coming up." As he turned away, he muttered, "Goddamn metrosexuals."

"Citiot," a man down the row said through a cough.

He recognized the "goddamn" well enough—such colorful curses here on the surface—but "citiot"? "Metrosexual"? Given the men's body language and tone of voice, the context didn't seem complimentary.

A trio of trills emanated from a small rectangular device sitting on the table in front of the coughing man, who picked it up and spoke. The device looked enough like the comm unit he'd left behind on the ship that he could probably bring his with him the next time he came down to the surface.

While the other man prepared his drink, Beddoe observed the room. What an odd mix of primitive and... even more primitive. Dead animal heads, stuffed and mounted, adorned the walls and stared at him with unblinking eyes. Brightly colored signs illuminated with ancient planetary gasses that buzzed and popped and hummed. Music throbbed from a colorful box in the corner. A gravelly voiced man begged someone to pour some sugar on him in the name of love. Up on the screen, men bashed a small, black, cylindrical object with hook-ended sticks.

The music was effective. He felt its pull at his

groin—or maybe the pull came from the woman sitting at his right, suckling on the round red fruit with her flexible pink tongue.

"Jesus," the man seated on his other side muttered, setting down his comm device. "It won't work, you know," he said under his breath to Beddoe. "The 'I'll have what she's having' thing. She's shot everyone down tonight."

Beddoe tensed. He couldn't see a weapon, but—

"You from The Cities?" the man continued.

The man stank of herb and frustration, but he didn't appear to be injured. *The Cities?* Beddoe remembered the man's previous comment. *Ah.* "Yes, I'm a Citiot."

The man cleared his throat, and his face turned ruddy. "Sorry about that."

The bearded man placed a reddish drink in front of him, setting it on a small absorbent mat. "Gonna watch the game for a while? Opening a tab?"

Payment. Dia, he'd arrived with empty pockets—not that they'd know what to do with his digital tender anyway. How had Minchin dealt with this issue?

"Let me get that for ya," the man said. "No hard feelings, eh?"

The small female spoke. "Put it on my tab, Tubby." Her voice was lower and smokier than he'd expected. "Any man who orders a raspberry cosmo in a northern Minnesota bar either has confidence to burn or a very odd sense of humor."

No one had ever accused him of having a sense of humor, but he wasn't about to contradict her. Not if it kept her talking to him. "Thank you," he said, picking up the drink and taking a careful sip. Tart, fruity sweetness exploded on his tongue. He narrowed his eyes, nodded in approval, and took another sip.

"Good, huh?" she said with a tiny feline smile. "These guys don't know what they're missing."

Before he could respond, a loud cheer suddenly rose from the screen where two warriors circled each other, drawing closer with a great sense of ceremony. They exchanged snarls, words, bumped chests. They threw the sticks, gauntlets, and helmets to the ground with quick, deliberate actions before lunging at each other, trading methodical bare-fisted punches.

On screen, the crowd roared even louder. "Kick the fucker's ass, Walloch!" Tubby called up to the device. "Ivy League pussy."

The two men fell to the slippery surface and grappled for position, the warrior in dark colors—Walloch—quickly gaining the upper hand. The man on his back fought bravely, but Walloch, clearly dominant, repeatedly smashed his fist into the other man's face. Blood spurted, staining skin, the man's garment, and the hard, white surface.

Beddoe's fangs tingled. This Lord Stanley certainly had fierce warriors fighting for the honor of his cup.

The men rolled, scrabbling for purchase on the slippery surface, and still, the punches flew. *First blood had been drawn. Why did they keep fighting?* Just as he thought it, two men wearing black-and-white striped shirts approached, pulling Walloch up and off the other man by his arms. As the victor was led away, the defeated man lurched to his hands and knees, head hanging, spitting blood.

On-screen, a melodious voice said, "And Walloch skates to the penalty box. Five minute major."

"Walloch couldn't let that check on his captain go unpunished, Robert," another disembodied voice added.

The warrior Walloch grinned, exposing bloody teeth, as he took a seat in a box that any youngling could escape. Beddoe tongued his fangs. *All that blood going to waste.*

"Look at that, Vance," Tubby said, pointing to the screen where several people had joined the defeated man, crawling on their hands and knees, peering closely at the white surface. "Dude lost a tooth."

Vance, the man who'd offered to pay for his drink, raised his own glass in a toast. "He should look for his sac as long as he's down there."

The small female rolled her eyes and set her empty glass on the table. "Hit me, Tubby."

What? Had she really asked the giant man to strike her? He outweighed her three to one. Why—

Tubby simply turned and prepared another pink drink. *Ah.*

Ramping up his glamour, Beddoe gestured to the empty chair between them, asking without words if he could join her. He'd bought and sold more flesh than he remembered, but this woman intrigued him. At her noncommittal shrug, he moved, not missing Tubby's poorly disguised disbelief when he set another beverage in front of her.

"Thanks, Tub." She turned and met his gaze. "Haven't seen you around here before."

He caught his breath. Her eyes were the color of a Saurian sunrise.

"I'm Paige," she said, extending her child-sized hand.

He took it, kissing her knuckles instead of shaking the hand, his fangs tingling at the sight of the tender veins and capillaries pulsing under the near-translucent skin of her inner wrist. *Dia*. "I'm… Robert."

"Robert," she repeated with a bemused smile. "Not Bob or Bobby?"

He shook his head. The name he'd heard the man on the screen call the other one was as good a name as any other, but if her smile was anything to go by, she approved. Her teeth were very small, and very, very white. The *TonTon's* customers always appreciated white teeth and fresh breath, and so did he. Still holding her hand, he gazed into her extraordinary eyes.

You're… smokin' hot.

Beddoe jerked back in surprise, dropping her hand. He'd heard the words, but her mouth hadn't moved. Faerie? Here?

"So you heard me. I thought so," she murmured. She drank deeply before muttering under her breath, "Damn vamps."

She knew.

"You're not one of Lorin's crew," she continued, skimming those extraordinary eyes over his body. "What brings you to this fine establishment? Opening a cabin for the season? Vacationing?"

Dia, she was looking at his hands, and he'd forgotten to remove Lorcan's Ring of Allegiance before coming down to the surface. "Opening a cabin," he repeated. Whatever *that* meant.

She brought the triangular vessel up to her lips, tipped it back as she had the other one, and drained it. He quickly followed suit. "Would you like to escort me home?" she asked, already sliding off the stool.

Would you like to feed?

His fangs shoved down in response. His pulse surged. Suddenly he had a cockstand like he hadn't had in ages. "Very much," he said.

They stood, and he escorted her toward the door with a light touch at the back of her waist.

"Paige?" the young Vampyr called from his table on the other side of the room.

"See you tomorrow, Mike," she said without turning.

Beddoe pulled the door open and followed her through it, ignoring the feel of the young Vampyr's eyes boring into his back. Once the door closed behind them, they both took a deep breath of the cold, crisp air. Paige laughed, tipping her head back to meet his eyes. "The smell can be a little overwhelming, can't it?"

"Yes." The light buzzing overhead illuminated tiny, pulsing veins. Saliva spurted in his mouth. "Where's home?"

"That way," she said, indicating the dark, tree-lined road.

He took her hand. "Let's go."

The beacon could wait.

~~~

Tipping off Gabe, Lorin sprawled, boneless, on her back in the cool, spongy moss, trying to catch her breath. Somehow they'd made it from the birch clump to the ground for Round Two, scattering clothes and shoes along the way. As far as physical comfort went, Gabe had definitely gotten the better end of the deal—she'd feel the bark scrapes on her lower back, the soreness in her muscles, for days—but she felt well-oiled, utterly fantastic, better than she had in months.

Against a birch clump, with endorphins and adrenaline coursing through both their systems? It had been a freaking collision. And once they'd dropped to the moss, she'd ridden them both into oblivion.

She'd never come so hard in her life.

She glanced over at him, lying on his back beside her, his lean, bare body gleaming with sweat in the bright moonlight. Though he was still breathing as hard as she was, his face was relaxed, satisfied, his eyes closed behind the lenses of his glasses. She felt inexplicably proud that she'd tired him out, that she'd ground the edge off his rough, uncontrolled need.

She wanted to feel it again—as soon as she could move.

"You okay?" He reached for her hand and clasped it.

Something about Gabe's gentle grasp rocked her, made some internal fault line slip. Other lovers—Rafe, for Freyja's sake—had done the exact same thing on countless occasions, but this was different somehow.

"Lorin?" He tugged, and she… went. She couldn't quite find the will to resist. Physically, her body hummed, like she'd had a particularly relaxing massage. She felt tired yet… oddly energized. As she cuddled up next to his side and rested her hand on his chest, he kissed her temple.

And the ground under her feet somehow stabilized. Realigned.

But then he sighed. "What are we going to do about this?"

"Repeat the experience? Now?"

He turned his head and met her eyes in the moon-dipped dark. "You really want a repeat performance?"

Freyja, how could he doubt his appeal? She leaned

over so she could see his face. She found his talented lips with hers, then suckled and nodded. "As soon as possible," she whispered.

He nipped her lip and licked away the tiny sting. When he skated his hand down her back, curved it over her butt cheek, she shivered, and not from the chill. "Sorry I was so quick on the trigger earlier." He gestured to the birch clump with a vaguely embarrassed wave of his hand. "It's been awhile, and—"

"Do you hear me complaining?" she murmured, suckling at his neck. Odd. She'd never felt the need to mark a lover before, but she did now. "I was pretty quick on the trigger myself."

His abs clenched as he lifted his head slightly. "What the…"

"Sorry—"

"No, not you. Look at these trees."

"Trees?"

"Look."

Lifting her head, she did—and caught her breath. The grove, the trees… they glittered in the moonlight, as if tiny shredded diamonds were embedded in the dirt and bark. "Wow. It's like a crystal fairyland."

"Or a crash site," Gabe murmured. "Look at the luminosity." Scrambling to his feet, Gabe walked to the nearest tree and examined the bark. Hands on his hips, naked—was that a grass stain on his ass?—he looked around the clearing, over to the odd rise that had captured his attention days earlier, and back to the trees again. "I think this is metal. Do you see my jacket?"

"Over there." Pointing to a mound of fabric near the birch clump, she quickly stood. "Damn, I wish I had a flashlight." Had she and Gabe had hot monkey sex at a second archaeological site? The one that might finally give their people the answers they'd sought for so long?

Goose bumps prickled. Gabe had been right. There'd been something here all along, and she'd missed it.

He retrieved his jacket—*definitely* a grass stain on his ass—and reached into the pocket. Her pulse jumped as he pulled out the Swiss Army knife he'd used to slice her leggings from her body. The blade clicked into place, and he carefully pried a piece of bark off the tree, tucking it into the other pocket.

She shivered as a breeze rustled the pine needles.

"I can see you gauging where to place the stakes already," he said, draping his jacket around her bare shoulders like a cape. "It might be nothing. Let me run some tests first."

"Come on, Gabe. Do you really think it's nothing?"

"No, but we need some information first. There's nothing else we can do here tonight." He nuzzled into her neck. "And I haven't had anywhere near enough of you yet."

This time, her shiver had nothing to do with the chilly breeze. She didn't want this night to end either. She hadn't come close to slaking her need for him, and she didn't know when she might. "Come back to the cabin with me?"

His eyes burned with an expression she couldn't read, as if some epic battle were being waged inside. Finally, he lowered his lips to hers and gave her a succulent, luxurious kiss that wiped away her thoughts.

"Hurry."

Gathering up their things, they did just that.

———※———

"So Paige, who's the mystery vamp?" Nathan called as he kneeled in the pit, a short-handled spade in his hand.

Shoring up the wall where she'd staked Pritchard's command box—and doing some surreptitious excavating when she could get away with it—Lorin eavesdropped. Paige had met someone last night? A vamp? Though it wasn't unheard of to run into one of their kind so far away from the Twin Cities metro, northern Minnesota wasn't exactly an Underworld hot spot.

Paige didn't look up from her laptop at the artifact cataloguing station. Instead, she ducked her chin into the neckline of her fuchsia turtleneck like a turtle pulling its head into its shell. "I don't know what you're talking about, Nathan."

Paige's voice was careless, but her expression was dreamy, besotted—the classic vamp glamour hangover. She was so pale she looked like she needed an immediate transfusion.

Lorin shot a glance at Mike, who pushed a wheelbarrow mounded with sifted dirt and extrusion toward their discard pile. She usually trusted his judgment, and his scowl made her stomach lurch.

Damn. Last night when she and Gabe had finally stumbled, wobbly kneed, back to camp, everyone had been in the bunkhouse, accounted for and asleep—which was good, because she'd been carrying her ruined running tights and relying on Gabe's longer jacket to cover the breeze-kissed essentials as they'd slipped into her cabin. When had Paige had time to hook up with someone?

One more mystery to solve.

Gabe was almost certain the fragments embedded in the trees at the grove were metallic. The same metal Pritchard's lockbox was made of? Gabe didn't know, but after his morning meetings were over, he planned to harvest more samples and run some tests.

Lorin propped her forearm on her sledgehammer, swiping her wrist across her sweating forehead. Command boxes, tech units, and now glittering trees. There were too many things she couldn't talk to the crew about, and the need for secrecy was driving her nuts.

"That's a vampire kiss on your neck if I've ever seen one," Nathan hooted. "Who slipped you the hard fang injection? Mike?"

Mike almost dropped a handle of the wheelbarrow. "Hell no."

Lorin winced on Paige's behalf.

"Ellenore…" Nathan singsonged to the only other vamp on their crew. "You and Paige hooked up last night and you didn't let me watch? I thought we were friends."

"Paige *is* adorable, but it wasn't me," Ellenore said from inside the shady gazebo as she scooped another cup of clay-laden dirt onto her sifting screen. The experimental sunscreen that allowed Mike to move freely about the site for several hours at a time unfortunately gave her hives. "Men and their deluded ménage fantasies." She sighed. Squinting, she picked up a fragment from the screen, squirted it with water, and set it aside for later examination. "When two women get it on, they're doing it to please themselves, not you. It's so refreshing to sleep with someone who knows their way around a clitoris."

Nathan stood with his hands on his hips. "Hey, I know my way around a clitoris just fine."

Ellenore poked at the dirt with a grubby finger. "Yeah, dude, you fascinate me."

Everyone burst into laughter. Ellenore's deadpan delivery of Neil Patrick Harris's classic line from *Harold and Kumar Go To White Castle* had been pitch-perfect.

When Nathan launched into a defense of his sexual prowess before the pack, Lorin shook her head. Werewolves. So damn predictable—except when they weren't. Why had she assumed that Gabe would be a careful, deliberate lover, and that she'd be in firm control of their sexual dealings? Her body still sang with a delicious soreness, and now she bloomed with a heat that had nothing to do with the quickly rising temperature. *Mind back on business, Lorin.* Dropping the sledgehammer, she chugged some water from her insulated canteen before joining Paige at the table sheltered from the sun by a tarp roof.

"Looks great," she said, using her height advantage to peer down the neck of Paige's shirt. Nathan was right. Though partially healed, the twin punctures on Paige's neck was a classic vampire kiss. And still half glamoured this far into the day? Paige had found a strong one.

She didn't know whether to be happy for Paige, concerned, or both. As she'd told Gabe, Paige was an adult, but in terms of real-world experience, she was a babe in the woods.

Mike joined them, leaning over to peer at Paige's neck—not being nearly as covert about his interest as Lorin had been. "Get away from me," Paige snarled.

Whoa. Lorin stepped between them.

"I just wanted to—"

"What you want doesn't matter in the least."

Mike's solicitous big brother act was going to push Paige over the edge. "Mike," she murmured. "I think Ellenore has another load of dirt ready for you."

"Okay. Yeah." Mike stared at Paige, finally stalking off.

"Everything okay here?"

Gabe. Lorin wheeled around.

"Everything's fine." Paige glared daggers at Mike's back.

Gabe smelled like pine trees, wind, wet soil, and man. He stood slightly too close to her, but she didn't have the strength or desire to nudge him out of her personal space. The rustle of fabric as their hips brushed sounded unnaturally loud.

"Okay," Gabe said agreeably, clearly not buying it for a minute. "Lorin, could you spare Paige for a couple of hours? I have some satellite data that I could use her help with."

The timbre of his voice swirled low, tugging at her core. She cleared her throat and nodded. "Sure." Good idea to get Paige away from the dig, away from Mike, and give her a chance to calm down. "Paige, are you at a good stopping point?"

"Yes." Paige saved her work, shoved her floppy pink hat and sunglasses into an already-bulging tote bag, and stomped towards camp.

"Is she okay?" Gabe asked.

"I'm not sure," she admitted, "but getting her focused on something else for a while can't hurt."

He trailed his fingertips over her hip. "How about a run after dinner?"

"Love to." There were hundreds of places along their running route where she could have him flat on his back in seconds.

Gabe's gaze dropped to her lips and back again. They stared at each other for several seconds before he finally turned with a curse and trotted down the same trail Paige had just taken.

"She left Tubby's with that vamp last night," Mike said from behind her.

Lorin stopped ogling Gabe's ass. "But she was alone when she got back to the bunkhouse?"

"Yeah."

She nodded. At least Paige hadn't been so besotted that she'd forgotten their rule against bringing guests back to the camp. There was simply too much to lose if information about what they were doing here got into the wrong hands. "She's an adult, Mike."

He stared at the trail. "Barely."

Linking her arm through his, she walked them back to the lip of the pit. "Come on, we've all had an ill-advised one-night stand or two."

Rather than laughing at her comment, or ruefully agreeing, his forearm tensed under her hand.

"Let's start getting things cleaned up," she called to the crew. "Anyone up for a swim?" She needed to do something to cool her jets until after dinner, when she and Gabe went running.

"Not me," Ellenore said with a shake of her head. "The ice is barely out."

Gretchen's horrified expression was answer enough.

"Mike?" she asked.

"Not tonight."

"Pussy," Nathan said around a theatrical cough. "I'll swim with you, Lorin."

Mike strode away from camp without a backward glance.

Ellenore raised an eyebrow at the wheelbarrow full of dirt that he'd left standing beside the gazebo. Gretchen stared after him but stayed at her station.

"What is *wrong* with people today?"

"Just let him walk it off, Nathan. I'll talk to him later," Lorin said as she lifted the handles of the wheelbarrow and pushed the load to the discard pile.

Later. When Gabe said the word earlier, its promise had floated on the air like exotic incense. Now?

It made her feel… uneasy.

—⁕—

Sitting in the workroom a couple of days later, Gabe and Julianna talked via conference call, methodically plowing through the list of items needing his attention. Personnel issues. Purchase requests. Test results and status updates. He smothered a yawn. How the hell did Alka ever get any actual work done?

"Add a dependency here?" Julianna mused aloud, not waiting for an answer as she updated the project plan.

He hadn't mentioned the bark samples. Not yet, not until he had a better idea of what they were dealing with—a challenging task given how little equipment he had on hand, and how poorly his eyes were working. So far he'd been able to confirm that the fragments he'd dug out of the tree were metallic, but that was all.

They had more urgent problems to deal with. For some reason, after initially agreeing that his staff could hold to the schedule, Krispin Woolf was dragging his feet. One more experiment. Staffing shortages. Unanticipated vacations delaying his team's move. "What's the problem this time?"

Three hundred miles south, framed in the rectangle of the conferencing software, Julianna threw up her hands. "The PM said there was an unforeseeable delay on their last remaining experiment. One more task, three days' delay. He assures me this one will be the last."

"That's what he said last time." Reaching under the lenses of his glasses, Gabe closed his eyes and rubbed the bridge of his nose. Maybe it was time to call in the big guns. He hated to do it, but... "I'll ping Mr. Sebastiani, ask him to help encourage the Alpha to keep things moving along."

Julianna nodded. "Some additional muscle couldn't hurt. This issue's escalating above our pay grade—" The screen blipped, and her voice and face winked out.

"Damn it." This was the second time today that they'd lost electricity.

Leaning back in the squeaky office chair, he rubbed his stiff neck, rolled his shoulders, and gave another jaw-cracking yawn. He needed to get his own ergonomic office chair up here, pronto, or he'd end the season permanently maimed. It would probably help if he got some sleep somewhere along the way.

Nah. He was enjoying his sleepless nights way too much.

And dusk was falling. It was night again. Despite his tiredness, anticipation booted him from his chair. He plucked up his Bat Phone, tapping out a quick email to Jules telling her what had happened with the electricity, that he'd check in with her tomorrow, and headed to the networking closet—the closet he and Lorin had spent too much time in a couple of hours ago, when the balky grid had crashed for the first time. Everyone's dinner had been delayed because Lorin had shoved him back against the closed door, dropped to her knees, unzipped his pants, and taken him to heaven with her wicked, wicked mouth before starting repairs.

The woman was going to kill him, but… damn, what a way to go.

They'd done more together than just have sex. No, there had been talking and laughter, and plenty of debate. He'd actually helped put in the dock and raft, and given the temperature of the water, it had damn well been a sacrifice. He'd taught and he'd learned; he'd worked solo… and in the midst of too many chattering voices. And… yeah. He'd had more sex. Lots of great sex. Mind-blowing, gut-busting sex. He'd never synced so quickly and so well with a new lover in his life.

And he learned things about her—intimate things. She hid her chocolate—the good stuff—in a tampon box but left the Hershey's out for Nathan to steal. She kept a supply of condoms in her bedside table drawer. She wore candy-colored lingerie under her utilitarian cargo shorts and tank tops, in every color but yellow. She hated the color yellow. She couldn't stay still long, flitting about the cabin, the dig, and the workroom like a sturdy hummingbird. She twitched in her sleep, her body expending energy even when she was at rest. He felt unaccountably proud that she'd fallen into an exhausted sleep next to him three nights running. That didn't mean she turned in her meticulous paperwork anywhere close to on schedule—"I have more important things to do"—but a guy could dream.

Being that it was nearly dark, very little natural light made it from the workroom's single stingy window to the dark room. Though he'd watched Lorin fix the equipment earlier and had memorized the repair sequence, there was no way he could do it in the dark.

The flashlight was in the cabin. With Lorin. He left the workroom, practically skipping across the camp's central clearing. Mike, Gretchen, and Ellenore were roasting marshmallows at the big fire pit, their hair wet from either a swim or a sauna. Though it was warm outside, they'd all changed into light pants and long-sleeved shirts because of the mosquitoes. Paige wasn't with them.

"Gabe, my man. Full moon tonight," Nathan called from the bunkhouse door. He was bare-chested, and his hand was at the button of his already-saggy cargo shorts. "Wanna go for a run?"

Undressing for a shift. Gabe shoved down a super-sized portion of resentment. "Not tonight, thanks." If Nathan only knew how much he yearned to join him, to crash through the underbrush muzzle-first, to frolic in the woods on four fleet feet while moonlight stroked his fur, but his vision was even worse when he was shifted. As long as he kept to human form, he could wear glasses to correct the nearsightedness.

His vision had been so bad for so long that he couldn't remember the last time he'd called his wolf.

"Okay, but you're missing out."

I know. "I have other stuff to do, but you have fun."

Nathan glanced at Lorin's cabin and grinned know-ingly. "Yeah. Find me if you change your mind." Turning, he went into the bunkhouse.

Gabe approached the fire pit, shooting a quick glance at Lorin's open window. "Grid's down again."

Ellenore rolled her eyes. "Paige's blow-dryer must have put us over the top." She held out a metal stick. Speared on its end was a lightly browned, perfectly roasted marshmallow. "Want one?"

"Sure." He'd managed to eat a hasty, wobbly kneed dinner earlier, but he'd passed on the blueberry pie be-cause he hadn't wanted to be late for his meeting with Jules. He carefully removed the hot, sticky treat, recog-nizing the roasting stick as one of the batch he'd grabbed to protect Lorin with the first day he arrived. Blowing on the marshmallow, he stuck the whole thing in his mouth, closing his eyes as his taste buds flooded with sweet, sticky sugar.

"How about a s'more?" Gretchen asked, already as-sembling one.

"I'll take one for Lorin." And share it with her. The gooey treat would taste better licked off her lips.

S'more in hand, he approached Lorin's cabin, half hard already—and little wonder, given how they'd nearly burned the place down last night. Thankfully she'd had more condoms, because they'd worked through his supply at record pace.

Jumping onto the cabin's low deck, he heard Lorin swear. He peeked in the window and grinned. She sat at the wooden table, a legal-sized document in one hand and a cheap, chewed-up pen in the other, surrounded by the blizzard of paperwork delivered by the courier earlier that afternoon—in a beat-up camper trailer, of all things. Though he'd received his own considerable pile of work papers and personal mail, Lorin's stack definitely had his beat.

Her head lifted, whipping to the window. "S'mores. Gimme."

"What's it worth to you?"

"Come here and find out."

His cock jumped at the lusty twist in her voice, and he couldn't open the heavy door fast enough. "The grid went down again."

She glanced at the front of his pants, and she quirked a grin. "And you don't sound the least bit grumpy about it." She peered at her open window, then tipped her head back against the top rung of the ladder-backed chair. "Kiss me."

"Am I that easy to read?"

"Yes," she replied, still smiling. "But in this case, we want the same thing. And I always ask for what I want."

And she wanted him, at least for now.

Need wound tighter with each step he took. Even though she was seated and he was standing, even though she'd exposed her delicate, delicious neck to him, there was nothing submissive about her position. Her eyes burned, and her hands clutched his ass with clear possession. The juxtaposition about blew the top of his head off. He set the s'more down on the table. Cradling her head in his hands, he bent his lips to hers… and gorged on her. There was no other word for it. Their lips clung and clashed, their tongues teased and tasted.

Lorin licked her lips. "Marshmallows." She shoved to her feet with a scrape of chair legs, wrapping her arms around him with a strength he'd have to work to escape—not that he was stupid enough to do any such thing.

He clutched her back with equal strength. Felt her breath hitch. With a quick pivot, he backed her against the table, stepping into the V created by her spread legs. Her clingy, navy blue leggings ended just below the knee, and a white tank top exposed both her muscular shoulders and distinct lack of a bra. It would take only seconds to remove the shirt, to feel the weight of her bare breasts in his hands—not that he needed them to be bare to touch and taste.

He bore her back against the table, his mouth quickly following. Her eyes drifted closed as she scooted her butt onto the edge of the table, lying back—right on the s'more.

Recoiling, she sat up quickly, but not quickly enough to save the pile of paperwork and the s'more from tipping onto the floor.

They both stared at the upside down paper plate before bursting into laughter. "There goes dessert," Lorin said woefully.

"Not necessarily." Gabe licked her shoulder blade, where she'd lain in the sticky treat.

Lorin let him take several laps before pushing him away, bending down to pick up the fallen papers with a sigh. "I promised Willem I'd have all this back to him tomorrow. The courier will be back to pick these up at first light."

The document at the top of the pile was an intriguing mixture of old-fashioned calligraphy and small point font. Must be Council stuff. "A deadline. Horrors."

"Shut up," she said without heat. "So the grid's down again?"

Gabe nodded. "Paige's blow-dryer."

"She must have a date with that vamp," Lorin muttered. "Damn it."

"What?"

She took a deep breath and determinedly straightened her shoulders. "Nothing." Crossing to the shelving unit next to the sink, she grabbed a flashlight and held it out to him. "Do you remember how I fixed the grid this afternoon?"

He remembered a lot of things about that afternoon. The feel of her tongue lashing his hard cock. The undulations of her throat as she suckled on him, swallowed down his hot seed. "You're not going to help?"

Was that rumbly noise his voice?

"Dr. Lupinsky." She sidled up next to him, so close he could feel her body heat. "Think about multitasking. Efficiency. While you get the grid up and running, I can finish up my work. Then"—she stroked her fingertip over his lower lip—"we can… play."

Jesus. He nipped the finger with his teeth, then drew it into his mouth, curling his tongue around the digit to soothe and madden. The scent of her humid need burrowed in his brain stem like a dart hitting the center of the target.

"Go," she whispered, giving him the flashlight and a hard nudge. "Hurry."

"Back soon," he said, giving her lips a short, hard kiss. As he left, he heard her cell phone ring. Then heard her answer it.

"Rafe? Hi!"

His euphoric mood darkened like a lunar eclipse. For someone who was in such a hurry to get her work done—so she could play with *him*—her voice sounded too damn intimate and inviting. He stealthily approached the window. He could barely see her in the dark.

"What kind of trouble are you getting into now?"

Damn it. He could barely convince Lorin to pick up the phone, but Rafe Sebastiani calls and she not only answers the phone, but curls up on the unmade bed— *their* bed, smelling of *them*—and settles in for a long, cozy chat?

Of course she did. The reality check clouted him upside the head.

He closed his eyes and tried to control his breathing, clenching the flashlight like a lifeline. Lorin might be the woman of his dreams, but that didn't mean he was the man of hers.

He had to remember that.

Chapter 9

GABE CAREFULLY SKIRTED THE PINE BOUGH THAT partially blocked the well-worn trail leading to the excavation site. The damn tree had drooled sap on him five days in a row. But not today.

Today, everything was going his way. The conference call he'd just navigated had run as long as a three-act play, but the hard work, the long days and nights, had paid off. The lab was ready—or nearly so. He'd get his hands on the command box two days from now.

Tomorrow, he'd be going home—home, with indoor plumbing, hot showers, air conditioning, and take-out. He could almost hear the delicate crunch of the Vietnamese egg rolls he always ordered with his *phô*.

Museums. Theatre tickets. Restaurants. Culture. He could wear his work clothes again, feel summer-weight wool draped against his skin instead of rough cotton. See for himself how Glynna was doing instead of relying on her assurances by phone that things were going well. No steel-toed boots, no pterodactyl-sized mosquitoes, no lingering scent of bug dope permeating his pillowcase no matter how hard he scrubbed in the sauna.

He'd be able to sleep in his own bed, a king-sized pillow-top he bought right after he and Kayla had broken up.

Yeah, he'd finally get test results from his retinologist too, but all things considered, he should be dancing a jig right here on the trail. So why wasn't he happier about the prospect? Because his chances of convincing Lorin to share the bed with him once they got home were lower than the odds of him discovering a new element on the periodic table.

Lorin wasn't his girlfriend, not by a long shot, and he couldn't let himself forget that he only shared her laughably small bed through proximity and sheer dumb luck. No way would she want to continue their arrangement once they got home. She'd be back in Rafe Sebastiani's bed again by tomorrow night.

The thought was a pickax to the gut.

He jammed his hands in the pockets of his shorts, crunching fallen pinecones under his boots as he approached the clearing where Lorin and the crew worked. Yes, the timing of this trip back home was excellent on many fronts. He needed to take a giant step back, because he was enjoying this—enjoying her—far too much. The WerePack Alpha's opinions about bonding outside of the pack were clear—ignorant, but clear.

The Valkyrie Princess wasn't his to keep.

Damn it, she'd told him right up front that their relationship was physical, and thinking with his dick, he'd mindlessly agreed with her. It wasn't her fault his feelings were—

His traitorous hearing picked out Lorin's low, throaty laugh over the pop and hiss of someone opening an aluminum can and the familiar rasp of soil being sifted through a screen. When he stepped into the clearing, he saw her immediately, wearing the black tank top, camo-patterned cargo shorts, snowy white crew socks, and leather boots he'd watched her put on that morning. Her

gloved hands rested lightly on the handles of a wheelbarrow Nathan filled with dirt he excavated from the pit.
As he watched, she snorted and doubled over laughing.

Nathan told some of the filthiest jokes Gabe had
ever heard.

Dragging his eyes from Lorin, he assessed the crew's
progress. What a difference a couple of weeks made.
The mud had dried, and the edges of the pit were notice-
ably vertical again, shored up with upright two-by-fours.
Wooden yardsticks were in place. With the colorful
gazebos erected, tarps stretched tautly over the active
work areas, and brightly colored coolers and five-gallon
beverage jugs resting in the shade, the site looked like a
tailgate party—until you noticed the shovels, tools, and
the line of laptops sitting at the worktable.

Gabe swiped his forearm against his sweaty forehead.
Spring had not only sprung but had gleefully trampo-
lined into summer. The pink calamine lotion Lorin
had dabbed onto his mosquito bites that morning was
already melting down his legs.

"Hey, Gabe," Paige called, lifting a can of Mountain
Dew to her lips. Her tank top and khaki shorts exposed
her neck, delicate collarbones, and thin legs. With her
pouf of pale hair pulled into a ponytail perched at the
top of her head, she reminded him of a baby bird. Her
light-sensitive eyes were protected by a pair of tiny,
Lennonesque sunglasses with dark lenses, so he couldn't
use her eyes to assess her mood. Her vamp bite was
completely healed, but she'd positioned her chair so her
back was to Mike, who was screening dirt in the gazebo
with Ellenore.

"Hi there," he said, approaching his little fly in the

ointment. "Why is Lorin pushing the wheelbarrow? I thought that was Mike's job."

Paige rolled her eyes. "Mike forgot to put on his VampScreen this morning. Now he's paying the stupid tax."

Through the gazebo's flexible door, Gabe watched the younger man grumpily scrape a length of two-by-four across a wood-framed screen, the extrusion underneath looking like soft spaghetti noodles, the signature of clay-heavy dirt. Every inch of Mike's exposed skin was slathered in nearly opaque white cream.

He sighed. Could they really leave responsibility for the dig in the hands of a vamp who forgot to apply his sunscreen, and the tween-sized faerie holding a Jolly Green Giant-sized grudge against him? Damn it, how could he and Lorin leave the dig if their two most experienced crewmembers weren't even talking to each other?

Lorin approached, still giggling at Nathan's joke, pushing the wheelbarrow filled with damp soil. Her shoulders, arms, and wrists flexed in the hot, ruthless sun. Though she used sunscreen religiously—he'd slathered it on her body himself that morning—Lorin spent so much time outside that she couldn't help but pick up some color. Freckles speckled her shoulders and upper chest, diving into her cleavage.

Last night, he'd played Connect-the-Dots between them with his tongue.

"Hey."

Her scent swirled into his nostrils. Sidling back from her a few crucial inches, he cleared his throat, mentally adding Coppertone to the growing list of everyday things that had somehow become aphrodisiacs. "Hi," he said. Her smile lit her face like sunrise. He desperately wanted to kiss the tip of her adorable, slightly reddened nose, but… Gabe steeled himself for what he had to do. "Have a minute?"

Her eyes flicked over his body. "What do you have in mind? And it had better take more than a minute."

His body hardened in a rush, urgent and primal. A red film floated over his spotty field of vision, and his mouth and lips suddenly tingled, like fire ants had taken up residence under his skin. His teeth pulsed and stung.

Ah, damn. He hadn't shifted in years, and his body chose *this* specific moment to pulse to life? A low growl rumbled in his chest. His muscles banded too tightly around his lungs.

It felt… wonderful.

Shove it back. Shove it down.

Lorin stepped in front of him with her body, resting her hand on the small of his back. Waiting, guarding. Of course she knew he was vulnerable. She'd probably had countless werewolf lovers who couldn't control themselves around her.

Her touch comforted him. Maddened him. Made him want to howl in recognition. In rage.

She wasn't his mate to claim.

"Gabe. Dude," Nathan called from the pit. "You gotta get a room for that shit, man. Hit the woods, drag Lorin off, go running or something."

Trust the other werewolf on the crew, one who shifted as frequently and carelessly as he changed his underwear, to know exactly what was happening to him—and to draw everyone's attention to the situation.

Paige hurled her half-full can of Mountain Dew at Nathan, splashing neon green liquid on his cheek, neck, and T-shirt. "You need a couth implant."

As Nathan pulled wet, clinging cotton away from his chest, Mike left the protection of the gazebo to stand at Paige's side.

"Keep out of this," Paige snapped, elbowing him aside so she could better see Nathan. "When will you grow up?"

Nathan eyed the thrown can lying on its side in the dirt. "You're a fine one to talk about maturity, there, Booster Seat."

Paige glared at him. "If I didn't like these shoes so much, I'd plant my foot up your ass."

"You should really get some professional help for that anal fixation, Paige."

Paige lunged at him, but Mike slung an arm around her waist, stopping her. "Damn it, let me go!"

"Enough!" Lorin's raised voice got everyone's attention. "Paige, calm down. Nathan, shut up. Everyone, just shut up." There was a pause in the mayhem. "Start breaking down for the day. Now."

Shoving Mike's arm away from her waist, Paige stalked toward the now-empty water coolers, grabbed two of them, and disappeared down the trail leading back to camp without a backwards glance.

Mike rubbed at the rib Paige had tagged with her bony elbow. "What the hell…?"

"Shark Week," Nathan responded knowingly. "She's on the rag."

Lorin wheeled toward him. "Shut. Up."

Nathan ducked, disappearing into the pit.

"Damn wolfy nose," she muttered.

Gabe had a damn wolfy nose of his own, and the scent of Lorin's sun-baked body was cratering into his head for the long haul. He cleared the gravel from his throat, hoping he could speak with something other than a rumble. His wolf was finally receding. "Lorin, I need a minute."

Her gaze cruised over his face. He wasn't sure what she was looking for, but there was no suggestive comeback this time. "Sure. Are you okay?" She pulled off her leather gloves and tucked them in her back pocket.

No. He missed her already. "Yeah. Sorry about…" He made a vague hand gesture toward his own body. "The place is crawling with hormones." *Yeah, nothing personal, Lorin.* He put some space between them and tried to get his mind on business. "I have an update from Elliott."

He and Lorin walked to the picnic table and sat down on the same bench. Remnants of the crew's lunch—clear glass salt and pepper shakers and plastic squeeze bottles of ketchup, mustard, and mayonnaise in red, yellow, and white—still sat on the table. Paper napkins fluttered under a fist-sized piece of ore. Without thinking, Gabe reached into the pocket of his shorts, extracted his lip balm, and passed it to Lorin, like he had so many times over the last couple of weeks.

She popped off the cap, slicked it across her lips, rubbed them together, and handed the black tube back to him. "Thanks."

Gabe dragged his eyes away from her moist lips—the lips that, just last night, had mapped his body with an explorer's gusto. "I just got off the phone with Elliott and

Julianna." He quickly ran down the high points of the meeting he'd just held. "The lower level lab is ready for us," he concluded. "It's ours for the foreseeable future."

Lorin's brows rose halfway to her hairline. "You booted Krispin Woolf's team out of the basement lab?"

"Elliott did the dirty work on this one." Though Krispin Woolf didn't work at Sebastiani Labs, or for Elliott Sebastiani in any capacity, Elliott let the WerePack Alpha use his facilities as a Council member courtesy. Elliott hadn't disclosed why Krispin Woolf, who didn't have a single scientific bone in his body, might need scientific research facilities in the first place, and Gabe hadn't asked. "We're scheduled to start work the day after tomorrow."

"So, you'll finally get your hands on Pritchard's command box."

He nodded, not bothering to call her attention to the assumption inherent in her statement. Pritchard's box, Lorin's box... statements of origin or ownership wouldn't impact his assessment of its physical makeup. And she was right; he was anxious to examine the box, which Wyland had placed in the mysterious archives for safekeeping. Gabe envisioned the box glowing serenely, napping in a crate, stored in a facility that looked a lot like the one at the end of *Raiders of the Lost Ark*.

"I want to compare the box's composition to the flecks of metal we found at the grove." Not looking at her, he buried her in status, data, minutiae, and the details of the tests he was going to perform, because if he didn't keep talking, his thoughts would clatter back to everything else they'd done in that grove—things that would never be repeated. "Wyland will deliver the box to the lab early Wednesday morning. I'll take exterior measurements and perform some initial tests before handing it over to you," he said. "After you document and catalogue its contents, I'll take it back and perform a more detailed analysis."

They sat quietly for a moment, listening to the sounds of the crew cleaning up their workstations. Nathan kicked the pop can Paige had hurled at him toward the recycling station between his feet, soccer-style. Mike stuffed Paige's forgotten supplies into her pink and black tote bag, slung it over his shoulder, and picked up a cooler. He placed both items in the bed of Lorin's truck for the short trip back to the campsite.

"So, we're leaving, going south tomorrow," Lorin finally said. "Just when the weather's getting nice."

Gabe nearly snorted in disbelief. She thought this lung-clogging heat and humidity was "nice weather"? Jesus, he preferred the frost, and that was saying something. "I'll appreciate a break from the mosquitoes."

Lorin glanced at the pink calamine lotion dotting his calves and ventured a smile. "It would help if you remembered to zip your tent."

Blood rushed to his cheeks, and body parts south, as he recalled how he'd acquired most of the bug bites in the first place. Yesterday, he'd been in such a rush to get Lorin flat on her back on his blow-up mattress that he'd forgotten to zip the tent door behind them, proximity of the crew be damned. He cleared his throat and shoved the memory aside. "We should be gone five days, maybe six. What do you suggest we do about supervision of the dig while we're gone?"

"Hmm?"

"Mike's head isn't fully in the game, and Paige's be-havior is erratic, to say the least. Throwing that can at Nathan?" He shook his head. "Completely unacceptable."

"Oh, come on," Lorin scoffed. "There are times when *I'd* like to throw a can at Nathan. And if Paige really meant to hurt him, she'd have thrown the pickax." She paused. "She was protecting you."

He fiddled with the snap on his pocket before look-ing at her again. "So, you're not the least bit concerned about Paige?"

She sliced him a look. "I didn't say that—"

"—and you're comfortable leaving the dig right now, knowing that she's hooking up with a strange vamp who leaves her a thralled, hormonal mess?"

"No. And speaking of hormonal messes, does fight-ing back a shift always leave you in such a pissy mood?"

Gabe choked back his anger. She couldn't know how rare—how bittersweet—shifting was for him in the first place. "Lorin, this conversation proves my point. Professional lives and private lives don't mix. We should be talking about who's going to manage the dig while we're gone, and here we are, fighting about"—he threw up his hands in disgust—"hormones and moods. Damn it, this is why people who work together should never—"

"Yes. Now we're getting to the real issue." Lorin sat ramrod straight on the rough picnic table bench. "Gabe, if our arrangement isn't working for you, all you have to do is say so. We can call things off right here and now."

Not working? It was working too goddamn well, and that was the problem. She made it sound as if halting their "arrangement"—gah, what an insulting word—wouldn't be any skin off her nose.

And it probably wouldn't be. She could have any lover she wanted.

"Enough said." When she rose to her feet, Gabe stood too. Her face was blank, her voice icily polite. He suddenly felt like he was thousands of years old, like his bones would crumble to dust if he so much as moved. "I'll talk to—"

"No. I'll coordinate arrangements for our departure. Who knows whether you'll even be making the return trip?"

In the heat of this miserable day, her words were like icicles dropping from a roof ledge. Not coming back wasn't a prospect he'd considered. He hadn't thought that far ahead. The very idea should make him jump for joy, but… it didn't.

He was already mourning.

"It probably makes sense for us to both drive our own cars south," she said. "I'll want my own transportation once I get to The Cities."

Gabe nodded. "Yeah." He knew he couldn't stomach a five-hour car ride with her now with this tensile-steel tension between them. "What do you want to do about Paige?"

"I'll take care of it."

Her expression was carved in rock, like the nearby petroglyphs. Was she feeling anything, anything at all? She'd completely shut down. Why did he feel like he was attending his own wake? "You'll be putting Mike in charge?"

For a moment, he didn't think she'd respond. Finally, she said, "Yes."

"How will Paige feel about that?"

"She'll deal with it," Lorin snapped. "I'll make sure that the work rotation is solid before we go, and I'll check in with them by phone while we're gone. It's not like we're going on an Everest expedition, Gabe. We'll be gone less than a week." Her gaze bored into him like a drill bit. "It's my problem, not yours."

"Lorin!" Nathan called from the driver's seat of her truck. "Your chariot awaits."

"Be right there," she called back. "I'll talk to Mike and Paige now, and update everyone else after dinner tonight."

The edges of his mouth tugged up reluctantly. "I think I heard you say you're going to call a meeting."

She didn't smile back. "Are we done here?"

"Lorin…" Nathan called again.

She turned away without a word.

Gabe stared at her. Yeah, they were done, all right. Mission fucking accomplished.

———⁓⁓⁓———

"Nathan." Lorin mentally counted to three. "If Ellenore wants to trade responsibilities with you, that's okay with me. You two figure it out." An eighteen-wheeler barreled by on her left, and her poor old truck shuddered in its wake. "I'm driving, Nathan. I've gotta go. Yeah. Yeah. Bye." Disconnecting the call with an extra-hard punch of her thumb, she tossed the phone onto the passenger seat.

"Christ on a cracker." Half the crew had called since she'd left the dig a little over two hours ago, either talking through minor problems she knew damn well they could solve for themselves, or saying they just wanted to keep her company as she drove.

She didn't want company. She wanted to be alone. She desperately needed to be alone.

Was Gabe's phone ringing off the hook? Was he as crabby about it as she was? Probably not. She wouldn't recognize his ear if it didn't have a phone clapped to it.

On the other hand, the endless phone conversations had kept her mind off how twitchy her body was getting, now that Gabe had ended their… whatever the hell their relationship was. First Rafe had called things off, and now Gabe.

Why couldn't she be attracted to women? Men were nothing but trouble.

She turned off her mind, turned the radio to the '80s station, and sang away the miles, the volume loud enough so she couldn't hear the phone ringing if she wanted to. When Jon Bon Jovi started wailing about shots to the heart and who's to blame, she snapped off the music with a curse—just in time to hear a clunk. Metal dragged against asphalt with an ungodly scraping noise. She looked in her rearview mirror.

She was spitting sparks.

Crap. Tailpipe? Muffler? Up ahead, like an oasis in the desert, she saw a green road sign: "Hinckley: One Mile." *Excellent.* She'd stop at Tobies, do some emergency repairs, and then have a cinnamon roll to reward a job well done.

Okay, two cinnamon rolls.

Wincing, she muscled the truck up the exit ramp and turned into the parking lot. The last six months had been a steady succession of emergency repairs. It was probably time to permanently park her old truck up at the dig and buy a new one, and she was more than a little depressed at the prospect. She'd bought the truck used back when she was a teenager, and half a lifetime of memories lay in every spill soiling the carpet, and every crack in the dash. The windshield had been broken and replaced countless times, and she'd taken her first lover on the roomy bench seat. A couple of Buttercup's doggy nose prints still smudged the back window, carefully framed by black electrical tape so she wouldn't wipe them off by mistake.

Princess Buttercup, her beloved, snaggletoothed bulldog, had gone to the Great Doggy Beyond over five years ago. Maybe it was time to get another dog.

Lorin wove her way through the busy parking lot, past the cars, trucks, vans, and people, to the relative quiet of the nearly empty overflow lot. Now that she'd stopped, she couldn't ignore the deep ache pulsing low in her abdomen. Examining the tree-rimmed lot with a critical eye, she considered running a few laps to bleed off some of the buildup.

Not that it would help much. *Damn you, Gabe.*

Stepping out of the truck, she stretched, then walked to the back of the truck and peered under the back quarter panel. Sure enough, the tailpipe was dragging, the back clamp rusted clean off. "I've got to have baling wire in here somewhere," she muttered as she walked to the passenger side of the truck. Twine or electrical tape would do. Hell, she'd MacGyver something with spit and rubber bands as long as it meant not calling Gabe, who couldn't be more than ten minutes ahead of her. Being that he'd barely said a word to her as their paths crossed loading their vehicles this morning, that trip would be pretty damn fun.

Not.

Her phone rang again as she rooted around in the toolbox tucked behind the passenger seat, and she snatched it up with a growl. If this was an indication of what the next five days were going to be like, she was going to—

She blinked at the display, but the numbers didn't budge. Her mother? Lorin had received a text from her the day before yesterday, letting her know that she'd arrived in La Paz, but she hadn't expected an actual phone call for, well, weeks yet. Unless something was wrong. "Mom? Are you okay?"

"Hello to you, too, dear." Amusement colored her mother's voice. "Yes, I'm fine."

Lorin plugged her open ear with a forefinger to block out a nearby semi's diesel whine. "Where are you?"

"I'm not precisely sure, dear. Let me ask the captain."

Captain? Her mother must be in the air, calling from one of the Sebastiani Gulfstreams.

"We're just north of Austin," Alka finally said. "We ran into a permit problem, so rather than cooling my heels at the hotel for a week or two, I decided I'd rather fly home and watch you and Gabriel work."

Great. Just great. Now her mother would have a front row seat to observe the wreckage of her working relationship with Gabe.

"When do you start? I saw that you'll be working in the basement lab."

"Tomorrow morning. I'm driving south from the site right now. I stopped at Tobies for some quick repairs and a cinnamon roll."

"That old truck," Alka said fretfully. "Lorin, when

are you going to get a new car? I worry about you driving on those remote northern Minnesota roads, broken down—"

"—and fully able to fix the problem myself?" Lorin deadpanned. "Mom, I'm fine. Don't worry. Gabe is less than ten minutes ahead of me, and I've got the phone."

"Which you rarely use. Why aren't you and Gabriel riding together? What a waste of gas."

"It was a… business continuity decision." Lorin strove for a lighthearted tone. "Put the two of us in a car together for almost five hours and only one of us is going to come out alive. You know it's gonna be me."

Alka's disappointed sigh was audible. "I really hoped you'd be getting along better with Gabriel by now."

Lorin fought back a wild laugh as she remembered Gabe pinning her to the grass with his tough, rangy body, feasting on her breasts like they were his last meal. "Don't make such a big deal out of Gabe and me driving home separately, Mom," she said. "We each wanted our own transportation back home, that's all. And after I fix this tailpipe, I'll be right back on the road."

"I'll let you go, then," Alka said with a sigh. "I'll see you tomorrow at the lab. Strictly in an observer capacity, of course." She paused. "Lorin, I'm so, so proud of you."

Lorin's eyes stung. Tomorrow was soon enough to shatter her mother's illusions. "Thanks, Mom. See you tomorrow."

She hung up, tossed the phone on the passenger seat again, and pulled on her sweatshirt so she wouldn't scuff her back on the asphalt. Snatching the baling wire, tin snips, and a pair of pliers out of the toolbox, she walked to the tailgate. After repairs, she'd clean up in the restaurant's bathroom, get some cinnamon rolls, and—

Gabe.

Gabe was walking out of the restaurant juggling a tall cup of coffee and a white pastry bag with one hand, holding a phone to his ear with the other. Whoever he was talking to made him grin like a fool; she could see his white teeth flash from here. He wore familiar-looking khaki pants, but he'd paired them with soft leather loafers instead of steel-toed boots. His pale green oxford shirt, unbuttoned at the neck and casually rolled up at the sleeves, made her crave mint chocolate chip ice cream.

Gabe threw back his head and laughed, the late morning sun glinting off those absurdly hot glasses. He looked relaxed. Happy. Edible, damn it. She wanted to drag him down to the nearest flat surface.

Who was he talking to? Who amused him so much? Not that it was any of her business. Not anymore.

Turning her back on him, she shimmied under the truck, pushing against the asphalt with the heels of her hiking boots, and unspooled a length of wire. Gabe probably had big plans for tonight now that he was returning to civilization. She should make some plans too. Going back to town opened up all sorts of options— for both of them. She could hit Underbelly with Andi Woolf and dance until dawn. With a single phone call, a shower, and a change of clothes, she could score a seat at Chadden's downtown restaurant, be fed by the tempestuous chef himself, share his decadent bed—and work off this jones she had for a tight-assed, half-blind, calamine-covered werewolf with a vengeance.

"There." With one last twist of the wrist, the tailpipe was solidly in place—not that it was actually connected to the muffler anymore. Scrabbling out from under the truck, she brushed tiny rocks off her shorts and bare legs. She returned her tools to the toolbox and eyed the phone.

Then picked it up and dialed.

———

"Can you see the source?" Beddoe asked from the command chair.

"Yes, Sirrah." Xantha Ta'al wiped her streaming eyes and coughed on acrid smoke. Lying on her stomach, her head and shoulders wedged under the science console, she found the tiny smoker she'd purposely dropped into the cabinet at the beginning of her shift. Pinching it off, she slid it under the wristband of her duty suit. "An overheating circuit, Captain. Shall I repair?"

"Please proceed."

"Certainly, Sirrah." Xantha took a shallow, careful breath to control her rocketing heart. Reaching behind her, she retrieved her ServiPak, then selected a tool she didn't need and the blank chip she most emphatically did. She blinked as she waited for more smoke to clear.

Moving carefully and deliberately, the blank held between two fingers, she wedged her hand deep into the crevices of the control panel, working by touch. Bumps: screws, slots, circuits. So many of them, and all so small—

There. There it was.

Not giving herself time to question her instincts, she quickly popped a chip and replaced it with the blank.

She held her breath.

Nothing from Beddoe.

Slowly exhaling, she extracted her hand, tucking the purloined chip under her wristband next to the smoker.

If the *Arkapaedis*'s beacon blipped again, Beddoe would never know about it.

Her boss would be pleased.

Chapter 10

"Lorin! Hello!" Willem Lund stepped out from behind the U-shaped desk defending Elliott Sebastiani's inner sanctum and hugged her.

"What? Am I late?" Lorin asked as she returned his embrace.

Willem stepped back, looking her up and down. "No, you're right on time. I'm just happy to see you looking so…" He paused, as if searching for the right word.

"Clean?" Lorin looked down at her well-used denim jacket, khaki pants, and boots.

"Healthy and whole, thank the universe. That last Council meeting was… brutal. I'm glad you're okay."

"Thank you." She gestured to Elliott Sebastiani's closed office door. "Is he ready for us? And where's Gabe?" Probably already in the office. Her temper spiked as she looked at the closed door. Who knew what Gabe was telling Elliott about their work so far? Damn it, she should have gotten here early.

"Gabe's running late, so he's all yours. Go on in."

Declining Willem's offer of coffee, Lorin tapped on the door with her knuckles, opening it when Elliott called, "Come."

Elliott rose from his mahogany desk and walked toward her with his arms extended. "Lorin," he said with a smile. "You look well." Elliott kissed her on each cheek, and then enfolded her in a hug.

Why did everyone expect her to be at death's door? Apparently she'd drastically underestimated the impact of her fuckup back here at home base.

"It's good to be back," she replied, "though I wasn't too happy to see the mound of paperwork on my desk when I swung by there a couple of minutes ago." Her office was a chaotic mess, but somehow Elliott's work area always looked more like an elegant salon than the power center of one of the most successful privately held companies in the world. His desk was tidy, an expanse where no dust mote would dare land, and nary a piece of paper strayed from ruthless alignment. One of the vintage fountain pens he collected lay across an open leather-bound notebook, and on his sleek monitor, pictures of his extraordinary family scrolled by: His children grouped around their long-deceased mother, Dasha, who held a newborn Antonia. A casual headshot of Elliott and Claudette Fontaine embracing at their bonding ceremony, celebrating the romantic relationship they'd finally allowed themselves to have after years of platonic friendship. And there were the Sebastiani siblings and the Fontaine sisters together, with a laughing Claudette at the center of the action, a bottle of wine in her hand.

There was a tug in Lorin's chest as she looked at the third picture. *The changes since then.* Annika Fontaine, snapped in mid-laugh, was no longer with them, leaving a horrible void. Lukas stared at Scarlett with a broody expression that would be painful to look at if you didn't know how happily it had ended.

As Elliott escorted her to the furniture grouping, Lorin looked back to the door, still slightly ajar. "I thought Gabe was joining us?"

"Gabe has an appointment that's running late."

Gabe hadn't mentioned that he had an appointment.

"I wanted to speak with you privately anyway."

Ah, hell, here it comes. Lorin sat up straighter in the slouchy leather chair. If she was going to be chewed out, she'd take it on the chin.

"How are things going?"

Elliott's gentle question took the wind out of her sails and yet at the same time set all her internal alerts shrieking. She knew what he was really asking: How were she and Gabe getting along? "Fine." She locked eyes with him. "All the tests came back clear, right?"

Exasperation flitted across his hawk-like face, there then gone. "Yes, you're fine, as far as we know. As a scientist, you're aware we can't test for things we don't have tests for." He leaned back in his own chair, watching her with eyes that, depending on the task at hand, could glow warmly, or slice with the blowtorch of his intelligence. "How many times over the years have you or a member of the crew run a metal detector over the very spot where you found the command box? Dozens? And yet it was there." Elliott spread his hands. "We don't know what we don't know—and if that box is what we think it could be, what we don't know is, unfortunately, a lot." Elliott's multiline phone chirped, barely audible, but he ignored it. "You were extremely fortunate that there was nothing biohazardous in that box, Lorin."

"It opened by accident, Elliott," she said defensively. "Worst-case scenario, I was breathing thousand-year-old air."

"It would have been fascinating to test its atmospheric composition."

But that opportunity is forever lost. Though Elliott was too polite to say it, she easily read it on his face. "Where's the box now?"

"Wyland is transporting it from archives as we speak. I really want Gabe's take on that metal."

"It does seem to have some unusual properties. The color is extraordinary, and the dirt flowed off of it like—"

The heavy door opened, and Gabe strode in. "Sorry I'm late."

Lorin hadn't seen Gabe since yesterday, in Tobies' parking lot. Dressed in a pair of tailored black suit pants, a bronze oxford unbuttoned at the neck, and carrying the matching jacket, his metamorphosis back to "city Gabe" was pretty much complete. His hair had a subtle, lustrous sheen that bespoke hair product of some type, and as he approached and sat in the chair next to hers, a hint of delicious, civilized scent wafted her way. She looked down at her own rumpled khakis and denim jacket—a definite step up for her—and sighed.

The men seemed to be having a nonverbal conversation of some type: a questioning eyebrow from Elliott, followed by a fatalistic shrug from Gabe.

Lorin waved her hand, breaking their sight line. "What's up?"

"Nothing." Gabe reached into the side pocket of his computer bag, extracted a file folder, and flipped it open. "I'd like to quickly review the latest work plan before we go down to the lab."

Elliott Sebastiani's nostrils were working overtime—and his attention was entirely focused on Gabe.

Nothing was up? Bullshit.

What the hell was going on?

———

"What a clusterfuck," Lorin muttered, nudging past Lukas so she could better survey the activity below. "Who are all these people?"

Standing on the open gantry overlooking the subterranean lab space, she watched far too many people swarm as industriously as ants at a picnic, carrying the last pieces of equipment from other labs to their temporary quarters. Bailey Brown lay on her stomach under the table running the length of the east wall. Gabe, stepping over her legs, gave instructions to people she vaguely recognized as working in geology and metallurgy. His minions hung on his every word, anxious to do his bidding, scuttling pieces of equipment down one of the many hallways branching off the main room to other areas of the subterranean lab. Julianna Benton was simply everywhere, pointing, directing, coordinating—and trying to smooth the very ruffled feathers of Dr. Anna Mae Whitman, the crabby genius of a woman who managed Sebastiani Labs' lab facilities with her tiny iron fist. Dr. Whitman was being relocated to temporary quarters and wasn't at all happy about it.

Her mother was having a quiet but animated conversation with Elliott on the other side of the control room, her signature jade and bone bracelet clacking with each gesture she made.

The subtle sound ground on Lorin's last remaining nerve.

All told, over a dozen people bustled in the lab below, and though the workers were too well-trained to ask unnecessary questions, the presence of Elliott Sebastiani and a good chunk of the Underworld Council was a huge tip-off that something big was going down.

"So much for confidentiality," she groused.

"They'll be leaving soon and won't have access to the lab after they leave," Lukas replied, looking at her far too closely. His nostrils were twitching up a storm.

Damn his incubus hide. "Will you back off?" She felt ornery enough to take him on today, and damn the consequences.

"Lover's spat?" Lukas asked, amusement lacing his voice.

"We are not lovers," she snapped.

Gabe's head jerked up to the gantry, and then he glanced away again.

"Yeah, right. The pheromones pumping off the two of you are off the charts, and you're about to twitch out of your skin." Lukas tucked his thumbs into the front pockets of his jeans, rocking back on his booted heels. "Drag him off somewhere and do something about it."

"We are not sleeping together," Lorin bit out. *Anymore.* "I'm fine." His raised eyebrow flat-out called her a liar. "Shut up," she said. "I'll be fine—" *Shit.* As soon as the words slipped out of her mouth, she wanted to snatch them back.

"Lorin—"

Ignoring him, she plucked her phone out of her jacket pocket and peered conscientiously at the screen. The thing wasn't even turned on, but he didn't have to know that. "Lukas, we have a lot of work to do here today. Let's just get on with it."

Down on the floor, Gabe pulled off his glasses and tiredly rubbed the bridge of his nose with his thumb and forefinger.

Lukas stepped closer to Lorin. "Is this how the two of you communicate?"

Lorin refused to think about some of the ways she and Gabe had communicated, and quite successfully too. "Would you quit"—she pushed at his big shoulder— "sniffing me!"

"Hard to avoid; you're reeking the place up something fierce."

Even though she knew Lukas was speaking figuratively—as an incubus, Lukas inhaled emotional energy for sustenance and could discern emotional nuances by smell and taste alone—her cheeks flamed with heat. What were her emotions telling Lukas? Maybe she should ask him, because Freyja knew *she* was coming up empty.

Jack approached. "Coffee, Lorin?" Before she quite realized what was happening, he'd drawn her away from Lukas and toward the refreshment table, where plates of fruit and glistening pastry surrounded an industrial-sized coffeemaker. "How are things going?"

Lorin choked back a hysterical laugh. She was in the doghouse with Elliott and Wyland because she hadn't followed procedure opening the box in the first place. Her mother was here, observing every move she made. She was more worried about Paige than she'd let on to either Mike or Gabe.

Gabe. She was even more pissed off at him today than she'd been yesterday. She'd met Chadden at his restaurant last night, with every intention of using his finely honed body to work off some of this outrageous energy building up in her system, but she'd inexplicably backed off.

She'd gone to bed alone, and it was all Gabe's fault. "Lorin?"

Jack's hand was on her shoulder. *Pull it together.* "Let's just say I'm overdue for some time in the cage," she admitted. She'd feel better if she could just whale on something—or someone. She eyed Jack, who she knew from experience sported some serious muscle under his impeccably tailored suit. Though he was bigger and taller, her stamina was better. In a fight they were pretty evenly matched.

"Name the time."

"I'll call you." She raised her clenched fist for a knuckle knock.

"It's a date." Jack tapped back. "Oh, hi, Gabe. You look like you could use a refill."

"Jack." The werewolf rumble at the edge of Gabe's voice vibrated straight to her core. Jack stepped aside, giving Gabe room to refill the mug he carried. Jack was right; Gabe definitely looked like he could use some coffee. Despite the crispness of his executive-casual wardrobe, he looked more visibly worn around the edges than he had an hour ago. His skin was drawn tightly against his cheekbones, and his hair stood on end.

Behind his rimless glasses, his ice floe eyes burned.

"Oh, here you are, Gabe," Julianna said, heels tapping as she joined them at the shiny coffeepot. The auburn bun on the back of her head sagged just a little, which was understandable. Going head-to-head with Anna Mae Whitman for any length of time was enough to take the starch out of anybody. Julianna consulted her watch then her clipboard, which clenched a familiar-looking spreadsheet between its teeth. "Mr.

Sebastiani," she said as Lukas joined them. "Do you have Wyland's ETA?"

"Call me Lukas. Please." He drew a vibrating Bat Phone out of his pocket and looked at the tiny glowing display. "They're here. The transport just pulled into the underground loading dock."

Lorin rolled her eyes. Lukas could ladle on the charm when it suited him. Why couldn't he cut her some of that same slack? "So you'll be leaving soon, right?" she muttered.

Julianna gasped at her tone, but Lukas? His eyes were dancing, damn it.

"Despite the… very interesting things going on here, yes—I do have other work I need to see to."

Jack looked down at the lab space still swarming with people. "We need to clear this area."

It took about twenty minutes for the workers to finish last-minute tasks, to gather their things, and finally leave. Anna Mae Whitman lodged one final protest and was finally escorted out—urbanely, and with a promise of a meeting—by Elliott himself. Finally, only Gabe, Julianna, Bailey, and Council members remained. "We're clear," Jack said.

When the heavy steel door between the loading dock and the lab space opened, Wyland wasn't pushing the cart as Lorin had expected. That honor went to Chico, who still sported a smudge of a black eye from their impromptu sparring session up at the dig. Behind him, Wyland escorted Valerian on a courteously extended arm. The Vampire First moved slowly but didn't allow his posture to be affected by his great age. Valerian had dressed for the occasion, resplendent in an Edwardian frock coat, narrow-legged, striped wool pants, and a wing-collared shirt. Slightly large at the neck and shoulders, the loose coat exposed how much weight he'd recently lost.

Annika Fontaine's death last fall had hit all of them hard, but Valerian most of all.

Pinning a cheerful look on her face, she enfolded Valerian in a gentle hug, inhaling the familiar mix of bergamot and cedar. "Great-looking kicks, V." He'd paired his suit with crayon-red athletic shoes that looked fresh from the box.

"Thank you, my dear. Wyland's always urging me to wear more supportive footwear. Even he can't complain about these." Standing at his side, Wyland merely blinked. "Congratulations, my dear."

"Thanks."

"Hey, pretty girl," Chico greeted her, kissing her on both cheeks and then on the tip of the nose for good measure. But even here, in the secure confines of the lab, he didn't remove his hand from the dolly carrying the wooden crate. "Today's the big day."

"Yeah, I guess so." And every eye would be on her... and on Gabe, who was suddenly standing way too close to her, being introduced to the newcomers.

Gabe bowed his head before extending his hand to Valerian. "It's an honor, sir."

"Gabriel," Valerian said, taking Gabe's hand in both of his and holding it instead of offering the customary handshake. "How nice to finally meet you. Are your parents enjoying their trip?"

Gabe's surprise was etched on his face. "Yes, very much, thank you."

"And how is young Glynna?"

"Much better now, thank you."

Lorin froze. Glynna had been sick? His parents were out of the country, his brother was working overtime hunting for Annika's killer, and Glynna was sick? Guilt slammed into her like a Mack truck. Her... little misadventure had pulled Gabe away from his family. Damn it, why hadn't he said anything?

Why hadn't anybody said anything?

"Are we ready to proceed?" Elliott asked.

"Um, yeah." Lorin gestured to the box. "Mom?"

Alka simply gestured back, her face glowing with pride.

Okay. This was it. Taking a deep breath and squaring her shoulders, Lorin accepted the handle of the dolly from Chico and led the group down the hall to the lab space that would be their home away from home for the next week or so. Gabe was suddenly flanking her on her left, and she thought she felt the slightest reassuring touch of his hand at the small of her back—there, then gone—before he opened the door and flicked a switch.

She squinted against the lighting as she and Gabe entered the lab. The studio-bright lights were a pain in the ass. She couldn't argue that it was important that their work be recorded for posterity, but she'd fought Lukas long and hard about his recommendation that the activity in the lab be recorded 24/7—and she'd finally worn him down, thank Freyja. Given her luck, the cameras would catch her digging a wedgie out of her ass, or itching her nose at such an angle that it looked like she was picking it, like in that episode of *Seinfeld*. She snickered at the thought.

"What's so funny?" Gabe asked.

"Nothing," she responded as she approached the stainless steel table equipped with the biohazard hood.

"Over here," Gabe said.

"We're not using the hood?"

Gabe shrugged. "You already breached the box, and the tests came back clean. Biohazard containment isn't a factor any longer."

"Okay." Looking around, she didn't recognize half of the equipment Gabe had requested be set up on the tables surrounding the perimeter of the room, but her own simple workstation was set up in the corner. Not that she'd have much to do initially but watch Gabe work. Today, he'd work with the exterior of the box, getting precise measurements and running some initial metallurgical, chemical, and photolithographic tests.

When she reached the waist-high table Gabe had indicated, he took a position on the other side of the dolly. Though she was more than capable of lifting the wooden crate onto the table herself, she nodded her head to indicate that she'd accept his help.

It seemed… the right thing to do.

"On three," he murmured.

After they lifted the crate onto the table, Gabe handed her a crowbar with a distinct sense of ceremony. The eyes of her mother, her Council, and her president prickled into her back.

"This is it," Gabe said softly. "Congratulations, Lorin."

Her throat slammed shut at his words. After a pause, she mouthed "thank you" in response. Speaking was beyond her capabilities at the moment.

Gabe seemed to recognize her difficulty, if not the reason for it. "Recording on," he said. "Go for it."

Lorin wedged the edge of the crowbar into a narrow crevice separating the top of the protective box from its sides and carefully pressed down. Nails squeaked. As Gabe carefully lifted the cover off, she looked down—and a soft snort of amusement escaped.

Wyland had cocooned the priceless object in bubble wrap.

After poking her finger against one of the bubbles until it broke with a pop—and receiving a deadpan look from Gabe in response—they lifted the box from the crate. Gabe bore the other pieces of the storage crate away, and then helped Lorin unwrap the box.

Finally, there the box stood, glowing green-tinged platinum under the bright lights. Though Lorin overheard snippets of conversation from the other side of the room—"the color"… "next to no surface drag, imagine the manufacturing possibilities"… "are you certain opening the box is safe?"—Gabe had the bulk of her attention.

It was his reaction she was interested in.

He extended a hand toward the box, then blinked and snatched it back. As he wandered around the table, muttering about photoluminescence, phosphorescence, and tensile strength, Lorin went to the supply container and snatched two pairs of gloves, handing him the XLs. He accepted them with an absent "thank you" and snapped them on.

When Gabe lightly stroked his fingertip along the box's edge, her core clenched like a fist—and Lukas's knowing and amused expression made her want to throttle him.

"Let's get to work," she said to Gabe. "What can I do for you?"

Gabe's head jerked up. The answer she saw in his
eyes… shocked her.

———— ‿‿‿ ————

Lorin was driving him nuts.

Somehow, she'd brought the scent of the north
with her—pine, wind, wood smoke—and he'd almost
reached for her several times during the long hours it
had taken to run initial tests on the exterior of the box.
Her hair was loose, spilling over her shoulders like a
waterfall. She sat across the room, at the small desk
she'd requested to perform her own work, fingers moving lightly over the keyboard. In the lab's bright light,
Gabe could see the double-grooved rumble strip of
concentration—or was it annoyance?—that creased the
skin between her eyebrows.

She'd ignored him all day, so he was pretty sure he
wasn't the cause.

While her back was turned, he removed his glasses
and carefully rubbed at his eyes, not that it would dissi-
pate the subtle, milky haze slowly but surely filming his
remaining field of vision. *Cataracts.* He'd known what
the diagnosis was before Dr. Mueller had opened her
mouth—they'd expected it, they'd been watching for
it—but… damn. As if the macular degeneration wasn't
enough to freaking deal with.

He closed his eyes and rubbed the bridge of his nose.
Working in the lab this morning had been a reality check,
revealing just how much his fine visual acuity had de-
teriorated. The tricks and coping mechanisms he used
for computer work—increasing the screen brightness
and font size, and tilting his head slightly to the left

to compensate for the gaps in the center of his field of vision—just didn't lend themselves to microscopic work.

Now was the absolute worst possible time for him to have surgery, but his work today had exposed how much he needed it.

Suddenly Lorin stood and stretched, long and lithe. "Gabe? I'm not doing anything here but watching you work. Do you really need me here?"

He slipped his glasses back on as she strolled toward him. Unfortunately—fortunately?—he could now see that little slice of belly her stretch had exposed. Her luscious scent perfumed the sterile air.

"I thought I'd hang around in case you needed something, needed some tests logged, needed water, needed *something*—but you haven't needed anything. Mumble, mutter, rub your eyes. You're doing fine without me."

Right. "Thank you for staying," he said. "I know you can't start working until I finish. I'm working as fast as I can." She was visibly fidgety and twitchy. Whomever she'd shared her bed with last night hadn't done a very good job. "If you have something"—*or someone*—"else to do, please. Go ahead." *Okay, that was surly. Throttle back.* "Wait. I *do* need your help with something. I need a small scraping." He indicated the box glowing under the lights like the priceless treasure it was. "Where the hell do I take it from?" Her gaze met his with an expression of horror. "Yeah. It's like deciding where to deface the *Mona Lisa*."

"Oh, man." Lorin raised her hand to her mouth and dropped it as she squared her shoulders. She took another breath. "How much do you need?"

Why did she have to keep talking about need? He

needed, all right. He needed to strip her bare, spread her out on that spotlighted table, and feast on her delicious body. He needed to twine his limbs with hers, fill his lungs with her scent. Know that she belonged to him, and only him.

But she didn't—and even if his mindless body didn't recognize the distinction, his brain certainly did. "Help me turn it over," he growled.

Lorin speared him with a look. "What is your damage?"

He took a deep breath, scraping back the hot embers of his temper. He was going to suffer whether she was here or not, albeit in very different ways. It wasn't her fault he'd let his feelings get involved. "I'm sorry. I realize this… situation is uncomfortable."

She stepped closer, so only the table and the box stood between them. "Gabe, I'm a big girl. I can take being dumped. But you have to shake off the bug that's crawled up your ass so we can work togeth—"

"Dumped? Please." Gabe laughed harshly. "Be honest. I just beat you to it."

"What?"

"Don't bother to deny it. Our 'relationship' was casual, strictly physical, and—"

"—and your problem is?" Her incredulous expression said louder than words that she couldn't understand a man not being happy with no-strings, casual sex.

Of course she couldn't.

"Gabe."

Damn it, this was not a conversation he wanted to have. "I know you needed… assistance when we were at the site, and I was the only reasonable choice. But now that we're back home, you have other options, and I—I can't sleep with you when you're sleeping with other men. I'm just not wired that way." He forced himself to shrug in a way that he hoped looked worldly and sophisticated rather than hopelessly old-fashioned and pathetic. "So go ahead and call Rafe or Chico or Jack. Not that you weren't free to do that anyway. You don't have to slum it anymore."

Lorin stared at him. "Slum it? What are you talking about? I haven't slept with anyone else since we've been together. Why do you assume I have?"

She looked angry and… hurt. What the hell? Without quite knowing why, he reached out with his hand, but she stepped back, out of range, fists clenched and lips pinched and bloodless.

"I need to go." Her voice cracked.

"Lorin, I—"

"Back. Off."

He disobeyed, stepping closer. When he touched her shoulder with his hand, she shook it off with a snarl, rearing back like a wild mare.

"I need to go." She whirled away—but not quickly enough to hide her glistening eyes.

"Lorin—" Ah, damn. He'd hurt her. He hadn't known he could hurt her.

What the hell had he done? Was it possible she—

The door slammed. "Damn it!" he shouted to the ceiling. Whose bed had he driven her to with his act of epic stupidity? Rafe Sebastiani? Chico Perez? Jack Kirkland? Someone else he didn't even know about?

He threw his clipboard across the room.

Chapter 11

"NICE SHOT."

"Nicer ass."

Lorin threw a look up to the ledge overlooking the racquetball court. She and Andi had drawn an audience.

"Match point," Andi called, grasping her racquet firmly. *Whap*. The small blue ball shot off her racquet with blistering speed.

She leaped to return serve. *WHAP*.

"Whoa," someone said.

Whoa was right, if she did say so herself. Wicked spin, paired with blistering pace. Better late than never, because Andi was kicking her ass.

The ball whizzed around the rectangular court during the long volley that followed, with both of them bumping off the walls, and each other, until Andi changed things up by tapping a soft shot to the front wall. "Damn it." Even as she dove, Lorin knew she'd get there too late. Her bare, sweaty belly squeaked against the thin-slatted wooden floor, and she tumbled into the front wall in a tangle of arms and legs. She hadn't even gotten her racquet on the thing. "Nice shot," she gasped to Andi as she flopped onto her back and stayed there.

Applause, hoots, and catcalls echoed from above. Their peanut gallery obviously agreed.

"That's match. Good hustle." Andi Woolf grinned, but the bitch was sucking air through her big white teeth.

Excellent. If Lorin had any doubts at all about how Andi's recovery was progressing, this balls-out racquetball game had removed them. Lorin and Andi hadn't played racquetball for ages—not since Stephen had nearly killed Andi, leaving her with a throat bracketed by surgical scars, and an anger she didn't know what to do with.

Andi extended a hand. Taking it, Lorin let Andi hoist her to her feet. Andi's arms and shoulders, exposed by the skimpy sports bra she wore, positively rippled with definition. Andi worked as a personal trainer, but had obviously stepped up her own use of the health club's facilities during her off-hours. Given that Stephen was on the loose, Lorin couldn't blame her.

"That wasn't even close," Lorin groused. "You absolutely thrashed me."

"Your jealousy tastes like candy."

"Yeah, yeah."

"Do you feel better now?" Andi asked as she opened the door at the back of the court. "You were about ready to stroke out when you first got here."

Lorin dropped onto one of the metal folding chairs right outside the door. Andi leaned against the wall as Lorin rubbed the stinging red circle imprinted above her right kidney.

"Sorry about that." Still grinning, Andi punched in a code, unlocked the storage bin, and extracted their gym bags. After tossing Lorin hers, she reached into her own, grabbed a water bottle, and guzzled.

"You're not sorry at all," Lorin said as she unzipped her own bag, hoping her reaction to her friend's permanently hoarse voice didn't show in her own. Ignoring her chirping phone, she grabbed a towel and rubbed it over her sweaty face, neck, and shoulders.

"I expected you to move out of the way, grandma."

Lorin snorted. "Don't think I didn't notice the assist you got from the wall as you sat down just now."

"You have no proof, only suspicions." Andi wiped at her own face and neck, working carefully around the fading incisions.

Lorin throttled back helpless anger. How many months had passed since Stephen had blown into their lives, leaving wreckage in his wake? Andi had been his first victim—had nearly died—and while Andi had been hospitalized, in an induced coma to aid her recovery, Stephen, posing as her lover, had gained regular access to her room, assaulting her again and again.

But Andi was alive, kicking, and recovering—unlike Annika Fontaine.

Andi pushed to her feet. "Come on, lazy bones." She extended a hand to Lorin again, yanking her up off her chair. "I want a smoothie."

"Okay." It amused her that Krispin Woolf, the fearsome WerePack Alpha, owned a health club that had a froufrou juice bar—even if the juice bar also served blood, either warmed or chilled.

They picked up a shadow as they tromped up the cement stairs to the main level of the health club. The man was about her own height, wearing the khakis and black polo shirt combo that the health club's employees wore, but his hard-soled shoes were completely wrong for the venue. Andi noticed the guy too, but instead of appearing concerned, she rolled her eyes instead.

The guy kept his distance.

Lorin didn't say anything until they'd pulled up two padded stools at the end of the juice bar, as far away as possible from a trio of fully made-up, hair-sprayed women who'd turned up their noses at Lorin and Andi's sweat-dampened clothes and lank hair. The buff vamp behind the bar acknowledged them, finished preparing the Mean Girls' drinks, then came down to their end of the long, curved bar. Lorin asked for some orange juice on ice, and Andi ordered a multi-berry smoothie with wheat germ, flaxseed, and so many other additives that Lorin couldn't imagine how it could possibly have a liquid consistency when it arrived.

Lorin indicated their shadow with a tilt of her head. "So what's with the tail?" The man had taken a seat at a table near the juice bar's entrance.

Andi sighed. "Bodyguards. My father insists." She raised her voice, calling across the room, "Bill, tell my father I said 'hi' the next time you report in."

A wisp of a smile crept across the bodyguard's mouth before he schooled his expression back into hard-assed neutrality.

So Andi had bodyguards. Good. Krispin Woolf was an epic pain in everyone's ass, but in this matter, Lorin agreed with him. As a victim still alive and able to testify against him, Andi was at risk until Stephen was recaptured.

"They're really starting to cramp my style." Their drinks were delivered, and Andi sucked on her straw. "A couple of Gideon's people are here too, but at least they're stealthier about it."

If the reports she'd heard were accurate, Gideon Lupinsky, who headed up their law enforcement

operation and had revived Andi at the scene after her as-
sault, was as detail-oriented as his younger brother was.

Andi fell silent, gazing pensively into the air.

"What's wrong?"

"When they're around, I can't forget. Not for a minute." Andi sat up straighter, lifted her chin, and huffed
out a breath. "Okay. Enough of the pity party for today."

"Are there any new leads?"

Andi shook her head. "It's like the bastard just disappeared into thin air."

"Disappeared into thin air" was a pretty accurate
description, Lorin thought as she sipped her orange
juice. Lukas and Jack were driving themselves nuts
trying to figure out how Stephen, his body swimming
with psychotropic meds, had escaped their high-security
treatment facility in the first place. Scarlett had worked
all her music industry contacts, had contacted mutual
friends, but if anyone had heard from or about Stephen,
they weren't talking.

"Speak of the devil," Andi murmured.

Adrenaline surged. "Stephen? Where?"

"No, silly. Gideon Lupinsky. Over there, on the
treadmill." Andi scowled slightly and sucked on her
straw again. "Pulling guard duty himself. I guess I
should feel honored."

On the other side of the room, Lorin watched Gideon
Lupinsky punch a button to pick up the pace on the
treadmill. From this distance, he looked a lot like Gabe.
His hair was dark brown where Gabe's was black, but
they had similar builds, with the same broad shoulders,
trim hips, and excellent ass. Lean muscle shifted under
a gray T-shirt dampened by perspiration. Commander

Gideon Lupinsky was no desk jockey—and he couldn't stop looking at Andi Woolf.

Interesting. "Are you two…" Lorin made a back-and-forth gesture with her hand.

"No." A bitter laugh escaped. "I'm a victim. To him, I'll always be a victim."

Lorin wasn't quite so sure. She recognized the heat, the interest, in Gideon's eyes. She'd been the recipient of the same expression from his brother on too many occasions.

"You're sleeping with Gabe, though. I smell him on you. How is he doing?" Andi shook her head sympathetically. "Tough news about his eyes. He just can't catch a break."

"What's wrong with Gabe's eyes?"

"His sister Gwen told me he needs cataract surgery before they can even think about dealing with the macular degeneration." Andi stared at her. "You really didn't know?" She shot a disgusted look to the ceiling and answered her own question. "Of course you didn't know. You just work together, sleep together, spend nearly every waking moment together. You Valkyries, with your 'food-fight-fuck.' You treat men like slabs of meat without a brain attached—not that they don't enjoy it immensely."

The observation stung. "I do not treat Gabe like a slab of meat. And his brain is stellar, thank you very much." But his eyes… weren't. And he hadn't told her.

"Don't you guys talk at all?"

Lorin's thoughts flipped like a slideshow: Gabe, clapping her body against the log wall of the cookhouse, kissing her silly. Her back, scratched and scraped by birch bark. Him, staring at her as she rode him like a cowgirl in broad daylight, not caring at all who might see them.

Nope. Not a lot of talking.

"Is the sex that good?" Andi murmured. She shot Gideon Lupinsky another assessing glance then scooted her stool a couple of inches closer. "Tell me everything."

Lorin sipped at her orange juice.

"No dish? What's up with that?"

What *was* up with that? She and Andi talked about their lovers all the time, in exacting, minute detail. But for some reason doing so now felt wrong. Not that Gabe was her lover any longer.

She swallowed as the orange juice she'd been enjoying so much started to climb back up her throat. Was Andi right? Had she made Gabe feel like a mere sexual convenience? Was that why he'd—

"Are you two dating, then?"

She hesitated, setting her glass down on the juice bar. "No."

"Another friend with benefits thing, like you have with Rafe?"

"*Had* with Rafe," she corrected. "I'm not sleeping with Rafe anymore, and damn it, I'm not just using Gabe for sex. I'm not. How insulting."

Andi eyed her innocently. "What's so insulting about it? It's pretty much your standard operating procedure."

Damn it. "We're… friends and colleagues," she finally said. "Who"—she gave Andi an annoyed look—"yes, have had sex. Note my use of the past tense. He ended it yesterday."

"Why?"

"He's always had a problem with me reporting to

him, about me being the Valkyrie Second, about me being 'out of his league'—whatever that means." She took a deep breath as she remembered Gabe's facial expression, the twist in his voice, when he'd said he couldn't sleep with her while she slept with other men. "He all but called me a slut."

"I'm sure he didn't say that."

"No," Lorin had to admit. "But I know he was think-ing it."

"Really." Andi's tiny, satisfied smile grated.

Lorin snatched up her glass of orange juice again. "I'm glad you find this so damn amusing."

"It's a relief to focus on someone else's issues for a change."

"Issues? I'm not having issues—"

"Lorin, *I* thought you were still sleeping with Rafe, so I can understand why Gabe might." Andi sucked hard on her straw, her cheeks hollowing as she drew the viscous liquid into her mouth. "I can also understand why he might back away."

"Huh?"

"Think about it. Weres tend toward monogamy in the first place, and Gabe has never been one to play the field. He's deliberate. Careful. If he started taking this"—Andi waved her hand—"thing between you more seriously than he thought you were, if he didn't think there was a chance for your relationship to go anywhere, he'd end it. When we mate, we mate for life."

We mate for life. Andi's words burned like a brand.

Andi took another drink of her smoothie. "So, now that Gabe's called things off, will you and Rafe pick things up again?"

Her stomach clenched. "No—"

"So who's the next lucky man? Chadden? He's made no secret of the fact that he'd love to share your bed." Andi shot her a sideways glance. "Or did you share it last night?"

Damn grapevine. "Can't a woman have dinner with a friend?"

"A candlelit dinner, cooked and served by the chef himself, at his private table? Sounds pretty romantic to me. Doesn't Chadden look positively edible in chef's whites? With that bandana lashed around his head? *Hoo*-boy." Andi fanned her face with her hand. "He looks like a debauched pirate."

"We didn't—I couldn't—"

"You didn't couldn't what?" Andi's grin grew. "Please, continue. This is most enlightening."

Lorin's mouth opened, but no words came out. Andi's information, however she'd obtained it, was spot-on. Last night, Chadden had set the stage for seduction, feeding her succulent, decadent tidbits, so artistically crafted that it almost—*almost*—seemed a shame to eat them. She appreciated the effort; she really did, but as the meal went on, the prospect of actually having sex with him had become so viscerally unappealing that she'd actually made up an excuse to leave the restaurant before he'd served her his signature Chocolate Wild Raspberry Bombe.

"Lorin, I've never seen you this scrambled by a relationship. Yeah, I said it—a relationship. I think your emotions are finally involved, and frankly it's past time."

Her diaphragm twisted in reaction. "We annoy each other to no end."

Andi's eyes danced. "Better annoyance than boring each other stiff."

"Don't say 'stiff' in my presence, please," Lorin muttered. Suddenly, she was starving. "Barkeep," she called to the vamp. "Do you have any raspberry muffins?" At his affirmative nod, she raised two fingers.

"Coming right up."

Lorin leaned back against the padded chair while Andi deliberated the offerings in the pastry case. A relationship. Maybe Andi was right. Spending time with Gabe was anything but boring. If pressed, she would have to admit that he could be good company—when she wasn't thinking about how to jump his bones. Truth be told, he more than carried his own weight up at the site, and… damn it, he made her think. Though their work styles were completely different, they built upon each other's ideas well. His legendary detail orientation definitely translated to lovemaking. She'd never had a lover who tripped her trigger quite so… efficiently.

Her thoughts sputtered to a stop. Backed up. When, exactly, had sex with Gabe become "lovemaking" in her mind? When the hell had *that* happened? It was a mental Freudian slip that even she couldn't ignore.

He'd hurt her feelings on numerous occasions. How could he hurt her feelings if they weren't involved in the first place? Was Andi right?

Was it possible that Gabe felt the same way? And what if he didn't? The very prospect sent nerves tap-dancing in her stomach.

The vamp approached with two plates, placing the one with two steaming muffins down in front of

her. Andi had chosen a plump croissant, shiny with
butter, with strawberries on the side. Murmuring her
thanks, Lorin dug in. Tart raspberries exploded on her
taste buds. "Mmm. You're right about one thing," she
mumbled to Andi around a mouthful of food. "Gabe
and I don't talk enough. If he has a health problem,
someone up at the dig should know about it. If not
me, someone."

"It's not like he's about to drop, or go spontaneously
blind." Andi narrowed her eyes. "I don't think."

The muffins she'd just eaten suddenly tasted like
sawdust. She shoved the plate away. "It's not like we
can just pick up and go to a hospital if something goes
seriously wrong while we're up at the site," she snapped.
The nearest hospital catering to their species was in
Minneapolis, a good three hundred miles south of the
dig. Should he even be driving? "Why the hell don't
we have a helicopter up there?" she fretted. "Not that I
know how to fly one, but I could learn—"

"Hey." Andi put a hand on her shoulder. "Calm
down. He's a smart guy. I'm sure he has his retinologist
on speed-dial."

Lorin made herself relax. *His beautiful eyes.* Deep
lakes of blue, covered by a thin sheet of ice. How much
of their unusual color was due to the cataracts? At least
now she knew why he blinked and rubbed his eyes so
much while he worked. It wasn't that he was reaching
the end of his rope with her.

Necessarily.

"I heard that he and Kayla Andersen broke up in
part because of his family's poor genetics," Andi said,
watching Gideon Lupinsky racking up weights at the

bench press station. "I'm sure she congratulated herself on the close call when the news about his eyes hit the grapevine."

"Bitch." She hadn't known Gabe and Kayla's relationship was quite *that* serious. The last time she'd seen Kayla had been in the hallway outside the VIP room at Underbelly, the night of Scarlett Fontaine's homecoming show last fall. Physically, Kayla Andersen was everything Lorin wasn't: small, girly, blonde, and delicate—everywhere except her bustline, of course. She designed handbags, for Freyja's sake. What had she and Gabe possibly found to talk about?

They probably hadn't talked all that much.

"Lorin." Andi waved a hand in front of her face to regain her attention. "Whether you're sleeping together right now or not, whether you're denying your emotions are involved or not, I'm glad Gabe's with you right now. Gwen worries about him being all broody and solitary up there in the northwoods."

Lorin snorted. "With the crew there, solitary is damn tough to come by."

"So, for real. Are things completely over between you and Rafe?"

Lorin knew that whatever she said next would hit the grapevine quickly, and then spread like wildfire. *Sorry, Rafe.* "Rafe and I aren't sleeping with each other anymore." He'd been the one to break off their sexual relationship too, and she still didn't know why.

First Rafe, then Gabe. It was enough to give her a complex.

Damn it, why had Gabe kept something so important from her? She needed to see him. Yell at him. Hug him.

Both, simultaneously. The stool screeched against the floor as she shoved to her feet.

Andi cocked her head and gestured to Lorin's gym bag. "Is that your phone again?"

"Probably." Lorin reached into the bag, extracted the annoying device, and quickly looked at the display. A text from Nathan lit the small screen: Dude. Where are you? Check in. She scrolled. "Hmm." Four text messages and a video from Nathan. A text and a voice mail from Mike, and a voice mail from Paige, all within the past two hours. "I'd better get these."

"A fate worse than death," Andi deadpanned as she stood and hugged her good-bye. "Go give him hell," she whispered.

Andi knew her too well. "Count on it."

As Lorin left, she saw Andi slam what was left of her smoothie, toss her shoulders back, and then approach Gabe's guarded older brother—undoubtedly to dish out a little hell of her own.

—∿∿—

Gabe took a deep breath and held it. *Don't drop it, don't drop it, don't drop it…* Moving slowly and carefully, he transferred the minute metallic scraping he'd finally taken to the SamplPak and quickly sealed it.

Then he released his breath.

Finally. After an hour of dithering, he'd finally—

The lab door crashed open behind him. "Gabe! You—"

He jerked, rapping his head on the corner of the monitor suspended over the table on a boom. The scraping tool dropped to the table with a clatter as he closed his eyes and clutched the top of his head.

Lorin dropped a gym bag and hurried to his side. "Are you okay? Let me see." She pulled his head down to examine his crown, pushing his nose right into her chest.

The initial, white-hot pain was already subsiding. The tips of her fingers stroking against his nerve-rich skull felt like heaven. Trying not to rest his cheek against her breast, he inhaled rosemary mint shampoo, floor wax, clean sweat, and... wolf.

"I don't see any blood."

He backed away several crucial feet, straightening his glasses. "I'm okay, you just startled me."

Now that he could see her, he couldn't tear his eyes away. Her hair was pulled back in a ponytail, highlighting her killer cheekbones and jawline. The clingy red workout clothes exposed yards of bare arms and legs, and hugged every dangerous curve. Dark patches of sweat on the midriff-baring top drew his attention back to her cleavage. She had an angry-looking floor burn on her stomach.

She'd walked through the halls of Sebastiani Labs looking like... that? The outfit had all the subtlety of a matador waving a red flag at a bull. He pointed to her stomach. "What happened?"

"Dove for a ball," she said absently. "Never mind that. Are you sure you're okay?"

He nodded.

"How is it going?" She indicated the table he'd been working at when she arrived, where the box glowed under bright lights.

That color. How to describe it? It was silver, fluid-looking, like the mercury in an old-time thermometer, with the slightest hint of green. Where had the metal been mined? It was unlike any alloy he'd seen. If this was Noah Pritchard's fabled command box, its composition might give them their first real data about the incubus homeworld. Then again, Pritchard could just as easily have obtained it at the intergalactic equivalent of Walmart.

He'd spent the hours since Lorin's departure testing the metal's optical properties, its ability to conduct heat and electricity, its possible malleability and ductility— but the test he'd been about to perform just as she'd walked in wasn't one that anyone would find in a scientific journal or text. Now that he'd taken the scraping, exposing fresh metallic molecules, the clock was ticking. He couldn't lose this opportunity. "One more test today, and I have to do it now. Can you step back a little? I need to clear my…" He indicated his nose.

"Sorry. I imagine I'm pretty ripe. I didn't shower before I left the health club." As Lorin walked towards the door she'd just come in through, he stared at the muscles and curves shifting under the clingy fabric. "Hurry, though," she said, stopping at the door and turning so she could watch. "I have news from up north."

Gabe fought his attention away from her ass. "Is everyone okay?"

"Yeah." A slight furrow creased her brow. "I think." She made a shooing motion with her hands. "Hurry. Do what you need to do, then I'll give you an update."

He walked to the worktable and pushed the monitor up and out of his way. Placing his gloved fingertip at the edge of the scraping, he took off his glasses, setting them down next to the box where he would be able to easily find them.

As the world blurred away, his sense of smell shoved to the forefront. Quickly, before he picked up Lorin's scent again, he lowered his head to the area of the box where he'd taken the scraping and inhaled deeply.

Nothing. How odd. No telltale sharpness, no metallic sting. Lowering his head, he touched the tip of his tongue to the minute scar. Still nothing. What the hell…? He'd never encountered a metal that didn't have either a scent or a taste.

He drew his tongue the full length of the scraping.

Behind him, Lorin gasped. The pace of her breathing had picked up, soft huffs of excitement he'd tried to erase from his memory but failed. He slowly inhaled. No more tests were possible, because the light salt of her arousal crowded out everything else.

He registered movement—a shift of shadows, a change in the quality of the light. As she approached, aspects of her appearance gradually came into sharper focus but were still covered by a milky film: her tanned arms, legs, and stomach, darker than the snow-white wall behind her. Her breasts and lower torso were a dangerous bright red.

His nose tingled. His teeth itched. His wolf was dangerously close to the surface.

"Gabe." Lorin leaned her face closer to his, her features blurry but familiar. She thrummed her thumbs up his cheekbones, stroking over his temples where his glasses typically rested. He slid his hands around her bare torso, resting them at the small of her back, and leaned into her touch with a rumble of pleasure. The light turned to shadow as she brought their lips together.

He sank gratefully into the kiss, which tasted,

delightfully, of oranges. What delusional thought process had ever made him believe he could walk away from her? From this? Who had he been kidding? If Lorin wanted sex, he'd give it to her—as much and as often as she could handle—and deal with the emotional fallout later. He must be at least competent at meeting her needs if she was coming back for more. Gabe lifted a hand and tugged on her ponytail, baring her neck to his mouth. He'd sleep with her as long as he could keep her interest, and be damn thankful for—

A throat cleared theatrically from the door.

"Mom. Hi."

Lorin stepped away from Gabe—but not before giving his lower lip a final, teasing nip that made him feel… claimed somehow.

If he wasn't absolutely mortified, he'd sit up and howl. Caught necking at work by Lorin's mother. The Valkyrie First. His—he gulped—boss. As Lorin greeted her mother, Gabe tugged his lab coat over his groin.

"Hello, Gabriel." As Alka kissed him on both cheeks, Gabe tried not to wrinkle his nose. Something she wore smelled like bad taxidermy. "Where are your glasses, dear?"

Suddenly his glasses were in his hand. "Thanks," he murmured to Lorin. He slipped them on, resting a hand on the table as his eyes fought to adjust.

"Did you get Nathan's messages?" Alka asked. "He called me when he couldn't reach either of you."

Lorin mouthed a curse. "Yes, I picked them up after Andi and I finished playing racquetball. I was just about to update Gabe."

Racquetball with Andi Woolf. He'd been so addled

earlier that he'd completely missed the fact that the wolf he'd smelled on Lorin was female.

He had it bad.

"What's happening?" Now that he had his glasses on, Gabe saw the origin of the gamy smell surrounding Alka. The belt slung around her ample hips was made of bleached bones and an animal hide of some type. Yak? Antelope? With Alka, one never knew.

"A new find." Lorin jacked her phone into her workstation, and with a couple of clicks, she played the short video clip Nathan had sent. His cheeks heated as they listened. He glanced at Alka and cleared his throat. "Did Nathan say—"

"—dildo? Yes, dear," Alka said matter-of-factly.

Gabe leaned closer to the monitor. There, half excavated, lying not two feet from where Lorin had found the command box, was a… capsule?—whose color was a visual match for the metal of the box glowing on his table. And yes, it looked very much like a sex toy. A giant's sex toy.

"Obviously Nathan thinks it's cross-contamination," Lorin said, laughing.

Gabe nodded. He'd worked with Alka and Lorin long enough to have heard them talk about how, even at ancient archaeological sites, it wasn't at all unusual to find current-era items such as cigarette butts or plastic bottle caps.

"Mike sent pictures of it *in situ*," Lorin said, scrolling through a sequence of still photos that exposed more of the artifact with each click. "We need to update Elliott and decide what to do next."

"We need to get it down here," Gabe stated. "Fast."

"Yeah," Lorin agreed. "It'll be safer down here. But I don't want to alarm the crew."

Alka glanced at her watch. "You could drive up to Isabella tonight, Lorin, see how things are going at the dig, and be back here with the find by tomorrow noon, easy." She rested a hand on his shoulder. "I know you want to get your hands on it as soon as possible, Gabe."

I want my hands on your daughter even more.

Lorin glanced at him, then at her mother. "Okay."

Maybe it was wishful thinking, but Lorin sounded as disappointed as he felt. He'd spent too many days out of her bed. He could manage one more night.

Couldn't he?

Chapter 12

"Shh. Be quiet," Paige whispered.

Beddoe nodded as Paige tugged him along the shadowy side of the building. He'd met her at Tubby's again, and after drinking raspberry cosmos together—tasty beverage, that; he'd have to offer them on board the *TonTon*—they'd walked, their arms wrapped around each other to fight off the chill, down the same tree-lined dirt road they'd sauntered down the last time they'd met.

But this time they walked the road to its end, and he hadn't had to thrall her to do it. Shivering as they'd left the warm, smelly bar, Paige said she knew a private place nearby. Beddoe never imagined that he might be thankful for the bone-chilling temperature, but it provided the perfect excuse to access one of their buildings.

A man didn't accomplish what he had without learning to trust his instincts. Something about the buildings down the road made his skin prickle. The *Arkapaedis*'s beacon—perhaps the *Ark* itself—was down here somewhere. Though currently quiet, the beacon could reactivate at any time.

He had to find it before it did.

Paige stopped at a darkened door. Despite the rough looking nature of the building—made of the stalks of the very trees lining the road!—he was glad there was shelter in his future. Here in the open, it was dark, dank, and colder than the rings of the Outer Pteralides. Though pleasure was definitely on the agenda, so was reconnaissance. He'd prefer to be warm and comfortable for both activities.

"Are we hiding?" he murmured against the delicate shell of her ear as he assessed his surroundings. The building he'd so carefully examined the last time he was here—the strapping woman's residence—was dark, with soft textile coverings blocking the windows, but the bigger building across the open clearing blazed with lights. Through the window, he saw a group of people huddled around a glowing screen. On the screen, a handsome man and his fur-covered copilot navigated a beat-up ship through a field of stars.

If they knew about space travel, why did they use such ancient technology?

"Yes, we're definitely hiding," Paige whispered, tilting her head to the side so he had better access to her neck.

He licked his way down her tender vein.

"You're not supposed to be here."

Beddoe glanced at the other building again. Though muffled sound escaped, the windows were closed to the chilly night air. No one would hear them. He had plenty of time.

"No guests allowed." Paige's low, smoky laugh wrapped itself around his groin like a hand.

He tugged the tiny dangle of her ear adornment into his mouth, then worried it between his teeth. As he suckled on it, a near-silent moan escaped her throat.

His incisors tingled in his mouth.

"Come on." Sidling away from his touch, she opened the door and disappeared inside.

He followed her into the building, quickly closing the door behind them. Though it wasn't much warmer than it was outside, at least they had shelter from the wind.

A single dim light. A wall of shelves, some empty and some not. A long table bisected the room, its top littered with simple hinged comps, imaging equipment, papers and writing implements, shallow trays, picks, and brushes. Though nothing gritted under his feet, the room smelled distinctly of soil.

What was this place?

The question evaporated as Paige slipped her chilly hand into his. Lifting their joined hands to his lips, he ran his tongue over her knuckles. Paige sagged back against the table as he nibbled his way up to the delicate veins in her wrist. *So very tiny.* He could crush her using only a fraction of his physical strength.

"Robert," she whispered.

Paige's voice soothed him like a balm and maddened him at the same time—he, who'd slept with some of the most beautiful creatures in the galaxy. What was it about her? Was it her fumbling, eager hands? The way she touched him with more enthusiasm than skill? How her expression shifted from supplication to dark dawning delight as he drove her to the heights of pleasure? In his world, sex was an exchange of services, but Paige seemed to want nothing from him but pleasure.

It was a novel experience.

Lifting her slight body up onto the table, Beddoe brought his lips to hers, sinking into her tempting mouth. She was so small, so delicate, but her taste was temptation incarnate. When she craned her neck, exposing that delicious, pulsing vein, his teeth shoved down in his mouth. "Will anyone interrupt us?" he asked, scraping his incisor against her neck.

"No," Paige gasped as she twined her legs around his hips. She lay back on the rough table, pulling his upper body down against hers with surprising strength. "Lorin and Gabe are gone, and everyone else is watching a movie." Their eyes met in the dim light. "Kiss me, Robert."

Her demand inflamed him. His incisors throbbed, and his staff surged to life under his rough pants. "Witch," he muttered against her petal-soft lips, flicking his tongue against the tender upper bow. He pressed her arms over her head, held her wrists in his hands, and simply stared. Her extraordinary hair spilled over the table in a nimbus of light. Tightening her legs around his hips, she writhed, making a soft mewing sound in the back of her throat—as if being denied his lips, his touch, caused her physical pain.

He wanted to pierce, to plunge, to lose himself in the tight clasp of her body. To possess her with both teeth and staff—a pleasure he had not yet permitted himself. Beddoe raked his gaze over the bounty of her stretched-out frame. Her outer garments covered most of her arteries, but even in the dim light, he could see the delicate capillaries tracing her temples, and the tender veins branching her wrists. Blood pulsed in her neck, and a vulnerable slice of bare belly was exposed by her writhing.

After a tongue-tangling kiss, he tugged at the waistband of her shirt, lifting it up her torso, baring her skin to the air. Her body arched as he kissed each inch of exposed skin. Her breath came in shallow pants the closer he got to her breasts. He jerked the bundle of fabric up and inside out—covering her head, trapping her arms, and exposing her torso. He examined every pale, unblemished inch, not touching her, until she groaned under the layers of fabric, pushing her luscious breasts toward his mouth.

"Please," she moaned from under the layers of fabric.

"Please what?" Her tiny pink nipples were hard, begging for his mouth. He lowered his head, his hot breath puffing against the tender curve of her left breast. She shivered violently, writhing against the constraints of her clothing. Under the layers, her head tossed back and forth. Her hips rolled against his staff, her torso arching even higher off the rough table, demanding a harder touch.

He gave the nipple a tiny lick, and then backed away. "Tell me what you want."

"Robert," she groaned.

Pulling back slightly, Beddoe waited. The lovers who came after him would thank him for teaching her to accept, and ask for, what her body wanted—but in the meantime, he'd train her well, and enjoy the fruits of his labors. Perhaps their liaison could continue after he claimed this territory.

With a groan, Paige shifted her weight and pushed the nipple into his mouth with unerring instinct. "Suck me!" she begged.

"Gladly," he murmured, finally latching on to her pink, crinkled skin, the delicious nipple. He tested its hardness with his tongue, suckling strongly to reward her.

"Ah!" Her entire torso lifted off the table in response. Tools clanked as she thumped down roughly. Her wrist hit the rim of one of the shallow pans littering the table.

Reaching over to push the pan out of range, he saw the familiar shape, the familiar glint of metal.

A cryotube? Here?

His thoughts raced. It was unmistakably a cryotube—an ancient one, given the rudimentary touch clasp on the blocky outcropping at the base. Such devices had long been standard equipment on ships making long-haul voyages. He rarely thought about his own seed and skin cells nestled in stasis alongside those of his command crew in a similar unit on board the *TonTon,* but in the event the ship went down and rescue wasn't possible, the 'tube's contents gave survivors a fighting chance to repopulate, to avoid extinction.

First a beacon with the *Arkapaedis*'s signature, and now a cryotube? No need to see the ship's physical wreckage; he'd found the *Arkapaedis*'s final resting place.

Had Captain Noah Pritchard breached the 'tube? Did it still contain the captain's own genetic material? Did his descendents, and the descendents of his command crew, walk this tiny, backwater planet? Beddoe swallowed hard. If he was clever—if he handled things very carefully indeed—he could be rich beyond measure.

Questioning Paige Scott was more important than ever.

Reaching to the waistband of her pants, he slipped the closure open, lowered the metal fastener, and delved his hand under the layers to touch her slippery, intimate heat. As she writhed, he gave a tiny mental push: *What is this place? What do you seek here?*

Paige reared up, scrabbling at the fabric covering her head.

Distract. "You like being teased," he purred, cupping her mound. "You're burning up."

She pushed the garment back down so she could see, blocking her precious breasts and all that fine-grained skin hidden from his view. In the dim light of the room, her sunset-colored eyes looked nearly black.

She nipped at the point of his chin with her tiny white teeth, a surprising sting that shrilled all the way down his spine. *Why do you want to know?* She punctuated her mental question with a lithe stretch of her neck.

Nothing she could do would affect him more, and her low, knowing laugh meant the little witch knew it. He latched his lips onto that tender juncture where neck met shoulder.

Her throat vibrated against his mouth as she spoke. "I'll answer a question if you do." She snaked her hands under his upper body garment, stroking up his abdomen, his chest—"What's this?" Her nimble fingers traced the barely discernible outline of his plant.

Dia. He shouldn't have allowed her to touch his body so freely. How could he explain? So far, he hadn't seen any evidence of even the most rudimentary comporganic intelligence. "What a waste of a question," he responded, scratching his teeth against her neck to distract her.

Plucking his hand out of her pants, Paige pushed him back so she could look at his face. "Do you have heart problems?"

"I've had it so long I hardly notice it anymore," he replied truthfully. Her conclusion, though incorrect, was better than any that he could come up with on such short notice.

"A vamp with circulatory problems? That can be life-threatening." She frowned, stroking the skin over the plant.

Vamp. Vampyr. There it was again—confirmation that she knew *what* he was, if not from *where*. He glanced at the ancient cryotube, gleaming in the rough wooden box not two feet away. How much did she know?

Beddoe stared at Paige, her eyes narrowed in worry, her pale hair snarled with passion, her lips glowing, pink and puffy, against her skin. Her hand rested over his beating heart.

His strain floated away under her talented fingers. "How do you do that?" he asked.

"Do what?"

"Ease me so easily."

Her smile was full of secrets. "We all have our skills."

Dia, he wanted her.

"Feed, Robert."

Though she whispered her demand, the need in her voice ignited a conflagration. Bloodlust sparked quickly, threatening to blaze out of control. Pushing her body back so she rested against the table again, he tugged at her unfastened pants, baring her lower torso to his gaze.

Under the tiny divot of her umbilicus, the tender curve of her stomach quickly rose and fell. Gleaming between her hip bones was soft body hair the color of flax. Tender arteries branched at each side of her private adornment.

As he lowered his head, her scent deepened, intensified: iron-rich blood, pulsing under tissue-thin skin. Her light floral perfume. The salty tang of the desire he'd called from her body with his touch. She groaned when his tongue traced the juncture where her leg joined her torso. Her outstretched hands clutched at nothing, nails scratching against the hard table as he suckled, drawing her rich blood to the surface—and marking her in the process.

As he swirled his tongue over the spot he'd chosen, she straightened her legs in a luxurious, sensual stretch, and then twined them around his body, bumping her hand against the shallow box holding the cryotube again. Lifting his head, he examined his mark. Gave it a final, prideful lick. And drove his teeth deep.

She cried out at the momentary pain, but her moans quickly changed tone as the transcendent effects of his bite buffeted her system. She vised her legs around his shoulders, clasping him tighter and tighter in a restless, shifting embrace. His knees nearly buckled when she grabbed his hair and yanked, trying to pull his head even closer to her body. As he scrambled to regain his footing, finally propping his elbows on the edge of the table to support his weight, her tiny fingernails bit into his skull.

Witch.

For long, timeless moments, he mindlessly drank her rich red nectar.

When his frantic suckling finally slowed, he had no idea how much time had passed—but her pulse still ticked reassuringly against his lips. Gently removing his teeth, he shifted to slow, luxurious licks, swirling his saliva into the wound to start the healing process.

Paige lay still under his mouth, gazing at him with an expression as deep as space. And… there it was again, that soft, narcotic calm. Was this peace? Contentment? Closing his eyes, Beddoe rested his cheek against her stomach and simply savored.

Until he heard a creak—right outside the door.

Paige pushed him away from her body, shoved off the table, and dropped to her feet, lithe as a feline. "Someone's checking the cookhouse," she whispered, jerking her pants up over her oozing bite. She pointed to a closed door on the other side of the room. "Hide. Quick."

No other option. He did as she asked, hearing a clatter and a rustle behind him as he struggled with the mechanical knob. As he pulled the door closed behind him, the last thing he saw was Paige sitting at the desk, her hands poised over the keys of her machine.

The outer door opened with a squeak. "Oh, it's you."

Male voice—and a big male, if the heavy footfalls were any indication. Beddoe cocked his head in the dark, straining to hear.

"Hi, Mike," Paige responded casually, a tone that he filed away for future reference. His little witch had shaken off the aftereffects of his bite very quickly indeed. "Locking up for the night?"

"Yeah, just making a last check of the buildings before going to bed." More rustles and footfalls. Clacking sounds. "What are you doing? Are you going to be here much longer?"

"Do you think I need an escort back to the bunkhouse? I think I'm capable of making it across the clearing."

"I didn't mean—"

"I'm working." Silence. "I'm trying to concentrate here," Paige snapped. "Go back to the bunkhouse and watch some Skinemax."

"Are you okay?"

"What?"

A pause. "I smell blood."

Her wound. Beddoe tensed.

Rather than answering, his little witch let the question twist in the wind. "Mike. Just go," she finally said.

"Paige…"

"Please leave. Just leave me alone." Her voice was barely audible.

There were a couple of beats of silence, and then the sound of heavy footsteps as the deep-voiced man did as she asked. The outer door opened and closed with matching soft squeals.

Finally, he heard Paige approach. When she opened the door, the dim light made him blink.

"You have to get out of here," she whispered urgently. "Go."

Beddoe nodded. Approaching the door, he snatched a kiss—and one last look at the cryotube, lying serenely in its shallow bed on the table.

He'd be back. For the 'tube, and for the woman.

Dawn was just brightening the horizon as Lorin's headlights swept across the dig's dark parking lot. Braking to a stop with a soft crunch of tires against gravel, she wrestled the truck's sticky gearshift into park, turned off the ignition, and—ignoring her screaming bladder—closed her eyes and dropped her head back against the top of the seat.

Though she'd stopped at her townhouse to try to catch some sleep before making the drive up north, her treasonous body hadn't cooperated, so she'd hit the road. She had an itch that only Gabe could scratch, but instead of picking up where she and Gabe had left off when her mother had so rudely interrupted them, she'd driven nearly three hundred miles to retrieve a *dildo*. Damn Nathan for planting that incendiary word in her head. Every other option she could think of to call it—a package? A unit?—made her inner twelve-year-old snicker. She had phallic euphemisms on the brain.

Someone tapped on her window.

She slapped down the driver's side door lock and was diving for the other door when she recognized the muffled voice.

"Lorin. It's me."

She raised a hand to her racing heart. "Mike, you scared the crap out of me!"

"Sorry. When you pulled into the lot and didn't get out of the truck, I thought something might be wrong. Why are you just sitting out here in the dark?"

Lorin unlocked the door and opened it. Blessedly cool air wafted over her cheeks and into the open flaps of her jean jacket. "Just trying to find the energy to move," she responded with a sigh, unfolding her body from behind the wheel. She eyed the sky. "Sun's rising."

Mike indicated the bag of blood in his hand. "I'm good."

Though a fresh infusion of blood temporarily jacked a vampire's immune system into overdrive, reducing the effects of UV damage, they didn't have an unlimited supply of blood up here at the dig. She glanced at the bunkhouse, where a light burned at the window nearest Paige's bed, and then back to Mike. He looked tired. "How have things been going?"

"Pretty well."

Yeah, right. She reached back into the truck cab, snagging the strap of her messenger bag. "Give me five minutes to drop this off, get a cup of coffee"—*and pee*—"and I'll meet you in the workroom. You can bring me up to speed."

"Ditto. Because that thing"—he jerked a thumb toward the workroom—"is *not* a dildo."

"Let's take a look, and I'll tell you what I can." Which wouldn't be much.

By the time she arrived at the workroom carrying a thermal mug of freshly brewed Crackhouse Blend, Mike had company: Paige and Nathan had joined him.

"Hi, Lorin," Nathan said around a jaw-cracking yawn. "Heard your truck pull in. Muffler trouble?"

"Yeah." She hadn't thought about the broken tailpipe since she'd temporarily fixed it in Tobies' parking lot.

"I'll take a look at it before you leave."

"Better work fast," she said. "I'm picking up your find, and then turning right back around."

"I'll set up the pictures," Paige said, walking over to the desk and firing up a laptop.

Stepping over to the table, Mike picked up a shallow tray lined with puffy synthetic quilt batting. Lying nestled in the stuff, tucked into a clear, labeled specimen bag, was an oblong capsule, about two feet long and six inches wide, with a blocky extension on one end, its metal the same color as the box Gabe was testing in Sebastiani Labs' basement. Sleek, aerodynamic, the capsule shrieked high-tech—and if their working hypothesis was anywhere near accurate, the thing had been buried in the ground for at least a millennia. While she'd been brought up on stories about their ancestors, and had spent countless hours staring at the petroglyphs in the nearby cave, actually finding a second physical artifact that might support the hypothesis packed a wallop.

"The metal's… odd," Paige said as she set the laptop down on the table, quickly displaying the familiar-looking sequence of pictures they'd taken of the capsule *in situ*. "The color is unusual, and the dirt brushed away so easily."

Lorin nodded noncommittally. Gabe's preliminary tests on the box had confirmed that the metal's surface tension was almost zero. He wasn't quite ready to say that the metal was completely unfamiliar because he didn't have most of the test results back yet. Gabe hadn't been willing to play "what if?" or even propose theories about the origins of the box until he had more hard data to work with.

While Nathan described the excavation—in typical Nathan fashion, the edge of the capsule had been exposed when he'd stumbled against the edge of the pit in the area Lorin had just gridded out—Lorin listened with half an ear. Sipping her coffee and supplying a nod or a "mmm hmm" here and there, she tried to assess Paige's condition as the younger woman clicked through the photos on the laptop. She was pale, so very pale—or maybe it was the turtleneck she wore, in uncharacteristic black. With the sun barely up, she was, logically, covered from chin to toes against the morning chill. If Paige had a fresh vamp bite, she couldn't tell.

Mike, standing back with arms crossed, finally spoke. "What do you think it is, Lorin?"

Finally, a question she could answer truthfully. "I have no idea."

"I know we're not supposed to make assumptions or draw conclusions on such sketchy data, but"—Paige indicated the capsule with her head—"that's some advanced freaking manufacturing."

"Yeah." Mike picked up the bag containing the capsule, neatly labeled with his own precise printing, and held it in both hands. "The Woodland peoples made pottery, had bows and arrows," he mused. "We know they used copper for making tools and for personal ornamentation, but—"

"—but not tools like that, and that ain't copper," Nathan said.

Lorin silently agreed. They definitely weren't looking at an artifact that could have been made by the Archaic peoples, or the Woodland peoples who came after them. "Well, I'll bring it down to Gabe and see what he makes of it."

Mike eyed her. "How are your meetings going? When are you and Gabe coming back?"

I don't know if Gabe is coming back. She shrugged. "You know how it is with meetings." They didn't ask any more questions. Sometimes being the Valkyrie Second really came in handy.

"Well, at least stay long enough to eat," Mike said. "Gretchen's making breakfast burritos this morning."

Lorin nodded. "Sounds good." Paige didn't flinch or roll her eyes as Mike mentioned Gretchen. Maybe things were settling down with Paige.

"Seems like an awful waste of gas to drive up and turn right back around," Nathan said. "We could have overnighted the thing to you—"

"—and gotten a personal visit from a very nice government agent after the container was X-rayed?" Paige shook her head in exasperation. "Please."

Lorin put a hand on Nathan's arm. "Could you wrap the capsule in bubble wrap for me?"

"Sure." Nathan stopped. "A capsule. That's a good thing to call it."

"Better than a dildo, that's for sure," Paige muttered.

Lorin chatted with Paige while Nathan and Mike wrapped the capsule. It was nice to catch up on what was happening at the dig, but Paige didn't mention anything about her hot vamp, and Lorin didn't ask. Before long, Nathan handed her the capsule, its glowing metal obscured by a layer of small bubbles and clear packing tape.

As she tucked it into her messenger bag, the smell of grilled breakfast meat wafted in from the kitchen next door. Her stomach growled loudly, making Paige giggle. The smaller woman tucked her arm through Lorin's. "Let's get you fed."

They walked to the noisy dining hall, and after a round of hugs and hellos from the rest of the crew, she and Paige finally sat down. Gretchen brought over a platter of breakfast burritos bursting with eggs, bacon, and a pepper/onion mix that made Lorin's mouth water.

"Wow. These look fabulous."

"Thanks, Gretchen," Paige said with a smile.

Gretchen smiled back.

Hmm, interesting. Lorin listened as Paige chattered about events at the dig with no trace of her previous sarcasm or sullenness. Maybe she was worrying about nothing.

But she'd talk to Mike before she left and find out what was what.

Chapter 13

MUCH LATER THAT DAY, LORIN WAS BACK AT HER DESK in Sebastiani Labs' subterranean workroom, scrolling through another set of pictures—of the command box's contents—even though the objects themselves now lay in individual shallow trays on an adjacent table just across the room. She replayed the slideshow from the beginning once again, gazing at the first shot: the contents of the box *in situ*. Even though the box had been transported, shifted, and jostled many, many times since she'd dug it out of the ground, she'd followed proper procedure anyway, documenting and measuring the position of each of the objects relative to each other immediately after she and Gabe had opened it.

Several hours had passed since then, hours during which she'd tried to throttle back a clawing, growing hunger that food wouldn't satisfy. Gabe, scribbling on a clipboard behind her, apparently had no such problem.

She zoomed in on a fragile curl of birch bark, the dozen or so kernels of what looked like wild rice, the doll—or perhaps it was a spiritual totem—lying next to two locks of hair, one black and fine, the other curly platinum blond, lashed together at one end with a near-translucent polymer that looked a lot like fishing line. And there, at the back, lay the tech unit—nearly invisible because the metal it was made from was a visual match to the box itself—looking like something she could buy from the freaking Apple Store. Handheld, maybe three inches by six, it was sleek and slick.

She glared at the device's tiny glowing light. Bailey had hovered so much during Lorin's initial documentation, and had been such an epic pain in her ass, she'd given the unit to the other woman as soon as she'd finished with individual pictures and measurements. Bailey had immediately absconded with it, disappearing into the adjacent computer lab, her face glowing like a child who'd seen Santa Claus's boots drop down the chimney on Christmas morning.

Across the lab, Gabe muttered as he consulted a clipboard. Lorin rolled her eyes. He hadn't said a personal word to her since she'd come back from Isabella. Work, work, work. Though she'd felt his gaze throughout the afternoon, apparently he wasn't in the mood to talk.

The silence grew oppressive and heavy without the beeps, cheeps, blips, and pings of Gabe's Bat Phone, which Bailey had decreed be powered down. Bailey's technical explanation about her reasoning had completely flown over her head, but Gabe was complying. Since her return, he'd snatched up the handset of the wall-mounted landline a couple of times, having a short, jargon-filled conversation with Julianna Benton, and then calling his sister to ask how things were going with her prosthetic. His guilty expression as he spoke with Glynna made her queasy.

Gabe was sacrificing so much to work on this project, and it was all her fault.

She threw a dirty look at the door leading to the Biohazard Lab. Though his interest had been clear as she'd removed the capsule from her messenger bag,

Gabe had ordered it placed under the hood for bubble wrap removal, lest they have what he'd called "an encore performance." He was right, damn his eyes, but that didn't mean she had to like it. And now the capsule she'd sacrificed sleep and probable sex to retrieve lay slumbering under a biohood. Untouched. Waiting.

Like her.

Ah, damn, now he was talking, taking copious oral notes as he moved the ProScope over each millimeter of the box. She shifted restlessly. Apparently his actual words didn't matter, nor did the fact that he'd directed so few of those words to her. His rumbly voice stroked her as thoroughly as his clever tongue had the last time they'd made love.

She could practically see his synapses snap as he picked up his clipboard, scribbling a notation in his heinous handwriting. When had she started finding concentration—thinking—so damned sexy? When had a days' growth of beard juxtaposed against a starched oxford shirt made her slicken with want? Damn it, she knew *exactly* how delicious that scruff would feel scraping its way up her inner thighs.

Gabe stepped away from the table with a sigh, rolling his head in circles to stretch his neck. Latex snapped as he removed his gloves. He raised his hands to his shoulders and rubbed.

She stood, approached him from behind, and covered his hands with her own.

He tensed for several endless seconds. Slowly, with a stroke of skin against skin, he removed his hands.

Placing himself in hers.

Lorin's breath quickened as she rubbed her thumbs

against his tight trapezoids. Gooseflesh rose on the back of his neck, and his silent exhale vibrated into the fingertips resting lightly on his Adam's apple. The sterile air suddenly seemed heavy, and her perfectly comfortable clothes pulled and scratched. She felt her sex soften, dampen, clench against emptiness. Taking a half a step, she closed the distance between their bodies, bumping the toes of her boots into the heels of his loafers. Gabe groaned aloud as her breasts made contact with his back. When she twined her arms around his chest, hugging him from behind, he reached back to clutch her ass in his long-fingered hands, yanking her more tightly against his lanky frame. He hissed a breath as she dragged her hands down his chest, over his abs, taking a meandering path to the waistband of his flat-front khakis.

Which were no longer quite so flat.

She groaned. It had been too long since she'd touched the hard flesh bulging under the soft fabric, forever since she'd felt his weight in her hand... tasted his essence on her tongue. Sidling around his body, brushing him with lips and breasts as she made the journey, she reached for the tab of his zipper.

His icy blue eyes burned with heat. He covered her hand with his—

"Damn it!" Bailey's frantic voice carried clearly from the adjacent computer lab.

Lorin dropped into a fighting stance—or tried to. Gabe's arms clamped around hers like a vice, impeding her range of motion. Intruder? Security breach? She had no idea, but the panic in Bailey's voice was real. "Move, damn it." Lorin shoved out of Gabe's arms. Stalking over to the entrance, she slapped the silent alarm button that would bring Sebastiani Labs' Security and Emergency Response teams running. The cluster of warning indicators on the panel above the button indicated nothing amiss.

Bailey bumped into her as she scurried into the lab, holding the tech unit in front of her at arm's length. She ran directly to the box, dropped the tech unit into it, and slammed the cover down.

Lorin quickly scanned Bailey from stem to stern. No blood. She was mobile, all limbs working. Breathing, talking. "Are you okay?"

Bailey looked at them like they were missing the brain regions responsible for critical thinking. "Guys. That *thing*"—she pointed to the box she'd slammed closed—"connected to my network."

Lorin looked at the now-closed box, and then at the laptops both she and Gabe were using. Both units were top-of-the-line, but their network access was nil. She could type up her notes, Gabe could update his spreadsheets, but that was it. Bailey must have a different setup for herself. Why hadn't she listened to the technical details more closely during all those meetings Gabe had helmed?

And now Bailey and Gabe were walking quickly, jabbering about LANs, RFID shielding, encryption, and jammers.

"Damage?" Gabe asked.

"Don't know yet."

Lorin brought up the rear as they entered Bailey's domain, the computer lab she'd explicitly built to test the unit she'd just slammed back into the box. Dimly lit, fans whirring, nearly a dozen laptops, monitors, and CPUs elbowed for space on the crowded L-shaped table.

Bailey dropped onto a wheeled backless stool, pushed off with a foot, and clattered half the length of the table, coming to a stop in front of a large monitor, where she pounded on a keyboard in frantic bursts that sounded like the rat-tat-tat of a machine gun. She bounced her Converse-clad feet as characters flew across the screen.

"Son of a bitch," Bailey finally muttered at a stream of letters and numbers that meant absolutely nothing to Lorin.

"What?" Lorin asked. "What do you see?"

"Actually, it's what I don't see," Bailey said, leaning in to peer at the screen more closely. "There's no sign of it now. It's gone. If the unit was still latched on, we'd see it, right"—Bailey pointed to a tiny stream of characters—"there. Damn it."

"Bailey, are you sure—"

"Yes, and now it's gone."

Gabe glanced to the door leading to the lab, and back at Bailey. "So you were working with the unit in here—"

"It was just lying there on the desk," Bailey said defensively. "I hadn't started my first test yet—"

"Hang on. When the tech unit was in here with you, out of the command box, it latched onto the network," Gabe said. "And now that it's back in the box, there's no sign of it?"

"Yeah."

"So… the box is blocking the signal somehow?"

"Like a Faraday cage? Maybe." Bailey chewed on her lower lip. "But what the hell did it do, what did it access, when it latched on?" Focusing on the screen again, she muttered something about viruses and payloads and core dumps.

Lorin was having trouble understanding the fine technical details, but Freyja, she got the gist. "How did you think to put the unit back in the box in the first place?"

"The box has been down here, closed, for several days now while Gabe ran his initial tests. My network's been clean all that time, was clean when I ran my last diagnostic a couple of hours ago. What's changed? The box was opened, and the unit was removed. I thought putting it back, turning back the clock, would be a good first thing to try." With a sigh, she whirled her stool back toward the screen, where white characters marched across a black background. "We're lucky it worked—or seems to have worked, at any rate—'cuz after that, I had nothin'."

"What's the risk of incursion into SL's network infrastructure?"

Lorin caught her breath.

"Unknown." Bailey looked up to the ceiling, where ten floors of *very* privately held corporation soared overhead. "We're shielded down here, but I won't know anything about the unit's range and capabilities until I examine it—"

"Which won't happen anytime soon," Gabe said darkly. "That thing's staying in that box until—"

"Shit," Lorin blurted. The day she'd found the box—the day she'd accidentally opened it, and noticed the unit and its red glowing light—she'd been attending a Council meeting.

"What's wrong?" Gabe asked.

"Council_Net," she said starkly. "The first time I opened the box, I was attending a Council meeting. I was logged into Council_Net."

Bailey's eyes widened as she considered the implications of a possible breach of the Underworld Council's confidential workspace. "I can't run Council_Net diagnostics from here. I—"

They heard a loud crack. Lorin ran back to the other lab, just in time to see the tread of Lukas's big boot slam into the tempered glass window of the outer door again, lengthening the fissure he'd made, but not yet shattering the glass. Elliott and a uniformed Sebastiani Labs security team stood behind him.

"Damn it. Hold on." Lorin opened the door.

Lukas shouldered into the room, his laser-beam gaze slicing into every corner. "What happened?"

"Get in here," Bailey called from the computer lab. "We've got a couple of problems."

Lukas didn't comply until he'd satisfied himself that everyone was okay, that the lab was clear. After he turned off the alarm and sent the security team back to their stations, she, Gabe, Bailey, Lukas, and Elliott congregated in the computer lab while Bailey explained what had happened. With five people in the small, dim room, space was at a premium. Lukas paced while he, Elliot, and Bailey had a convoluted, jargon-laced conversation about the lab's proprietary shielding technology, and the capabilities of the prototype jammer Bailey had thought to install. Lorin scooted up onto the table to free up more floor space.

Lukas summed up. "So, bottom line, the tech unit may have breached SL and Council_Net."

"That about nails it," Bailey said grimly. "I need to go back to Sebastiani Security to run a Council_Net diagnostic."

"Go," Elliott ordered. "I'll get our network team going here to verify that our shielding held. We'll bring it down until we have more information."

Lorin gulped at Lukas's nod of agreement. An SL network shutdown? This was serious shit.

Bailey shoved tiredly to her feet. "Lorin, Gabe, I'll need your phones."

"Huh?" Though her phone was off most of the time, the prospect of being without it was unexpectedly disconcerting. "It's powered down in my bag next door."

"I need to check them out," Bailey said. "Not that I actually know what the hell I'm looking for yet."

Bailey walked over to Gabe and held out her hand.

"Shit," he muttered. Color flushing over his cheeks, he glanced at Elliott. "Sorry."

Elliott smiled slightly. "I've heard the word before."

Reaching to the holder at his waistband, Gabe slowly handed over his Bat Phone, as reluctant as a parent leaving his child with a babysitter for the first time.

"Oh, you have a prototype."

"I don't appear to have it anymore."

"Nope," Bailey responded without sympathy. To Lukas, she said, "This would be a great opportunity to probe Council_Net for other susceptibilities. As long as I'm—"

"Bailey, there are too many projects on your plate as it is. Most of them are behind schedule."

"Just pointing out that there's a silver lining here. C'mon, who needs sleep?" Bailey quipped.

You do. Bailey looked like she'd pulled too many all-nighters as it was. So much responsibility rested on the shoulders of this single, frail human.

"Are you done down here for the day?" Elliott asked Gabe. "I have a couple of questions about that proposed budget you sent last night."

Gabe shot Lorin an apologetic glance. "Sure, Elliott."

So, he *hadn't* forgotten what they'd been up to before all technological hell had broken loose. She sighed heavily. Damn. Even without computers, even with a possible breach, business went on. She had some work to catch up on herself. "Touch base with me later, Gabe."

As Lorin turned over her phone to Bailey, she wondered if Gabe would hear the invitation in her words—and if he heard it, would he take her up on it?

"Aah…" Even as his legs collapsed, even as the floor tipped up to smack him, Beddoe closed his eyes to protect them from the searing light. He'd materialized into a dark, seething cauldron: sharp spears of light. Ozone. A huge shock wave of sound built, rolling and rumbling, threatening to cleave the world in two. He clapped his hands over his ears.

Had Minchin finally made his move, sending his captain to a fiery death?

Suddenly the room… quieted. Stilled. Hesitantly opening his eyes and dropping his hands from his ears, he sat up and checked his 'comp: *Thunderstorm. A seasonal weather phenomena comprised of rain, lightning, thunder.*

As he read further, the workroom's shapes and shadows formed, grounding him: the wall of shelves. The window, flashing with strobes of light. A table leg. He'd fallen near the table where, last night, he'd suckled from

Paige's body—a delicacy that still thrummed through his body and mind.

Outside, projectiles pounded, rhythmic and musical. Dragging himself up from the floor, he carefully walked to the window. He peered out and grabbed onto the windowsill to keep from falling again.

Clean water—*rain*—fell from the sky. The planet was so abundant with water that it fell from the sky and flowed freely over the land.

Rain. Such a simple word to describe a treasure beyond price.

Dia. Even if he never found the wreckage of the *Arkapaedis* and couldn't claim the bounty, possessing the cryotube would more than meet his needs. If the cryo's precious cargo was still viable, he could claim this world—so many worlds—as his own.

All he had to do was take it.

He flicked a tiny button at his wrist, illuminating the tabletop with a narrow-beamed light. He swept the light over its surface—its clean, empty surface. *Where was...* Shoving down the panic, he searched the shelves, the desk and its drawers, even the tiny room that Paige had hidden him in last night.

Nothing. The cryotube was gone.

Lorin jerked awake at the light touch on her shoulder. "Gabe?"

"No, dear," her mother said softly. "It's me. Are you expecting Gabriel?"

Lorin sat up, disgusted to find that she'd fallen asleep at her desk with her hand buried in a bag of Cheetos.

Was she expecting Gabe? "No, not really." She'd hoped Gabe might seek her out after his meeting with Elliott was over, but she'd worked for several hours, waiting, hitting the snacks like an addict did his pipe. "What time is it?" she asked while she stretched, glancing to the big window overlooking her mother's desk. It was full dark outside, but that didn't tell her much.

Alka glanced at her slim, black-banded watch. "Just past 1:00 a.m."

And no Gabe. Had he called? She reached for her messenger bag, stopping with her arm extended. She didn't have a phone anymore; Bailey had taken it. She had Gabe's, too. He'd need to use a landline to call her, use someone's desk phone—duh, desk phone. She glanced at the whiz-bang machine sitting, dusty and neglected, on the corner of her desk. The thing had so many features that frankly, it intimidated her, but she'd managed to use it earlier to retrieve Elliott's message notifying SL employees that their technology use would be limited to internal communications and local work until further notice.

The message light was dark. And she was staring at the phone like a lovesick teenager.

Suck it up, Schlessinger.

Sitting up with a lurch, she stuck her forefinger in her mouth to suckle off the neon orange Cheetos dust, taking in her mother's simple black linen pants, matching tunic, and stunning fire-opal necklace. The large collar covering most of her upper chest was priceless, an ancestral piece, but her mother wore the ornate jewels with a royal's casual confidence.

"How was your dinner with Valerian?" she asked.

Alka snagged the Cheetos bag for herself, walked to her own desk, and sat down. "Just fine. Valerian was quite the raconteur tonight, in fine form. But that might have had something to do with the wine. Oh my stars, the wine."

While her mother rhapsodized over the vintage Wyland had selected from Valerian's incomparable wine cellar, Lorin's thoughts turned bittersweet. Even for a species as long-lived as vampires, Valerian was ancient. While deteriorating health was to be expected at such a great age, Valerian's condition had taken a marked turn for the worse this year, prompting urgent action by both Alka and Wyland. Most of their peoples' known history had been catalogued by this one man, written in his distinctive, sprawling script as he whispered into rulers' ears from behind countless royal thrones, in innumerable smoke-filled rooms, sitting on the periphery of history, influencing it on their species' behalf. Plumbing his fading memories had become an urgent priority. Alka had started recording his oral histories during a series of weekly dinners, a digital recorder lying beside the heavy Georgian cutlery, catching every word of their wide-ranging conversation. Wyland, Valerian's chosen successor, had all but moved in to Valerian's hulking old house, perched on the cliffs overlooking the St. Croix River, to maximize their time together.

"Why are you here, not at home?" Lorin asked around a jaw-cracking yawn.

"Wyland makes a vicious espresso. I'm wide awake." Reaching over, Alka carefully extracted a single Cheeto from the bag. "I thought I'd catch up on some work. I never figured you'd be here."

Lorin told her mother about what had happened in the lab earlier in the day, that Bailey suspected that the tech unit had somehow attached to her test network. "You don't seem surprised."

Alka shrugged fatalistically. "Carl always said that math might be the closest thing we have to a universal language." Though Council Humanity Chair Carl Sagan had died before Lorin took her own Council seat, she'd spent many happy hours simply sitting at his feet as he'd examined the petroglyphs up at Isabella. "I miss Carl," she said. "I could really use his counsel right about now."

"So could we all," her mother said, reaching into the bag. "So tell me how things are going up at the dig. Did the site winter well? How is the crew this year?"

As they munched, Lorin updated her mother on the significant happenings up at the dig, telling her about the capsule Nathan had unearthed, and the odd, metal-flecked trees she and Gabe had found. She didn't reveal to her mother just what she and Gabe had been doing at the time of discovery. "And Paige has a boyfriend."

"Really? Did Mike finally make a move?"

"Nope. Dude's a vamp she met at Tubby's." Lorin shrugged. "I'm not sure Mike quite knows what to think. I don't know what to think either. We don't know anything about this guy."

"They're adults with their own lives," Alka gently reminded her. "There's a line."

"Yeah. Speaking of which…" Reaching into her lower desk drawer, Lorin withdrew a bag of fun-sized Snickers and tore it open, scattering candy bars over the top of her desk. "Why didn't you say anything about Gabe's eyes, his macular degeneration?"

"Lorin, his medical condition is none of my business, unless it influences his job performance. It's his news to share, or not." A pause. "Damn it," Alka muttered, snatching a candy bar. "I know he had an appointment with his retinologist this week. How did it go?"

"Mom, he hasn't said anything at all—and we've worked together in that damn lab, alone, for two days straight. He's had every chance in the world to bring it up, and he hasn't. What I *do* know, I heard from Andi." As she told her mother about Gabe's cataract diagnosis, she kept her hands busy unwrapping candy bars. How in the world could anyone call these microscopic tidbits fun-sized? They were way too small. "His family seems to have a lot of health problems."

Alka sighed. "It's a problem for the wolves in general. If they bonded and bred outside their species more often, their genetic line would grow more resilient, but Krispin—gah." She threw up her hands. "There's no talking to the man."

"Nope." Lorin tossed a candy bar into her mouth and chewed. Though not codified by any law, Krispin Woolf, and generations of alphas before him, had made their strong preference for wolf/wolf mating bonds crystal clear.

"Speaking of mating, how are you and Gabriel getting along?"

Lorin coughed on her candy bar then held up a hand as she choked it down. "Geez, Mom."

"If that clinch I interrupted down in the lab is anything to go by, I'd say very well indeed. His quiet strength, your exuberance. I knew you two would be a good match."

"A good match? Mother, we fight like lions in a

cage." At her comment, Alka laughed—so hard that she reached for a tissue to wipe tears from her eyes. "I'm so glad I amuse you."

"My poor, deluded darling. Lorin, the sexual tension between the two of you has been brewing for ages. So, have you done anything about it?"

"Mom. Not going there."

Alka fanned herself with her hand. "Those wolves. Even the betas are such… vigorous lovers."

Up against a tree. On the pine needles carpeting the forest floor. On her firm mattress. *Vigorous? Hell, yes.* "Mother…"

"Ha! No denials from you."

How could she explain all the factors at play? "Mom, it's… complicated."

"Most worthwhile things are," her mother said serenely. "So, you're a problem-solver. What do you want to achieve, and what's the biggest obstacle standing in your way?"

"What do I want?" Her mother's question had a very simple answer: Gabe. She wanted Gabe. What did she want from him? *More.* The word jumped into her head, no thought required. More than a working relationship, more than a sexual relationship. She wanted… more.

Ah, damn, Andi was right. Her feelings *were* involved. She raised a hand to her suddenly queasy stomach.

"It'll be okay, Lorin."

Her mother's voice didn't soothe. How would it be okay? "I have no idea whether he wants the same thing. Hell, I *know* he doesn't. He might want me sexually, but this is Gabe we're talking about. He doesn't think it's ethical to get involved with a subordinate."

Alka frowned. "But—your reporting relationship is a formality. You're peers. You handle the site work, he handles the paperwork."

"Gabe doesn't see it that way. I still don't know what caused him to change his mind about us sleeping together, but he did. We—" Her cheeks flushed again. "We were having what I thought was a mutually satisfying physical relationship, but just before we came back south, he ended it. Now?" She shrugged. "He seems like he might be interested again. I just don't know what's going on in his head."

Alka smiled. "I think this is the first time I've heard you express interest in what a lover might be thinking and feeling."

"Physical's always been enough in the past," Lorin groused. "I don't like this… emotional stuff. I don't understand it. It makes me feel really… off-balance."

Alka laughed merrily, and Lorin heard not one whiff of sympathy. "I envy you, my darling. Though I've known some fascinating men in my life, I've never come close to falling in love again since your father."

Love? Freyja help me. "Ugh." She shoved the candy bars away with a groan. Her wrist bumped her mouse, deactivating her screen saver, revealing a small window on her desktop that hadn't been open when she'd last looked at it.

Instant messages. From Gabe.

And she'd slept through them all.

Chapter 14

INSIDE THE CONTAINMENT HOOD, SOMETHING NUDGED Gabe's wrist.

"Shit," he blurted, yanking his hands out of the integrated gloves. He stared, openmouthed, as the blocky assemblage at one end of the capsule—the end he'd just finished measuring, using what he thought had been a very delicate touch—pivoted on a hidden axis, rotating away from the body of the unit.

An inner compartment slid out, exposing approximately two dozen slim, translucent vials.

"Holy…" His gaze flicked to the recording equipment to ensure it was functioning. Was the unit mechanical? Pneumatic? It hadn't made a sound, not one that he could hear, at any rate. Two of the vials were clearly damaged, their contents dried and brown. One vial's protective lid had cracked off entirely.

He leaned in with a squint as the biohood's ventilation system hissed and pumped, carrying the potentially contaminated air up and away, capturing it for later study. His glove, thankfully, appeared intact. He now knew exactly how Lorin had felt when she'd accidentally opened the box up at the Isabella site.

"Cameras running, containment intact," Anna Mae Whitman confirmed from the other side of the table as she studied the readout on the monitor adjacent to the hood. "Look at that CO_2 level, and organic matter in the tubes. Ain't that a fine howdy-do."

And Lorin had transported the thing here in a freaking messenger bag. Jesus. It was sheer dumb luck that the capsule hadn't opened, leaving her breathing potentially tainted air.

"No toxins—that we have tests for, at any rate. Containment's still holding." Slipping her hands back into her set of integrated gloves, Anna Mae lightly touched one of the unbroken cylinders. "Come over here. Look at this."

He rounded the table. Once he looked at the vials from Anna Mae's vantage point, he saw what she did. Each vial sported a set of characters—or were they symbols?—he couldn't decipher. "A label of some type?" he theorized.

Anna Mae nodded. "We're gonna need linguistic anthro."

His poor project plan was already into triple-digit revisions, and he'd revised it again late last night, after his meeting with Elliott was over and Lorin hadn't responded to his instant messages. Given yesterday afternoon's technological misadventure, Bailey Brown's task list ran nearly two pages on its own—and now, with a single touch, a silent slide, he'd need linguistics, biochem, and probably mechanical engineering.

Managing this project had somehow turned into two full-time jobs.

"I should be able to determine the biochemical composition of what's in those vials pretty quickly, but for mechanical, you'll want Elliott." She removed her hands from the gloves again, smiling. "Let's get him down here."

Gabe blinked, quickly following as she walked toward the phone hanging next to the door separating the biohazard lab from the air lock and changing room. "You can't just dial him up, Dr. Whitman." Between his responsibilities as the CEO of Sebastiani Labs and his Council presidency, Elliott Sebastiani's schedule was so tight it squeaked.

"Sure I can," she said. "I do it all the time. Believe me, he'll want to see this for himself."

She was right. Not fifteen minutes later, Gabe watched, bemused, as Elliott Sebastiani arrived, already slipping off his suit coat. Opening a locker—his own?—he extracted a lab coat and shrugged into it. After slipping shoe coverings over his Italian loafers, he dipped his hand into the lab coat's right pocket, snagging a black elastic band, which he used to lash back his hair.

"Gabe." Elliott greeted him with a handshake and a slap on the shoulder. "Just what kind of shenanigans have you and Anna Mae been up to this afternoon?" They approached the brightly lit table. "Well." Elliott walked around all four sides of the table, carefully assessing the tightly hooded tableau, and then glanced at the monitor. "Interesting CO_2 reading," he commented to Anna Mae.

She nodded. "Especially given how little atmosphere was released from the capsule in the first place."

The hair stood up on Gabe's forearms as he finally comprehended the implications of Anna Mae's previous comment. The atmosphere released from the capsule had changed the composition of the air in the biohood.

The atmosphere in the capsule could be Earth's, from over a thousand years ago.

Or it could be from someplace else entirely.

The hours passed without notice. Elliott and Anna Mae worked like a well-oiled machine, analyzing the capsule, its contents, and the atmospheric data with plenty of theorizing and debate. Gabe, after initially feeling pretty damn useless, was the one to discover the ingenious touch pad that opened and closed the capsule. While he took close-up photos of the vials and their labels, he heard a muffled pounding at the lab door.

From the changing room, the intercom crackled. "Elliott. I need a word. Now."

Alka. Alka and Lorin, standing at her mother's side. Arms crossed over their chests, standing tall, the Schlessinger women looked battle-ready and bent on vengeance. Without quite understanding why, Gabe lifted the camera and clicked.

What were they doing here? Alka had told him earlier in the day that she and Lorin were going to be busy with Council matters. Now, Lorin scoured the lab's ceiling and corners with hard, flat eyes.

Elliott stood ramrod straight. The relaxed lab partner Gabe had spent the afternoon working with transformed into his CEO and Council president between one breath and the next. "Start shutting down," he ordered, stripping off his lab coat as he strode to the door.

"Shit's hit the fan," Anna Mae murmured.

Alka and Elliott talked in the changing room, their heads close together as they examined a sheet of paper Alka held. Suddenly, Lorin waved her arms overhead to get his attention—as if his attention had ever really left her in the first place. Geez, with her arms raised like that, how could he look anywhere other than—

Lorin rolled her eyes, pointing to her own head in a classic "eyes up here, buddy" gesture, but he noticed her amusement—dare he think it was pleasure?—for just a moment before she rested her upraised forefinger over her own lips.

The universal signal for silence. What the hell…?

She twirled her finger, indicating the lab.

Then mouthed "bugged."

—◦◦◦—

"How the hell did this happen?" With a clack of keys, Elliott retrieved the email Krispin Woolf had sent to every member of the Underworld Council not an hour before—the same email that had sent Alka and Lorin hightailing downstairs to the lab—and displayed it on the large monitor mounted on his office wall near the conference table.

"Don't know yet." Lukas's voice was controlled, locked down tight. "A team is tearing the lab apart as we speak."

Lorin stared at Krispin's email. She and her mother had been reviewing their presentation for tomorrow's Council meeting when Krispin's demand for an updated agenda had arrived. The command box and its contents were nothing new—every member of the Council had watched her accidentally open the box at their last meeting—but the potential breach of their network by the tech unit? The discovery of a metal capsule, a capsule that had unexpectedly opened, potentially exposing toxic organic material? That was information that even *she* didn't have. She'd hightailed down to the lab with her mother to make sure Gabe was okay. She'd never been so relieved to have her rack ogled in her life.

So how the hell had Krispin come by his information? That was the question that had ratchetted everyone up to DEFCON 1.

"Are you sure you're okay?" she murmured to Gabe, sitting next to her on Elliott's sleek leather love seat. She touched his chino-covered thigh just above the knee. He felt solid, reassuringly warm. Alive. Hearing that the capsule had opened while he worked with it, exposing cracked vials filled with gawd knew what, chilled her blood.

"It opened under the hood," he responded, covering her hand with his own. "I'm fine."

She stared at their joined hands. Did he realize what he'd just done? In front of her mother? In front of Elliott?

He twined their fingers together, sandwiching her chilly digits in blessed warmth. "Hey, at least I'm not dialing into this meeting from quarantine."

"Not funny."

"Sorry. Bad joke. It's just sheer dumb luck that the capsule opened where and when it did, and not when Nathan was excavating, when Mike was cataloguing, or when you transported it down here in your messenger bag. Keeping the crew in the dark is making me very uncomfortable."

Nodding her agreement, she gestured to the screen where Krispin's email mocked them. "So much for confidentiality."

Lukas looked spitting mad. His sweeps hadn't picked up any monitoring devices, and there had to be one somewhere. Thank Freyja that she and Gabe had never actually made love down in the lab. It was disgusting enough to think that Krispin Woolf had probably watched them touch each other fully clothed.

"Can we watch our recording again, please?" Alka asked from her seat at the small conference table.

With a couple of clicks of keys, Krispin's email disappeared, replaced by nine squares, one for each camera, displayed in classic Tic-Tac-Toe formation, recording every action that took place at the work surfaces, biohood, and entryways. Very few blind spots, Lorin noted with a sinking stomach. The capabilities and location of Krispin's monitoring equipment was still a wild card, but it seemed highly likely that at least one of their own cameras had recorded the… extracurricular encounters she'd had with Gabe.

It was *way* too easy to forget about the damn cameras.

Elliot selected one of the boxes, enlarged it, and with a couple of clicks, there was Gabe, earlier in the day. As Elliott fast-forwarded, Gabe pulled at his hair, wrote on a clipboard, and punched data into a handheld computer like Speedy Gonzales. Lorin glanced at her mother, then Elliott. Had either of them noticed how often Gabe removed his glasses to rub his eyes?

"Gabe, can you walk us through?" Elliott asked.

"Sure."

Lorin gave his hand a quick squeeze.

The timestamp in the corner showed a little after 1:00 p.m., barely three hours ago. On-screen, she watched Gabe and Anna Mae work—carefully, and following biohazard protocol to the letter. Beside her, Gabe's body tensed, telegraphing what was coming. Even though she knew what to expect, Lorin gasped as she watched the blocky end of the capsule slowly rotate, nudging an unsuspecting Gabe on his gloved hand. On-screen, he jumped. Swore. Stared in awe as an inner compartment slid smoothly from the capsule's outer covering.

Translucent vials, standing upright. Two of them brown and crusty, clearly breached.

"Thank Freyja the capsule was under the hood," her mother said.

They watched as the on-screen Gabe talked with Anna Mae Whitman, and as Anna Mae crossed the room to call Elliott.

Elliott paused the playback. "After I came down, we worked for—oh, two hours?" He looked to Gabe for verification of his estimate. Gabe nodded. "And before you ask, Lukas," Elliott continued, "no one left the lab, even to use the bathroom. We didn't leave each other's sight. None of us could have contacted Krispin."

At her side, Gabe stilled.

She twisted around in her seat to stare at Lukas, who leaned against the wall by the door, arms crossed over his chest, studying Gabe like he was a smear under a microscope. Krispin Woolf was Gabe's alpha, and Lukas's job was to be a suspicious son of a bitch.

Gabe gestured to the screen. "You can roll the play-back to confirm," he said evenly.

"I will," Lukas said without apology.

"Lukas, Gabe couldn't have contacted anyone if he wanted to," Lorin snapped. "Bailey took our phones last night." Turning to Gabe, she asked, "Have you replaced your phone yet?"

"No. I fell asleep in my office last night. I haven't left the building since yesterday morning."

The IMs he'd sent—the messages she'd stupidly slept through—had asked her to join him there. Though the words had been circumspect enough, they'd shimmered with intent. He'd wanted her. She hadn't responded. And now, here they were, holding hands, tense as two kids at their first dance.

She was so confused.

"Speaking of phones…" Lukas levered himself off the wall, reached into the black leather bag he'd dropped next to the door when he arrived, and extracted a Bat Phone. Walking to the love seat, he bypassed Gabe and handed it to her instead. "Sorry, Gabe, your replacement isn't quite ready yet. Bailey's still retrieving your email and contact lists."

Gabe nodded.

Lorin sighed in relief. Lukas wouldn't be giving Gabe another prototype if he seriously suspected him of a security breach. When Lukas handed her the phone, she pointedly reached for it with her left hand, leaving her right clasped in Gabe's. "Thank you."

"You're welcome." As he walked around the back of the couch, he scrubbed his big knuckles against the top of her head.

"Stop it," she muttered, batting his hand away.

"Children." Elliott yanked off the black elastic band holding back his hair. "Can we get back to the business at hand?"

"Sorry." She studied the freeze-framed playback, which showed Gabe staring down in awe at the open capsule glinting under the hood. Noting the timestamp in the corner, she raised a brow. "Look at the time Krispin sent the email."

Lukas nodded grimly. "He's got to have a real-time feed."

"Gabe." Her mother spoke from the conference table. "Have you spoken to Krispin about this project in any way? Even—"

"Not one word, Alka," Gabe broke in. "I never talk with the alpha about my work. He has only the vaguest idea of what I do here."

"He knows more now." Lukas picked up his chirping mini. "Jack." The longer he listened, the more his expression darkened. "Hang on a sec." He pointed to the monitor, still displaying Gabe's freeze-framed face. "Can you get me a live feed?"

Elliott re-retrieved the nine-camera view. Click, click. Each box now displayed Lukas's security team, probing, scanning, and examining the floors, walls, and work surfaces with equipment Lorin wasn't familiar with. Ceiling panels rested against the walls, and any equipment that had previously been attached to the walls now lay on the floor. Jack stood next to the phone Anna Mae had used to call Elliott, a stoic expression on his face. The reason for his expression stood on the other side of the closed door. Supervising from the changing room, Anna Mae Whitman banged on the window with her fist, ripping Jack a new one via intercom.

"Camera Two?" Lukas asked. Elliott maximized the view Lukas had requested—just in time to see heavy boots and jean-clad legs emerge from a hole in the ceiling, right over the biohood.

No wonder Anna Mae was swearing so much.

Chico dropped onto the table with a thunk, straddling the biohood like it was a bull he was about to take for an eight-second ride. "Parallel feed, manually patched into the main," he reported to Jack.

Overhearing, Lukas's big fist clenched.

"Very low tech," Chico continued. "Sweeps wouldn't have caught it."

"Rip it out," Lukas said to Jack. "The whole thing, his and ours. Now."

Jack relayed the message to Chico. Reaching up with both hands, Chico levered himself back up into the hole over the biohood. The tip of his steel-toed boot brushed against the housing of the hood's ventilation system.

"Be careful!" Anna Mae squawked over the intercom. "Do you have any idea how expensive—"

The feed went to static.

Gabe sat still and tense at her side as Lukas asked Jack to haul the recording equipment back to Sebastiani Security. Her mother, sitting closest to the hissing monitor, snapped, "Can you turn that off? Please."

Elliott complied, redisplaying Krispin's email.

Lukas hung up, looking at his father with disbelief. "Dad, why the hell do you let Woolf on the property, much less give him lab space?"

Elliott eyed Lukas. "You've heard the saying, 'Keep your friends close and your enemies closer'? If he's working here, I know what he's doing."

"And now he knows what *we're* doing."

"Yes," Elliott acknowledged, leaning back in his office chair, steepling his fingers. "He likely installed the equipment to monitor his own people while they worked—"

"Dad—"

"But he left the equipment installed after they vacated, and that I can't abide."

The tension in the room rose, a river about to over-flow its banks.

Her mother finally asked the billion-dollar question. "Elliott, what was Krispin doing down there that was worth taking such a risk?"

"Genetic research," Elliott responded. "He's trying to get some insight into his wolves' deteriorating health."

Gabe flinched again, the action rippling into her body where their thighs and shoulders touched.

"Damn it, Dad, why didn't you tell me?" Lukas paced at the back of the room. "I can't do jack shit without complete information."

"Elliott, why doesn't the Council know about this project?" Alka asked.

Elliott stared at Krispin's silent email message with a gaze as sharp as honed steel. "He's sequencing his own DNA, and funding the work himself. He asked for my discretion. But he's abused my trust for the last time."

Lorin's eyes widened at his tone.

"Change of plans for tomorrow's Council meeting." Elliott studied Gabe, then said, "Gabe, I'm sorry for putting you in such an untenable position with your alpha. Please accept my thanks—"

"No," Gabe blurted. "The work's not done yet. I want to stay with this."

"Gabe," Lorin said softly. "Krispin's going to be pissed enough that you didn't tell him what you were working on."

Gabe's laugh was humorless, ragged around the edges. "Let's get real. My family has no political standing to consider or preserve. I'd like to stay on."

Elliott considered Gabe, then looked at their still-twined fingers. Finally he nodded.

Lorin squeezed Gabe's hand. She'd taken on Krispin Woolf before—and she'd do it again if it meant protecting Gabe from his alpha—but Elliott's support was no small matter.

Elliott clicked on the "Reply All" button to respond to Krispin's request. The only sound in the office was the soft tap of fingers against keys as he typed a short, succinct message, and hit "Send."

"Ah, crap," she breathed. Elliott had requested an agenda addition of his own—a status update on Krispin's genetic research project—copying everyone on the Council.

This was going to get ugly.

⁓⁓⁓

When Gabe told Elliott that he wanted to stay on, he hadn't anticipated being pulled into an all-nighter with most of the members of the Underworld Council—nor had he expected to wake up the following morning on his office couch, the sun shining through his window, holding Lorin Schlessinger in his arms again.

Some things were worth incurring his alpha's wrath.

Still asleep, she tried to shift her weight, tugging on the corner of the blanket he'd hastily pulled over them after they'd stumbled, wordless, to his office after finishing long hours of work. The couch he'd spent many a night upon by himself was a very tight squeeze for two, so all she accomplished with her movements was to snuggle her ass more closely against his groin—which shouted that it was wide awake and ready for action.

Closing his eyes again, he tightened his arm around her torso, tugging her long frame away from the edge and back against his own body, savoring the sensation of simply holding her again. Her surfer-girl hair was loose, sprawled over most of their shared pillow, exposing the nape of her neck.

Gabe bent his head and wallowed in her scent, a combination of rosemary-mint shampoo, sea salt body scrub, and warm skin. Even though they'd been away from Isabella for days, he still smelled the mildest hint of pine.

He stilled when she shifted her head on the pillow. Gulped when she clasped his hand with an inarticulate murmur, tugging it up so it rested between her breasts.

And then she settled back to sleep again.

She was exhausted and needed to sleep. He should be sleeping too. The day to come would be challenging, to say the least.

Should I call Mom and Dad? Gideon? At least give them a heads up? He sighed as he imagined the conversation: "Mom, Dad… there's good news and bad news. The good news is that I'm making my first presentation before the Underworld Council. The bad news? As soon as it's over the alpha will likely boot me from the pack."

There was sure to be some blowback from what he was going to do later today, but he'd protect his family to the best of his ability. And after last night, he knew he'd have all the help he could get.

How had he acquired such high-powered allies? He could call Elliott on the phone, call him by his first name. Alka, the Valkyrie First, called him "dear." And Lorin, the Valkyrie Second? He looked down at the sleeping bundle, blinking against the milky haze that never quite cleared. In some ways, he knew her intimately, but in so many others, she was a complete enigma. One thing he was sure of? Lorin had his back.

When the hell had *that* happened?

Last night, long into the night, he'd worked alongside some other members of the Underworld Council he didn't know as well. Barely an hour after they'd watched Elliott send his succinct reply to Krispin, the CEO's office looked and sounded more like a cocktail party in full swing than a meeting location. Elliott's bondmate, Siren First Claudette Fontaine, had been the first to arrive, with Elliott's daughter, Incubus Second Antonia Sebastiani, in tow. Lukas's bondmate, Scarlett Fontaine, pulled in a few minutes later—and yeah, he'd covertly stared at the famous singer whose public profile had dropped to near-zero since she'd become the Siren Second. Thanks to Alka, he'd been fortunate enough to attend Scarlett's last public performance at Underbelly last fall, the night her sister Annika had been killed.

The night he'd ended his relationship with Kayla.

After kissing Lukas hello—a greeting so lengthy and enthusiastic that they really should have taken it somewhere else—Scarlett had picked up Elliott's desk phone and placed a monstrous order for Vietnamese food. Jack Kirkland came upstairs from the lab. Elliott's assistant, Willem Lund, had magically produced a huge urn of coffee, and then conferenced in Valerian and Wyland from Valerian's place near the Wisconsin border, their faces peering into the room from the monitor hanging on the wall. Lorin finally reappeared, carrying her messenger bag and the memory stick she'd gone to her office to retrieve.

Elliott, Claudette, and Antonia. Alka and Lorin. Lukas and Scarlett. Jack and Willem. So many Council members crowded into Elliott's office that they didn't have room for everyone to sit, but that didn't seem to matter. Lukas tugged Scarlett onto his lap, and Antonia perched, cross-legged, on the corner of her father's desk. Jack leaned against the same wall Lukas had earlier, in a position so similar it was uncanny.

Krispin had sent a warning shot over the bow with his initial email, and Elliott had returned fire—but the bare-knuckled tactical and strategic firepower on display during the session that followed quite frankly exhausted him. He and Lorin had huddled side by side behind Elliott's desk, muttering and murmuring, incorporating the long hours of strategy into Lorin's presentation— now *their* presentation—as it was displayed on the large screen for everyone to see as they typed. Sequences of events were brainstormed, analyzed, their risks assessed, and argued out to their logical, sometimes brutal, con- clusions. Lukas scribbled flowcharts on Elliott's huge e-board, with Antonia often challenging her father's or brother's analysis, displaying intelligence beyond her years and a stunningly Machiavellian mind-set. By the end of the meeting, the possible outcomes listed in the boxes crawling along the bottom of the e-board ranged from "Defer topic to next meeting" to "Imprison WerePack Alpha." And he'd overheard so many details about the Council's other activities during breaks and casual side-conversations that he yearned for some brain bleach. No wonder Lorin needed so much downtime. He

would, too, if he had to deal with the same nasty crap
that apparently greeted her every time she logged on
to Council_Net.

Finally, after much stretching and yawning, the presentation was complete and the strategy set—and without discussing it, he and Lorin had stumbled to his office
together, collapsed on the couch, and fallen asleep.

And now it was morning, the sun was shining, and
Lorin was shifting, turning in his arms so she faced him.
Settling again. He lifted his arm momentarily, bringing
his watch close enough to his face so he could read the
large digital display: 7:10 a.m. The Council meeting
started in three hours.

Nerves eddied in his stomach. Shit, he was making
a presentation before the Underworld Council. And
despite a couple of stolen moments in the lab—despite
her presence on this couch—he and Lorin hadn't
settled a damn thing between them yet. He hadn't told
her that he'd made a mistake, yearned to share her bed
again, on whatever terms she wanted. And if he wanted
more than sex? If his emotions had gotten a little more
snarled up in the situation than hers had? He'd keep it
to himself.

"Gabe." With a soft, sleepy sigh, she cuddled closer,
bringing her breasts flush against his chest.

He stilled, breath snagging in his throat. Was she
still asleep? Did she know what she was doing? The sun
slanted into the open window, spilling bright, unforgiving light over her hair and face. Her thickly lashed eyes
were still closed. The tensions of the day hadn't caught
up with her yet, so the twin grooves that sometimes appeared between her slashing eyebrows were nowhere to

be seen. The corners of her bare lips were tipped up in a sleepy, satisfied smile.

Had he ever seen her wear a lick of makeup? He didn't think so.

Lorin's hand emerged from under the blanket, stroking up his cheekbone and sliding into his hair. "You're not wearing your glasses," she murmured against his jaw.

"I usually don't when I'm sleeping."

She stroked his temple, where the bow usually rode. "But you usually do when we make love."

Something in Gabe's chest leaped at her words. "I can't see very well without them," he finally said in the understatement of the decade, trailing his fingertip over her eyebrow. "And when we make love"—he repeated her words gingerly, experimentally—"I want to see every inch of you."

There was no panicked expression, no rush to correct him. Instead, she brought their heads together, nuzzled his lips with hers, and looked at him with mossy green eyes filled with sleepy desire. "Where are they?"

"Never mind," he whispered. "I'm pretty good working by touch." There wasn't an inch of her body that wasn't burned into his memory, and he wanted to revisit every one.

A tiny sound came from her throat, a release of breath escaping. "Yes, you are." She licked the corner of his lip with her agile pink tongue. She suckled at it, then started unfastening the pearl snaps of her denim work shirt, working her way down, exposing her bright purple bra. The shirt finally unbuttoned, and Lorin wrestled out of it, her writhing and shifting bringing their bodies into electrifying contact at the groin.

She was destroying him, one molecule at a time.

Leaving her to fight with the cuffs, he cupped her satin and lace-covered breasts, closing his eyes as the tender weight filled his hand. Lorin might live in denim shirts, fleece, cargo pants, and work boots, but his kick-ass Valkyrie Princess wore silk and satin against her skin. He never knew what kind of girly confection he'd find under her utilitarian clothes.

Her shirt now gone, Lorin climbed atop him and made quick work of his. His oxford shoved aside, she jerked his snowy white T-shirt out from his waistband, shoved it up under his arms, and threaded her fingers through the hair on his pecs, tugging so deliciously that he moaned. Her mouth replaced her hands, nibbling and suckling, stroking the sensitive skin under his arms before continuing oh-so-lightly down his sides.

He shivered at the sensation, clenched his teeth. Who knew his sides were erogenous zones? The things this woman taught him. His cock punched against the layers of fabric separating their bodies, and he grabbed her hips to tug them more tightly together. She leaned down, and suddenly his nipple was in her mouth. "Jesus." His fingers clutched her head convulsively. His hips churned, seeking a firmer touch. He shuddered as her lips curved against his hypersensitive skin, shivered when her long, streaky hair dragged over his chest and abs as she transferred her attention to his other nipple.

With a twist of his hand, her bra was unfastened, sagging off her shoulders. Lorin lifted her torso, sending the silky garment sliding down her arms to drape over his rib cage. As she wrenched at the fastening of his pants, he blindly reached for hers. Not being able to see what he was doing heightened his sense of touch. He felt the hard disk of the brass button, could practically read the raised words ridging its rim. Smaller brass buttons marched down the fly under a placket of fabric.

He knew these pants, soft and pliable from countless washings. All he had to do was tug. When he did, the buttons slipped open easily, exposing more purple fabric.

Matching panties. Gabe closed his eyes, rested his palm against the silky fabric. Above him, Lorin gasped, stilled momentarily, then finally located the tab of his zipper, drawing it down with a soft gnash of metal teeth. Gabe sighed in relief as the fabric loosened, gaped.

Her downward progress was impeded by her own body position. Suddenly, Gabe wished—violently— that he had his glasses on so he could better see her hand, poised next to his at the V of her legs. Rising up on her knees, she shifted down his body a couple of crucial inches, the movement causing her pants to sag at the back.

I'm a dead man. But what a way to go, because she was finally touching him, cupping him, measuring every inch of his rampant need with her clever, clever hands. When she leaned down, her hot breath caressed him. His abs clenched. Clenched again as she edged her rough fingers under the elastic waistband of his boxer-briefs.

And something… snapped, broke apart inside, something natural, violent, and inexorable, like ice heaving in the spring, leaving open water in its wake.

His mate.

Chase. Taste. Take.

Clamping an arm around her waist, he tumbled them off the couch and pinned her to the floor, his hips nestled snugly between her spread legs and his hands pinning her wrists to the floor over her head. At this distance, he could see her eyes, the mossy green nearly obliterated by her dilated pupils.

She twined her legs around him. "Love me, Gabe."

I do. But instead of saying it with words, he said it with his hands, tearing off the rest of her clothing, then his own, snagging a condom from his wallet and quickly donning it. Told her with his mouth as he kissed and licked every inch of skin he uncovered. Told her with his body as he plunged into hers, over and over again, until they finally shattered in each other's arms.

Chapter 15

LORIN WATCHED KRISPIN WOOLF PACE THE SEBASTIANI Labs boardroom, his rising voice a tip-off to his growing frustration level. No matter how loudly he repeated his arguments, he hadn't changed anyone's mind. Breach the vials in the capsule and accelerate the pace of genetic research, on the off-chance that one of the vials contained lupine DNA? Gene splicing? No fucking way. On the other hand, Krispin's proposal meant that he accepted the possibility that the capsule might have originated on the *Arkapaedis*, a theory he'd discounted for years.

"Krispin, please calm down. Certainly you can see—"

"I'm immune to your siren's wiles, Claudette."

Lorin's fingers curled, forming fists under the boardroom table. Sitting at her side, Gabe gasped—whether at his alpha's tone or at his words, she didn't know. What she *did* know was that Krispin Woolf, having failed to make his case with questions, arguments, declarations, guilt-mongering, patriotism, and vocal brute force, had now resorted to name-calling. He'd just skated uncomfortably close to calling the Siren First, the Council president's bondmate, a whore, implying that the rest of the Council was operating under her vocal influence.

"Father. Control yourself," Jacoby Woolf said, his voice switchblade-sharp.

Krispin's nose and mouth twitched as he glanced at his wheelchair-bound son. Was Krispin about to shift?

Here? Adrenaline surged, pulling her upright from her comfortable slouch. Shifting in the boardroom was forbidden, tantamount to making a physical threat.

Lukas inhaled, his chest expanding to linebacker proportions as he assessed the room's emotional energy. Jack rose from the table to stand beside Elliott. Lorin stood and joined him, flanking Claudette, weight balanced lightly on the balls of her feet.

Gabe sat wide-eyed, and rightly so. When they'd worked their flowcharts last night, no one had really thought "Imprison WerePack Alpha" was a likely possibility.

"Okay, everyone, it's been a long, stressful day. Let's calm down." Scarlett's voice saturated the room like an anesthetic balm, and Lukas shot her an annoyed look that Lorin completely understood. Though Scarlett had defused the standoff, they'd all be fighting off the effects of her voice for minutes to come, rendering their physical protection less effective. On the other hand, Krispin would feel similar effects.

"Willem, could we take a short break, please?" Claudette asked.

"Certainly."

Krispin turned his back to the room, and Lorin hoped he was making a sincere effort to pull himself together. He had four minutes left on the clock, and then they'd finally be able to vote and get this over with. Any more time than that, and she was sure he'd stroke out.

"Please, take your seats," Elliott murmured to her and Jack. Jack nodded and sat, but the adrenaline coursing through her system was waging a royal battle with the effects of Scarlett's velvet-covered bludgeon of a voice. She needed to move.

She strode to the refreshment station set up along one of the conference room's side walls and poured herself half a cup of coffee. Keeping one eye on Krispin, she paced, sipping caffeine she certainly didn't need. After the meeting was over, she'd work the excess energy out of her system with a vengeance. Eyeing Gabe's wide suit-covered shoulders from behind, she knew exactly how she wanted to proceed.

She looked around the room, where people still milled about after Krispin's near breach of protocol. As Scarlett had noted, it had already been a long, stressful day, with every Council member attending the meeting in person. Two additional seats were filled by Gabe, who sat between Lorin and her mother, and Bailey Brown. They'd started the day hours ago, working through their regular agenda, with Krispin predictably finding "insurmountable" issues with the latest candidate being considered for the open Humanity Chair. Personally, Lorin thought that the very appeal Krispin had cited as a negative in mediagenic physicist Brian Cox was a huge, huge asset. They'd need someone with a firm grasp of media relations if their existence was ever outed to humanity; Dr. Cox's boyish mein and adorable English accent wouldn't hurt one little bit. Voting as a bloc, they'd managed to table further discussion of his candidacy until the next meeting.

Lukas's update on the search for Stephen had been terse and short: "No change since last report." Wyland and Bailey's presentation on the data archiving project showed some forward progress, but the effort was seriously behind schedule due to competing demands on Bailey's time. They'd voted to greatly restrict the Internet privileges of a teenaged were who'd posted a picture of a friend, mid-shift, on a popular social media site.

After breaking for a short lunch, she and Gabe had been up, with her providing a verbal update on the work at the Isabella dig while Gabe clicked through the sequence of pictures they'd chosen: the closed command box as it sat on the cabin's rough wooden table. The open box, a downward shot, taken in the downstairs lab. A sequence of photos of Nathan discovering the capsule, each picture exposing more and more of its freakishly clean, greenish-platinum metal. After much debate, they'd included a picture of the latest discovery, made by Paige just last night, of a stack of silvery, sharp-edged metal pieces found not two feet from where the capsule had been found. Vertically stacked by size, with the largest resting on an intricately woven mat, the pieces had clearly been arranged by sentience rather than by chance. There'd been a collective gasp as Gabe showed some of the nighttime shots he'd taken of the metal-flecked trees, and he'd picked up the presentation from there, displaying one of the samples at extreme magnification. The jagged edges suggested violent manipulation of the metal.

"We also found traces of an unknown accelerant," he said, "supporting the working theory that these pieces may be remnants of the *Arkapaedis*." Gabe suspected the same could be true of the pieces that Paige had just found. With Elliott's full support, they'd asked Anna Mae Whitman to helm the next phase of the lab work, freeing them up to return to Isabella early tomorrow morning. Too many important finds were being made solely by their student crew.

"You have no proof," Krispin had challenged.

"As I stated, Alpha, it's a working theory. There's a lot of work to do yet—both in the lab and at the site."

He'd clicked through more pictures taken down in the Sebastiani Labs basement: the tech unit. The locks of hair. The small totem, the kernels of rice. Bailey then supplied a pithy update on the tech unit's theoretical breach of the Sebastiani Labs and Council_Net networks. "No damage noted so far. Still analyzing." They'd ended their presentation by playing the recording of the capsule opening at Gabe's touch—which Krispin Woolf didn't bother to pretend he hadn't seen before.

Then it was Krispin's turn to reveal details about the genetic research he'd been performing in Sebastiani Labs' basement lab facilities. It was an oral report— the WerePack Alpha was notoriously reluctant to put anything in writing—with each detail being pried out of him like rusty nails from a board, and ending with his unexpected zinger of a demand: access to the organic material in the capsule Nathan had found. His request had been summarily shot down, lighting the fuse on the fireworks still whizzing around the room.

"Let's settle, please," Willem requested. He waited for the room to quiet. "Mr. Woolf, you have four minutes remaining."

Now facing everyone again, Krispin glanced at the clock—and then directly at Gabe.

Trouble. Lorin quickly strode to the table, taking her seat at Gabe's side.

"Gabriel, I don't understand why you, of all people, would disagree with this proposal."

Earlier in the meeting, Gabe *had* disagreed with his alpha—diplomatically, and using the language of science—but publicly, and on the record. The tension which had subsided slightly during the break was now back with a vengeance. At Gabe's other side, her mother's knuckles whitened around her pen. Elliott, Lukas, Jack, and Jacoby had all straightened in their chairs.

The air felt combustible.

"Your own family has been disproportionately impacted by genetic issues," Krispin continued in a voice as smooth as buttercream frosting. "Your eyesight is failing as we speak. I understand surgery is recommended but that a successful outcome is by no means assured. Surely you, of all people, see the benefits of accessing heritage genetic material—"

"Alpha, thank you for your concern, but the condition of my eyes isn't nearly that dire." Using an even, respectful tone, Gabe repeated the arguments he'd made earlier. "We don't yet know what kind of organic material the vials contain. It could be plant or animal matter. We don't know whether it's viable. It could be toxic."

"Even if it's lupine and viable, we don't know how long it might take to sequence the DNA," Elliott said. "The samples themselves might be genetically modified or biohazardous in ways we can't predict. Krispin, I—we"—he gestured to everyone sitting at the table—"share your concern about the wolves' genetic degradation, but you must understand that we have years of research and investigation ahead of us before—"

"You don't know—"

"You're right," Lukas interrupted. "We don't know. We don't have enough information to make an informed decision about your proposal today—a proposal that might put your wolves at greater risk, not less. Even if the capsule contains viable lupine DNA, it will take years of work to refine the technology to the point where we can entrust our people's safety to the process."

Gabe sat, tense, at her side. While every Council member knew there was no love lost between Lukas and the WerePack Alpha, they always presented a united front to their people. Gabe had likely never heard anyone speak quite so frankly to his alpha before.

Krispin's cagey glance now encompassed them both. "Gabriel, now that you've engaged the... ah... interest of the Valkyrie Second, wouldn't you find it worthwhile to investigate ways to improve the health of your future offspring?"

He'd watched them. Of course he had. Lorin's skin crawled, and a flush washed over Gabe's sharp cheekbones. Damn it. Krispin knew Gabe's sore spots, knew exactly where to poke his stick. Reaching under the table, she clasped his hand more tightly.

"Lorin?" Krispin indicated Gabe with a negligent wave of the hand. "Would you taint the Valkyrie line of succession with his issue?"

Sitting in his wheelchair across the table, Jacoby Woolf's expression froze.

"'Taint'? His 'issue'? Krispin, how medieval," she drawled. How in the world could she explain to a man who didn't realize he'd just insulted his own son? "Gabe is smart, loyal, capable, and contributing to the good of our people. Krispin, is Jacoby any less a son, a family member, a friend, a Council member—a man—because he has a motor neuron disease? No, of course not," she answered before he could recover from her conversational sneak-attack. "Neither is Gabe." Pausing, she looked around the jam-packed conference table. "Aren't loved ones loved regardless of the condition of their chromosomes?"

"Any of us who are fortunate to live a long life will develop abnormalities simply due to age," Valerian said with a serenity leavened by nearly nine hundred years of age.

Gabe sat, unmoving as one of Rafe's bronze sculptures, and understandably so. When he'd taken his seat at the boardroom table earlier that day, he couldn't have predicted that his private medical data and his sex life would be on the meeting agenda—or that she'd claim him, publicly and on the record, as her lover.

No, the actual words she'd used were "loved one." She closed her eyes. No wonder he looked stunned.

Opening her eyes again, she took a shaky breath. She'd spoken nothing less than the truth. *In for a penny, in for a pound.* "I could crash my truck and die during tonight's evening rush," she said. "Tomorrow is promised to none of us. I don't know about you, but I'll take today, imperfections and all." She indicated the clock. "Time's up. Let's vote."

Elliott glanced at the clock and nodded. "Willem?"

Up on the large screen, Willem displayed Krispin's proposal. "A 'yes' vote authorizes fast-track genetic research on the contents of the capsule. A 'no' vote tables the topic pending additional analysis." He paused. "Council members, please issue your votes."

Reaching for the conference table's integrated touch pad with her left hand, Lorin selected "no." As the other Council members issued their votes, Gabe's fingers finally, slowly, curled around hers.

She squeezed back and looked at him. When she met his eyes, she caught her breath at the emotion roiling in their icy blue depths.

"All votes have been cast," Willem finally said.

There was an odd quality to his voice that she couldn't place. Elliott's, Lukas's, and Antonia's nostrils were twitching up a storm.

"The votes are now displayed."

Her mother gasped.

When Lorin raised her eyes to the screen, her jaw dropped. One "yes" vote, and eleven "no"? Across the table, Jacoby Woolf's face was expressionless.

The WerePack Beta had voted with the majority. Against his father.

And the shit was about to hit the fan.

⌀

"What did you say?" Lorin yelled at Andi Woolf, standing less than an arm's length away. She could see her friend's lips move, but the music thumped so loudly that she couldn't hear a damn thing. The dance floor was packed. Bodies jostled and writhed, and the scent of pheromones drifted like exotic smoke. Finally, admitting defeat, she simply pointed toward the back bar.

Andi nodded and took off, elbowing through the writhing bodies like a roller derby jammer.

Why had she let Andi drag her to Underbelly? And where the hell was Gabe? She should have touched base with him before coming, made plans for later, not simply have taken Andi's word for it that Gabe's siblings had made big celebration plans with their brother tonight.

After being asked for a private word with his alpha

after the council meeting, celebrating was probably the last thing Gabe was in the mood to do.

Was he okay? Plucking her phone from her pocket, she impatiently checked messages. Nothing. *She* couldn't call *him*, because Bailey was still configuring his damn phone. How frustrating!

Lorin took a deep breath. She could try his desk phone again. Then, when she reached Underbelly's back bar, she'd ask Flynn to pour her the biggest, stiffest—

An arm snaked out of the crowd, yanking her against a tall, hard body. "Damn it." Someone's testicles were about to be kneed clean up to their eyeballs.

"I have a bone to pick with you, Lorin."

Chadden. She relaxed slightly—but only slightly. He had yard-long arms, and both of them were wrapped around her like octopus tentacles. His voice vibrated against the tender skin under her ear, his sharp teeth an inch away from her jugular.

She met his gaze squarely. "What makes you think I'm interested in your bone, Chadden?"

His eyes lit with self-deprecating humor. "Who isn't, darling?"

Ah, hell. While she wasn't deluded enough to think him harmless, she let his arms stay where they were and started dancing with him. She had to bleed off some of the outrageous buildup of energy coursing through her body somehow, and dancing would do for now.

"I understand that your arrangement with Rafe Sebastiani has ended."

She ignored the hard bulge at the front of his leathers. "Calling my relationship with Rafe 'an arrangement' makes it sound so... cold-blooded."

"Well, it looks like you didn't break his heart," he said, gesturing with a sideways tip of his head that sent his dark hair sliding sensuously over his shoulder.

Twenty feet away, next to the DJ booth, Rafe danced with Bailey Brown. Though they barely touched each other, she could smell Rafe's familiar pheromones from here.

Rafe, a human? What the hell are you getting yourself into?

"Speaking of offended"—Chadden's voice dipped to a rumble—"Gabe Lupinsky? Lorin, I'm desolate."

She stiffened in his arms. If Chadden said one nasty thing about Gabe or his family—

"He's way too straitlaced for my rowdy, randy Lorin."

A visual of Gabe lashing her lips with his talented tongue popped into her head. She considered telling Chadden that there was something to be said for devastating focus and precision, but she decided not to. Her only answer was an enigmatic, secretive smile.

Chadden kept them dancing, but his arms loosened just a little. When Lorin looked at his face, his expression had relaxed, shifting from predatory hunger back to flirtatiousness. "I bet he brings his phone to bed. In one of those hideous waistband holders."

She laughed lightly, shaking her head. "We don't actually make it to a bed very often."

Chadden raised an approving eyebrow. "Mr. Lupinsky has hidden depths—and he's sitting at the back table. Despite his delightful female company, he doesn't look like he's having a very good time."

Her head whipped. Gabe was here?

Chadden whispered a kiss onto her temple, a touch

that comforted rather than seduced. "I wish you luck, my friend."

"Thank you. I think I... may need it." She returned his hug, but true to form, it didn't take long for Chadden's hand to drift south, from her hip to the curve of her ass. She giggled, shoving him away. "You're incorrigible."

He grinned, flashing his fangs. "If things don't work out with the werewolf, you know where to find me."

"You're such a humanitarian, Chadden."

"No need to be insulting." A cacophony of female howls split the air. "Someone needs to cut those bitches off."

Lorin glanced over to the curved leather banquette, where nearly a dozen dressed-to-kill werewolf females celebrated. Two women seated at the center of the pack wore faux balls and chains attached to their ankles, and sparkly collars and leashes adorned their necks. "Bondmate celebration."

"Kayla Andersen is staring you down."

Kayla was here? Where? After the hellacious day she'd had, throwing down with Gabe's ex-girlfriend sounded... okay, it sounded great, but... hell. Diplomacy wasn't exactly her strong suit. Her eyes cruised the partygoers milling around the edges of the banquette, looking for small, blonde, and stacked. "Where is she?"

Chadden pointed. "Ball and Chain Number One."

Lorin blinked and looked to the center of the raucous celebration. Yes, there Kayla was, all right.

Wearing a sparkly pink leash, and holding hands with her brand new wife.

—⚡—

Gabe turned away from the dance floor as Flynn approached Underbelly's big back table with a loaded tray. Who'd ordered tequila shots? Whoever had done so had read his damn mind. He needed alcohol, a lot of it, and fast.

"Hello, Lupinskys," Flynn greeted them, setting the tray down in the middle of the table. "Ready to celebrate?"

Gabe shot a baleful look over his shoulder. "Yeah." Having his loyalty to the pack questioned by his pissed-off alpha had been no treat, but coming here to find Lorin dancing with a slinky vampire who had his hands all over her? *Jesus.* As Flynn handed him one of the small, clear glasses filled with beige liquor, the vamp slid his hand onto her ass. She must want it there, because otherwise the guy would be eating teeth. "That's just great."

Why had he let his family drag him to Underbelly? After being dressed down by his alpha, Gabe had let himself hope that Lorin might be waiting for him. But she hadn't been—nor had she been in her office, in Elliott's office, or in the downstairs lab. Going up to his own office to ponder what he should do next, he'd discovered his brother and sisters in his office—there, according to Glynna, to kidnap him. "Congratulations! Mom told us about your presentation to the Council today! We're all going to Underbelly to celebrate. Now." After a slight hesitation, he'd allowed himself to be dragged along. On their way out, Gideon, ever the investigator, bent toward the couch, scooping up a handful of purple satin. *Lorin's underwear.* Dropping them on Gabe's desk, Gideon said, "Interesting work you do here, bro."

Going out to a loud, noisy club was the last thing he wanted to do, but Lorin was MIA and Glynna wanted to dance. There was dancing, all right—and thankfully enough liquor to temporarily distract him from the sight of Lorin in another man's arms. Fumes stung his nose as he lifted the tequila shot up to his lips and knocked it back. It burned all the way down, setting fire to his throat. "I'll take another."

"Who ordered these?" Gideon asked.

"Does it matter? It's alcohol."

Andi Woolf plopped down in the empty chair next to Gideon, pushing waves of dark hair away from her face. "Well, look at this. The Lupinskys are on the prowl." She indicated the tray. "This round's on me."

Gideon cursed under his breath. Gabe spoke up before his brother did something stupid, like send the tray back. "Thank you, Andi." Krispin Woolf's daughter wanted to buy him drinks after the horrible day her father had caused. It was karma.

"None for me, thanks," Gideon said, crossing his arms over his chest.

Andi rolled her eyes at Gideon. "No roofies, no drugs, Commander. Just liquor, glorious liquor."

"Where's your security?" Gideon looked over her shoulder.

She shrugged, her careless gesture contradicted by the annoyance in her eyes. "No clue. It's their job to watch me, not the other way around." Turning her back on Gideon, Andi chatted with Gwen and Glynna.

A familiar laugh drew his attention back to the dance floor. No, it wasn't a laugh, it was a… giggle. The Eurotrash vamp had whispered something to Lorin that made her giggle like a schoolgirl. Gabe tossed back the shot he was holding, savoring the liquid smolder. "We're going to need another round," he called to Flynn.

Howls echoed from the far side of the dance floor, louder than the pounding music. "What's up over there?" he asked Flynn. Bless the man, he'd brought the bottle.

"Bondmate celebration." Why was Flynn looking at him so strangely?

Andi gestured grandly. "Please send them a round, kind sir."

"As you wish, Princess." Flynn's white teeth flashed in a smile. "You're mighty generous with the liquid cheer tonight."

"Too generous," Gideon muttered.

Andi reached for one of the glasses remaining on the tray. "I'm celebrating tonight."

"Celebrating what?"

When Andi simply smiled, Gideon picked up a tequila shot of his own.

"Shit." Glynna rarely swore, and now she exchanged a worried look with Gwen.

"What's wrong?" he asked.

Gwen hesitated, then said, "Kayla's here."

He felt a jolt of surprise, but it quickly passed. "So?"

Another pause. "That's her bondmate celebration over there."

He craned his head slightly and finally saw her, sitting in the midst of a pack of howling women, wearing a sparkly collar and leash, and a fake ball and chain around her ankle. So, Kayla had finally found a guy whose lineage was acceptable to her tight-assed family. Good for her. Reaching to the tray, Gabe picked up a shot to make a toast. "To Kayla," he said. "Gawd help the poor bastard."

Silence ensued as his sisters exchanged another loaded glance. "Bitch," Glynna finally said.

Gabe chuckled. He could always count on his family. "It's okay, Glyn. I wish her well. Really."

A baffled expression flitted over Glynna's face. "Gabe, her bondmate's a bitch. A woman. A werewolf female."

Whoa. The floor tilted momentarily, and then leveled off. Someone—Gideon?—handed him another shot glass. He peered at it, considering. Three shots in less than ten minutes? Four?

Hell, Gideon was driving.

He tipped the glass back quickly, vaguely noticing the embers on his tongue. Lorin, his lover, was dancing with another man. Kayla and her bondmate celebrated across the room.

His track record with women was less than stellar.

"Hey." Lorin sidled up behind him, holding out her hand. He could do nothing but take it, and she tugged him out on to the dance floor without saying a word. Gabe didn't recognize the song that was playing, but it beat like a heart against his skin. Its rhythm required nothing more than swaying, which suited him just fine. Thudding music, laughter, and voices swirled together in a frothy cocktail. The world blunted off, growing fuzzy around the edges as the liquor hit. Holding on to her as much for support as to dance with her, he inhaled the scent of her hair—and smelled that long-haired vamp. He rubbed his mouth along her neck to eradicate the other man's scent, licking and snuffling. Instead of rebuffing his unspeakably primitive actions,

Lorin simply tilted her head to the side to give him better access.

Other wolves in the room might perceive her gesture as submissive, but he could feel her strength in the fists she clenched in his hair. She had wide shoulders, curvy hips, firm muscles, and long, sturdy bones. Her strength intoxicated him, liberated him. He could ride her—hard—all night long. He could be as rough as he wanted to be.

He was suddenly hard as a rock.

"Gabe."

What the hell was his brother doing on the dance floor, surrounded by writhing bodies?

"Hello, Gideon," Lorin responded serenely.

Gideon tried to tug his hand off Lorin's muscled ass. *Nope. Not moving it, bro.*

"I apologize for my brother, Lorin," Gideon said. Tug. "Gabe's had a little too much to drink tonight, and he's getting"—tug—"grabby."

"Your brother's hands are right where I want them to be, Gideon. Yours, however…?"

Gideon snatched his hand away.

Grinning at her imperious tone, Gabe smacked a kiss onto the tip of her adorable nose. "That's my Valkyrie Princess. Off with his head!"

Clearing his throat, Gideon stepped back. "Will you please see that he gets home?"

"Yes."

"Yes. Now go find your own woman," Gabe said, burying his nose in the crook of her neck. The other man's smell was drifting away, slowly being replaced by his own.

Gideon tapped his shoulder again. Gabe looked at him with exasperation. "What?"

"We'll talk tomorrow." His brother's tone indicated that the conversation would be an inquisition of monumental proportions.

"Yeah, yeah. Now go away. Ask Andi to dance."

Gideon left the dance floor, not dignifying his suggestion with a response.

He rested his chin on Lorin's broad, bare shoulder, nudging the purple satin bra strap back under her shirt.

"We're leaving for Isabella first thing in the morning, no matter how hungover you are," she murmured in that amused tone typically reserved for misbehaving children.

"I won't be hungover," he replied testily. "I've had three tequila shots." Or was it four?

"Okay." She wrapped her arms more firmly around him. Her warm breath bloomed against his ear, making him shiver.

"I couldn't find you after the meeting," he said. "You disappeared on me." He gathered Lorin more closely to his body to ensure it didn't happen again.

"I'm sorry. Andi told me your brother and sisters were waiting for you in your office," she replied. "How did things go with Krispin?"

"Let's just say that if he could have fired me, he would have."

"Elliott would just hire you back," she replied. "I think Krispin was more pissed off at Jacoby than he was with you. I called Andi after the meeting, gave her a heads up about what happened."

Gabe nodded. "Then I get here, and you're clamped against some oily vamp."

Lorin grinned. Grinned, damn her. "Chadden's not oily. He… glistens."

"Well, he wants you," he grumbled.

Lorin didn't deny it. She didn't say that the other man was merely a sparring partner, or that she tolerated him only because of his ability to keep her refrigerator stocked with very high-end food. The important information was telegraphed by her body, swaying languidly with his, plastered together from torso to knee. The music lilted and throbbed, harmonizing angels celebrating their glorious fall from grace.

"Hell, who wouldn't want you? You drive me crazy," he muttered mindlessly, dipping his mouth to the juncture of her shoulder and neck. He bit, and then licked away the sting. Her moan vibrated onto his tongue, a decadent treat.

She clasped his hand. "Let's get out of here." The urgency in her voice inflamed him, and her eyes blazed with lascivious intent.

Restrooms. Stairwell. It was finally going to happen, and he couldn't wait.

Someone tapped him on the arm. "What?" he snapped, not tearing his eyes from Lorin.

"Gabe?"

He blinked. "Kayla?" His former almost-bondmate stood before him, resplendent in her light pink collar and leash, the traditional tongue-in-cheek apparel for bondmate celebrations amongst the wolves. Behind him, chairs scraped against the floor as his siblings stood.

Did they think he couldn't handle this?

"Kayla," he repeated, leaning down to hug her

gingerly. She felt like she would break in his hands. "I understand congratulations are in order."

"Yes. Thank you," she said, glancing back at the banquette, where her new bondmate watched them carefully.

Hell, a lot of people were watching. Though the music still played, the people closest to them didn't even pretend to hide their curiosity. Kayla seemed nervous, more nervous than he was—maybe because Lorin had just wrapped her long arm around him, her hand skimming along his hip bone with proprietary weight. Gabe felt a kick of satisfaction.

"Congratulations, Kayla," Lorin said with a smile while her fingers did a wicked, wicked dance at his pocket seam. "Ready for the big celebration next weekend?"

Kayla's gaze flicked back and forth between them, probably wondering why the Valkyrie Second had her arm wrapped around her former intended. "There are still dozens of details to attend to," she finally responded, "but we'll be ready. I'm sorry you won't be able to make it."

"Gabe and I will be up at Isabella," Lorin replied, her fingertips slipping into his pocket.

How could Lorin just stand there chitchatting when her hand was burning him alive? "I wish you well, Kayla," he said, leaning down to kiss her cheek. "Ready to go?" he murmured to Lorin. He shot Kayla an apologetic look. "You caught us on our way out."

"So I see." Kayla took in their now-clasped hands, and the bulge pressing against the fly of his dress pants.

"Congratulations again, Kayla." After kissing Kayla on the cheek, Lorin waved toward Underbelly's back table without looking. He felt hundreds of eyes boring into his back as they walked to the elevator that would bring them to Underbelly's underground parking garage.

"Well, that ought to hit the grapevine at warp speed."

She watched him carefully as she pressed the elevator call button. "Are you okay?"

He answered her question by yanking her against him and delivering a swaggering, marauding kiss. He speared his tongue deep in her mouth, thrusting and parrying with hers. He didn't want her concern. He didn't want her pity. He wanted her hot, open, and writhing underneath him. Now.

The elevator doors opened, and he backed her in. As the doors shut behind them, she snaked a hand between their bodies and cupped him, measuring every inch of his need. He hissed like he was in pain—the kind of pain a man wanted to experience over and over again, world without end, amen.

When the elevator reached the lower level and the doors opened, she backed away and took his hand. "Come home with me?"

He nodded. He could do nothing but follow.

Whatever Gabe had thought Lorin's home might look like, it wasn't what they walked into a half hour later. The upscale townhouse complex tucked into thick woods just west of the 494 loop in Minnetonka? Yeah, that he'd expected. But given how comfortable she seemed roughing it up at the Isabella cabin, he hadn't expected the explosion of color, texture, and sheer coziness he saw in her living room. A leaning tower of mail balanced precariously on a glossy Arts and Crafts table next to the front door, and next to it, a huge houseplant towered from a squat rust-colored pot. No dust on the leaves.

"Who takes care of your plants while you're gone?" he called. No answer, but he heard her pressing buttons and rustling with something near the garage entrance they'd just stumbled through. So he explored—as much as he could, anyway, using the illumination provided by the tiny, clever lights set into the wide custom base-boards. As he walked along the long island separating the kitchen from the living room, trailing his hand for balance, he brushed against an open bag of snacks. Snatching one—Doritos—he munched as he wandered to the end of a short hallway. To the right, there was a closed door. To the left, a stairwell, leading up to her bedroom, he hoped. The stairway wall was covered with black-framed pictures. He grinned at a close-up of Lorin hugging a drooling white-and-black bulldog whose head was bigger than hers. Both she and the dog were wearing hats and sunglasses.

"Hey."

"There you are," he said. He gestured to the picture. "Cute dog. Who looks after your place when you're gone?" Before he realized what was happening, she'd grabbed his hand, tugged him up the stairs, and down a short, dark hallway.

"The couple next door," she finally answered. "They're snowbirds. I keep an eye on their place while they're gone in the winter, and they do the same for me during dig season."

Did the couple next door know that their neighbor was practically royalty? And not human, to boot? He wanted to know more about this couple who had a key to Lorin's home. If Lukas hadn't already done a deep background check on them, he'd ask Gideon to do some quiet poking around. Couldn't be too careful.

"Gabe." Her throaty voice pulled him along as surely as her tugging hand. Surely there was some siren blood in her lineage. He couldn't walk away from her right now if his life depended upon it. She was smoking hot, incisively intelligent, could be cranky and sulky as a child, and had generations of service bred into her very bones. It would take a lifetime—longer—to learn her moods.

She was the lover of his most secret dreams, and given her comments at the council meeting earlier in the day, she… just might love him back.

Light from the near-full moon streamed into the room, illuminating the clean Scandinavian lines of her bedroom furniture. He couldn't see colors, just shadows, but he smelled soil, and fresh growing things—ah, hell. Lorin stood silhouetted in the moonlight, stripping off her shirt. Removing her bra. With a groan, he cupped the tender flesh with his hands, supported her for his mouth. Lorin moaned at his touch, clutching his hair in her strong, callused hands.

He'd sacrifice every hair on his head if it meant he could keep his mouth right where it was.

She tipped her head back as he suckled, the milky light caressing her stubborn jawline as she surrendered to the pleasure he gave her. "You're so beautiful," he murmured against her skin.

"I'm glad you think so," she said with the slightest hint of amusement. She touched the rims of his glasses. "Mind if I take these off? Wouldn't want them to get broken."

His pulse jumped. Broken? Just what did she have in mind?

Did it matter? "Go ahead."

His breath quickened as she slipped the glasses off, as what little he could see in the shadowy room blurred to fog. He heard soft twin snicks as she folded the titanium bows against the lenses. A click as she set the glasses down on what must be a bedside table.

She grabbed the fabric at the unbuttoned neck of his oxford shirt and yanked. Buttons flew, skittering against the hardwood floor. She dragged the shirt down his arms, baring his chest to her touch, leaving his hands stuck in the sleeves.

And then her mouth was on him. He jumped as her teeth grazed his nipple. She latched on, suckling strongly, and he felt the rhythmic tugs all the way to his balls. A growl pushed up out of his throat, rough and ragged. She was destroying him.

He fought with the cuffs of the shirt, tore them, frantic to touch her. He had to touch her. Had to. Every muscle in his body was coiled tight, ready to spring. But when he finally freed his hands, dropping the ruined shirt to the floor, he cupped her cheekbones instead of her breasts. Tipped her head up. Blinked against the last of the liquor swimming through his system. Did she know who she was with? Did she know how much he—

"Love me, Gabe." Her mossy green eyes were shiny in the moonlight. "Love me."

His heart leaped at her words, and his body quickly followed suit. Tipping them both back onto the soft bed, Lorin's breath left her chest with a *whoof* of surprise. Rather than scrabbling for the dominant position, she wrapped her arms and legs around him, pulling him more firmly into her embrace.

Skin. He needed to feel her skin.

After a couple of mindless yanks and tugs, their clothes were gone. They rolled on the moonlit wreck of a bed, over and over again—skin to skin, hand to hand, mouth to mouth. He gasped as her legs twined around him, groaned as his naked, violently aroused flesh nudged her lush, wet center. After a tiny, helpless roll of his hips, he pulled back. Condoms. In his wallet—

She leaned over to the bedside table, grabbed something. A soft tearing sound, the scent of latex, and then her cool hands stroked a condom onto his cock. Pulling their bodies back into perfect alignment, she tightened her legs around him. Tugged. Hard.

And then he was inside her, thrusting and lost… lost in time, in the feel of her inner muscles milking him, in the humid puff of her breath against his shoulder, in the desperate cling of her strong arms and legs.

"Harder," she moaned.

He pulled out, flipped her onto her stomach, and pulled her up on all fours. Ranging his body over hers, he touched her with every inch of skin he could.

"More, Gabe. More. Love me…"

Her words made his seed boil, his head swim, his balls pull up tight. Not holding back, using all his strength, he mindlessly thrust into her from behind, over and over and over again.

"Mate with me, Lorin. Mate with me."

He loved her, as she asked, until they both broke apart.

Chapter 16

WHAT A BED HOG.

Lorin scooted back from the edge of the mattress she'd awakened to find herself clutching. Gabe sprawled over most of the bed, and if his even breathing was anything to go by, he was still deeply asleep. Sunlight flooded the room, painting a pale yellow stripe across the foot of the bed.

So much for that early start she'd threatened him with. Oh, well. They'd given each other a hell of a workout last night, and the featherbed felt like sin. No need to wake him up. Burrowing her head more deeply into her pillow with a contented sigh, she abandoned her ambition to get up and close the blinds.

At her side, Gabe snored softly.

She smiled. Gabe really couldn't hold his liquor worth a damn, but thankfully his personal brand of inebriation leaned toward tactile and adorable rather than loud and obnoxious. On the drive home from Underbelly, the last tequila shot had hit him like a Mack truck, and he'd turned into a chatterbox, hopping from one subject to the next like a jackrabbit: How relieved he was that Glynna's new prosthesis was working. How worried he was about his traveling parents, especially his mother. How he wished that Gideon would just jump Andi Woolf's bones already and be done with it. Something about Gideon and purple panties. During this amusing, largely one-sided conversation, she'd had her hands full just keeping the truck on the road, because his kept wandering from the passenger seat over to hers, cruising her body, their usual skill and precision in no way impacted by the tequila swimming in his system.

She'd allowed it.

Once they'd reached her townhouse, they'd spent an entertaining couple of minutes in her attached double garage, kissing, fumbling with their clothes, giggling like kids, until the overhead light timed out, plunging them into darkness. Taking hold of Gabe's hand, she'd found the door, tugged him inside, and he'd wandered off while she dealt with the security system. She'd found him at the foot of the stairs, grinning at her favorite picture of Buttercup, Butter drooling through her massive bulldog underbite.

They'd kissed their way up the stairs. Heated murmurs, muttered demands, his lips and clever hands branding her skin. After removing her shirt, she'd torn his from his body—and her action had triggered something within him, something feral and urgent and so, so beautiful. In the lost hours that followed, Gabe had unleashed a positively alpha display of erotic skill and dominance—and she'd… allowed it. Reveled in it.

A breath of a moan escaped. Without opening her eyes, she reached over to his pillow and twined her fingers in his hair. She wanted to allow it again, right now.

Would he remember half of what he'd said—half of what they'd done—last night? Would he remember the incendiary words he'd whispered, barely audible in the dark?

"Mate with me, Lorin. Mate with me."

Had he… proposed to her? If so, he hadn't waited for an answer. Instead, he'd turned her onto her back again, stretched her arms over her head and covered her, full-length, imprinting her with his scent. And then, with their gazes locked, he'd brought their lips together and filled her, the long, slippery strokes making her gasp in dark delight until they both tipped over the edge.

Had he meant it, or had it been the liquor talking? Maybe he hadn't sobered up on the drive home as much as she'd thought. And why hadn't his words sent her hauling ass from the bed, scuttling away from danger? Because she hadn't. Nope, she'd stayed right there, in the dark nest of the bed, taking everything he offered and making some heated demands of her own.

Lazy languor filled her, a low, luxurious ache. Her hand drifted south, stroking from Gabe's head to the nape of his neck to his upper back. There was something to be said for lazy mornings in bed. Maybe she'd—

She stilled her hand against Gabe's upper back. His… very hairy upper back. Tipping her head on her pillow, she opened her eyes.

There was a wolf in her bed.

Adrenaline spiked but quickly subsided. It was unmistakably Gabe: about two hundred lean, muscular pounds, a glorious black pelt, with that same small blaze of white behind his ear that he had in his human form. He lay sprawled on his side, four legs extended outright toward his side of the mattress. His breath puffed lightly out of an aquiline snout. One big paw twitched as he dreamed.

She stroked the white blaze behind his ear. He huffed a sigh in response but remained asleep.

She drifted back to sleep too, her heart filling her chest like an over-inflated balloon.

—⁓—

"This thing's going to break apart if you push it much harder," Gabe said from the passenger seat of Lorin's ancient Ford truck. The vehicle seemed held together with little more than primer and Bondo, and produced so much ambient noise that they could barely talk— which was good, because he was still mortified she'd had to haul his drunk ass home with her to her place last night. They were whizzing north on I-35 approaching Hinckley, and traffic clogged the highway like arterial plaque. All around them, cars, trucks, and RVs jockeyed for position as people drove north to cabins and camp-grounds for the weekend.

Lorin turned down the old-school Bon Jovi blasting out of a stereo system worth more than the rattletrap truck. "What?"

He indicated her speedometer. Not that it worked. "Can you slow down a little?"

"Sorry." Lorin eased her foot off the accelerator and rolled her head to stretch her neck. "How's the head?"

"Fine," he said testily.

His head was fine. What *wasn't* fine was that he'd woken up in her bed that morning in wolf form. Thankfully, he'd shifted back before she woke up, before she climbed on top of him and rode him, long and lazy, into glorious exhaustion. Two shifts and making love all night long had taken energy reserves he wasn't used to expending. The huge breakfast they'd shared at Lorin's place that morning had long since burned off, and he'd missed lunch.

"Feel like stopping at Tobies to eat?" he asked. The exit was just ahead, and he was hungry enough to gnaw through the truck's ratty upholstery.

"Sure." Lorin hit the blinker, checked her mirrors, and muscled the truck to the right-hand lane.

Despite their plan for a morning departure, the day had gotten away from them. After leaving Lorin's place, they'd stopped at his, but then what was supposed to be a quick stop at Sebastiani Labs to pick up a few things before heading north to Isabella had turned into a couple of impromptu meetings instead—including one with Elliott, who'd wanted to make sure there'd been no unfortunate fallout from Gabe's discussion with his alpha after yesterday's Council meeting. When he'd finally made his way to his own office, he found a fully configured Bat Phone sitting on his desk, right next to the purple satin panties Gideon had so thoughtfully set there the night before.

Living in a tent. Panties on his desk. Feeling Lorin up on a crowded dance floor. His life sure had taken some unexpected turns since Lorin opened that box.

The old truck rattled and shuddered up the exit ramp. Lorin had somehow convinced him to take only one vehicle up to Isabella—they'd save on gas—but why did the one car have to be hers? He was now completely dependent upon her for mobility, and what sounded like a busted muffler rendered her environmental argument completely moot.

He glanced at her, a suspicion sparking to life. Damn it, he could still see well enough to drive—in the daylight, at any rate. There was no need for her to treat him like he was damaged. Feeble. "Lorin, we could have taken my car."

"You wanted *more* scratches in that paint?"

Her reasonable answer doused the embers of his annoyance. She had a point, which was… annoying.

Lorin parked in the overflow lot, and they walked to the restaurant. The scent of cinnamon rolls and grilled beef hit him as soon as he opened the door, making his stomach growl. The hostess seated them at a table for two near the windows and handed them plastic-coated menus. While he loved fine dining, he also appreciated casual family cafés like this one, with their bright lights, worn Formica tables, plastic tumblers of ice water, and the menus featuring meatloaf, hot beef sandwiches, and BLTs.

He needed meat.

He picked up the menu, opened it—and the words swam, then disappeared into the void. *Damn it.* He held the menu out at arm's length, and when that didn't work, he brought it close again. He tipped his head to the left, the trick he usually used to work around the gaps in his field of vision. No go.

"Need some help?"

Her matter-of-fact offer made his diaphragm clutch, but after a blink and another tilt of his head, the blurry black letters finally formed words. "I've got it, thanks."

When the middle-aged waitress came to take their order, Lorin said, "I'll have the meatloaf with double mashed potatoes and gravy, a side of onion rings, and…" She pursed her lips. "A piece of apple pie with extra whipped cream, please."

The waitress didn't blink at her order, just scribbled on her pad. "And how about you, sweetie?"

Gabe shoved aside thoughts of what he could do with

extra whipped cream. "Hamburger and fries, please."
He'd snitch a bite of Lorin's pie for dessert.

As the waitress walked away, Lorin smirked. "No
green salad?"

Was he really so predictable? "I decided to indulge
myself. I'll run it off tonight."

Indulging. Running. Ordinary words suddenly
seemed spoken in bold font, and Lorin's dilated pupils
indicated that she felt it too. Shifting in her red vinyl
chair, she fiddled with her napkin-wrapped silverware,
removing the paper ring that secured the bundle. Her
breathing was a little fast, and her pulse throbbed at
her neck.

Just the two of them, sitting at a restaurant. No
weathered picnic table, no noisy, rowdy crew, no blar-
ing tunes. No paperwork, no ticks and mosquitoes, no
meeting agenda.

It felt like… a date.

Gabe glanced out the window, trying without suc-
cess to ignore her luscious scent. So much had happened
within the last twenty-four hours. Gabe's presentation to
the Council—which, under most circumstances, would
be a career highlight—somehow seemed… insignificant
now. The tense discussion he'd had with the alpha after
the meeting barely registered. What lodged in his mind
like a sliver was Lorin's response to the question that
Woolf had asked. "Loved ones are loved ones, regardless of their health issues." Was it possible that Lorin
didn't see his genetic weaknesses as a barrier to a relationship? Or had she simply been making a point about
the alpha's attitude toward his own son?

Could both be true?

Then last night at Underbelly. He'd been eaten up with jealousy watching Lorin dance with that slinky vamp, but he hadn't felt even one tug of regret seeing Kayla with her new bondmate.

Later, in Lorin's bed, he'd shifted spontaneously in his sleep after making love with her. His wolf had known it was safe sleeping at her side.

Must be love.

He watched her shred her paper napkin. They could never turn the clock back, pretend they were simply work colleagues anymore, even if he wanted to. But now what? So many things were yet unsaid, but if he said too much—asked for too much—he'd lose her for sure.

"Why didn't you tell me about your eyes?"

Her soft question, and the slight hint of hurt feelings under the surface, blindsided him. All these issues swirling around them, and *that's* what she wanted to talk about?

"You'll need surgery soon?" she prompted with an ideal balance of interest and concern. Not too blasé, but… not wigging out either, prompting him to offer comfort rather than accept it, as was usually the case. Before he knew it, he was actually telling her about the blurriness, the black voids in his field of vision, and in more detail than he'd felt comfortable sharing with anyone except Gideon. His head-tilt trick. How driving was sometimes a challenge, especially at night. That he'd discovered in the lab that using an old-school microscope was now pretty much beyond his capabilities. That only yesterday, he'd been forced to increase the default font size on his laptop.

She reached across the table to twine their fingers

together. "Schedule the surgery, Gabe. What's up at Isabella has been there for hundreds of years. It can wait a little longer." As she asked pointed questions about the procedure, risks, and aftercare, her expression riveted him. Soft, caring, yet battle-ready. Willing to fight on his behalf—and apparently willing to postpone at least some of their work until he'd recovered and could join her again.

Their work.

A weight he wasn't aware he carried lightened. Tangling his feet with hers, he leaned in closer to the table separating them.

"Is your vision better or worse when you shift? Could you see me this morning?"

Shock rocked him back in his seat. She'd... seen him? Seen his wolf? And she'd still made love with him, with such sheet-tumbling abandon? "I'm blind when I'm shifted," he admitted. He indicated his glasses. "Until Sebastiani Labs creates glasses for wolves, or implant-able vision correction lenses that can bridge a shift"—he shrugged fatalistically—"I'm shit out of luck. At least in human form, glasses can help with the myopia."

"But your other senses aren't impacted? Scent, touch, hearing?"

Of course she'd focus on capabilities instead of deficiencies. Despite claiming to possess not a single molecule of sentimentality in her spectacular body, she was definitely a glass-half-full girl. And she cared for him. The question was, how much?

He had to know. "Lorin, what are we doing here?"

"Eating?"

"You know what I mean."

"Shagging each other senseless?"

He couldn't let her joke her way through this conversation. "I'm serious, Lorin."

"Believe me, so am I." Under the table, her sneaky foot stroked north along the inner leg seam of his jeans. "Excellent sex is no laughing matter."

The waitress approached, carrying a circular serving tray. "I'd say not." She looked at their linked hands as she set steaming plates on the table. "You folks enjoy," she said, departing with an amused backward glance.

At the table next to theirs, a toddler screamed, gleefully pounding silverware against the tray of his high chair.

Hell. Why had he broached such a sensitive topic at the busiest roadside restaurant in the state? No matter how the conversation went, he and Lorin would have to spend three more hours together in the tight confines of her truck—unless she decided to turn right around and drop his sorry ass back at his place.

For an intelligent man, sometimes he wasn't very smart.

"You're my lover, Gabe."

The tone of her voice as she said "lover" made his stomach jump. He heard a banked sensual heat, exasperation, and affection—as if, maybe, he wasn't just the most convenient candidate for the job. He said as much.

She shot him an annoyed look. "Gabe, I'm capable of sleeping alone if I choose. If I didn't want you in my bed, you wouldn't be there."

"What about your adrenal condition?" he asked. "You need to leach off the excess hormones somehow."

"There *are* other ways I can deal with it," she replied, exasperated. "Run. Chop wood. Masturbate. Spar. Mike won't spar with me, but nothing's stopping me from driving south once a week and playing racquetball with Andi, or hitting the cage with Lukas, Jack, or Chico."

His thoughts were still snagged on "masturbate," but… "A cage?"

"Yeah. Have you ever watched mixed martial arts? There's a sparring cage in the basement at Sebastiani Security."

He thought back to the down-and-dirty fight Lorin and Chico Perez had been having when he first arrived at the dig. Her mud-soaked clothes had clung to her like a second skin. How barbaric—and how utterly, undeniably hot. "Is there mud in this cage?"

"No." The toe stroking up his leg delivered a hard nudge, uncomfortably close to some sensitive flesh that had just woken up to join the party. "Sorry. No mud, no Jello, no chocolate pudding."

"Pity."

She picked up a plastic bottle of ketchup from the collection of condiments, adorning her meatloaf with a decorative squiggle. "Men have some very odd fantasies."

Gabe didn't waste energy denying it, but now he had one more thing to worry about. Lorin and Chico were pretty evenly matched. She and Jack probably were too; Jack was big but human. But the thought of Lorin fighting with Lukas—even as a workout—turned his stomach.

Those damn Sebastianis. Picking up his fork, he asked the question that had been picking at him for ages. "Is your relationship with Rafe Sebastiani over?"

Her hand stilled, holding the ketchup bottle momentarily suspended. "Of course." She set it down carefully.

"Gabe, my relationship with Rafe was a friends-with-benefits thing. Pleasurable, convenient, until it was time to move on." She shrugged. "He wanted to move on."

Rafe had ended it? "How could he not want you?" he blurted.

"Want wasn't the issue, Gabe."

The amusement in her voice made him visualize long hair and long limbs tangled together in artistically rumpled silk sheets. Hell. Rafe was an incubus—a frickin' sex demon—with a reputation for hedonism even among his kind. How long would it be until Lorin felt the need to take advantage of her friend's... benefits again?

Lorin put down her fork. "Gabe, Rafe and I are friends. You're my... lover. The lover I choose. The lover I want."

"For how long?" How could a half-blind werewolf with zero lineage and damaged genetics ever be enough for her? "I've gone and fallen in love with the Valkyrie Princess. Isn't that a fucking laugh."

She stilled. "You... love me?"

As Gabe dropped his head into his hands, the toddler next door shrieked again. Perfect timing, because he'd just dealt their fledgling relationship a deathblow.

"Gabe? Look at me. Please."

Would she let him down easy, or chop him off at the knees? He'd almost prefer the chop. Surely some sort of obvious physical injury should accompany the pain that was already rising, ruthless as the tide.

Steeling himself, squaring his shoulders, he did as she asked—only to find her staring back at him with an expression he couldn't read. At least she wasn't laughing, or looking at him with the sympathy that signaled an "it's not you, it's me" kiss-off.

"I think about you when I should be thinking about other things. I look for you when you're not with me. I can't get enough of your body. You make me think. You make me feel. Damn it, Gabe. I don't know what to do with this. With"—she gestured with a violent hand—"us. You scare the shit out of me."

What? "I'd never hurt you, Lorin."

She picked up her fork again, stabbing at her ketchup-coated meatloaf. "You… could. And that's what scares me."

Goose bumps sheeted over his body despite the room's perfectly reasonable temperature. "Will you quit torturing that meatloaf and talk to me?"

She dropped her fork with a loud clank and glared at him. "I suck at this, Gabe. I suck at relationships. I don't have the experience or the vocabulary."

He swallowed down the laugh that pushed up in his throat. Damn, the woman could jerk him from sorrow to delight to feral need to inappropriate humor in seconds. *My woman.* His face and fingertips started to tingle, but he fought it back. Taking her hand, he kissed it, licked her inner wrist with an ownership that he couldn't hide, stared at her, knowing that his need and his love shone, undisguised, in his eyes.

She stared back, her dilated pupils shoving the mossy green out of the way. Muttering a curse, she stood, the legs of her chair scraping loudly against the tile floor. "Can we leave? Now?"

Lorin, leaving a full plate of food behind? He wanted to howl in triumph. Reaching into his back pocket for his wallet, he dropped a random wad of bills on the table, then grabbed her hand and tugged her toward the building's entrance.

"Do you know how many gravel side roads there are between here and Isabella?" she murmured. She wrapped a proprietary arm around his waist as they reached the door.

"No, but I'm glad you do." He nuzzled the delicate skin where her shoulder met her neck. He nipped. Her gasp of response grabbed him by the balls. His body pulsed, his muscles pushing and shoving from the underside of his skin.

"Hey!" their waitress called from the door, waving bills. "You paid too much."

Not slowing down, Gabe called back, "Keep it."

Hand in hand, they nearly jogged to the nearly empty overflow parking lot. Standing at the truck's passenger door, fingers on the handle, he scanned the area. Hinckley's city streets trailed off to forest and fields pretty quickly. There was a decent motel adjacent to the parking lot.

No way would he make it even a mile down the highway.

Lorin pushed him back against the passenger door of the truck, slamming her mouth to his, clutching at his hair so hard it stung. Without thinking, he pivoted, flipping their positions so her body was pinned to the sun-warmed metal door. Plowing his fingers into her surfer-girl hair, he held her head in place and plunged his tongue back into her mouth.

Her taste. He couldn't get enough. His eyelids drifted closed when her tongue slid alongside his and back into her own mouth, teasing, drawing him in. Their bodies clicked together like puzzle pieces, aligning soft to hard, concave to convex, give to take. But under the softness, she was strong—strong enough to take his full weight, strength, and outrageous demand. He pinned her against the metal from torso to knee, pressing so hard that her soft skin must surely bear the imprint of his shirt buttons.

His breath dragged in and out of a throat that suddenly felt too small for the job. Denim rasped against denim as her showgirl leg twined around his upper thigh. Thousands of tires hummed and sang from the nearby highway. Birds chirped, doors slammed, and her soft moans of excitement, of need, seemed plucked straight from his most fevered dreams.

She pushed him away momentarily and fumbled with the door handle, cursing when it took several tries to open it. Finally, he heard a metallic click, the door swung open, and he found himself falling, tugged on top of her long, lithe body as she lay back on the truck's big bench seat.

A hungry growl rumbled from his throat. His hips gave an instinctive lurch as he landed between her upraised knees, in the cradle her body made for him. Her demanding groan nearly unmanned him. He could smell her arousal, almost taste it on his tongue.

He yearned. He burned. She hadn't said the words, but his mate wanted him.

"Gabe," she whispered against his lips. "Close the door."

"Huh?" Fighting the lust pounding through his system, he tried to focus on her words.

"Get the door."

Shit, his feet were hanging out of the car. Scrambling to a sitting position, he yanked the door closed. Being that Lorin had parked in the overflow lot, there were no other vehicles parked nearby. Her industrious hand was making very quick work of the button at his waistband, tugging down his zipper. Its opening whoosh sounded unnaturally loud in the quiet cocoon of the truck cab. Reaching into the V she'd created, she burrowed under the elastic waistband of his white cotton briefs, cupping his erection in hot, possessive hands.

"Are we really going to do this here?" he asked between gritted teeth.

"You can wait?" Tilting her head, she shot him a sideways glance that sent her hair drifting over his cock.

He gulped, staring at his mate's strong, capable hands stroking him with a distinct aura of ownership. The civilized man inside told him to stop this now, to take her someplace more romantic, but damn it, there was nothing civilized about the frantic need rocketing through his body, coalescing in the hard, blunt flesh surging in her hands.

"Have you ever made love in a car, Gabe?" she murmured.

Her expression was positively riveting. Lust. Humor. A hot, edgy hunger—and a tenderness that shredded him. She'd said "made love"—again. Suddenly he felt ten feet tall, like she'd handed him the magic sword that would slay all of her dragons. He stared at his glorious mate, the woman he loved.

"Gabriel, I asked you a question."

He gulped as her hot breath teased his violently aroused flesh. "No. I can't say I've had the pleasure."

A tiny, feline smile curved her lips. "You're about to." And she took him into the wild heat of her mouth.

—⁓—

For long minutes, Lorin lost herself in textures, tastes, scents, and sounds: iron-hard flesh under hot, silky skin,

so soft and slippery in her mouth. Her own harsh breathing. The tip of her nose brushing against a tangle of hair
with every downward stroke. Salt on her tongue. Musk,
sultry and deep, mixed with the rain-clean scent of the
fabric softener sheets he'd dried his clothes with.

Gabe clutched her head, his fingernails biting into
her skull with a delicious sting. "You're killing me,"
he strangled out. With a growl she felt and heard, he
tugged on her head, pulling her up and away from his
lap. She released his cock with an audible, wet pop,
and found herself bodily lifted, tipped, and laid flat on
her back, her elbow bumping into the truck's cracked
plastic steering wheel. Gabe pulled her T-shirt up and
off, and the front clasp of her bra dissolved under his
touch. He peeled the cups back, stared at her bared flesh
with hot eyes, and then possessively cupped her breasts
with his hands.

Her groan of reaction blended with his. So warm, so
strong. His fingertips plucked at her nipples. Before she
could moan, before she could clutch at his broad shoulders, he tore at the button fly of her jeans. The jeans
were old friends, flour-soft from too many washings,
and the buttons easily slipped free. A frustrated growl.
Tug, tug. She felt the slick vinyl truck seat against her
bare ass.

Lifting her legs, Gabe yanked off her shoes and pants,
dropping them carelessly to the passenger side floor.

Hmm. Her position opened up a lot of room on the
truck seat—and created some intriguing possibilities.
Leaving her legs upright, she slowly spread them, planting her feet against the ceiling of the truck cab, exposing
her damp need.

He simply… stared. His fingers twitched, like he couldn't wait to touch her—but for some reason, he held himself back.

What did he see with that hot, possessive gaze? Could he see how much she loved him? Reaching up, Lorin cupped his lust-flushed cheekbone in her palm.

Gabe shoved his jeans and underwear down around his hips, scrambled into place between her legs. But instead of plunging, he licked her jawbone, the tendons in her neck, the underside of her chin, her ears.

And her lips. Oh, he licked her lips like she was a decadent treat before slipping his tongue inside. His succulent kiss, his gentle touch, was positively maddening. His hot, blunt flesh teased the wet opening to her body.

"Lorin," he whispered against her lips.

That's all he said—her name—but something in his rumbly voice, something about the voluptuous pleasure etching his face, made her blink back tears.

Finally, he lifted his head and opened his eyes. After one final, hot stare, he lowered his head and carefully clamped his teeth against the sensitive juncture where her shoulder met her neck.

His teeth tightened. His cock plunged. And he rode them into sweet, frantic oblivion.

Chapter 17

AS BEDDOE STRODE THROUGH THE DARK AND CROWDED gambling den, the clatter of credits clacking off on the machines barely registered. His breath dragged through pinched nostrils. His heels punished the floor with each step. His fangs were buried in his own inner lip, but even the taste of blood couldn't temper the sting of failure clawing up from his stomach.

All the deprivation. All the secrecy. After all his careful plans, all the risks he'd taken, Lorcan had just waltzed in and—

"Captain Beddoe! Captain! Did you see? I won!"

Beddoe stopped and stared at the meaty hand resting on his forearm. He raised his head to gaze, expressionless, at the man's sweaty, excited face.

The eagle-eyed employee accompanying the man to the Winner's Circle shot him a wary look. "Come with me, Sirrah."

"But—"

She tugged the man safely out of range with a too-bright smile. "Let's go claim your winnings!"

He resumed walking again, his hard cadence at odds with the opulent surroundings. Delicate scents masked the pheromones and chemicals pumped into the air to reduce inhibitions and erode judgment. Scantily clad, galaxy-class beauties carried trays of food and drink to customers attired in glittering gowns, elegant formal wear, skinsuits, and jumpsuits. But it was a mirage. An illusion. Open the wrong door and you'd see the grime, hear the ominous clanks.

What else could possibly go wrong?

"Captain?" Ta'al had drawn alongside him, and he hadn't noticed. Her hair was pulled back in a severe twist, throwing her cheekbones and jawline into sharp focus. The duty suit hugged her curves faithfully, lending the utilitarian uniform a sensuality that its designer likely hadn't intended. She could easily work the entertainment floors if she wasn't such a talented officer and pilot. How lucky he was to have her in his service.

"Yes, Ta'al." He looked at his timepiece. Minchin should have come on duty over a cycle ago.

She handed him a commchip. "Urgent confidential communication from Lorcan Industries, Sirrah."

My new assignment. With some fast thinking and even faster talking, he'd convinced Lorcan that a thorough territorial survey should be undertaken before Lorcan Industries considered making such a significant expenditure, buying himself more time to find the cryotube. Lorcan had agreed, stating that he'd have the most recent territorial survey materials sent to him at the *TonTon.*

He clicked the chip into his comm plant and quickly skimmed. The last survey, performed from far orbit over three hundred Earth years ago, described an agrarian society, population approximately 700 million humanoids, and a planet in pristine condition. A planned fact-finding expedition had never occurred, citing budgetary issues. Beddoe pursed his lips. Lorcan was, of course, most interested in water, but his scientists were excited about the opportunity to study a civilization on the cusp of technological breakthrough.

They'd missed observing the nascent event for themselves by mere decades, but the environmental damage that almost always accompanied the key cultural stepping-stone had already started. He'd exaggerate the damage when he filed his own report.

He honed in on the most recent update: "Smugglers' network reports homing beacon, possible signature Pritchard/*Arkapaedis*. Investigate and report."

There was his trump card, exposed and played.

This was what else could possibly go wrong.

———

"Andi, you have to help me out here."

Lorin punched the speakerphone button and hung up the cabin landline's handset, leaving both hands free to repair the balky kerosene lamp. Andi must be psychic. Her call had come at just the right time—Gabe was stuck on a conference call, dialed in from the workroom—and right about now, talking to a wolf couldn't hurt. After almost a week of hot days and even hotter nights—with Gabe fulfilling every sexual desire she'd ever had and some she hadn't been aware she possessed—she still had a restless, edgy twitch she just couldn't shake no matter how many miles she ran.

This was no mere adrenal system spike. These jitters were emotional in origin, and she didn't have the first clue what to do about them.

She held a hand to her jumpy stomach. "Why do I feel this way?"

"You really don't know?"

"No," she nearly snarled. "Please enlighten me." Andi's merry giggles echoed from the phone's speaker. "You are *such* a bitch."

"Thank you," Andi said. Her laughter gradually subsided. "Baby, you're in love."

"That's what I was afraid you were going to say." She gave the screwdriver a vicious twist. "Scattered, jumpy, half sick to my stomach. Why on earth do people yearn to feel this way?" She hadn't gotten much work done in the last week. Her concentration was absolutely shot.

"You're so spoiled."

"What?"

"You heard me. You've dated and discarded so many extraordinary men, with every relationship entirely on your terms. No one's ever asked you for more. No man's ever pushed you to offer them more than your hot bod. To work at it. You've always been the one to set the terms, and to move on first."

"I work plenty hard at it, and it wasn't enough," Lorin snapped. "Gabe's already broken it off once."

"It's okay to be scared, baby—"

"And what about Rafe? He's the one who called things off between us, not me."

"Rafe doesn't count," Andi scoffed. "You were both between lovers, scratching a mutual itch. He's safe. Gabe isn't."

Silence hummed while she filled the lamp with kerosene. "Gabe wants me to tell him how I feel, to share my emotions?" she grumbled. "Why was I practically the last person to find out what was wrong with his eyes?" Even Krispin Woolf had more information than she'd had, and that really chapped her ass. "He's a fine one to talk. The one time I saw his wolf, he acted like it hadn't happened at all."

"You saw Gabe's wolf?"

"I woke up to Gabe's wolf," she corrected. "Then I fell back asleep, and by the time I woke up again, he'd shifted back. Pretended nothing happened." Then they'd made love, so slow and sweet that the memory of it still—

"You saw Gabe's wolf," Andi repeated.

"Yeah." What was the big deal?

"Lorin, it's been years since even his *family* has seen his wolf. I know for a fact that Kayla never did. She complained about it to anyone who'd listen. It was a sore spot in their relationship."

"What a bitch," she muttered. Gabe was well rid of a girlfriend who had such loose lips. "So he didn't shift just because he was drunk?"

"Lorin, think. He's so vulnerable when he shifts. No glasses, remember? He can't see." Andi paused, considering. "I think he felt safe with you."

Something inside her warmed, stretched.

"Lorin, the man told you he loves you, and you haven't said it back. Seems to me that he's taking all the risks here." She paused again. "Do you love him, Lorin?"

"I—"

"Jacoby told me what you said at the Council meeting, about tomorrow being promised to no one. Were they just empty words?"

No—and having nearly died herself, Andi had reason to know.

"He loves you, Lorin. You love him. What would your life be like without him in it?"

Empty. Lonely. "Damn it," she whispered.

"Find your gonads and go get him, girl. Call me when you come up for air." Andi hung up without bothering to say good-bye.

Sweat bloomed on her upper lip, and her stomach writhed like a clutch of garter snakes. Andi was right. She was being a coward. She loved Gabe, and the next move was hers.

If she could only figure out what that move should be.

—⁓—

Gabe backed away from the open window, leaning against the picnic table on the cabin's deck. They say that eavesdroppers never hear anything good about themselves, but sometimes they do. Yeah, most people wouldn't consider a muttered "damn it" a declaration of love, but he and Lorin weren't most people.

He'd hurt her feelings by not telling her about his eyes, trying to shield her from the gory details.

The door suddenly opened. "Gabe." Lorin stopped short, almost dropping the kerosene lamp she carried. She glanced at the open window, then back at him. "How long have you been standing out here?"

"Long enough."

"Hmm." She looked him up and down, taking in the T-shirt, loose sweatpants, and running shoes he'd changed into after his meeting with Julianna had ended. Lorin didn't seem upset that her conversation might have been overheard. If anything, she looked relieved—or maybe that was wishful thinking on his part. Her expression seemed settled somehow, resolved, like she'd come to a decision of some sort.

When she sidled closer, he inhaled deeply. Her body's scent was a rich, heady perfume he'd never get enough of.

"Looks like you're dressed for a run." The twist she put on the final word made his face flush, his body pulse.

She hurdled off the deck, shooting a naughty smile over her shoulder.

Chase. Taste. Take.

He leaped after her, every molecule howling.

She'd already opened up a lead, disappearing into the tree line. He heard her crashing through the woods over the sound of his own huffing breath, taking the trail to the dig site, a trail now so familiar to him that he could probably follow it without wearing his glasses.

He hoped to hell she had condoms with her, because he sure as hell didn't.

His heart pounded in time with his shoes slapping against the dirt path. As he slowed to a quiet, stalking walk, opening up his senses, he glanced at the thunder-heads towering in the sky to the west. He could carry her off to the petroglyph cave, get some shelter from the rain, because once he got his hands on her, he wasn't going to let go—

A grunt from up ahead. The unmistakable smack of fists against skin.

The hair on the back of his neck lifted in primal warning as he approached the dig—and saw Lorin shoved to her knees, and a man holding a gun to the back of her head.

Chapter 18

"WHERE IS THE BEACON? THE CRYOTUBE? YOU WILL show me now."

Lorin fought to control her breathing despite the adrenaline blasting through her system like an F5 tornado. Damn it, she *knew* better. She knew better than to lose awareness of her surroundings, but she'd been so focused on the chase, stripping off her T-shirt on the run, that she'd been easy pickings. She'd gotten one good punch in, but the weapon he held against her head was… persuasive.

Kicking the dropped kerosene lamp out of his way, he jammed the weapon into the notch at the bottom of her skull. His silky brown hair brushed against her bare shoulder. "Where is the 'tube?"

Vamp. Trained fighter. Paige's vamp? His melodious baritone slipped and slithered, and she blinked hard against the pull of his glamour. "I don't know what you're talking about."

Something clicked, and the metal pressing against her head grew uncomfortably warm. Fighting not to flinch, she flicked her eyes to the trail. *Stay back.* She wouldn't be able to take this guy down if she was worried about Gabe's safety.

"The ship. Where is it?" he asked.

"Ship? Lake Superior's a good sixty miles away from here."

His big fist cracked against her cheekbone, rocking her head sideways. "The beacon blipped—here. Where's the *Arkapaedis*? Pritchard's box? The cryotube? I saw the 'tube with my own eyes, but now it's gone. Where is it?"

Another fist to the face. She tasted blood.

Cold. No emotion. Trained interrogator? Paige might have let some information slip about the capsule Nathan had found, but she didn't know anything about the box they suspected was Pritchard's. And a beacon? What the hell?

"Talk." Jerking back on her ponytail, he jabbed the barrel of the weapon under her chin. Another click.

"Shit," she gasped. The weapon burned her skin like a lit cigar.

"Robert?" Paige stepped out of the gazebo, tugging earbuds out of her ears. "What on earth—"

Lorin threw her body against the vamp's legs. The vamp pivoted, using her own momentum against her, sending her sprawling flat on her stomach. He dropped on top of her before she could scramble to her feet, his knees grinding her breasts into the dry, scrubby grass.

"Don't do that again," he said matter-of-factly, jamming the weapon against her right temple.

"Aah!" She smelled her own crisping skin.

"Come here, Paige."

The vamp's glamour eddied in waves. Paige approached jerkily, like a marionette on strings. Her eyes snapped with resistance and a dawning pain.

Fight, Paige. Fight.

"Up." The vamp stood, yanking on her ponytail like reins on a horse. She scurried to her feet, gritting her teeth against the weapon's crackling heat. His hot breath stung the burn already blistering on the back of her neck.

"Robert?" Paige said in a tiny voice as she approached.

Lorin shoved the searing pain to the back of her mind, waiting for her preternatural fighting equilibrium to kick in. Sooner or later, there'd be a split-second lapse in his grip, his focus. She just had to wait for it.

If the damn weapon didn't burn her to ashes first.

There was a slight rustle at the trailhead. Shoving Lorin away, the vamp fired at a wolf, black and sleek, with Gabe's squinting ice-blue eyes. The bright humming stream nipped the tip of Gabe's ear, showering sparks into the dry grass behind him. Gabe growled, baring his canines.

Her leg snapped up, kicking his weapon away. The vamp came at her quickly, tackling her to the ground, knocking the breath from her lungs. They rolled, over and over again. Time oozed like molasses, like it always did when she was fighting, pinning everyone else down but leaving her free to move. But the guy was fast. She dodged a fist the size of a Christmas ham with a sideways jerk of her head and heard him curse as his knuckles cracked into rocky soil instead of her face. He cursed again when her elbow slammed into his nose, crunching bone and cartilage, spraying her with his blood.

He manacled her wrists, pinning them to the ground. Smoke drifted into her nostrils as he ground her hips and tailbone into the dirt with his heavy body. Blood from his nose dripped onto her face in soft, wet splats. He was pulsing with glamour, and hugely erect.

She blinked again, fighting against the languor turning her body and will into mush.

He flicked his slick pink tongue against his upper lip, tasting his own blood. "A worthy opponent," he murmured. His eyes, the color of bitter chocolate, assessed her abs, breasts, and arms like he was buying a cow at a stockyard before pausing at her throat.

Another flick of his tongue. His mouth—his ridiculously sensuous mouth—opened slowly, a drawbridge lowered on silent hinges. His fangs flashed. His head descended—slowly, so slowly.

Her instincts screamed at her to hunch her shoulders, to protect her vulnerable neck. Craning it instead, she drifted a hand over his muscled ass.

Wait. Wait.

Soft lips brushed against her neck—once, twice—before he settled in to suckle. She choked back a moan as his supple tongue licked and swirled, preparing her skin for his bite. There was a slight pause as he inhaled, positioning his fangs over her pulsing carotid. The slightest sting—

She drove her knee into his balls.

His high-pitched wheeze started before she shoved him off her body, tipping him to the ground, where he clutched his crotch and shriveled into a fetal curl. She scrabbled to her feet and scoured the tree line, searching for Gabe. He'd been hit. Her own wounds burned like hell on fire, and the vamp hadn't even fired the weapon at her to inflict them.

A moan from the ground. Twitching feet, churning knees—the vamp was recovering quickly, and Paige was crawling to his aid. She needed some rope, fast.

She ran to the supply shed, scanning the cluttered shelves before snatching a handful of bungee cords. By the time she went back outside again, the vamp had pushed himself to his hands and knees, his head hanging down, shoulder blades heaving. He fought to his feet, shoving grass-flecked hair out of his face. After a slight stumble, he gained his balance and assumed a fighting stance.

Lorin dropped the bungee cords, freeing her hands. If looks could kill, she'd be a smear on the—

A blur of black fur exploded from the woods, taking the vamp down from behind.

"Robert!" Paige screamed.

Wolf and vamp rolled and writhed in a ball of fur, fabric, fists, fangs. Growls. Grunts. Groans. Gabe sank his teeth into the vamp's calf, shaking his head to rip and tear, and soon the vamp's shredded pants were wet, saturated with blood. The vamp kicked at Gabe with his uninjured leg, clubbing at him with joined fists.

Suddenly Paige was between them.

"Get back!" The minute Lorin hollered her warning, she realized it wasn't necessary. Gabe now stood, panting, several feet away. His teeth and tongue were stained red.

With a sob, Paige slapped her hand over the vamp's calf, trying to staunch the flow of blood.

The vamp grimaced and fumbled at his wrist. "Ta'al. Transport. Now!"

With a percussive pop and a flash of white light, they both shimmered away.

They'd vanished.

Lorin rushed to where they'd lain not seconds before. "Where are they?" she hollered at Gabe, waving her arms through the air. She sniffed, though her nose was

nowhere near as sensitive as Gabe's was. Flint? Ozone?
The air felt crackly, oddly energized. She rubbed at the
hair standing upright on her forearms.

Gabe sniffed the blood on the ground—blood that reassured her that she hadn't been hallucinating—before
trotting to the tree line.

No, this was no hallucination. There was the vamp's
weapon, dropped in the grass, gleaming in the fading
daylight. Her knuckles were scuffed, her burns oozed,
and blood from the nick of a fang trickled wetly down
her neck. The scent of Gabe's singed fur stung the air.

Standing by the trees, Gabe barked sharply.

Fire. Sparks crackled in the dry, scruffy grass, float-
ing into the air. Greedy flames licked at the ground. If
they made it to the tree line, they could gobble for miles.
Running to the shed, she grabbed two fire extinguishers.
She eyed the flames again.

They needed help.

Plucking her phone from the holder at her waistband,
she hit autodial to call Mike. Nothing. No dial tone. She
scowled at the display—the completely dark display.
Dead battery. "You piece of shit." Tossing the phone
aside, she aimed the fire extinguisher at the flames nearest the tree line. "Gabe! Go to the bunkhouse and get—"
She heard her truck barreling up the logging road. It ca-
reened into the clearing, with Nathan behind the wheel,
Mike riding shotgun, and three or four crewmembers
bouncing in the box.

"We smelled smoke," Nathan called as he jumped
out of the cab.

She pointed at the towering pines closest to the fire.
"Start there," she said as the rest of the crew spilled out

of the truck. "Get more fire extinguishers from the shed. These are nearly empty." The last thing they needed was for the fire to expand, bringing every well-meaning volunteer fire department in the Arrowhead to the dig. "Be careful. Don't get closer to the fire than you have to." Who knew what the hell the weapon had fired? The mere touch of the weapon's barrel against her skin had left it seared and branded. The burns hurt like hell.

"Lorin, sit down," Nathan said as he trotted by with fresh fire extinguishers. "We've got this."

He was right. The fire was almost contained. As Gabe sniffed the tree line around the perimeter of the clearing, still trying to pick up Paige's trail, Lorin grabbed an orange crate from a nearby pile of boxes and casually approached the weapon she'd kicked away from the vamp. About the length of her hand, gracefully curved and with no trigger that she could see, it glowed an otherworldly silvery green. Flipping the crate over, she placed it over the weapon, hiding it from view of the crew, and sat.

"Damn it," she breathed, putting a hand on her twisting stomach. Where was Paige?

A snout nudged her hand. Gabe, done with his tree line reconnaissance, stood at her side, holding a wad of black fabric in his mouth. He dropped it in her lap with a growl and a glance back at the crew.

Her T-shirt. Luckily the crewmembers were so busy fighting the fire that they hadn't asked her why she was wearing only a hot pink bra that was more lace than coverage. "Thanks," she murmured as she tugged it over her head, wincing as the fabric scratched the burn at her temple.

She felt as much as heard the soft rumble from his

throat before he lapped away the blood staining her face with delicate strokes of his tongue.

Why were her eyes stinging? Must be the smoke.

With a final lick, he moved back slightly, dropping to his haunches. Then he… shifted. Muscles wrenched. Ligaments and tendons snapped and popped. Paws and claws became hands and nails. His black pelt receded, leaving skin and his familiar sparse body hair in its wake. The shape of his face changed, rearranging into the features she recognized. Soon the man knelt at her side, breathing heavily, gleaming with sweat, and naked as the day he'd been born.

Gabe took her hand, raised her scuffed knuckles to his mouth, and suckled. "Looks like you got a few licks in." He squinted at her burns. "I can't see a goddamn thing."

She stroked the singed hair, careful not to touch his blistered ear with her filthy hands. "Where are your glasses?"

"Back on the trail with my clothes. Are you okay?" His voice was tight, controlled, but his eyes seethed like whitecaps on a lake. Still squinting, he brailled her for injuries, carefully skimming his fingertips over her forehead, cheekbones, and jawline, not touching her burns directly. He skated his big hands over her shoulders, down her arms and torso before peering myopically at her burns again. "Where's the first aid kit?"

"He singed your skunk stripe," she murmured.

"Huh?"

"The white patch of hair over your ear. It's burned."

"Forget my hair. Where's the first aid kit?"

She gestured to the same storage shed she'd retrieved the bungee cords and fire extinguishers from. While Gabe retrieved the first aid kit, Gretchen and Ellenore emerged from the trail on foot, Ellenore carrying a bundle of clothing that had to belong to Gabe.

Gretchen ogled Gabe's bare buns as he disappeared into the shed.

"Hey." Lorin snapped her fingers to get her attention.

"Wow. Who knew Gabe looked so great naked?"

"I did. Eyes front, ladies."

"Here." Ellenore handed over the wad of fabric, gingerly extending Gabe's glasses by a mangled bow. "Sorry, I think I stepped on these."

"I probably broke them myself when I dropped them to the ground," Gabe grumbled.

Whether by luck or design, Gabe carried the red plastic first aid kit in front of his groin, covering the essentials but no more. Disregarding the clothes, he examined his glasses instead. The lenses and right bow were intact, so he put them on. They listed drunkenly—adorably—on the bridge of his nose.

"Better than nothing," he said with a shrug.

Lorin snatched the bundle of clothes from Ellenore and thrust it at him. "Get dressed." Ignoring Gretchen's "you go, girl" smirk, she stepped in front of Gabe, blocking their view as he dragged on his discarded underwear and sweatpants, shoved his feet back into his running shoes, and yanked his T-shirt over his head.

She wanted nothing more than to find some privacy and reverse the sequence, stripping him completely, carefully examining every inch to make sure he was okay before losing herself in him for hours.

Gabe's Bat Phone rang. Plucking it from the holder attached to his waistband, he looked at the display. "It's Lukas."

He'd probably sensed the fight. Crap, he must be worried sick.

"What happened?" Ellenore asked as Gabe answered the phone. "How the hell did a fire start up here?"

Lorin looked over to the crew, busy with fire extinguishers, shovels, and sand. The fire was nearly out, and it was just a matter of time before Mike and Nathan picked up the scent of the vamp's spilled blood if they hadn't already. The vamp's weapon, lying under the orange crate not two feet away, beat like Poe's telltale heart.

She couldn't tell them the truth, damn it. She couldn't tell them a thing. "Gabe and I were running, started playing around, and I dropped the kerosene lamp," she said. "Stupid of me, I know."

As they watched Nathan and Mike finish putting out the fire, Gretchen looked around the site with a frown. "Where's Paige? Off with her vamp?"

Lorin bit back hysterical laughter. *Yeah, you could say that.*

Gabe approached. "Gretchen, could you collect the empty fire extinguishers, make sure they get down to the workshop so they can be refilled?"

"Sure."

He waited until Gretchen was out of hearing range. "Lukas wants us to collect what evidence we can, send pictures, and then call him once we get back to the cabin." He sighed. "He isn't happy with either of us."

"Why?"

"He knew something was wrong, and neither of us answered our phones when he called." He gave her hand a squeeze. "Can he really discern shifts in emotional energy at such a distance?"

She nodded.

Gabe looked to the sky. "We don't have a lot of time. Good job, everyone," he called to the crew. "Let's finish up here, then get back to the bunkhouse."

They scurried to respond. Gabe's lecture-hall tone had derailed additional questions—for now, anyway.

"I'm sure Paige's fine," he said, drawing her into his arms.

She hugged him back, as tightly as she could, knowing he was trying to convince himself as much as her.

Chapter 19

WHEN GABE DROPPED INTO A CHAIR AT THE CABIN'S small table a half hour later, he was struck by a distinct sense of déjà vu. Lorin paced, debating with Lukas via speakerphone, much like she had with Elliott the day he'd arrived at the dig.

Only this time, he wasn't annoyed. He was stunned.

They were about to be shut down. He'd be going home. The writing was on the wall, and he had no idea what to do with this yawning hole in his stomach, deep as any quarry he'd ever explored. He'd counted on having the entire summer to ease Lorin into a relationship, to help her get over her skittishness, see that—

"Lorin, be reasonable," Lukas snapped. "A student is missing. You can't—"

"Do *not* tell me what I can't do." Lorin's words were as crisp as hoarfrost. Being reamed out by Lukas for not answering her phone hadn't exactly gotten the conversation off to a collegial start.

Elliot broke in. "Lorin, tell us exactly what happened."

Gabe sighed, scrubbing his hands over his evening beard. Slouching in the ladder-backed chair, he gazed tiredly at the boxes he and Lorin had just lugged from the site, racing against the clock to gather as much evidence as they could before the thunderstorm boiling to the west washed everything away. After the crew left, they'd done their best in the dying light, taking pictures of the weapon, the spilled blood, and the burned grass *in situ*, and zapping everything to Lukas. He'd called back immediately to advise them how to collect the blood-soaked soil and burned grass for later analysis.

Outside, the thunder rolled, matching Lorin's glowering expression as her long strides ate up the floor. Dirt smudged her knees, her hair was a snarled mess, and a nasty bruise was developing on her cheekbone. She sported a trio of weeping, angry burns, and a thin trail of blood had dried on her neck, where the vamp's fang had nicked her.

She was glorious—and she was staring right at him.

"Were you planning on joining this conversation anytime soon?" she hissed before turning back to the phone. She took a deep breath. "Lukas, I don't think mobilizing a team tonight would accomplish anything. It's about to start pouring. Gabe was shifted, and even he lost their trail."

"Gabe?"

"There wasn't even a trail to follow," he admitted to Elliott. "It just… disappeared, just like they did. Lorin's right. There's nothing anyone can do here tonight." And he wanted this night with Lorin. "You might want to send an environmental impact team. The weapon fired a… stream of something rather than shooting projectiles. The stream burns to the touch. Analysis of the grass should give us an idea of whether it's chemical, electrical—"

"Gabe got hit," Lorin blurted.

He glared at her. "And Lorin has some contact burns, but we're both okay." Truth be told, his ear burned like a bitch. Both he and Lorin had put off first aid so they could gather samples and clean up the scene before the rain started.

Lukas swore. "Lorin, why are you wasting your breath arguing with me about shutting the place down?"

"Show me your injuries." Elliott's curt tone brooked no disobedience.

"Elliott—"

"Pictures or video. We'll wait."

Lorin sighed. "Hold on." She approached the table, picked up his Bat Phone, and stepped closer. Raising the device to her eye, she aimed. Then hesitated.

"What?"

"Your hair," she murmured. "A piece of your hair is stuck in your wound. Let me loosen it with a wet—"

He flicked it out of the way, ignoring the sting.

"Okay, that wasn't necessary." She snapped several pictures and extended the phone to him. "Take mine." Their gazes snagged as he took it from her hand. Despite the argument she'd been having with Lukas—hell, maybe because of it—he read her edgy, lusty intent.

Of course. After the night's events, her adrenaline and hormone levels must be off the charts. How fricking convenient for her that he was here. "Turn around," he rumbled. Was that his voice? Where was this seething, helpless anger coming from? "Let me get the back of your neck."

She turned around and flipped her messy ponytail out of the way, exposing her supple nape. The contact burn was circular, about an inch in diameter, nearly cauterized around the edges. Wincing, he raised the phone with a hand that shook. Valkyries were known to have a high pain tolerance, but Lorin's must be off the charts. Did she even feel her injuries? If she did, he couldn't tell.

"Guys?"

He started at the sound of Lukas's voice. "Yeah?"

"Swab all your wounds after we hang up. Use gauze pads from the first aid kit, one pad per wound. Put each one in its own Ziploc bag and label it."

"Okay."

She shuddered a tiny tremble. She was so sensitive on the nape of her neck. He'd mapped it with his tongue, caressed every baby tendril that curled at her hairline, and now he'd have to make do without—

"Gabe."

Lukas's patience was apparently coming to an end. Stabilizing his hand, he took the damn pictures and sent them. "Incoming."

"Thanks." Lukas paused, then said, "Lorin, you know we have to shut the site down. You and Gabe were attacked, and a student is missing. You have to get those kids out of there until we figure out what happened to Paige Scott."

Guilt roiled like a polluted river. A student was missing on his watch. Lukas was right, and Lorin knew it as well as he did. He saw it in her posture and body language as she stared out of the window.

"Lukas. It's full dark here, and the sky is about to split open. Having the crewmembers hop in their cars and drive south in a thunderstorm is a lot more risky than them staying here tonight."

She'd accepted Lukas's decree.

"Most of these kids sublet their apartments for the summer, or don't have families in the area they can stay with until school starts again," she continued. "We have to make sure everyone has a place to go." A bolt of lightning cracked, punctuating her words. "We need until tomorrow, Lukas."

She silently scrutinized him as Lukas and Elliott conferred in soft murmurs. "Okay," Lukas finally responded. "We'll mobilize a scene crew at first light."

Being that he didn't have his car here, he'd catch a ride home with Lukas tomorrow.

So that was that, then. They had tonight.

As Lukas instructed Lorin to put her clothing in a bag so they could process it for trace evidence, Gabe looked at the cabin that had become his home away from home: the stubborn stove. The chipped porcelain ladle used for dipping water from the pail. The picture she loathed still lying facedown on the bookshelf, now joined by a print he'd made of the shot he'd taken of Lorin and her mother that day in the lab. He wandered over to the bed, rumpled from their early morning lovemaking.

"So, we agree we'll reassess this decision after you've analyzed the scene."

"Yes." Lukas's response sounded like Lorin had pulled it from his throat with a pair of rusty pliers.

Gabe raised a brow. How had she managed *that*? How much of the conversation had he missed while he mooned like a lovesick pup?

"See you tomorrow, then." She stabbed at the button to hang up. "Hell." Crossing to the kitchen area, she snatched a box of Ziploc bags and a large paper sack off the open storage shelves, retrieved the first aid kit, and came over to the bed. "Can you open up some gauze pads?" she asked, handing him the first aid kit before shaking open the paper bag and setting it on the floor. "Crap. I really like this T-shirt, and I know I'll never see it again."

She peeled it off and dropped it in the bag, exposing her candy-colored bra.

A rumble of thunder shook the walls and floor, and spats of rain hit the roof. Gabe simply stared, savoring every second. Why had he taken their time together for granted?

"Gabe? What's wrong?"

The work-rough fingertips she raised so tenderly to his cheekbone cleaved his chest in two. He sucked in a careful breath and schooled his expression. Turning away from her, he reached under the bed, extracting his duffel bag. "I should start packing."

"What? Why?"

"The project's been shut down, Lorin. You don't need a PM anymore."

Her throat slammed shut. Not need him? She still shook from watching that weapon nearly take his head off. She needed him like she needed her next pulse of blood, her next gasp of air. She grabbed his arm, whirling him back to face her. "What the hell are you talking about?"

"You don't need me anymore." A ghost of a smile tipped his lips. "You never really did."

"So, this is just about work for you now?"

"No. It's not. And that's why I have to leave." He barked out a humorless laugh as he dropped his duffel bag onto the bed. "Come on, Lorin. Did you really see this working for the long haul?"

"Yes." The word popped out, no thought required. She loved him. He loved her. Didn't he?

"The mutt and the Valkyrie Princess? People would kill themselves laughing."

Relief wobbled her knees. The problem was insecurity, not that he didn't love her. "Freyja, don't scare me like that," she muttered, pushing him onto the bed and sitting down beside him. "Gabe, who are all these 'people' you keep talking about? The only person other than Krispin Woolf who's expressed the slightest reservation about our relationship is you. This 'mutt and princess' thing is all in your head." She met his eyes. "Isn't it what *we* feel that's important?"

"Lorin, I don't know how you feel from one minute to the next." He sighed, reaching for her hand before snatching it back. "You're like... quicksand. I need some solid ground under my feet."

He needed the words. He... deserved them. Andi was right—it was time to find her gonads.

I can do this.

She opened her mouth, but nothing came out.

"Lorin, it's okay—"

"No. It damn well isn't," she snapped. His resigned expression just... slayed her. He was so ready to sublimate his own needs, to make her comfortable despite his own discomfort. "Just... give me a second here."

"Okay."

The wisp of amusement in his voice calmed her slightly. Freyja, she was such an emotional basket case. It was amazing he wasn't running for the hills. She breathed deeply, in and out, stilling her body like she did before fighting with Lukas, who'd wipe the floor with her ass on sheer principle if he thought she was fighting one whit below her full abilities.

I can do this.

She cradled his face in her hands, taking care to avoid his ear—the ear that had been burned when he'd dived into the fray, blind, to protect her. She might not need physical protection very often, but it meant everything that he'd offered it.

She swallowed heavily. "I love you. I love you, Gabe." *In for a penny, in for a pound.* "Will you be my bondmate?"

He stilled. Didn't answer.

Shit, wolves mated for life. Why had she assumed that he'd want to—

"Yes." His lips latched on to hers in a clinging kiss, a kiss that made countless promises. "Yes. Sorry," he murmured against her mouth. "I thought that tonight was our last night together. A proposal was the last thing I expected."

"Why?" That damn inferiority complex again. She'd spend a lifetime pushing him to expect more—and kill herself making sure she provided it.

"Did you mean it? Are you serious?"

"Yes." She whapped his shoulder with her fist. "Did *you* mean it?"

"What?"

"That night at my place. You asked me to be your mate. Did you mean it?"

He stilled, eyes widening. Ruddy color swept over his cheekbones. "I thought I'd dreamed that."

"Nope. You said it, and then you fell asleep." She raised a forefinger. "Correction—we both came like gangbusters, and then you fell asleep."

He dropped his forehead onto his fingertips. "Classy."

"Hot," she corrected, pulling his hand away from his face. "It—*you*—were so freaking hot."

Whatever he saw in her face, or heard in her voice, must have reassured him. "Yes, I meant it. Then and now."

She lifted a hand to his red and oozing ear. "I've never been as scared as I was when that vamp shot at you."

"How do you think I felt seeing you with a gun held to your head? And Jesus, you didn't look scared at all," he marveled. "You were... steel. Capable. Tough. Absolutely magnificent." He drifted his lips along her jawline. "Can we not talk about that right now? I really need to make love with my bondmate."

His bondmate. She swallowed, hard. With his "yes"— with a single word—they were bondmates. She'd asked, he'd answered. A done deal, an oral contract between the two of them.

I have a bondmate.

She waited for the panic to crash down, for the hyper-ventilating to start. But it... didn't. She felt certain. Strong. Ready to step into the cage and take on all comers.

Ready to take him, over and over again.

She pushed him onto the pillows, tugging on the hem of his T-shirt as Gabe dealt with the button at his waist-band. As he sucked in his stomach to better deal with the zipper, his abs rippled.

She knew what the end result of thousands of crunches looked like. "You've been working out." Lowering her head, she licked in admiration. "Why—"

A knock at the door.

Gabe dropped his hands to his sides with a sigh. "Already being interrupted by the kids."

A snort of laughter escaped. "Don't move." Tugging

his discarded T-shirt over her head while she walked, she opened the door to Mike, who quickly ducked inside to get out of the rain. He carried Paige's tote bag.

Ah, damn.

"Hey. I found this in the gazebo—oh, sorry. Hi." He waved at Gabe, now sitting on the bed. "I didn't mean to interrupt."

"Hi, Mike. No worries."

"Paige left this up at the site," Mike said. "I didn't want it to get rained on."

"Oh. Um, thanks." An uncomfortable silence fell. What else could she say? She couldn't explain Paige's disappearance to herself, much less give Mike the reassurance he so clearly needed. "Why don't you bring it to the bunkhouse, put it on her bed?" Where it would lay, unclaimed, until Paige returned.

If she returned. What were they going to do when tomorrow morning came, and Paige's big bed hadn't been slept in?

Mike plucked Paige's tiny block-out sunglasses out of a side compartment and held them up. "She takes this bag with her everywhere she goes. Why did she leave it behind today?" He eyed them. "You both have oozing wounds. Lorin's been fighting; her knuckles are scuffed, and she's going to have a hell of a bruise on her cheek. Someone—vamp—bled up there, I fucking smelled it." He glanced at the cardboard boxes stacked against the wall. "I smell it now. Don't insult my intelligence."

Damn Elliott's decree. If she said a single thing, gave Mike even a single explanation to help ease his mind, he'd work the edges, prying the lid off their shoddy story with the crowbar of his intelligence.

"So that's it? Really?" Mike snapped. "One more thing you can't talk about?"

"Mike…" Lorin raised a tentative hand—to comfort? To apologize? She had no earthly idea.

Mike jerked away. "You two enjoy your evening." The cabin door closed behind him with an accusing snap, and his footsteps hammered against the wooden deck as he strode into the pounding rain.

"I hate this!" she yelled to the ceiling.

"I know." Wrapping his arms around her from behind, Gabe rested his chin on her shoulder. "I know."

She wanted to pace off her frustration, to punch something—hard and repeatedly—but leaned back against him instead. "Where did that vamp come from? He knew too much about what was going on here— more than even Paige knew." She turned in his arms. "A beacon? What's he talking about? Why does he seem to know more about what's going on here than we do?"

"I don't know."

"Do you think Paige is okay?" She stared at the window up to the sky, obscured by the driving rain. "They disappeared like something out of freaking *Star Trek*, Gabe. What the hell is going on?"

"I don't know."

"There's too damn much we don't know," she grumbled. "I think—"

"I think"—Gabe's arms tightened around her—"we need to set it aside for the night. One thing I *do* know is that I need you." With a sneaky shift of his weight, he tipped them both onto the bed. "Right now."

Their clothes seemed to dissolve, until the only item

remaining was Gabe's bent glasses. As she reached for them, he blocked her hand. "No. I want to see you."

Her insides melted, just oozed all over the place. Was that her heart going pitty-pat? Yup.

How freaking girly.

Gabe tugged her on top of him and eyed her knowingly from behind the thick lenses. "Show me what you've got, mate."

A challenge. Her lips twitched. He knew her too damn well. "Are you sure you're up for this?"

He lifted his hips and gave her a single teasing nudge, right where she needed it most. "Positive. You?"

"Bring it."

Lowering her lips to his, she stepped into the cage and slammed the door behind her.

And started wreaking havoc.

Chapter 20

"Ready?" Lorin said as they went outside.

"I can see your breath," Gabe grumbled, closing the cabin door behind them. "Can't we wait until the frost burns off?"

"You're the one who left this until our last day," she said matter-of-factly.

Too matter-of-factly. She was trying too hard to disguise her concern.

He and Lorin had decided to come back to the dig after his surgery so he could heal in peace and quiet. Now, a month later, he was, for all intents and purposes, recovered. The soreness at the incision and injection sites was a thing of the past, and the milky film was gone, but there was one final test to undertake. His retinologist had given him the all clear, but—

"What time does the Council meeting start?" Lorin asked.

She knew very well what time the meeting started; she'd reminded him of the time before they went to bed last night. The first in a series of special Underworld Council meetings had been called to discuss the ramifications of some of their early test results, including the fact that the kernels of wild rice they'd found in Pritchard's command box were almost four thousand years old instead of one thousand. What did they really know about what had come before?

Their peoples' entire oral history had been called into question.

He sighed. Three months had passed since they'd shut down the dig, spending the summer in the lab, working on the Pritchard finds, and every damn test result raised more questions than answers. Despite an astronomical reward offered by her family, the school year had started without Paige Scott, and Lorin was worried sick. Mike Gill had dropped out of school to initiate his own search.

"Two o'clock, and it's a five-hour drive back," he said, rubbing her shoulder.

She leaned down into a quad stretch, hissing as her bare fingertips touched the frost-coated wood. Though the leaves had barely started to change into their fall colors, last night northern Minnesota had had its first hard freeze of the season. "Come on, city boy. Let's get this done."

"Let's? I don't see *your* clothes coming off." Crossing his arms in front of him, Gabe pulled his black fleece jacket and waffle-weave thermal shirt up and over his head. He gasped as the air chilled his skin.

"Would that help?" Without waiting for an answer, she quickly and efficiently stripped, leaving her standing gloriously nude in the unforgiving morning sun. Her nipples hardened, sharpening to delicious points. Gooseflesh sheeted her skin.

But her eyes burned like a bonfire.

His pulse kicked into high gear. He quickly unbuckled his belt and shucked his jeans. They hit the deck with a metallic clank.

"Ready?"

Sighing, Gabe glanced across the clearing over to their favorite running path, the one that led to the glittery copse of trees where they'd made love for the first time. "I'm still as nearsighted as ever. You'll probably have to come looking for me."

"You'll find me," she said, unconcerned. "Just explore, sniff around, have some fun."

He eyed his naked mate. He knew Lorin wanted him to find pleasure in his wolf again, but frankly he preferred a man's. Yes, he very much planned on having some fun—with her, later, under the warm down comforter, thank you very much.

But first things first.

"Ready?" she asked again.

"As I'll ever be." He slipped off his new glasses, very carefully setting them on the picnic table. When he turned back to where he knew Lorin stood, all he saw was a fuzzy beige column. He could barely differentiate her from the tree trunks, but he could hear every nervous breath whooshing in and out of her lungs. He could smell rosemary-mint and sea salt, and his own scent on her body.

His teeth and nails stung as the shift came on. Skin and bone shifted and popped, rearranging in a timeless rush. Tooth became fang, nail became claw, flesh became fur.

Finally, he was wolf.

The deck's old wooden boards flexed and creaked as she approached. Her luscious scent intensified, became more pungent. Cupping his muzzle in one hand, she cautiously raised the other to his temple. "Any sharp pain? New shadows or gaps?"

He shook his head once.

"Sure?"

Her elemental scent intoxicated him. Maddened him. Drowned out everything else. She was right. He'd have no trouble finding her at all.

"Okay." Turning away from him, she presented him with a close-up view of her bare buttocks. With a quick shift of her weight, she sprang off the deck. "Chase me."

Chase. Taste. Take.

Always.

Forever.

He leaped into the blur and followed.

Read on for an excerpt from

TASTE ME

Now available from Sourcebooks Casablanca

HE WAS DESPERATE FOR A HIT. JUNKYARD DOG DESPERATE.

Stephen eyed the late night sky as he drew closer to the grimy club bordering Block E. Thunder rumbled like timpani, and the chains on his motorcycle boots rattled as he walked. Rubbing at the gnawing behind his breastbone, he unconsciously paced his movement to the beat thumping out of the club called Subterranean.

He stopped dead when he turned the corner. An overflow crowd seethed in the Indian summer heat, and two huge bouncers flanked the door like implacable marble columns. It had been a long time since he'd had to wait on the wrong side of the velvet rope, and he wasn't about to start now. Christ, he needed something, anything. His skin felt ready to burst off his bones.

He took a shaky breath, knowing that he'd have to play the "do you know who I am?" card and hope for the best. How low could you go? But he had to get in. Now. Straightening his shoulders, he walked alongside the line, his eyes flitting over the people who waited. Where were the couples with their hands on each other's asses? With their tongues down each other's throats? Right now, even inhaling some secondhand lust might ease the clawing and scratching on the backside of his ribs.

"Stephen! Is that Stephen?" The woman's high-pitched squeal floated into the humid night air, setting off a chain reaction that sounded like birds chirping in an aviary. Excitement pulsed. He huffed quickly, but it was there and gone. He turned on a carefully calibrated showman's smile, dripping accessibility and "so pleased to meetcha!" to pull more of the crowd toward him.

It worked better than he'd hoped. He was quickly surrounded, then swamped. Energy swirled, momentarily soothing the infernal gnawing behind his sternum, but it didn't last long. He desperately worked the crowd like the pro he'd become, shaking hands, accepting kisses, dodging a few wandering tongues, suckling on a few choice others. Energy surged, and he inhaled greedily. *More, more.* Men wearing baggy jeans and black T-shirts knocked knuckles with him and flashed devil horns while their friends' camera phones clicked. Snippets of conversation eddied around him: "Steve, Stephen? Stefan? I don't care what his name is, I just want to…" "Drummer for Scarlett's Web, idiot." "He's a lot… smaller than he looks on stage."

Two women bookended him and kissed his cheeks as their friend snapped pictures. He felt a hand creep along his hip, then cup his groin. "You're going commando, aren't you?" the chick on the right breathed into his ear.

He grinned but didn't answer, setting off more squeals.

No one noticed that the grin didn't meet his eyes; they never did. Dread rose like water in a leaky boat. *Her hand is right on my dick, and I don't feel a thing.*

The pulsing music beckoned, crooked its finger from the door. If touch alone wasn't doing the job, maybe a music chaser would do the trick. He waded toward the door, pulling the crowd along in his wake. An elbow tagged his kidney, and he felt fingers yanking at his shirt. Someone grabbed a handful of his ass. "Leave me some skin, love," he called back, a smile pasted on his face as he tugged his butt out of the man's grasp. *This could get ugly.*

All momentum stopped when a glacial blonde stepped in, pushed a black Sharpie into his hand, and pulled up her halter top to expose her world-class Scandinavian rack. A small space cleared around them, and cell cameras clicked as he grinned, cupped her right breast in his trembling hand, and scrawled his autograph just above her stiff pink nipple. A punch of lust glittered in the air—hers, for him, and the crowd's, for her—but once again, the energy dissipated too quickly. It was there, then gone. His frustration surged.

"Hey!" the blonde said, recoiling from the shock he'd delivered with his hand.

He kissed her cheek in apology, shoving down the panic. *What the fuck was that?* His body was acting like a blown transformer, sparking and crackling. Not normal, not good. "Sorry, love." He had to get inside. Now. He raised his arm and caught the eye of one of the three-hundred-pound badasses at the door. The bouncer dove into the melee and snagged him around the waist, half carrying him out of the crowd to the door.

"Thanks, man," Stephen said, tucking in his rumpled shirt. "That got a little more out of hand than I thought it would."

The bouncer grinned and straightened his immaculate suit coat. "No problem. Everyone's excited about tomorrow night's show."

"Well, thanks. You really saved my skin." He tried to slip a folded bill into the man's kielbasa-fingered hand.

The bouncer waved it off and unhooked the black velvet rope. "Glad I could help. You enjoy your evening now, sir."

Curses, squeals, and offers of blow jobs rained over him as he shouldered his way into the club. The thing in his chest had nibbled on appetizers, but now it was simply ravenous. Standing in the cave-dark entryway, Stephen wiped at his clammy forehead with his T-shirt sleeve and let the tsunami of sound pound over him.

A small zing, then... nothing.

Sex, then. He'd have to hook up with someone.

Oooh, what a horrible problem to have. He almost laughed. He was living the life, nailing groupies left, right, upside down, and sideways, but the sad truth was he didn't even enjoy it anymore. Nope, shuttling his dick in and out of a warm, willing body had become a means to an end: Just produce the orgasms that would feed the beast. And it had been fun at the beginning of the tour, grand fun. Men, women, anything in between—it didn't matter. Two at a time, three at a time, groups—hell, whole parties. A week ago he'd been so desperate he'd had a three-way in a fetid festival Porta Potty. Their road manager was still scrubbing the pictures off the Internet.

The thing was always hungry, never satisfied. But

now that the band was back on home turf, he didn't have to make do with weak humans anymore. He just had to find… some of *them*.

A cloud of the club's energy—gutter-glam techno, grinding dancers, blinking lights, and the scents of spilled beer, stale cigarettes, and hot, clean sweat—drifted over him as he walked from the entryway into the club. Pheromones permeated the place like sweet chloroform, and he huffed greedily as he approached the dark wood bar. *Yeah, this is more like it.*

"Diet cola, no lime, please." While the pierced and tattooed bartender poured his drink, he scoped the place out, mentally sorting energy into groups: light and shadow, sound and silence, smells, people touching each other. They all produced energy which he could use, but tonight he needed… *Ahhh. Jackpot.* A good dozen patrons who had that something extra blipped strongly on his internal radar.

The bartender—a vamp, he thought, but having escaped to the planet only a few years ago, he was still learning these nuances—placed his drink in front of him and waved off his money.

"On the house, man," he said, acknowledging Stephen's identity with a nod. He held out his black-nailed hand for Stephen to shake. Bracelets clanked. "Welcome home. When did you guys get back to town?"

"The tour bus just pulled in," Stephen answered, taking a sip of his drink. Were their comings and goings really the source of so much interest? "I thought I'd reacquaint myself with the nightlife before Scarlett starts cracking the whip."

The bartender moaned playfully. "Jesus, don't

torture me like that." He acknowledged the approaching waitress's hollered order with a nod and gestured back to Stephen's drink. "Let me know when you're ready for another."

Stephen thanked him, dropped a ten-spot onto the bar, and turned toward the dance floor. Bodies blended and writhed to the bass-heavy beat, and his toe automatically tapped like he was behind his kick drum. Humid colognes drifted through the cramped space, and Stephen scanned the crowd. Who would it be tonight? The leather-clad, Cuervo-sipping redhead eyeballing him from the end of the bar? The Beckham-looking guy drinking beer who sat with his dark-haired friend at the table tucked into the corner? Both of them? All three?

A laugh drew his attention back to the dance floor, where a tall brunette danced with two friends. She was dressed like most of the other women in the club, in low-riding jeans and a knit halter top that clung to excellent breasts and exposed a taut stomach—but in his eyes, she lit up like she was radioactive. Her pleasure and happiness crackled through him like a Fourth of July sparkler. He watched her whirl and grind in time to the blinking lights for a good half hour, saw her cheerfully decline offers to dance from three men and one woman. She finally separated from her friends and peeled off to the restrooms.

She was the one. For tonight, anyway. He levered himself off the bar and followed.

Acknowledgments

While writing a novel is a solitary endeavor, producing a book is a massive undertaking which could not be accomplished without the support and expertise of countless others. As always, many thanks to my eagle-eyed critique partner Brenda Whiteside, and to my agent Cherry Weiner, who keeps me on an even keel. At Sourcebooks, special thanks to my editor Deb Werksman, to publicist extraordinaire Danielle Jackson, to Susie and Aubrey, and to all the people whose talent and expertise make my book a stronger piece of work. Thanks to research archaeologist Bruce Koenen from the Minnesota Office of the State Archaeologist for information about four-season archaeological practices, and for so generously sharing his insights into Minnesota's geological and archaeological history. Any errors and extrapolations are, of course, my own. To my Midwest Fiction Writer chapter mates and my blogmates at The Ruby Slippered Sisterhood, thanks for your friendship, wise counsel, and for always having my back.

Last but definitely not least, endless thanks, again, to Mark—for holding down the fort, for herding the cats, and for the gift of time.

About the Author

Tamara Hogan loathes cold and snow but nonetheless lives near Minneapolis with her partner Mark and two naughty cats. When she's not working as a quality and process engineer for a global networking company, she writes urban fantasy romance with a sci-fi twist. A voracious reader with an unapologetic television addiction, Tamara is forever on the lookout for the perfect black boots.

Before its publication, Tamara's debut novel, *Taste Me,* won the Daphne du Maurier Award for Mystery and Suspense, and was nominated for the Romance Writers of America's prestigious Golden Heart award.

Tamara loves hearing from readers! Visit her on the web at www.tamarahogan.com.

Tempted

by Elisabeth Naughton

―᷾᷾―

DEMETRIUS—*He's the hulking, brooding warrior even his fellow Guardians avoid. Too dark. Too damaged. And given his heritage, he knows it's best to keep everyone at arm's length.*

Isadora is missing. The words pound through his head like a frantic drumbeat. For her own protection, Demetrius did all he could to avoid the fragile princess, his soul mate. And now she's gone—kidnapped. To get her back, he'll have to go to the black place in his soul he's always shunned.

As daemons ravage the human realm and his loyalty to the Guardians is put to the ultimate test, Demetrius realizes that Isadora is stronger than anyone thought. And finally letting her into his heart may be the only way to save them both.

―᷾᷾―

"Naturalistic, snappy dialogue, endlessly twisting plots within plots, a cast of complex and eminently likable characters, and a romance as hot as it is complicated make this an entertaining and smoldering read."—*Publishers Weekly* Starred Review

For more Elisabeth Naughton, visit:

www.sourcebooks.com

Enraptured

by Elisabeth Naughton

———

ORPHEUS—*To most he's an enigma, a devil-may-care rogue who does whatever he pleases whenever he wants. Now this loose cannon is part of the Eternal Guardians—elite warriors assigned to protect the human realm—whether he likes it or not.*

Orpheus has just one goal: to rescue his brother from the Underworld. He's not expecting a woman to get in the way. Especially not a Siren as gorgeous as Skyla. He has no idea she's an assassin sent by Zeus to seduce, entrap, and ultimately destroy him.

Yet Skyla herself might have the most to lose. There's a reason Orpheus feels so familiar to her, a reason her body seems to crave him. Perhaps he's not the man everyone thinks…The truth could reveal a deadly secret as old as the Eternal Guardians themselves.

———

"Filled with sizzling romance, heartbreaking drama, and a cast of multifaceted characters, this powerful and unusual retelling of the Orpheus and Eurydice story is Naughton's best book yet."—*Publishers Weekly*

For more of the Eternal Guardians series, visit:

www.sourcebooks.com

Untouched

by Sara Humphreys

--~~--

She may appear to have it all, but inside she harbors a crippling secret...

Kerry Smithson's modeling career ensures that she will be admired from afar—which is what she wants, for human touch sparks blinding pain and mind-numbing visions.

Dante is a dream-walking shapeshifter—an Amoveo, who must find his destined mate or lose his power forever. Now that he has found Kerry, nothing could have prepared him for the challenge of keeping her safe. And it may be altogether impossible for Dante to protect his own heart when Kerry touches his soul...

--~~--

For more of the Amoveo Legend series, visit:

www.sourcebooks.com

Kiss of the Goblin Prince

by Shona Husk

The Man of Her Dreams

He is like a prince in a fairy tale: tall, outrageously handsome, and way too dark for her own good. Amanda has been hurt before, though. And with her daughter's illness, the last thing she needs right now is a man. But the power of Dai King is hard to resist. And when he threads his hands through her hair and pulls her in for a kiss, there is no denying it feels achingly right.

In a Land of Nightmare

After being trapped in the Shadowlands for centuries with the goblin horde a constant threat, Dai revels in his newfound freedom back in the human realm. But even with the centuries of magic he's accumulated, he still doesn't know how to heal Amanda's daughter—and it breaks his heart. Yet for the woman he loves, he'd risk anything…including a return to the dreaded Shadowlands.

Praise for **The Goblin King**:

"A wonderfully dark and sensual fairy tale."
—Jessa Slade, author of *Seduced by Shadows*

For more of the Shadowlands series, visit:

www.sourcebooks.com

Hold Me If You Can

by Stephanie Rowe

Without her passions, she has no magic…

It's unfortunate for Natalie that Nigel Aquarian is so compelling. With his inner demons, his unbridled heat, and his "I will conquer you" looks, he calls to her in exactly the way that nearly killed her.

But losing control means losing her life…

That he's an immortal warrior and that her powers rise from intense passions would seem to make them a match made in heaven, but unless they embrace their greatest fears, they'll play out their final match in hell.

With a unique voice that critics say "carves out her very own niche— call it paranormal romance adventure comedy," Stephanie Rowe delivers an irresistible pair of desperadoes dancing on the edge of self-control and pure temptation.

For more Stephanie Rowe books, visit:

www.sourcebooks.com

The Danger That Is Damion

by Lisa Renee Jones

—⁓—

Lethally passionate, wickedly dangerous…

Renegade warrior Damion Browne is a soldier of soldiers, an enforcer of the code of honor. With ruthless precision, he calculates risks as deliberately as he does his lover's satisfaction. Now it's up to him to defeat a new generation of female Super Soldiers, including the one woman perfectly programmed to be his downfall.

His enemy… or his soul mate?

Lara Martin has never felt powerful, until she's brainwashed to destroy the one man who can help her find the answers she so desperately seeks. Alone and embroiled in lies, Lara must turn to Damion for the key to the truth…

—⁓—

Praise for **The Legend of Michael***:*

"A thrill ride of nonstop action, intricate suspense, and scorching love scenes!"—Stephanie Tyler, *New York Times* bestselling author of *Hold on Tight*

For more Lisa Renee Jones, visit:

www.sourcebooks.com

Stud

by Cheryl Brooks

—⁓—

They're galaxies apart…

Even for a Zetithian, Tarq Zulveidione's sexual prowess is legendary. Believing it's all he's good for, Tarq sets out to perpetuate his threatened species by offering his services to women across the galaxy…

But one force can bring them together

Lucinda Force is the sensitive dark horse in a self-absorbed family, repeatedly told that no man will ever want such a plain woman. Lucy longs for romance, but is resigned to her loveless lot in life—until Tarq walks through the door of her father's restaurant on Talus Five…

—⁓—

Praise for The Cat Star Chronicles:

"You will laugh, fall in love with an alien or two,
and be truly agog at the richness Ms. Brooks brings
to her worlds." —The Long and the Short of It

"A phenomenal series that just gets better and better. It's
sexy space travel at its finest." –Night Owl Romance

For more Cheryl Brooks books, visit:

www.sourcebooks.com